PRAISE for…

Hit & Mrs.
If you're in the mood for a cute chick-lit mystery with some nice gals in Montreal, Hit & Mrs. *is just the ticket.*—Globe and Mail

Crewe's writing has the breathless tenor of a kitchen-table yarn….a cinematic pace and crackling dialogue keep readers hooked.—Quill & Quire

Ava Comes Home
She expertly manages a page-turning blend of down-home comedy and heart-breaking romance.—Cape Breton Post

Shoot Me
Possesses an intelligence and emotional depth that reverberates long after you've stopped laughing.—Halifax Chronicle Herald

Relative Happiness
Her graceful prose…and her ability to turn a familiar story into something with such raw dramatic power, are skills that many veteran novelists have yet to develop.—Halifax Chronicle Herald

LESLEY CREWE

Her Mother's Daughter

Vagrant Press is an imprint of
Nimbus Publishing Limited
PO Box 9166
Halifax, NS   B3K 5M8
(902) 455-4286
nimbus.ca

Printed and bound in Canada

Cover design: Heather Bryan
Author photo: Sarah Crewe

This novel is a work of fiction. Names, characters, places, and incidents are either the product of the author's imagination or are used fictitiously. Any resemblance to actual persons, living or dead, events or locales is entirely coincidental.

Library and Archives Canada Cataloguing in Publication

Crewe, Lesley, 1955-
Her mother's daughter / Lesley Crewe.
ISBN 978-1-55109-774-9

I. Title.
PS8605.R48H47 2010   C813'.6   C2010-903050-8

We acknowledge the financial support of the Government of Canada through the Book Publishing Industry Development Program (BPIDP) and the Canada Council, and of the Province of Nova Scotia through the Department of Tourism, Culture and Heritage for our publishing activities.

 Mixed Sources
Product group from well-managed forests, controlled sources and recycled wood or fiber
www.fsc.org Cert no. SW-COC-000952
© 1996 Forest Stewardship Council
FSC

To my daughter, Sarah…
who took her first breath of life,
and saved mine.

❀

CHAPTER ONE

2000

Bay Gillis shovelled compost out of her ancient wheelbarrow and scattered it between the rows of vegetables in the garden at the back of the house. Her neighbour Flo hung sheets out to dry in the next yard. At the sound of tires squealing, Flo shook her head.

"Teenagers. They'll be the death of me yet."

Bay smiled to herself. Everything was going to be the death of Flo, but nothing in her sixty-five years had succeeded yet.

Bay became aware of her sore back and put down the shovel. She reached behind, placed her hands above her hips, and had a stretch before wiping her brow with the sleeve of her shirt. She surveyed her work. Bright green sprouts of cucumber and beans and peas popped out of the dark soil.

Flo headed for her back door with the laundry basket. "You've got a nice garden this year, Bay."

"My luck, the slugs will eat everything."

"Put plates of beer around and that will be the end of the slugs."

"I can't. Merlin gets drunk when I do that."

At the sound of his name, Merlin raised his shaggy head and tilted it to look at Bay. She reached down and gave the top of his head a pat. "Don't you, you silly dog."

"It's not Merlin who drinks the stuff. It's that no-good drunk I'm married to." Flo threw open the door and marched inside her house.

Nothing ever changed. Bay remembered Flo complaining about poor Ira when she was a young girl. Bay's mother used to roll her eyes whenever Flo came across the yard with that look in her eye, the one that said she was going to kill him.

At the thought of her mother, Bay's heart ached. Even a year later, Bay couldn't believe she was dead. Her mother had loved this garden. Bay used to take a cup of tea out to her in the early morning, so they

1

could sit together on the swing and decide where to stake the tomatoes and how many pumpkins they might need for the fall fair.

This was the first planting without her.

Bay looked past the garden and Flo's flapping sheets to the water in the harbour beyond, but the noonday sun made it hard to see, so she raised her hand to shield her eyes. Seagulls circled the lobster boats as they returned to the Louisbourg wharf, but she didn't hear their sharp cries, as the wind was blowing out to sea. She thought of the many times she and her mother had watched from this vantage point, waiting for her father's boat to come back to shore loaded with catch.

And seared in her memory was the day he and Bobby died out there on the water.

Her reverie was interrupted by the sound of the phone ringing through the open kitchen window. She hurried to the back steps, but Merlin got there first. When she opened the screen door, he charged in ahead of her. She made it to the phone on the fourth ring.

"Hello?"

"Bay, it's Ruth." Matt's mother.

"Hi, Ruth. What are you up to?"

"Trying to track down my son. Is he there?"

"No. Ashley's still asleep."

"Well, where is he? He practically lives at your house. He yelled that he was taking the car and jumped in it before I could tell him I need it to go to a funeral in Sydney this afternoon."

"I'll ask Ashley and see if she knows. It's time she was up anyway."

"Thanks."

Bay put down the phone and raced up the stairs. She knocked lightly on the bedroom door and then pushed it open. The usual chaos greeted her. How on earth did that child sleep in a bed piled high with clothes, wet towels, magazines, and stuffed animals? She approached the lump underneath the duvet.

"Honey." Bay reached out to put her hand on what she thought was her daughter. When the soft covers gave way, Bay was startled for a moment. She picked up the duvet. There was nothing there except the huge panda bear Matt had won for Ashley at the circus.

"That little minx." Bay threw the covers back on the bed and rushed to the phone.

"She's not here either."

She heard Ruth sigh. "This is getting out of hand, Bay. They're only seventeen. It frightens me how attached they are to each other."

Bay held up her forehead with her hand. "I know. Lately she's become such a handful. I try and talk to her, but she tunes me out. It's almost as if I don't matter anymore. What do you think we should do?"

"I know one thing," Ruth said. "I've scrimped and saved to get that boy to university, and he's damn well going. I'm not going to let Ashley or any girl ruin his future."

Bay sat up in her chair. "Well, excuse me, but I can say the same thing. Do I need some boy getting her pregnant? It's worse for a girl, Ruth. She'd be the one left with a baby."

"Then I suggest you put her on birth control."

"And I suggest you tell your son to keep his pants zipped."

"If you told your daughter to stop wearing clothes that are so tight you can see everything God gave her, then maybe he wouldn't be sniffing around."

"Excuse me?"

"You heard me."

"And here I was going to offer you the use of my car. Well, you can damn well walk into Sydney."

Bay hung up the phone in Ruth's ear and covered her face with her hands. Why wasn't her mother here? How was she supposed to raise Ashley without her? She felt a soft wet nose press against her thigh. She looked down at Merlin. He always knew when she was unhappy. She reached out to ruffle his ears.

"What would I do without you, eh?"

Merlin put his head on her lap.

❉

"Are you sure we can find our way back?"

Ashley sat between Matt's legs, nestled against his chest, his arms around her as they both leaned against a tree and looked out over a small cove neither of them had seen before. Privacy was hard to find, even in a small town surrounded by miles of fir trees, so they'd ventured off the road and walked down an unfamiliar path towards the water.

Matt kissed the back of her head. "I don't care if we ever go back."

Ashley smiled and snuggled against him. "Me neither."

She was happy. She hadn't thought she'd be happy again, after finding her grandmother on the kitchen floor with an oven mitt still on her hand, tea biscuits scattered around her. The shock had been so great; she didn't speak for days, even when her mother begged her to. Ashley knew that if she opened her mouth, she wouldn't be able to stop screaming.

It was Matt who broke her silence. Day after day she went to school and day after day her friends steered clear of her, unsure whether to approach her or not. Ashley knew Matt but didn't normally hang around with his cool crowd, so when he came up to her one day as she waited for the school bus, she was startled.

And then he put his arm around her.

"I know your grandmother died, Ashley, and I know how sad you are. It kills me to see you look so sad, but I know how it feels. My grandmother died too."

Her eyes filled with tears and she didn't want him to see. She looked away and bit her lower lip hard to keep herself from feeling anything. He reached out and touched her cheek, making her look at him.

"It was awful to find her like that, wasn't it?"

She couldn't breathe. When she tried to get away from him, he kept his grip on her shoulder. "Tell me, Ashley. Tell me how awful it was."

Ashley hit him. She pounded on his chest and he let her. Tears scalded her eyes and she tried to keep it in but finally had to open her mouth, because she couldn't catch her breath. And when she did, a guttural sound escaped from deep inside. She didn't recognize it as her own voice and it frightened her. But Matt was there, and when she had no energy left and started to sink to her knees, he pulled her up and let her cry into his sweater. He held her close and muffled those horrible sounds, so she didn't have to be frightened anymore.

That was last summer. They'd been inseparable since.

Ashley took her index finger and traced the words *I love you* in the palm of Matt's hand.

"I love you too," he said quietly.

She swivelled a little so she could see his face. "I'm never afraid when I'm with you."

"That's an odd thing to say. Are you usually afraid?"

She looked away again. "Yes."

"Of what?"

"Everything."

"Why?"

"What if my mom dies?"

"She's not going to die. She's too young to die."

"My dad died when he was twenty-two."

"God, that's my brother's age. He drowned, right?"

"Yeah, with my grandfather."

"You never knew them, did you?"

"No. I was born about six months later."

"That must have been awful for your mom, and your grandmother."

"Nana used to tell me about my grandfather and the silly things he did. I have a picture of him in his boat. But Mom doesn't talk about my dad very much. Whenever I ask, she says he was sweet and he had big hands and the world's best smile. Then she usually walks out of the room and goes outside to sit on the swing. I always see her looking out over the water and she looks lonely. I don't want to be alone. Ever."

"You're never going to be alone. I'm here."

She held his hands in a vice grip. "What if you die?"

"Silly girl, I'm going to live forever and be the greatest hockey player the world has ever seen."

"Oh yeah, I forgot," she laughed.

"Besides, you must have some other relatives kicking around. Everyone does."

"My mom has a younger sister, but I've never met her. Well, I met her once when I was three, but I don't remember. She could be in Outer Mongolia for all I know."

"You've never met her? Didn't she come home for your grandmother's funeral?"

"No." There was nothing else she could say.

Matt filled in the silence. "We have a family reunion every year and I get pinched and prodded and kissed by all my old aunties. It's horrible."

Ashley laughed and turned right around so she could face him. "It's horrible to be kissed, is it? Well, how about I make you feel downright miserable?"

She put her arms around his neck and kissed him hard as he pushed her back into the soft moss and lay on top of her. She wanted to stay there until the stars came out, one by one.

"Don't ever leave me, Matt," she whispered against his skin as his hand pushed up her shirt and encircled her ribs.

"Never, ever." And then he kissed her until she was dizzy.

Bay was waiting for her when Ashley finally walked into the kitchen. It was almost suppertime.

"I'm starved. What's for dinner?"

Bay folded her arms across her chest and leaned against the sink. "Where were you?"

"Out."

"You'll have to do better than that."

Ashley threw her jacket on the table. "Aren't I getting a little old for this? Everyone else I know is allowed to go out with their friends without getting the third degree."

"It's only common courtesy to let me know your plans. You should've told me."

"I couldn't find you."

Bay pushed herself away from the sink. "You didn't try very hard then, did you? I was only in the garden." She sat at the kitchen table. "I want you to sit down. I need to talk to you."

Ashley rolled her eyes and opened the fridge. "We're always talking. I'm sick of talking." She reached out and grabbed a wrapped cheese slice.

"Sit down."

Ashley sighed and plunked into the chair on the other side of the table. She busied herself opening the cheese wrapper.

It gave Bay a chance to look at her, and when she did, a chill ran up her spine. She'd seen that face before.

"You were with Matt, weren't you?"

Ashley shrugged. "So?"

"Matt's mother was on the phone and she was fit to be tied because he took off with her car."

"She's always fit to be tied. She's nuts."

"No. She's a worried mother, like I am. We think you and Matt are spending much too much time together, and it's not healthy."

Ashley looked up at her. "Not healthy? What's that supposed to mean?" She started to rise and when she did, Bay tapped the table-top.

"Sit down, young lady. I'm not finished talking to you."

Ashley stayed standing and threw the cheese to Merlin. "Well, I'm finished talking to you. I'm not seven years old, Mom. I'm seventeen, and I love Matt, and if I want to be with him I will. He's the only one around here who knows me."

"I know you—"

"No, Mom. Nana knew me, not you." And with that Ashley turned on her heel and stormed out of the kitchen.

Bay sat very still and listened to the clock tick. There was no other sound. She should get up, but what for? She wouldn't see Ashley for the rest of the night. She'd prefer to hole up in her room to punish her mother. Going to bed hungry was preferable to coming downstairs and chancing another meeting.

Bay had never felt so alone in her life. She went outside and sat on the garden swing. She heard her neighbours go about their business getting supper ready. There were six houses on their side of the lane, and the backyards all melted into each other. For the most part, shrubs and clotheslines and garages marked the property borders. The bottom of the lawns met the farmer's field, which was covered with wildflowers at this time of year. Beyond that, alders grew close to the rocky shoreline. There was no sand to speak of, and the drop-off was so steep that none of the kids in the neighbourhood used it as a beach.

The wind was still up and Bay could taste salt in the air. On top of that, the fog that blanketed the coast rolled in and made her shoulder-length wavy hair completely unruly. She felt the tiny dew-like drops cover her head like a veil, as the grey mist crept over the house.

She thought she should get up and tell Flo to take her sheets in before they became too damp. Just then, Flo threw open her back door and hurried down the steps.

"Bloody weather," Flo grumped. "It'll be the death of me yet."

Bay stood up and gave her a hand, starting at one end while Flo took the other. They worked in silence until they neared one another.

"A little birdie told me you're seeing Dermot Fraser," Flo smirked. "Now there's a fine man. You could do worse."

"I'm not seeing him." Bay passed her a folded sheet. "He's a friend."

"Ain't they all, until ya marry the buggers. You need to get out more, Bay. You're only a young woman. Your ma wouldn't want you moping away forever."

Bay didn't want to talk about it.

Flo pointed across the yard. "Speak of the devil, isn't that him now?"

Bay looked and saw Dermot walk around the back of her house. He never came to the front door. Most people didn't. It was the village way.

"I'm over here, Dermot."

Dermot stopped and waved. Bay knew he wouldn't venture over to Flo's yard. He was a little afraid of Flo, but then so were a lot of people.

"You go now, child," Flo said cheerfully. "Thanks for your help."

Bay passed her the last of the sheets. "See you tomorrow."

"Maybe. Maybe not. I could die in my sleep."

Bay walked over to her own yard, where Dermot stood and waited for her. He was a little taller than she was, with a hard, compact body and a mop of dark hair. He had an interesting, rugged face, with an intense gaze that unnerved her at times. He didn't smile often, but he was kind.

"Hi, Dermot."

"Hi, Bay."

She stopped in front of him. "Have you had your supper?"

He nodded. "I wouldn't say no to a cup of tea."

"Sure, come on in."

They went into the kitchen and Dermot sat down as Bay put the kettle on. Dermot and Merlin had a great reunion. Merlin flopped on the floor and exposed his belly so Dermot could scratch it.

Bay straightened up a little, aware that the countertops were filled with her junk and Ashley's. She couldn't seem to keep the house tidy. At least not since her mom died.

"You'll have to excuse the mess. Teenage daughters are not conducive to clean homes."

"It looks better than my place." Dermot lived in a rambling old farmhouse his father had left him. It was in desperate need of a coat of paint, but the bones were still good. Everyone in town said the only thing it needed was a woman's touch, but so far Dermot remained a bachelor. Naturally there was speculation in some corners that he was gay, but most pooh-poohed that idea. As Flo said, no fairy she'd ever come across knew how to fix a car engine, and since Dermot was a mechanic who ran the only gas station in town, that let him off the hook.

"You look tired, Bay. Are you all right?"

She brushed her bangs out of her face with a sweep of her hand and took a quick glance in the mirror that hung by the kitchen sink. Her lovely hazel eyes had dark circles under them. She was only thirty-six, but felt fifty. She pretended otherwise.

"I'm fine." She made the tea and brought it to the table. "I didn't bake today. Would you settle for an Oreo?"

"Nothing, thanks." Dermot sipped his tea. "I was wondering if you were up to going to the show on Friday night?"

Bay sipped her tea so she didn't have to answer him right away. A part of her wanted to go badly, but another part couldn't be bothered. She just didn't want to hurt his feelings. When she looked down at his hands she knew he'd gone to a lot of trouble to get the grease from underneath his fingernails before he came over. It made her feel worse.

She put down her teacup. "I'll have to see what Ashley is doing. Can I get back to you?"

Dermot didn't answer and his silence bothered her. "I'm sorry, okay? What do you want from me?" She got up quickly and took her cup to the sink. Dermot rose from his chair and stood behind her.

"You know what I want. I've told you long enough, but you put up roadblocks whenever I come near you. I've just about had it."

She spun around. "You've had it? What are you talking about?"

Dermot grabbed her shoulders. "You know how I feel about you, Bay. Everyone in this damn town knows how I feel about you. I've waited and waited and I don't know how much longer I can wait."

She lowered her head. "I'm sorry, Dermot. I don't feel anything anymore. Not for you, not for anyone."

"Let me show you." He held her face in his hands and kissed her. She resisted at first, but suddenly didn't care anymore. She didn't have the strength to object.

He raised his head and looked into her eyes. "Let me help you, Bay. You don't have to be alone."

"I'm not alone. I have Ashley."

"You need a man to love you. Let me be that man."

She felt his warm body against her and it was tempting to let him take her. His lips found hers again and she began to lean against him. When he kissed the hollow of her throat she gave a little gasp.

That's when Ashley cleared her throat.

Bay pushed Dermot away. He looked confused and then realized Ashley was in the room.

"Honey, I—"

"Don't bother, Mom. You're such a hypocrite. You don't want anyone to love me, but you let anyone who walks in off the street kiss you. At least Matt and I have the decency to go somewhere private. He doesn't do me in the kitchen."

Dermot raised his voice. "How dare you speak to your mother like that?"

"Dermot, please."

"Your mother is the most decent woman I've ever met and you have no right to upset her."

"Why should I listen to you?" Ashley yelled at him. "Who are you to me? You're the greasy guy who runs the gas station. Why don't you take her out for dinner before you take her to bed?"

Bay walked up to Ashley and slapped her across the face.

Ashley gasped and covered her cheek. "I hate you. Why didn't you die instead of Nana? Why wasn't it you?" She turned and ran out the front door.

Bay went after her. "Wait, Ashley. Come back!"

But Ashley didn't stop. She ran up the street and disappeared.

Bay stood in the front porch and covered her face. She rocked back and forth, not knowing what to do. Then she felt Dermot's hand on her arm.

"Bay…"

She didn't look at him. "Please go. Just go."

"I want to help you."

She uncovered her face then. "You've done enough, thank you very much. I don't want your help. I don't need anyone's help. Now leave me alone!"

And with that she ran up the stairs and disappeared behind her bedroom door.

CHAPTER TWO

Tansy Gillis stood at the top of the stairs and surveyed the scene below. Their guests were arriving. The strains of the string quartet hired for the occasion were heard quietly in the background, as the hum of voices and bursts of laughter gathered strength in the foyer. The women looked divine in their haute-couture gowns and the men even better. Was there anything more delicious than a man in a tuxedo?

Tansy never got tired of this. She lived for the moment she descended the stairs and all eyes looked up to watch her grand entrance. She had practised just such a scenario in the wooden tree fort she and Bay built beyond the farmer's field back home. Although she was the younger sister, Tansy was always the queen and Bay the servant. Neither one of them questioned it.

She stepped away from the railing and turned around to take one last peek in the large mirror in the hallway. Her blonde hair was pulled away from her face and caught up in a chignon. Dangling diamond earrings fell to the length of her chin. Her lips and eye shadow were the palest of pinks, to go with her salmon-coloured satin gown. She smoothed the corset top with her hands, circling her tiny waist. She wouldn't be able to take a bite of the delicious spread downstairs, but who cared about food? Everyone knew you never ate at a party. Someone might take your picture and sell it to the tabloids.

Tansy wanted this evening to be special. It was Charles's seventieth birthday and everyone who was anyone in New York was here in his fabulous penthouse apartment that overlooked Central Park. She spent weeks going over every detail with the event planners. He'd tell her not to make such a fuss, but she'd put her finger on his lips and tell him to hush. He'd smile and throw his hands in the air. "Fine then, do your worst."

A quick glance at her watch told her it was time to get going. She gathered up her gown and hurried to his dressing room, expecting him to be inside fiddling with his bow tie, but when she opened the door and called his name, no one answered.

Checking everywhere, she finally tried his study. She reached for the handle and was about to go through when she heard voices behind the door. She didn't want to interrupt if he was consulting with one of his many business partners, but when she heard a female voice laugh softly, the hairs on the back of her neck stood up. She leaned her ear against the door. There it was again.

Tansy carefully pushed down the handle and opened the door slightly. Charles was at his desk, a gorgeous young thing sitting in his lap. She had her arms around his neck and his hand was on her thigh. When it disappeared up her skirt, Tansy threw the door wide open.

Charles looked startled, but only for a moment.

"How are you going to explain your way out of this one, Charles?"

Charles carefully removed his hand and said to the young woman, "Would you excuse us, my dear?"

"Of course." She slipped off his lap and smoothed down her skirt. Then she gave Tansy a withering look before turning back to Charles. "Will I see you later?"

Charles didn't answer, so Tansy had to be content with that. The woman held her head up and walked past Tansy with a smirk on her face.

Tansy looked over her shoulder at the girl's retreating back. "Don't look so smug. He does this on a regular basis."

The door slammed shut.

Tansy turned back to Charles. "Why tonight?"

Charles's silver hair glowed in the light of the banker's lamp on his desk. "Tansy, it's my birthday. Can't a man have a little fun on his birthday?" He rose from his chair and walked out from behind his desk. He approached her with outstretched arms. "Don't be cross. Come give Daddy a kiss."

Tansy's stomach turned. "I deserve better than this, Charles."

He frowned slightly, reached over, and took her chin in his hand. "You deserve everything you get." Then he kissed her and made her kiss him back. "And you do get everything, don't you? I hope I don't have to tell you how lucky you are."

Tansy thought of the guests downstairs, the wonderful party she'd organized for him, and how the society pages would be filled with gossip about tonight. As much as she wanted to poke his eyes out, she had too much on the line to throw it away. She took a deep breath and smiled at him.

"I do know how lucky I am. I'm a lucky, lucky woman."

Charles patted her cheek. "Good girl."

Tansy walked down the stairs on Charles's arm to the sounds of applause and the singing of "Happy Birthday." Once they made their entrance and greeted everyone with air kisses, Tansy threw herself into the role of hostess. She laughed and tittered, smiled and cajoled, as she made sure the servants plied everyone with Moët Champagne and Russian caviar. She stood with groups of guests and had her picture taken. She'd sidle up to Charles and he'd put his arm around her waist, kiss her temple, and tell everyone what a lucky man he was to have such a beautiful young woman in his life.

And as much as she knew she was admired and envied by the celebrities in the crowd, she felt the eyes of high-society matrons boring into the back of her very pretty head. No matter how hard she tried, she couldn't fool these old birds. They knew class when they saw it, and the little girl from a small town in Cape Breton didn't have it, no matter how successful her party.

At one point, Charles held court by the buffet table. He waved Tansy over and introduced her to the CEO of one of his subsidiaries.

"I was telling Earl here that you flew in these lobsters from Nova Scotia." He pointed to the fresh lobster meat sitting on ice in a crystal bowl. "My special request."

"I understand you were born there," Earl said to her. "You must love lobster."

"I don't, actually."

"Nonsense!" Charles laughed. "Everyone loves lobster. Besides, it cost me a pretty penny." He picked up a fork and speared a large morsel, holding it up to Tansy's mouth. "Go on, take a bite."

"No, thank you."

Charles kept the fork in the air. "I insist."

Tansy was grateful when the CEO looked away as she opened her mouth and took the meat in her mouth. Charles looked triumphant. He put his arm around Earl's shoulder and steered him away from the table. Tansy hurried to the downstairs powder room and spit the lobster into the toilet before flushing it down.

Three hours into the party, she couldn't stand it anymore. She slipped away and grabbed a bottle of bubbly out of the small fridge in the back pantry and then sat on a stool and poured herself glass after glass, downing each of them with one toss of her head. One of the waiters watched her every time he came back into the kitchen to have his tray filled. He smiled at her and she raised her glass to him in a silent toast.

She'd finished the bottle when he slipped into the pantry and shut the door behind him.

"A pretty lady like you shouldn't be drinking alone."

"No, I shouldn't, but there you have it." She drained the last glass and held it out for more. "Why don't you give me another bottle?"

He came closer to her. "Why don't I give you something else?"

Tansy laughed. "I'm afraid I'll have to pass."

"Why?"

"Do you have millions of dollars?"

"If I did, I wouldn't be waiting on tables, now would I?"

Tansy tried to focus on his face. "I like you. You've got spunk."

He reached for her waist and pulled her close. "I have a feeling you're pretty spunky yourself."

"I was once."

"Let's find out if you still are." He locked the door.

❦

The waiter slipped out first. Checking to see if the coast was clear, Tansy raced up the back stairs to her dressing room. She had to fix her hair. It fell out of its bobby pins, but because she felt decidedly queasy by now, her hands trembled and she couldn't do it properly.

As she fussed in the mirror, her eyes fell upon the framed picture on her dressing table. It was of her mom, Bay, and Ashley, laughing together on the family swing. "Please don't look at me," she whispered.

She had to hurry. Charles would notice her absence and figure out a way to make her pay.

When she went back downstairs, some of the guests had already left. Charles was seated on an ottoman, swaying and singing "New York, New York" with his cronies.

A cold finger tapped her on the shoulder. She turned around and came face to face with Charles's eldest son, Philip.

"Don't think you're fooling anyone, Tansy. I know what you've been up to."

"I haven't been up to anything."

"I beg to differ. I'm sure my father would love to know the truth."

"What truth?"

"That you were having a party of your own with the hired help."

Tansy stayed very still. "What do you want, Philip?"

"I want what my father has."

"Meaning?"

"You."

She blinked. That was the last thing she expected him to say, especially as his wife was ten feet away. Tansy drew her shoulders back. "Say that again and you'll regret it. You're not the only one who can run to your father with tittle-tattle." She moved away.

"Blood is thicker than water," Philip reminded her. "Who do you think he'll believe?"

Her head throbbed. She was so damn weary of the lot of them. "You know what, Philip? I really don't care."

She left the room.

The next day, Tansy returned home with shopping bags filled with new summer clothes from Prada. The chauffeur was behind her with the bags she couldn't carry.

She took everything up to her suite and laid the clothes on the bed. Maria would put them away later. She fingered the silk camisoles and the linen suits. The wraparound dresses and party outfits were so beautiful that she was dying to show someone, but that would have to wait. When she glanced at the clock on the bedside table, it was four o'clock; time to get ready for this evening. The mayor was having an intimate dinner party and she wanted to look her best.

After a leisurely soak, she was wrapping herself up in a bath sheet when there was a knock on the bedroom door.

"Yes?"

She heard the door open. "Excuse me, Madam, you're wanted in the study."

"Thank you, Maria."

Charles never asked to see her in his study. The last time was when he presented her with keys to her very own Porsche. That's when it hit her. It was her birthday tomorrow. He'd remembered.

She took pains to look especially beautiful and didn't wear jewellery in case that was her gift. She pictured herself bending her neck to let Charles fasten the clasp of an exquisite necklace, or holding out her arm as he placed a diamond and sapphire bracelet on her wrist.

Tansy sprayed his favourite perfume, Chanel No. 5, on her throat. Taking one final look to make sure her lipstick was perfect, she jumped up from the vanity and hurried to the study. She knocked on the door softly.

Charles said, "Come in."

She opened the door and gave him a smile. Charles sat behind his desk with papers in his hand. When he looked up, he frowned.

She was unsure what to do. "You wanted me?"

"Yes. Sit down."

Closing the door, she walked toward him. "It's gloomy in here. Why don't you turn on a light?"

"Fine. If you would, Philip."

Tansy spun around as the light came on. Philip sat in a wing chair beside a small table, the lamp chain in his hand.

"Tansy, I asked you to sit down."

She looked back at Charles and then slowly walked to the chair in front of his desk. She sat. "What is this, Charles?"

"Philip told me something interesting last night, didn't you, Philip? Something about you entertaining a waiter instead of my guests at the party."

Tansy turned her head to look at her accuser.

"Don't look so surprised. I told you I would."

She glared him. "You've waited for this, haven't you? Why do you hate me so much? What have I ever done to you? It's not like I'm in line to inherit his money. I'm not a threat."

Philip lit a cigarette. "Oh yes, you are."

"How? I'm his lover, not his wife."

"A lover who can get pregnant any time it suits her. And we can't have that."

"Your father beds every woman he sees. If it's not me, it'll be someone else. Your inheritance isn't safe."

Charles glowered at her. "What I do with my free time is my business. As you say, you're not my wife. But we've been together now for two years, the longest I've been with anyone other than his mother. And I expected loyalty."

"Loyalty? Is it loyalty when your son asks me to go to bed with him?"

"I did no such thing. She's lying to save her own skin."

Charles stood and came around the desk, then grabbed her arm and made her look at him. "You live a life most people can only dream of, and this is how you repay me? By screwing a waiter on my kitchen floor?"

"That's not true."

He slapped her face. "Fifty bucks and a bottle of scotch loosened your waiter's tongue, so don't lie to me."

She put her hand up to her stinging cheek. "I'm sorry."

He turned away and walked over to the floor-to-ceiling window, where the bright lights of New York shone in the dark. There he stood for quite a while before he said, "Leave us, Philip."

"But Dad—"

"Go."

Philip got up reluctantly and gave Tansy a disgusted look before he walked out the door.

Charles turned his head from the window. "Why, Tansy?"

She looked at her hands. "I was drunk and stupid and jealous of that young girl…"

"You hurt me."

"I know that."

His face softened. "Come here."

Tansy got out of the chair and walked over to him. He took her hand.

"I love you, Tansy. You're the one I want by my side."

"And I will be."

Charles reached out and held her tight. "Let's go to your room."

They left the study to walk to the bedroom. He kissed her once more before she opened the door and then quietly closed it behind them.

❃

She dreamt she was running through the farmer's field behind their house, Bay in front of her laughing. She was happy and the sun shone brightly on her face. It was so bright it became uncomfortable.

Tansy woke with a start. Early morning light filled every corner of the room. She gave a great stretch and then relaxed with her arms over her head. She hadn't expected to see Charles this morning. He told her he had an early meeting but to get herself dolled up for dinner tonight. He was taking her somewhere special for her birthday.

Tansy turned over on her belly. She smoothed the satin sheets with her hand, but her limbs felt heavy, like they did after a session in the gym. There was a good reason for that. Last night Charles had surprised her. She'd never known him to be so imaginative or so demanding. Her cheeks grew hot when she thought of it.

She'd done it. She'd escaped by the skin of her teeth. The fright of last night made her realize that she had to work extra hard, but it would be worth it. Before they'd fallen asleep he'd mentioned a world cruise.

At the thought of it, she jumped out of bed and hummed as she went into the bathroom. She was pinning up her hair when she noticed it.

There was a hundred-dollar bill sticking out from under a can of hairspray.

And a note.

Get out of my house.

CHAPTER THREE

Bay watched Wendell Bonaparte stagger up the street towards the post office. As she sorted the mail, she kept her eye on him through the front window. Every morning Wendell lurched his way down Main Street and every morning Bay was sure he'd be hit by a car. But drunks and fools must have someone looking after them, because he always managed to make it.

She prepared herself. The door flew open and Wendell came flying in with it. The only reason he stayed on his feet was Verna Bradford's enormous bosom. He careened into her and steadied himself against her soft bulges.

"Morning, Verna. Grand day, wha'?"

Verna hit him with her newspaper. "Get off me, you great oaf."

Wendell took several steps back and removed his ball cap to reveal his greasy comb-over. He waved his hat about with a flourish and bowed. "So sorry, me lady. No offence meant."

Verna didn't look impressed. "Get yourself into detox, Wendell, for your poor ma's sake. I can't for the life of me figure out why she doesn't boot your arse all the way from here to Halifax."

Wendell blinked several times as he swayed in front of his opponent. "Well, my dear, that may be because my arse isn't nearly as large a target as yours."

Verna gave an indignant shout and tore off out the door.

Bay bit her lip to keep from laughing. Wendell weaved his way over to her. He leaned on the counter and winked.

"That wasn't very nice, Wendell."

He put his ball cap back on. "No, sadly, it wasn't."

"No cheque for you today, I'm afraid."

He winced. "Goddamn government."

"They don't come in until Thursday."

Wendell's head went back. "Isn't today Thursday?"

"Nope."

He sighed and the smell of alcohol almost made her eyes water.

"You better go home, Wendell. Your ma will be looking for you."

He saluted her and did the two-step over to the post office door. He shouted over his shoulder, "When are you going to marry me, Bay?"

"When pigs fly."

"Righto." And out he went.

Bay shook her head and kept sorting. She was about to grab another bundle when she heard the school bus approach. Most days Ashley sat on the right side of the bus and would wave at her as they rumbled by. For the past week she was nowhere to be seen. There were only eight days left before both she and Matt graduated from high school, so this endearing ritual was quickly coming to a close. It hurt not to see her grinning face in the window.

Once more Bay steadied herself for Ashley's rejection, but there she was. She gave a small wave and a half-hearted smile, but they meant everything to Bay.

When her best friend, Gertie, came up the walk, Bay was smiling from ear to ear.

"Hey ho," Gertie cried. Gertie was single and very pretty, but because she was a large gal, that's all people saw. Her uncontrollable frizzy hair didn't help matters. She was always on a diet, yet managed to gain more and more weight as the years went by. She told people she still had her baby weight on, but didn't tell them her baby was a cat named Jeffrey.

"Hi, Gertie. What's up with you?"

Gertie leaned her plump elbows on the counter. "Same old, same old. Ashley talking to ya yet?"

Bay nodded. "Well, sort of. She waved at me this morning."

Gertie rolled her eyes, but Bay was used to it. Gertie didn't know how hard it was to be a mother and that you had to take your small victories when you could get them.

"What she needs to do is crawl on her hands and knees and beg your forgiveness for being so damn rude."

"I did slap her."

"Too right you did, and she deserved it."

"Okay, let's drop it, shall we?"

Gertie always took the hint. She straightened up. "Any mail for me?"

Bay walked to the back of the postal boxes and took out a couple of grocery store flyers. "This is it."

Gertie was the only one she knew who was happy to get them. Gertie grabbed them out of her hand and flipped through the pages.

"Oh, goodie. Ice cream's on sale this week."

"So's celery."

"Your point?"

"Don't have one."

"Good…oh mercy, look who's coming."

Bay looked up and saw Dermot approaching with his postal key already in his hand.

"Oh great, just what I need. He never leaves me alone."

"He's allowed to pick up his mail, isn't he?"

"No, he's not." Bay pretended to be busy, and Gertie pretended she was reading the flyer.

Dermot pretended he didn't see them at all. He walked up to the mailbox, opened it, took his mail, and left.

The two women looked at each other.

"Oh, shit."

"Bay, what is wrong with you? That's one good-looking man when he's not in his grimy overalls. He cleans up real good, if you ask me."

"I didn't ask you."

"Well, since you're a stupid bitch, I guess you don't mind me taking my chances with him."

Bay's head shot up and when it did Gertie pointed a finger in her face. "The thought of that scared ya, didn't it?"

"Don't be ridiculous. Look, Gertie, I have work to do, so you better vamoose."

"Okay then." Gertie headed for the door. "I think I'll doll myself up and run over a box of nails with my car. Might have to get my tires fixed at the garage."

"Get goin'. And remember, supper's at six."

"I'll be there." Gertie gave her a wave and was gone.

Bay and Gertie met in sixth grade. Gertie's family moved into their grandmother's house after the old lady died and because her parents were older, they'd shoo her out of the house at every opportunity. Gertie was left to fend for herself, which was deadly, since she was the new, fat kid in town.

The first week of school was hell. The school bully was overjoyed to have a new target to practise on. Bay would watch from the sidelines, too afraid to intervene as Bradley taunted Gertie about her fat ass and jelly belly. Once Gertie looked at Bay with tears in her eyes, as if to ask, why don't you help me? The only reason she didn't was that Bradley had just started to leave her alone after ribbing her for weeks about her knobby knees and stick legs. No way did she want that to start over.

And so she was ashamed when her little sister, Tansy, came out of the school one day and happened to witness Bradley point at Gertie and laugh at her, calling her names while a group of kids stood around and watched the show.

Even though Tansy was in fifth grade, she marched up to Bradley and kicked him in the shin. When he bellowed and started after her, she held her ground and said for all to hear, "You dare hit me, Bradley, I'll tell your da I saw you cryin' in the principal's office."

That stopped him dead.

Tansy went up to Gertie. "You okay?"

Gertie nodded.

"Good." Tansy walked away and so did everyone else once the fun stopped.

Bay stayed behind and smiled at Gertie. "Want to come to my house? My mom makes good cookies."

Gertie sniffed and nodded as she shuffled along beside Bay. "Wasn't that your little sister?"

"Yeah."

"I like her. She's pretty, and really brave."

"I know."

Tansy didn't become Gertie's friend. Tansy wouldn't be caught dead with a loser. Gertie thought she came to her rescue because she didn't like to see injustice, but Bay knew it was because Tansy loved being the centre of attention. No matter. Gertie became Bay's best friend and if it weren't for Tansy it might not have happened.

Whenever Bay thought of her sister, it was as if she were remembering a character in one of the fairy tales their mother would read to them at night, more illusion than flesh and blood. She didn't talk to anyone about her sister and hadn't seen her in years. People in town were scandalized when Tansy didn't show up for her mother's funeral. They never said as much to Bay, but she knew by the hints that were dropped while they licked envelopes and stuck stamps on parcels.

"Must be hard to be on your own, dear, with only your daughter to comfort you," they'd say in a variety of ways. Bay would nod and change the subject. Only grouchy old Mrs. Skinner had the nerve to say it to her face.

"I think it's dreadful that Tansy wasn't there to say goodbye to your ma. A finer woman I've never met, but I'm afraid I can't say the same about your sister. Stuck-up little trollop she was, always parading around and chasing anything in pants. You mark my words, no good will come to her. No good at all."

Despite incidents like that, Bay loved her job. She had her finger on the pulse of the whole town. People would sometimes open a letter in the foyer, and then turn around with happy faces or looks of dismay. She knew everyone's secrets because people knew Bay never gossiped. They themselves talked about everyone else in town while they waited in line or leaned against the counter before heading off for work or household chores. Just by being quiet, Bay learned more than she often wanted to know about her fellow citizens.

Finally it was five o'clock. Bay was anxious to get home and talk to Ashley before Gertie arrived for supper. She wanted to give Ashley a hug and tell her how wonderful she was, despite their differences. Bay was tired of being on the outs with her daughter. Life was too short for that kind of nonsense.

She closed up the post office and hurried down the street before remembering she didn't have any milk, and tea without milk was a sad thing. She opened the door of one of the local shops and headed right for the cooler. With two cartons of 1 percent milk in her arms, she waited impatiently for Dolena Bagnell to hurry up and find the correct coins in her change purse. She knew she was in for a long wait. Dolena was as blind as a bat.

"I can't seem to find another nickel," Dolena told the bored teenager behind the counter.

Bay searched her pockets and found one. "Here, Dolena, take this."

Dolena waved her off. "No, dear, I'm fine. I won't be but a moment."

The teenager and Bay looked at each other in misery. There was nothing for it. Dolena would not be moved until she found her nickel. As she fumbled around pushing aside change she spoke up.

"Did any of you see that movie star drive down the street this afternoon?"

The bored teenager perked up. "Movie star?"

It sometimes happened that the odd famous person was seen walking or driving around; Louisbourg was a tourist town, famous for its historic fortress.

"Oh yes, I'm sure of it. Beautiful, she was."

"Who was it?" Bay asked, since she had nothing else to do.

"Oh, I'm sure it was that one who was in that movie...oh, what's the name of it...you know the one I mean."

"Ah, no. I can't say I do."

"She's blonde..."

The teenager shouted, "Reese Witherspoon?"

Dolena looked puzzled. "Who?"

"Kirsten Dunst?"

"Dunst?"

"Never mind, Dolena," Bay almost shouted. She looked at the clerk. "Can you put this on my bill instead?"

"Sure."

Bay headed for the door. That's when Dolena remembered. "Grace Kelly."

Bay turned around. "Grace Kelly is dead."

"Well, it looked like her, back in the days before she married that foreigner. Driving down the street in her fancy car, she was."

"You don't say." Bay hurried outside and kept going. As she neared her street she passed Eldon, an old widower who liked to carve rough little animals out of wood, paint them bright colours, and sell them to unsuspecting tourists as real folk art.

"Hi, Eldon."

"What's goin' on, girl?"

"Not much." She didn't want to stay and chat. "Sorry El, gotta run. I'm having company for supper."

"They've already arrived, I'm afraid."

She stopped. "What do you mean?"

"I mean there's a big fancy car in your driveway."

"Really?"

"Yep."

"I better go see." She left Eldon behind. She couldn't for the life of her figure out who it might be. Gertie drove a Dodge Shadow. As Bay got closer she saw the beautiful sleek silver car and despite her curiosity her steps slowed down the closer she got to it. She wasn't sure why. It was a feeling. Her heart started to pound and her mind went blank.

It couldn't be.

She started up the back steps and that's when Flo poked her head out of her kitchen window. "As I live and breathe, you'll never guess who's back."

No.

Bay looked through the screen door. Ashley sat at one end of the table looking happy and almost in awe. A beautiful woman sat opposite her. They were laughing together and both turned when they heard the door open. Bay stood there and held the heavy plastic bag down by her side.

Ashley couldn't contain her excitement. "Mom, look who's here."

Tansy stood and faced Bay. "Hi, Sis."

Bay couldn't find her voice.

"Aren't you glad to see me?"

Bay dropped her bag onto the counter. "Of course, how are you?"

The sisters gave each other a brief hug and stood awkwardly for a moment. Ashley broke the silence.

"I can't believe you two are sisters."

They looked at her.

Ashley pointed at Tansy. "I mean, you're so glamorous..."

"And I'm a bag lady," Bay frowned. "Thanks, kiddo." She sat at the table. It was either that or run out the door. Tansy sat too.

"You know I didn't mean it like that," Ashley said.

"I always thought your mother was the prettier sister," Tansy smiled.

Bay glanced at her. "You always did, didn't you?"

"So why are you here?" Ashley asked. "Where do you live? Are you a model? Why didn't you come home for so long?"

Bay put up her hand. "Enough."

"That's okay," Tansy laughed. "I don't mind."

Bay turned to her. "Oh. Then why the heck are you here?"

"*Mom.*"

Tansy held up her hands. "Now girls, don't fight."

"We're not fighting."

Ashley made a face. "We always fight."

"That's not true."

"We do so, Mom. You don't have to try and hide it."

Bay got up and slipped off her jacket. "I'm not hiding anything. I need to get busy and make supper."

Tansy watched the two of them with amusement. "Nothing changes. I used to fight with my mother. Remember, Bay?"

Bay had her back turned towards the counter and didn't answer.

"Is that why you didn't come home when Nana died?" Ashley asked. "Were you still mad at each other?"

Bay froze. Tansy didn't say anything at first. She looked down at her hands in her lap. "That's part of it, I suppose, but I was far away when it happened and couldn't get here in time."

Bay abandoned her post by the sink, coming closer to the table. "I hear airplanes are very fast these days. Have you heard of them?"

"*Mom.*"

Bay gave Ashley a look. "You 'Mom' me one more time and you can leave the kitchen."

"I'm not a little girl. You can't..."

"Please," Tansy said. "You both have every right to be furious with me for not coming to the funeral."

"You can say that again," Bay said.

"I'm sorry."

"You were always sorry. It really doesn't mean much."

Tansy sighed. "Can we just drop it? I'm tired and I've had a long day. I'm so happy to see you both. Please, Bay, let's be friends."

Ashley stared at her mother. Bay's jaw twitched. She was about to open her mouth when the door opened and in walked Gertie.

"Holy shit, whose car is that?...*Tansy*?"

"Hi, Gertie."

Gertie looked at Bay before answering. "Holy cow, Tansy, nice to see you again after so long. What have you been up to? Still kicking boys in the shin?"

Tansy gave a delighted laugh. "Oh yes, only now I aim a little higher."

Thank God Gertie was there. She kept the conversation going, which was just as well since Bay couldn't think. She busied herself getting everyone's supper ready while the other three talked. Finally she served them homemade macaroni and cheese with cornbread. When she placed it in front of her sister, Tansy looked at it.

"Is something wrong?" Bay asked. "I thought you liked macaroni and cheese."

Tansy looked up at her. "It smells like Mom's."

"It is Mom's. It's her recipe."

Tansy jumped up from the table. "I'm sorry." She ran out the door and through the back garden. By the time Bay, Gertie, and Ashley got to the porch, Tansy was running through the farmer's field, her hair falling down around her shoulders.

"What's wrong with her, Mom?"

Bay didn't answer as she watched her little sister fade from view.

It was Gertie who pulled Ashley away from the screen. "Let them be. They both need a little time."

"Time for what? It seems to me they've spent enough time apart."

"How about you show me your prom dress? Your mother says it's lovely."

"It is. I'll show you."

When Gertie and Ashley disappeared upstairs, Bay went out to the garden swing. She kept her eyes focused on the trees at the other end of the field. She knew where her sister had gone. The remnant of their old fort was still there, even after all these years. Tansy used to hide from everyone when something bad happened to her, and their mother would send Bay to fetch her.

What was she doing here? Why now?

Bay sat on the swing a while longer before she sighed and went in the house. She called the other two down for supper and put Tansy's plate in the microwave. Gertie opened the fridge to get some milk and whispered to Bay out of Ashley's earshot, "Are you okay? Do you need smelling salts?"

"I'll live."

"What the hell is she doing here?"

Bay shrugged.

As they ate their supper Ashley couldn't stop talking. "She's beautiful. Why didn't you tell me how beautiful she was?"

Gertie slathered butter on her cornbread. "She wasn't that gorgeous when she left. Did you see her toes? And her fingernails? And that skin. She's definitely been pampered."

"She's obviously rich," Ashley said. "Maybe I'll get an expensive graduation gift."

Bay pushed the food around her plate. "Don't count on it. She's always been tight with her money."

"Maybe that's why she's got some." Gertie popped another piece of cornbread in her mouth.

Ashley shoved her plate away. "You don't like her, do you, Mom?"

"Don't be silly."

"Well, look at your face. That tells me everything."

Bay placed her fork on the plate, put her elbows on the table, and leaned towards her daughter. "I know you're young, Ashley, but even at your age you must realize that life is rather complicated. If you must know, I'm in shock more than anything else. My sister has stayed away from me for almost fifteen years, and suddenly she pops out of nowhere. No explanations, no excuses, just waltzes in the door and says 'I'm back.' Where's she been? Why didn't she come home to comfort us when Nana died? I could've used some help a year ago. But she didn't bother, so yes, I am a little annoyed with her at the moment, but it doesn't mean I don't love her. She's my sister and she'll always be my sister, good or bad, happy or sad. Okay?"

Ashley blinked. "Okay."

"Well, I for one am ready for dessert," Gertie announced to no one in particular.

Neither Bay nor Ashley said anything, so Gertie looked down at the rug by the back door. "How about you, Merlin? Would you like an ice cream cone?"

Merlin woofed that yes, he'd love one, so Gertie got up and put everyone's dishes in the sink. She took out a carton of ice cream and served Merlin first. He had a great time licking maple walnut out of his dish.

"Last chance, girls." Gertie plopped two scoops on her cone.

"No, thank you," Bay and Ashley said in unison.

Gertie put the ice cream away and came back to the table. "I hate eating alone."

"You eat alone every night," Ashley said.

"No, I don't. Jeffrey is great company."

Ashley smiled. "How come you never married, Gertie?"

"Look at me. Who'd have me?"

Bay was annoyed. "Stop putting yourself down all the time. You're the nicest woman I know."

"I may be the nicest, but I'm also the fattest and fat ain't sexy."

Ashley clapped her hands. "Wait a minute. There's a website for fat people. Some guys get off on it, apparently."

Gertie put down her ice cream. "No one who lives around here. Do tell, o wise child."

"They have conventions and everything."

"Conventions for what?" Bay frowned.

"All these fat people get together and dance and stuff."

Gertie sucked on her ice cream. "What's the name of this website?"

"'Fat R Us', I think, or maybe 'FatSoWhat'?"

"I think she's onto something, Bay."

"But they only have conventions in Las Vegas and places like that," said the young know-it-all.

"I've got Air Miles. What the hell else am I going to use them for?"

The three of them looked at each other and giggled. Then they laughed out loud because it was ridiculous.

That's when Tansy opened the screen door and smiled. "What's so funny?"

It was easier after that.

Gertie and Ashley talked about nothing and everything, so Bay and Tansy were able to be together without having to confront each other. They both knew there would be lots of time for conversation when they were alone.

But it was Gertie who brought up the one thing Bay wanted to know.

"How long are you here for, Tansy?"

The silence was deafening. Even Merlin stopped licking himself.

"That depends on Bay."

Bay furrowed her brow. "It does?"

"I may be a lot of things, but I'm not a freeloader. I'm between engagements, shall we say, and I thought I could use a rest before I start on my next venture. It seemed to be the perfect opportunity to come and stay for a while, if you'll have me."

"Of course we'll have you!" Ashley cried. "This is so exciting. That means you'll be able to meet Matt and come to my prom and everything. Isn't this great, Mom?"

"Great." It sounded a little half-hearted, so Bay added, "You know you're welcome here anytime."

"I'll pay my own way. I don't want you out of pocket."

"What exactly is your next venture?" Gertie asked. "It sounds intriguing."

"I haven't narrowed it down yet. I'm too burnt out from the last project."

"Which was?" Ashley wanted to know.

"A mistake."

With that pronouncement, Tansy gave a great yawn and stretched her slender arms over her head. "Would it be possible to have a bubble bath? I'm fading as we speak."

While Tansy was in the tub, Gertie went out with Bay as she watered the garden.

"You must have nearly died when she walked in," Gertie said.

"You could say that. I honestly thought I'd never see her again."

"Did she...you know...say why she never came home for your mom's funeral?"

"She told Ashley she was too far away. Hello? What kind of an answer is that?"

"Obviously she's not going to say anything in front of Ashley, but it will be interesting to hear her excuse. I wonder why she stayed away so long."

Bay didn't answer.

❁

Ashley was upstairs in her room looking at her prom dress when Matt arrived.

"Anyone home?"

Ashley ran down the stairs and into his arms. She kissed him.

"I missed you."

"I missed you more."

"I love it when you say that."

"I can't stay long. I have to go to—"

"Never mind that, you're not going to believe it. My aunt showed up tonight."

"I was going to ask who owned the awesome car out there."

"She's beautiful. Wait till you meet her."

"She's not as beautiful as you are." He kissed her and they were still kissing when Tansy came down the stairs in her robe. Matt opened his eyes and gave a start. He pulled away from Ashley. "Sorry, we didn't see you."

"This is Matt, Aunt Tansy—"

"Please, call me Tansy." She walked down the last few steps and held out her hand to shake Matt's.

"It's nice to meet you, Matt. I can see why you like him, Ashley. He's very good looking."

Matt nodded and shook her hand, blushing profusely.

Ashley put her arms around his waist. "I know. And he's mine."

Matt pulled away as gently as he could. "Uh, I've got to go."

"Do you have to?"

"Yeah, Mom's waiting in the car. What colour is your dress? I have to order my tie and cummerbund."

"Am I supposed to tell you? Isn't that a secret?"

Tansy laughed. "You're not getting married."

"Okay, it's pink."

"That's all I needed. I'll call you later." Matt hurried out.

"Isn't he the sweetest?"

Tansy nodded. "Why don't you show me your dress?"

"Okay."

They went up the stairs and into Ashley's room. She took a garment bag out her closet and unzipped it, pulling the dress out into plain view. "What do you think?"

Tansy looked at the simple pink dress. "It's lovely. Where did you buy it?"

"Mom made it."

"Did she? She's very talented."

"She is. She can do anything. She hooked that rug you're standing on, and she made the quilt on my bed."

"Imagine. Is everything you have homemade?"

"Well...sort of. We don't have tons of money."

Tansy sat on the bed. "Does that bother you?"

Ashley quickly put her dress away. "Sometimes."

"Do you feel selfish for wanting more?"

Ashley walked over and sat at her desk. "Sort of."

"You should always want more." Tansy went to the window and peeked through the curtains. "This used to be my room and I always dreamed of having more."

"Really?"

"I didn't want to be stuck in a small town. I couldn't breathe."

"I can't leave Mom. I'm all she has."

"Aren't you going away to university?"

"I'm going here."

"Oh."

"I wouldn't mind going away, but we can't afford it."

Tansy came back to the bed and sat down. "Tell me about your young man."

Ashley's face immediately lit up. "He's wonderful."

"You're obviously in love."

She nodded. "But Mom and his mom think it's puppy love or something."

"That's what mothers are supposed to say. But I don't think your mother has any reason to talk. She was nineteen when she married your father."

"So you remember him?"

"Of course."

"What was he like?"

Tansy rubbed the quilt on Ashley's bed. "He was quite something. Your mother was a lucky woman."

"It's not fair that he died."

"No."

Before Ashley could say anything else, Tansy said, "I should put some clothes on. Excuse me." And with that she left the room.

❁

Bay was outside for a long time after Gertie said her goodbyes, looking over her plants and pulling out the odd weed from the garden. Flo came out her back door and hung up her dishtowels. It gave her the opportunity to grill Bay.

"So? Why's she here?"

"I don't have a clue."

"She must have said something."

"That something was pretty vague. Apparently she needs a rest before her next big adventure."

"It's all right for some," Flo snorted. "I hope you gave her a blast for staying away so long."

Bay walked over and shut off the valve on the water hose and started to reel it in. "I haven't really talked to her yet."

"Well, when that child of yours goes to bed, demand some answers. You need to stick up for yourself."

"I know you mean well, Flo," Bay smiled sadly, "but I need to do this my way."

Flo patted her arm. "Of course you do, duckie. Don't mind me. I just hate to see you looking down in the mouth."

Flo's back door opened and Ira stuck his head out. "Where the hell's the rum, woman?"

"I poured it down the toilet. Add a bottle of Coke and sup it through a straw if you're that desperate."

"You miserable old hag."

Flo took off across the lawn. "Get back in that house, you, before I set the dog on ya."

Ira disappeared and two seconds later so did Flo.

Bay had no more excuses to stay outside. She and Merlin went indoors and Bay washed her hands at the kitchen sink. All was quiet. She went upstairs and peeked in Ashley's room. She was reading.

"Studying for your last exam?"

Ashley nodded. "It's Biology. I hate science."

Bay went over to the end of the bed and sat down. Ashley put her book on her stomach.

"Honey, I don't want to fight anymore. So many nice things are going to happen to you in the next few weeks. I want to be able to share them with you."

"I know. Me too. I'm sorry I mouthed off at Dermot."

"I expect you to apologize to him the next time you see him."

Ashley made a face. "Great."

"Ashley..."

"All right, all right, I will."

"And I'm sorry I slapped you. There's no excuse for that."

"Okay."

Bay nodded and absentmindedly picked lint off the hem of her sweater.

"Are you okay, Mom?"

"Yeah."

"You know, you don't have to worry about Matt and me."

Bay gave a little smile. "I don't?"

"No. I'm not stupid."

"I know you're not stupid. I just don't want your heart to get broken."

"Matt loves me."

"You're young…"

"So were you."

"I know," Bay sighed, "but your dad was also three years older than I was."

"That doesn't matter."

Bay didn't want to get into another argument. "I better let you get back to it." She got up and started for the door.

"It's fun to have Tansy back, isn't it?"

She didn't turn around. "Yes. Goodnight, honey."

"Night."

"And don't stay on the phone too late, missy."

"I won't."

Bay went across the hall and walked into her room. Tansy stood by the bureau looking at a picture of their mother. She turned quickly when she heard Bay approach.

"Sorry, I didn't mean to barge in. Do you think I could get a copy of this?"

"You don't have that picture?"

"No."

"Well, you left in a hell of a hurry, Tansy, so I guess that's your fault."

"Isn't it always?"

CHAPTER FOUR

The next morning, Bay and Ashley's routine was thrown into chaos. Tansy, awake since five thanks to the crows cawing outside the bedroom window, had used up all the hot water with her twenty-minute shower, and was downstairs trying to make breakfast for everyone.

Since she hadn't cooked in years, the only one benefiting from her efforts was Merlin. He had a full breakfast from the stuff that fell on the floor. When Bay and Ashley roared downstairs to grab their usual glass of juice and granola bar, they were greeted by Tansy, who stood over their plates of burnt pancakes and undercooked bacon, as pleased as punch with herself.

"Breakfast is served."

"Gosh," Bay grimaced, "we don't usually stop for breakfast. Ashley has to catch the school bus and I have to be at work in ten minutes."

Tansy looked crestfallen.

"It looks delicious though," Ashley piped up. "How about I take a pancake for the road?" She reached out and grabbed one, taking a big bite.

"Don't you want syrup?"

Ashley couldn't answer. Her mouth was stuck together with batter. She rushed over to the sink and spit it out. "Yuck." She cupped water into her mouth to rinse out the glue-like substance.

"Oh dear, I suppose these are all horrible," Tansy fretted, poking them with a fork.

Bay smiled. "Don't worry about it. It takes practise."

Ashley agreed, once she'd wiped her mouth on a paper towel. "Pancakes are hard."

Bay looked at her watch. "You better run, Ash. Good luck with your exam. I'll keep my fingers crossed."

"Thanks." Ashley grabbed a banana, kissing her mother and then her aunt before she raced out the door. Tansy held her hand up to her face.

"She likes me."

"She does."

"I don't deserve it."

Bay looked away. "I'll see you tonight."

"Can I do anything for you today?"

Bay turned back. "Okay. Buy something for supper, and we need milk, dog food, and more granola bars."

Tansy ran to the pad by the phone and muttered the list. "Okay. I can walk the dog, too. And maybe I'll vacuum. I haven't done that in years."

"Wonderful. That puts me in a great mood, knowing you haven't lifted a finger in ages."

"I paid dearly for the privilege."

The sisters looked at one another. "See ya later," Bay said.

"Bye."

Once Bay was gone, Tansy looked around. "Well, Merlin. I think I can fix this place up. I picked up a hint or two from decorators over the years. What do you say we try and put our stamp on things?"

Merlin wagged his tail.

She didn't do the dishes or make the beds. Instead, she spent her morning moving furniture around and taking pictures off the wall only to hang them again, several inches lower than they were originally. The fact that there were now glaring nail holes showing mattered not a whit.

"All right, Merlin. I'll walk you first and then I'm off to hit the shops."

Tansy got dressed in her casual clothes, a cashmere sweater set and four-hundred-dollar jeans. She reached for her sunglasses and put Merlin on his leash. Then off they went, just in time to run into Flo scrubbing her front walk.

"Well, well." Flo threw the scrub brush in her bucket. "Look who the cat dragged in."

Tansy stopped. "It's look who the dog dragged out, unless you're blind, what with being old and everything."

Flo's mouth dropped open. "You always were a handful, Tansy Gillis. Your ma used to say so."

"And Mom used to say you were a windbag. I can see nothing's changed. Come on, Merlin." Tansy walked past the flustered Flo.

"You break your sister's heart and you'll have me to reckon with," Flo shouted.

Tansy waved but didn't look back.

She ran into Eldon next, sitting on his doorstep.

"Hey, girlie."

"I'm not a girl anymore, Eldon."

"Eh?"

She kept going.

Merlin made several stops at telephone poles, fence posts, and garbage boxes. But when he did his business on Kay Cathcart's newly sodded lawn, the shit hit the fan. Kay came down her front steps at a clip.

"Excuse me. Excuse me!"

Tansy and Merlin turned around. "Yes?"

"Your dog left his calling card on my new lawn. Didn't you see the sign?"

"What sign?"

Kay pointed at the big sign not ten feet away. "The one that reads 'No dogs, kids, bikes, Rollerblades, or salesmen.'"

"Merlin's not a dog."

Kay screwed up her face. "Not a dog? That hairy beast?"

Merlin looked away.

"That's right. He's my nephew."

"Your nephew? What kind of game are you playing at? Now pick up that mess before I call the cops."

Tansy stood there. "Make me."

Kay looked one way and then the other. She opened her mouth and then closed it. She was so stymied she froze.

Tansy waited.

Kay huffed and puffed and nearly blew up from the aggravation, but in the end she just stood there.

"Good day." Tansy and the dog walked away. When they got a

little further down the street, Tansy told Merlin, "Let that be a lesson to you. If you want people to know you've arrived, give them something to talk about."

Once Tansy dropped her nephew off at the house, she got back in her car and drove down the street. That's when she noticed she was almost out of gas. She turned around and went in the opposite direction until she saw the Irving sign.

Tansy pulled in alongside the gas pump and turned off the engine. She then reached in her purse and took out her lipstick, manoeuvring the rearview mirror until she could see her lips. She was applying the first coat when a man wearing coveralls sauntered over to the car wiping his hands on a greasy rag.

"Nice car."

"Thank you."

"Is there anything I can do for you?" Dermot asked.

Tansy put down her lipstick. "I'd like some gas."

"This is a self-serve station."

She smiled at him. "I'm quite capable of servicing myself, but why bother when there's a handsome guy here to do it for me?"

Dermot gave her a quick look and then a small smile. He put the rag in his back pocket, and reached for the nozzle. "It'll be my pleasure."

"Yes, it will."

Dermot smirked and started to fill the car. "You're not from around here, are you?"

Tansy decided to get out. She opened the door and stood up in one fluid motion, then shut the car door and leaned against it. "Not now. I was in New York. You?"

"My family is originally from Louisbourg, but I only moved back three years ago."

Tansy crossed her arms. "Don't you go crazy in this small place? Aren't you tired of servicing Tercels when you can service this?" She tossed her head towards her Porsche.

"It is tempting," he smiled.

"I'm Tansy, by the way."

"Dermot."

"Hello, Dermot." She held out her hand.

He shook his head. "Sorry, I'd get grease all over you."

"That could be fun."

Dermot laughed out loud. "You're not shy, are you?"

"Life is too short," Tansy sighed. "Would you like to take me out for a drink?"

"Well, I'm…"

She looked for a ring. "…married?"

"No."

"I'm in luck, then."

"I have to work until nine." The pump stopped and Dermot put back the hose.

"I'll pick you up at nine-thirty, back here."

"I'm…"

"…looking forward to it?"

Dermot stood awkwardly for a moment and looked down the road, before he said, "Why not?"

She took out her wallet and paid for the gas with cash. "Thank you."

"You're welcome."

She got back in the car and drove off.

❈

When Bay got home she had a fit.

"Tansy Gillis, get down here!"

She heard a hair dryer drone above her head, so Bay dropped the mail and keys on the sideboard and ran upstairs. Her sister was in the bathroom and Bay nearly killed herself on the cord plugged into the outlet across the hall. She lurched into the doorway.

"Are you insane?"

Tansy shut off the dryer. "Oh hi. I've got supper started…"

"What have you done to my house?"

"Do you like it?"

"Who gave you permission to come in here and move everything around?"

Tansy put down the dryer. "I'm sorry. I thought—"

Bay stamped her foot. "About yourself. You don't care about anyone else."

"Hey, calm down. I wanted to help."

"Don't do this to me. Before long, you'll tell me I should change my hair and quit my job and criticize the way I've raised Ashley."

"That's not true, Bay. I haven't come here to do anything but introduce myself to your family and spend some time with you."

"Where were you last summer? That's when I needed you."

"I'm sorry I wasn't here."

"So am I." Bay turned around and ran downstairs. She was going out into the garden but had to stop in the kitchen because there was a pot boiling over and smoke coming out of the stove. "Oh, for the love of…"

The smoke alarm went off and Merlin howled just as Ashley and Matt came through the door. Chaos reigned for a few moments, as Bay ran to the back door with a flaming pan of lasagna. Ashley took a tea towel and waved it under the alarm while Matt flapped the front door back and forth.

When the noise stopped, Ashley gushed over the furniture arrangement. "I love it. Look at this place. It's so cool."

The sisters reappeared at the same time at either end of the kitchen.

"Don't you love what Tansy did with the living room, Mom?"

"Oh yes, I love it." She put the casserole on top of the stove.

"Is supper ruined?" Tansy asked. "I'll go and get us something else, if you like."

"No. I'll go." Bay grabbed her wallet off the counter and left the house.

Ashley crooked her thumb at the back door. "What's up with her?"

"Nothing. Come and tell me about your day."

When Bay came back with a pizza, everyone was in the kitchen. Tansy and Ashley were talking a mile a minute, while Matt sat back with a grin on his face. Bay took a deep breath before she placed the pizza on the table.

"Eat up, everyone."

Matt looked up at her. "Thank you."

The other two smiled but continued to talk, so Bay got the plates and glasses and Pepsi. Matt jumped up to help her.

"Thanks."

"No problem."

Bay cut the pizza and put a slice on everyone's plate. "How was your exam?"

Ashley didn't hear her, so Matt jumped in. "Mine wasn't too bad. One more to go."

"That's great. I bet you can't wait for high school to be over."

Matt ate a big bite. "You can say that again."

"Do you have a summer job?"

Matt nodded. "I'm working for my uncle at his construction company. I'm the designated slave."

Bay smiled at him. "You're young enough to recover."

"I hope so."

As they ate, both Bay and Matt looked over at the other two, but they were talking about fashion and Tansy was telling Ashley about every store in New York. Ashley looked spellbound.

Matt smiled at Bay. "She likes your sister."

Bay agreed.

"I'm happy for Ash. It makes her feel better to have another family member around."

"She said that?"

Matt nodded. "You know how she worries."

Bay frowned slightly before she leaned closer to him. "Does she worry often?"

"More than she should."

Ashley looked over at Matt as he finished his pizza. "Are you talking about me?"

"Nope."

"You better not be," she smiled.

Matt wiped his mouth on a napkin and stood up. "I better get going anyway. I have to study. Thanks for dinner."

"You're welcome," Bay said.

Ashley rose from the table. "I'll walk you out."

"Bye, Matt," Tansy said.

Matt waved and they were gone.

"I wish Ashley could visit New York," Tansy sighed. "She'd die of excitement."

Bay didn't say anything as she got up from the table and took the dishes to the sink.

"You'd come too, of course," Tansy added.

"Some day."

Tansy stood up and went over to Bay. "Don't take this the wrong way, but do you think Ashley's dress is fancy enough for the prom? Don't young girls like sparkles and tulle?"

Bay turned on the tap and added dish liquid to the sink. "I wondered when you were going to say that."

"The dress you made is lovely, Bay. You know it is. But she seemed a little sad when she showed it to me."

Bay looked at her. "She did?"

"Well, she didn't say anything; it was more a feeling than anything else. I know you can't afford to buy one, but would you mind if I did? It could be a graduation present."

"Must be nice to have money to throw around."

"When you have no one to spend it on, it adds up."

Bay stared off into space. Then she took her hands out of the sink and wiped them on a towel. "Do you mind washing these? I'll be back in a little while."

"Bay…"

Bay grabbed her car keys and left out the back door. She hopped in the car and quickly waved at Ashley and Matt, who were still talking on the front step. She drove without thought until she got to the rural cemetery where her parents and husband lay. Once out of the car she headed straight for her mother's grave.

She sat on the grass in front of the granite stone. "Mom, I miss you. Tell me what to do. Please. I can't think. She's come back and I'm frightened. Ashley loves her already, but she'll leave, like she always does, and then what will I do?"

She listened to the evening breeze whisper though the giant fir trees that surrounded that quiet place. If she sat still long enough, her mother's voice would come back to her.

Eventually she kissed the grass between her mother's and father's graves and walked over to Bobby's stone. "I'll miss you forever."

Silence was the only sound.

She blew a kiss and went home.

When she got back to the house, Tansy was standing in the vegetable garden, watering the plants. As soon as she saw Bay, she dropped the hose and ran over to her, throwing herself in Bay's arms. "I'm a creep. I never should've suggested such a thing. Of course she should wear your dress."

They held each other for a long time. Bay was the first to pull away. "I've been thinking. You're right, that dress isn't anything special. We can go together and let her pick out something beautiful."

Tansy clasped her hands together. "Do you mean it?"

Bay nodded.

Tansy jumped up and down. "Oh, I can't wait to tell her."

"Go then."

Tansy ran back in the house shouting Ashley's name. Bay walked over and picked up the hose. Two minutes later Ashley ran out of the house and across the lawn.

"Are you sure, Mom? Because I'm perfectly happy with your gown."

The look on Ashley's face was all Bay needed to see. "I'm sure."

Ashley jumped into Bay's arms. "I love you so much."

When Tansy told Bay she was going into town for the evening to see the sights, Bay was relieved. She got on the phone and called Gertie.

"May I come over?"

"Only if you bring a huge chocolate bar and a bag of Doritos."

"You've got it."

Gertie lived in the upstairs apartment of an old house on the edge of town. When Bay arrived, plastic bag of treats in hand, Gertie was on the front porch sitting on the top step.

"You sounded like you needed help instantly," Gertie smiled.

Bay walked up the steps and sat beside her friend. She passed her the bag. "Here ya go."

"You're a saint."

The two friends sat together and breathed in the salt air. Neither one of them spoke. It was enough to be together as they listened to the foghorn groan nearby. Gertie broke the silence. She reached in the bag and opened the Doritos, passing them to Bay.

"Want some?"

"No, thanks."

Gertie took a handful. In between crunches she said, "So, what's up?"

"I hate that she's back and I love that's she's back. I want to wring her neck while I'm hugging her. I can't seem to relax when I'm with her."

"For pity's sake, Bay, she just got here. You both need time to get used to being in each other's lives again before you can talk. Once you do, I'm sure this emotional stuff will sort itself out."

"I guess so," Bay sighed.

"Why are you here and not with her?"

"She went into town."

"Already? Alone?"

Bay laughed. "If she's still Tansy, it's probably not alone, but I can't see her working that fast. Even she's not that good."

"What does Ashley think of her?"

"She's in love with her."

Gertie continued to crunch. "And you're afraid you're not going to measure up, is that it?"

"Something like that."

"Of course Ashley's going to be thrilled with her. You guys have been missing your mom for a year, and now a relative comes home who's beautiful, sophisticated, and exciting. I'm sure to Ashley she's the epitome of everything cool. But for heaven's sake, you're her mother. She's not going to love Tansy more than you."

Bay looked away. Gertie stayed quiet, except to rattle the bag every so often. Bay glanced at her pal. "I'm letting Tansy buy her a prom dress."

Gertie's eyes got big. "What do you mean? You made her one. It's adorable."

Bay shrugged. "Not adorable enough, apparently. When Tansy

suggested it and I agreed, Ashley ran out of the house and was so excited. I hate that I can't provide things that put that kind of smile on her face."

"Gee whiz, you worked hard on that dress. How easy is it to slap down a Visa card? I think that's crummy."

Bay smiled. "I knew you'd stick up for me. But when you're seventeen, it's all about looks. I want her to be happy."

"But..."

"It's done."

"Okay." Gertie rolled up the bag of Doritos, put them beside her, and then licked her fingers clean. "So, Bay, can I ask you something?"

"Shoot."

"If I ever have a daughter, will you make her prom dress?"

Bay leaned her head against Gertie's shoulder. Gertie patted her knee.

❀

When Tansy drove to the gas station there was no one there. She looked at the time. It was 9:40. She decided she'd wait for five more minutes and if he wasn't there by then, she'd continue on alone.

Every time a car went by she wondered if it was him. Finally it was. A truck came towards her and parked beside her car. He smiled at her but sat for a few seconds as if debating whether to get out. It unnerved her. Most men jumped at the chance to be in her company. She looked at those dark brooding eyes and decided his uncertainty made him more attractive.

When he got out of the truck, she tossed her head towards the passenger door of her car. Dermot walked over, opened the door, and got in. He smelled heavenly, which was a complete surprise.

"Hi."

"Hi, Dermot. It's good to see you."

He looked nervous and awkward in her fancy car. He said, "You look nice."

"Thank you."

He slapped his knees. "So, where to?"

She took the keys out of the ignition. "How about we go in your truck?"

He seemed surprised. "Oh, sure." He looked around. "But you better not leave your car here. How about I put it in the garage? That way it will be safe."

"Okay," she smiled. "Whatever you think."

He got out of the car and went over to the garage doors to unlock them. She fired up the engine and manoeuvred the car through the tight space. When she turned it off and opened the door, he held out his hand to help her out.

"Thank you."

They walked out together and he pulled the garage door down and locked it. He opened the truck door for her. "I'm afraid it's not very clean."

"That's okay. Don't worry about me."

He helped her in and shut it behind her. When he sat behind the wheel, he turned to her. "Before we go, I need to ask you something."

Tansy crossed her bare legs. "Ask me anything you like."

"Are you with me because you like slumming it?"

"Excuse me?"

"A woman like you doesn't go with a guy like me unless she's into having an adventure she can laugh about with her friends over lunch."

Tansy smiled. "You're not stupid, are you, Dermot?"

"No, I'm not."

"Believe me. I won't be telling anyone about this. My family wouldn't approve."

"Of me, in particular?"

"Not at all, but they live in a Betty Crocker world."

"And what world do you live in?"

"Madonna."

Dermot laughed. "Looks like I'm in for a wild ride."

"That's a promise."

They spent the evening in Sydney, going to a few clubs, but it was obvious to Tansy that Dermot was extremely uncomfortable in places where there was loud music and dancing. She tried to get him up on the dance floor, but he begged off. When he looked at his watch, she said, "Let's get out of here."

They talked easily all the way back to Louisbourg. When they neared the garage, she turned to him. "Take me home with you."

Dermot stared straight ahead, but the truck got slower and slower.

She held her breath and waited.

When they passed the garage she smiled. Without a word between them he drove into his yard and they got out of the truck. He preceded her up the back steps.

"This is a lovely old house." She took in the old porch and peeling paint. "You should fix it up a little."

"I work a lot." He opened the door and went through ahead of her. He turned on the kitchen light and she saw that his dishes from breakfast were still on the table.

"You need a wife."

"I know."

Dermot threw his keys on the counter and put his hands in his back pockets. He looked everywhere but at her. She placed her purse on the table and walked over to him. She put her arms around his neck and made him look at her.

"I don't bite, you know."

He looked away. "It's not that. It's just..."

"If you don't want to, that's fine. I'm not going to beg."

He looked at her then. "I need to explain something."

She pulled her arms away. "Go ahead."

Dermot gave a big sigh. "I'm in love with someone."

"A girlfriend?"

"No. A friend."

"And she doesn't know this?"

"Yes, she does, but she's..."

"...a fool."

Dermot shook his head. "She's no fool. She's lost at the moment."

Now it was Tansy's turn to sigh. She turned away from him and walked aimlessly around the room, as if to gather her thoughts. Then she stood in front of him and took his hands.

"Dermot, I can tell you this in all honesty. I don't want your heart. I gave mine away a long time ago, so keep your heart for your friend.

No one will know about this. It's you and me and something we can share to keep the night at bay. I'm lonely and I think you're lonely too. You're not betraying her. I want your body, that's all."

She put her arms back around his neck. "Now be very quiet and let me kiss you." She pulled his head towards hers and almost touched his mouth but not quite. Her lips opened and she waited. He groaned and kissed her. A shock of electricity shot through them both. Everything and everyone else was forgotten.

He eventually led her upstairs and the rest of the night was filled with the soft sounds of skin against skin and their breathless whispers.

It was daybreak when Dermot got up from the bed and went over to the window. He stood there for a long time. When he finally looked back, she was awake.

"Hi."

She smiled. He walked over to the bed, grabbed his jeans off the floor, and put them on.

"You're a dangerous man, Dermot."

He pulled up his zipper. "Why's that?"

"You made me feel too much."

Tansy let herself in the back door quietly. She wanted to go upstairs and put on her bathrobe, so she could walk back downstairs and put the coffee maker on for Bay. But that idea was thrown out the window, because as soon as Tansy stepped into the kitchen carrying her sandals Bay waylaid her.

"Did you have a nice time?"

Tansy jumped. "God, you scared me."

"Sorry."

"I hope you didn't wait up for me."

"Of course not. I couldn't sleep and noticed your car wasn't in the yard. Where have you been?"

Tansy threw her shoes in the corner and sat at the table. "I'm not sixteen and you're not Mom," she laughed.

"No, but you're still my house guest. I was worried."

"Is that what I am?" Tansy frowned. "A house guest? I'm not your sister who grew up in this house too?"

"You might be my sister, but you're almost a stranger and I don't know how long you're staying. You won't tell me. Maybe you're here just long enough for Ashley to learn to love you before you disappear again. And I'll be left to pick up the pieces."

"Stop, Bay. Stop making me feel guilty all the time. Don't you think I feel badly that I didn't come back for Mom's funeral? That I regret it? Do you think it's easy to come into this kitchen and not miss her like crazy? You lived with her. I didn't."

"And whose decision was that?"

"I had no choice."

"Bullshit."

Tansy stood up. "I couldn't come back to this house when I knew she was dead. I would've gone out of my mind. Trust me on that, Bay. You were better off without me."

"I needed you, even if you'd been no help at all. I needed someone to hold my hand while I held Ashley's."

"Stop it!"

They turned. Ashley was in the doorway looking frightened. "Mom, stop fighting with her. You'll make her leave."

"I'm not—"

"You are. Don't do this to me."

Tansy stepped towards her. "Sweetheart, it's not your mother's fault. It's mine."

Ashley shook her head. "She always does this. She's always sad and she has to make everyone else sad around her."

"Is that what you think?" Bay whispered.

"It's true, Mom. You're not happy about me and Matt. You're not happy that your sister's finally come home. Why can't you just be happy?"

"Excuse me." Bay went out the back door.

Ashley yelled after her. "Fine, go sit on your stupid swing. That's all you ever do."

"It's okay, Ashley. Come sit down." Tansy pulled her to the table and made her sit. "Listen to me. Please don't be angry with your mother. This is between us. It has nothing to do with you, okay?"

"I'm so happy that you're here. I want her to be glad too."

"Then don't be hard on her. She doesn't deserve that, because she's had a terrible time of it and she's right. I should have been here for her."

"Okay."

"Go to her."

Ashley nodded and went outside. Tansy pressed her palms into her eyeballs. Her head ached. She slowly went upstairs and closed the bedroom door behind her.

CHAPTER FIVE

It didn't take long for the locals to express their displeasure with Tansy. Bay got an earful from Flo, Mrs. Cathcart, and Eldon. She listened and nodded sympathetically and went back to work. What they wanted her to do about it she didn't know. Her sister had always caused havoc. It wasn't anything new.

When she saw Dermot get out of his truck the next morning, Bay's heart raced. Something had to be done. She hated being on the outs with him. As he walked towards the post office, she thought he looked different. Aloof, almost, and it was because of her.

He entered the foyer and went straight to his box. When he didn't look at her and was about to turn and leave, she shouted, "Dermot!"

He looked up and she beckoned him over. He opened the door and came through. "What is it?"

Bay cleared her throat. "How are you?"

"Okay."

"Look, Dermot, I'm sorry I yelled at you the other night. I haven't been myself and I took it out on you. I shouldn't have done that."

He continued to look at her but didn't speak.

Bay became uncomfortable. He wasn't making this easy. "I hope we're still friends."

"Yes, Bay. We'll always be friends, won't we? I'm sorry, I have to go."

He turned around and walked out. She stared open-mouthed as he got in his truck and squealed his tires leaving the parking space.

When Gertie came to see her on her lunch hour, Bay told her about it.

"Hmm. What would a *Cosmo* girl do?" Gertie wondered.

"What?"

"You know. What would a girl in *Cosmo* magazine do?"

"Who gives a shit? They're not real. It's a stupid committee of preppy editors who sit around with their café mochas and pretend they have vastly superior sex lives to the rest of us."

Gertie shrugged. "Well, they do."

"Oh, shut up, Gertie. You're no help at all."

"How exactly did he look when you apologized?"

"He looked annoyed."

"Hmm, that's not good."

"You don't say."

Gertie reached into her pants pocket and pulled out some Mentos. "Want one?"

"Okay." Bay reached over and Gertie squeezed two into her hand.

"I think you have to make the next move. He has every right to be mad at you; all he did was tell you he liked you, that he wanted to be with you, and you basically told him to take a hike. That must have been great on the old ego."

Bay chewed her mints at a furious pace. "I'm a real jerk sometimes."

"Sometimes? I beg to differ. You're a jerk quite frequently."

"That must be why I hang around with you," Bay smiled.

"Listen, do you think I should do that internet thing Ashley talked about?"

"Meeting someone over the internet is quite common these days. There's nothing wrong with it."

"I'll think about it."

"You've got nothing to lose."

"Yes, I do. My virginity."

Bay stared at her. "You're kidding. You never told me that. As a matter of fact, you told me you did it with what's-his-face...that fellow who came here one summer."

"I lied."

"Oh, Gertie."

"I'm only human. You and Bobby were driving me crazy the way you were all over each other. I was jealous. And it didn't help that your sister had every boy in town following her like she was the Pied Piper. Why I don't hate the two of you intensely is beyond me."

Bay shook her head. "What am I going to do with you?"

Gertie laughed and headed towards the door. "Gotta run, or saunter, as the case may be. Listen, call Dermot and ask him over for supper. That's what I'd do. And then make something really nice, like Cornish hen and baked Alaska."

"I'll make spaghetti."

"You're too stubborn for your own good."

Later that afternoon when all was quiet, Bay called the garage.

"Irving."

"Hi, Dermot. It's me."

"Yes?"

"Would you like to come over for supper tonight?"

There was a long silence. "Sorry, Bay. I have plans tonight."

"Oh, of course. Well, another time, perhaps."

"Right. See ya." He hung up.

Bay looked at her cellphone because she couldn't believe it. He blew her off, just like that. She put the phone in her purse and walked out to the small mirror in the back room. She looked long and hard at herself. Hazel eyes and pretty heart-shaped face, freckles across the bridge of her nose. She looked tired, but maybe if she put her hair up and tried some makeup...

The thought that Dermot was fed up with her made her stomach knot. Dermot not being there was something that had never occurred to her, and the fact that it hadn't made her feel worse. She was the last person on earth who should take people for granted, since she knew only too well how fleeting life could be.

She needed to smarten up.

About everything.

Rain was falling when Bay left work. Before she closed up for the night, Tansy's car appeared in front of the post office. Bay ran to it and hopped in.

"I knew you'd get soaked, walking home in this," Tansy said.

"Thanks."

"Want to go out for supper? My treat."

Bay leaned her head back against the car seat. "That would be great, actually." She looked over at her sister. "I'm glad you're here, you know. Sorry I've been difficult."

Tansy smiled and looked over her shoulder before she drove into the street. "That's okay."

Bay looked out the side window. The rhythm of the wipers soothed her.

"Are you all right, Bay? I mean, do you feel okay?"

Bay watched the passing scenery, the familiar houses and stores of the town she grew up in. She knew it like the back of her hand, which was a blessing and a curse.

"I don't know if I feel anything."

"And how long has this been going on?"

"Since Mom died...I miss her."

"God forbid I sound like an old busybody, but you should see a doctor."

Bay swivelled her head to look at her sister. "What for?"

"I think you're depressed."

"Nonsense. I'm sad, that's all. Aren't I allowed to be sad?"

"Yes, Bay. You're allowed to be sad, but believe it or not, you're also allowed to be happy."

Bay didn't say anything, so Tansy continued. "If not for your sake, then for Ashley's. It hurts her to see you like this."

"So now you're an expert on Ashley. That didn't take long."

Tansy pulled up to the house and parked in the driveway. "I've got eyes, haven't I? Look, let's drop it. Run in and get Ashley and she can decide where we'll eat."

Bay nodded, got out of the car, and disappeared around the corner. She went into the kitchen and hollered for her. A muffled "What?" came from the bedroom. Bay went to the bottom of the stairs.

"Do you want to go out for supper?"

"Sure, can Matt come too?"

"Yeah, we'll pick him up."

Ashley and Matt appeared at the top of the stairs. "You won't have to. He's here."

Bay gave her a look and Ashley gave her one back. Bay's look said *You know how I feel about Matt in your room* and Ashley's said *Lighten up, why do you always think the worst?*

When Matt passed her on the stairs, he gave her a quick smile and rushed by, as if afraid she'd reach out and grab him by the collar.

"You better call your mom and tell her we'll bring you home after dinner."

"Okay, thanks." He went to the phone. It gave the other two a chance to stare each other down. Ashley was about to open her mouth but Bay put her hand up.

"Never mind. Let's go and have fun."

Ashley smiled. "Okay."

When Matt got off the phone, Bay quickly fed Merlin and then they ran out the back door and around the house and realized too late that they'd never fit in Tansy's sports car, so they got soaked as they switched vehicles.

"Great," Tansy pouted. "I look like a drowned rat." She checked the mirror in the sun visor. "I should've worn waterproof mascara. What a ridiculous place this is. Rain, fog, drizzle, wind—you name it, it's here."

Bay backed back out of the driveway. "Are you telling me you didn't have weather in New York?"

"Not destructive, damp, stupid fog."

"You're in for a great time, then." Bay turned onto Main Street and started to pick up speed, when she noticed Gertie walking along the sidewalk, head down, with four grocery bags in her hands.

"That silly woman's going to catch her death," Bay tsked.

"Doesn't she own a car?" Tansy asked.

"Well, not really."

"What do you mean, not really?"

"She has one but it needs gas."

Ashley and Matt laughed at Tansy's expression. "Do you mean to tell me she's too cheap to buy gas for her car?"

Bay nodded. "She'd rather buy nachos. We'd better pick her up."

Tansy looked around at the back seat. "Where on earth will you put her?"

Ashley solved that. "I'll sit on Matt's lap."

Bay pulled over to the curb ahead of Gertie and honked the horn. Gertie was wearing an accordion plastic head scarf on her head, which made her look eighty. She tried to wave, but her hands were full. The kids opened the back door and she hurried over to the car.

"Take these," Gertie shouted. "My boxes of doughnuts are getting soggy."

Matt grabbed the bags and Gertie grunted as she squeezed into the back seat. She took off her headscarf and shook it. Tansy cried out in dismay.

"For heaven's sake, Gertie, you're not a dog. Watch my hair."

"Sorry. Look, Tansy, could you push your seat up a tad? My knees are up to my chins."

Tansy pulled her seat forward. "Is that better?"

"Not really, but never mind."

"Want to go to dinner with us, Gertie?"

"That would be great. Anyone want a doughnut?"

After arguing about where they should go, they decided on Swiss Chalet. They had a horrible time trying to get Gertie out of the back seat of the car. Even Gertie seemed distressed by the episode.

"I think I'm going to have to go on a diet." She stopped for a breather before they got through the restaurant door. But once she was seated, she sniffed the air. "Oh darn, smell that chicken. Maybe I'll start my diet tomorrow."

"There's no time like the present," Tansy announced. "If you mean what you say, then act on it. Starting tonight."

Gertie looked dismayed. "You mean I get invited to a restaurant with someone else picking up the tab and you're going to make me eat a salad?"

"That's what I'm having," Tansy replied.

"Oh, brother. But the fries are so good here."

Tansy patted Gertie's hand. "Listen, Gertie, my sister loves you very much and right now she can't afford to lose anyone else in her life, so let's get you into shape. You don't want to have a heart attack while walking home one night carting twenty pounds of Doritos, do you?"

"Well, no..."

"We'll start an exercise routine as well. I'll teach you everything you need to know. It'll be fun, and I'm not taking no for an answer."

"I forgot how bossy you were."

"Suck it up, Gertie. Okay, everyone, what are you guys ordering?"

Everyone looked at Gertie's long face and no one had the heart to eat in front of her, so they all had a salad, even Matt. The waitress gave them a funny look but otherwise did what she was told. While they ate, Tansy waxed poetic about healthy diets and vitamin supplements. It was a pretty quick dinner, as everyone was anxious to go home and stuff their faces. Gertie, Ashley, and Matt had a devil of a time trying not to make any noise while opening the packages of doughnuts in the back seat. They'd managed to wolf down three each by the time they got back to Louisbourg.

When Bay dropped Gertie off, Tansy reached behind the seat and grabbed the remaining bag of doughnuts. "Ah, ah, ah. Remember. No sweets. I'll be over tomorrow morning at seven-thirty sharp. We'll start our walking program."

"Flippin' wonderful," Gertie groused. "Thanks for taking me along, Bay. A firing squad would've been more enjoyable."

"Sorry," Bay grimaced. "Do you still love me?"

"No."

Gertie huffed up the porch stairs and slammed her front door.

Tansy looked at the others. "You have to be cruel to be kind. You know I'm right."

"I know," Bay sighed. "It's just that she has nothing else in her life."

"She'll get a life once she loses some weight and starts to feel better about herself."

When they got back to the house, Ashley said she'd drive Matt home, so Bay and Tansy said goodnight to Matt and went inside. Ashley drove over to his place and parked outside his house.

Ashley rubbed her hands gleefully. "I can't wait for the prom. Aren't you excited?"

"I'm excited about what's going to happen after the prom, mostly."

"You don't care about the grand march and all that?"

"Guys don't get as freaked out about stuff like that."

"Well, I can't wait. Tansy is buying me a dress."

"I thought your mom made you one."

Ashley rubbed the steering wheel with her thumbs. "She did, but it wasn't fancy enough."

"You liked it before your aunt showed up."

"I know…"

"Don't change who you are because of her."

Ashley frowned at him. "I'm not. Mom said it was okay, so don't make a big deal out of it."

Matt leaned over and put his hand in hers. "You look hot no matter what you have on, but you look even hotter when you wear nothing at all."

Ashley laid her head on his shoulder. "I wish we could spend the night together."

"We will."

She sat upright. "What do you mean?"

"The prom is the perfect opportunity to be together. We're supposed to go to Ryan's party, but I've made arrangements to go somewhere else instead. Just you and me."

Ashley squeezed his hand. "Oh, good. Where?"

"Never mind. It's a surprise."

"Oh, I love you." She kissed him then, and they were so wrapped up in each other that neither of them saw Matt's mother, Ruth, come over to the car and knock on the car door window. They jumped.

Matt opened the door slightly. "Mom, you don't need to scare us like that."

"And I don't need you two steaming up car windows in my driveway. I think you'd better go home, Ashley."

"Okay, sorry." Ashley gave Matt a guilty look. "Bye."

"Bye." He got out, shut the door, and turned to face his mother as Ashley backed the car out onto the street. "Don't embarrass me like that."

"Me embarrass you? I think you have it the wrong way around, buddy boy."

"Why do you hate her so much?"

Ruth rolled her eyes. "I don't hate her, Matt. I think you're too young to be so involved, that's all."

Matt walked away. "I'm not too young and I know what I want."

Ruth followed him. "You're going to have to cool things down anyway. You're off to university in the fall, don't forget."

Matt swung around. "You say that at least three times a day. Well, for your information, I don't know if I want to go away in September."

Ruth blanched. "You're not serious."

"I'm deadly serious."

"I knew that girl was trouble."

Matt gave her a dirty look. "You make it sound as if she's asking me to stay here, but she's not. It's my decision, not hers and certainly not yours. Now leave me alone." He stormed into the house and nearly took the hinges off the screen door when it hit the wall.

❀

At seven-thirty sharp the next morning, Tansy was at Gertie's door. She had on a fabulous Lycra workout suit that hugged her curves. Gertie answered the door, looked at Tansy, and put her hands on her hips. "Are you for real?"

"What?"

"I'm supposed to go walking with someone who looks like Pamela Anderson? My ass is the size of a barn door compared to yours."

Tansy pointed at her. "Stop making excuses. And for your information, I'm a 34 B and my breasts are real. Now let's get a move on."

"Wait, I need a jacket." Gertie left Tansy standing in the doorway. While she was gone, the ugliest cat Tansy ever laid eyes on sauntered up and gave her the once over. She tried to shoo it away, but it wouldn't budge. "What are you looking at?"

Jeffrey growled, so Tansy backed up. "What's wrong with your cat?"

Gertie arrived back on the scene. "I told Jeffrey about last night and he wasn't impressed by your strong-arm tactics." She reached down and picked up her baby. "Mommy will be back soon...I hope. If I die, you're well provided for in my will." She kissed the top of his head and put him back down, closing the door behind her.

"Oh God, can we take a few back roads? I don't want to be seen by the whole population of Louisbourg."

Tansy started down the stairs. "Don't be foolish. You live in this town. Why should you go slinking around the backwoods? Who cares what anyone thinks?"

"I do."

"Well, you need to get over that. The only person you have to please is yourself."

Gertie tried to keep up with Tansy as she marched down the road. "If I wanted to please myself, I'd still be in bed with a couple of cinnamon raisin bagels and a mug of hot chocolate."

"Stop talking."

Gertie made a face behind Tansy's back.

The rest of the walk was an exercise in frustration. Tansy walked too fast and Gertie walked too slowly. Tansy spent most of their session walking briskly up the street, only to have to turn around and walk back to join Gertie. In the end, she walked a mile and Gertie walked a block. Tansy relented and told Gertie to turn around and head for home. She walked beside her.

"I'm worried about Bay," she confessed.

"So am I," wheezed Gertie.

"She gets annoyed when I say anything."

Gertie took a tissue out of her pocket and wiped the sweat off her face. "Well, she would, wouldn't she?"

Tansy gave Gertie a quick glance. "Why's that?"

"Why do you think? You've stayed away for years and suddenly you come back and order her around. I'd be pissed too. As a matter of fact, I *am* pissed, because I'm about to have a stroke, thanks to you."

"Hardly."

"If you don't mind my asking, why did you stay away so long?"

Tansy looked straight ahead. "I couldn't be here."

"Why?"

"Memories."

"Of what?"

"A man."

"Who?"

Tansy stopped. "Look, Gertie, you're a great gal, but I don't plan on spilling my guts, to you or to anyone. I'll save that for my shrink."

Gertie continued up the street. "Fine. But I'm a good listener, if you ever need one."

Tansy gave her a pat on the back. "Thanks. I'll keep that in mind."

CHAPTER SIX

"You look adorable," Tansy smiled.

Ashley turned around in front of the store mirror and looked over her shoulder. "How does it look in the back?"

"Gorgeous. Don't you think so, Bay?"

"Yes, it's lovely."

They'd spent an hour trying on prom dresses, and Bay was decidedly weary. She wanted Ashley to choose one so they could leave, but she knew that Ashley and Tansy were having the time of their lives, so she sat on the one chair available and let them go at it. Trouble was, every one Ashley tried on was better than the last.

"I can't decide," Ashley laughed. "I love them all."

"I like this one the best," Tansy said. "Violet isn't a common colour and with your gorgeous hair and blue eyes, it looks perfect. Right, Bay?"

"Right."

The saleslady concurred. "I think your daughter looks beautiful in this dress."

"She's not my mother."

Bay stood up. "So, are we finished?"

Tansy busied herself with her purse, and then passed an American Express card to the clerk. "A gift from a proud auntie."

"Of course."

Bay was quiet on the way home, but when she saw Tansy and Ashley exchange glances, she gave herself a mental boot up the backside. She looked in the rearview mirror. "You'll be the prettiest one at the prom."

Ashley gave her a big smile. "Do you think so?"

"I know so."

"Thanks, Mom."

As usual, the heat in Sydney started to dissipate the closer they got to Louisbourg. Bay felt it as the air rushed by her open window. She loved the cool misty atmosphere that lingered over her hometown. The smell of the ocean rode on the gusts of wind and refreshed her spirit. She drank it in as they sped by the tall evergreen trees lining the side of the road. She started to relax.

"I always forget how isolated we are out here," Tansy said. "Doesn't it drive you mad in the winter?"

"No. I love it."

"You need to get out of here. There's more to the world than a small coastal town in Cape Breton."

"This small coastal town suits me to a T. I don't need to go anywhere."

"How on earth did we come out of the same womb?"

"Beats me."

When they got home, the first thing Ashley did was call her friends to tell them to come over and see her dress. Ten minutes later a gaggle of girls ran up the stairs and excited shouts rang from the bedroom. Bay and Tansy sat at the kitchen table with mugs of tea and smiled at each other.

"Thanks again for the dress," Bay said. "You've made her very happy."

"She's a wonderful girl. You've done a great job bringing her up."

"I didn't do it alone. Mom was so good with her."

Tansy cleared her throat. "I wish I'd seen them together more." She looked sad, so Bay reached over and grabbed her hand.

"Mom was exactly the same way she was with us growing up; kind, patient, and loving."

"I always ruined everything," Tansy sighed. "I was such a miserable teenager. I don't know why she didn't hate me."

Bay smiled. "You were a challenge."

"I was a pain in the ass."

"You still are."

They laughed together.

After supper Tansy came downstairs and said she was going out for a while. Bay looked up from her newspaper. "You're dolled up. Where are you going?"

"I'm not sure. Just out."

"If you're looking for something to do, we could go to the movies."

"Nah, I hate sitting in the dark. See you."

"Tansy?"

She turned around.

"I thought you were here to see us."

"What? Twenty-four seven?"

"Well, it's nice to be together, isn't it?"

"Of course it is, but I was with you all day." She walked back in from the porch and sat at the table. "Bay, can I ask what a great-looking girl like you is doing alone on a Friday night? Why don't you have a boyfriend?"

"I don't know."

"Aren't men interested?"

Bay shrugged. "Some are, but I can't be bothered."

Tansy crossed her arms. "Are you telling me you haven't been with a man since Bobby died?"

Bay didn't say anything.

"Well?"

She put down the paper. "I was sort of with one once."

Tansy's mouth dropped open. "In almost eighteen years, you've only been with one man? Are you crazy?"

Bay got defensive. "I loved Bobby with all my heart. It was hard to be with anyone else. The thought of…" She couldn't continue.

"The thought of sleeping with someone else bothered you?"

"Yes."

"Did you go to bed with this man?"

"I tried. It didn't work."

Tansy sat back in her chair. Bay looked at her. "I couldn't…you know. I was nervous and on edge. He was annoyed. It was humiliating."

"He was a jerk. Not all men are jerks."

"No. Not all of them."

Tansy stood. "That's my next mission. I'm getting you a date with someone nice. By the time I leave here, Gertie will weigh 150 pounds and you'll be engaged."

"Don't be stupid," Bay laughed.

Her sister headed for the back door. "Make a list of eligible bachelors in town and we'll start first thing in the morning. Don't wait up."

The door shut behind her.

Bay picked up the paper and smiled. She'd make up a list, but there would only be one name on it.

❊

This time Tansy and Dermot didn't go anywhere. She parked around the back of his house and no one was the wiser. He opened the back door and let her in. She smiled and walked past him slowly, knowing his eyes were on her. Placing her bag on the kitchen table, she stood with her back to him, waiting.

Dermot came up behind her and put his hands on her hips. He lowered his head and kissed her right shoulder. She leaned to the left, giving him access to her neck. There was a quick intake of breath as his lips touched her, his tongue warm against her skin. He kissed her perfumed flesh. It was unhurried, endless. She wanted more. She tried to turn and face him, but he wouldn't let her.

"Please," she whispered.

"Wait."

His right hand came up and covered her breastbone, while his left slid around and held her belly, pressing her against his body without releasing his grip, bringing her closer. She wanted to melt into him. Her head fell back against his shoulder. She was breathless.

"There are a lot of things I can teach you, city girl."

"Do it."

It was almost dawn when Tansy got out of his bed. He pulled her back for a moment. "What are we doing?"

She reached out and brushed his hair away from his forehead. "I thought that was obvious."

"This is not what it was supposed to be."

She touched his cheek with the back of her hand. "And what was that?"

"A one-night stand."

She laughed. "Now don't go ruining everything by falling for me, Dermot."

"Hey!" He reached out and messed up her hair. "I think it's the other way around."

"Stop it, you!" She grabbed his hands, but he pushed her back down on the bed and leaned over her.

"Say it."

Tansy smiled. "Say what?"

"That you think I'm the greatest guy you've ever been with."

"Why would I say that? My last guy was a multimillionaire, not a grease monkey."

"You told me grease could be fun."

"I did?"

"You did," Dermot laughed. "Two minutes after we met."

"That was a mistake. I'll be more circumspect in the future."

Dermot grinned and sat at the edge of the bed, holding out his hand to pull her up. "Look who's showing off with her fancy language."

Tansy gathered up her clothes and held them in front of her. "I'm proceeding to the lavatory to expunge your pungent odour from my epidermis."

"What you really need is a shower."

Tansy threw her camisole at him.

When she arrived at home she tiptoed upstairs, closed her bedroom door, and waited until seven o'clock to call Gertie.

"Sorry, Gertie, I can't make it for our walk this morning."

"Can't say I'm sorry."

"I want you to go for a walk without me."

"What? That's no fun. Are you sick?"

"No, had a late night."

"And I bet it wasn't in front of a television set."

"You know me so well. Now remember, twenty minutes at least."

"Goodbye, Commandant."

Tansy put down the phone and went to sleep.

❦

Bay poked her head into Tansy's bedroom before she left for work. She wanted to make sure her sister was home. Despite the fact that she'd been awake for a long time after she went to bed, she hadn't heard Tansy come in. Bay had spent the time thinking up a game plan, because Tansy was right. It was ridiculous that she never made an effort. A dried-up old prune is exactly what she'd be if she didn't soon change her ways.

She was about to go downstairs when she heard a noise in the bathroom. She went over to the door and knocked softly. "Is that you, Ashley?"

"Yeah."

"Are you okay?"

"I feel kind of crummy."

"Really? Let me feel your forehead."

"Mom, I'm not a baby. I have an upset stomach. Probably nerves about the prom tomorrow."

"You've never changed. You always had a delicate stomach."

"I'll be fine. You're going to be late."

"Okay, sweetheart. Feel better."

"Thanks."

Bay ran down the stairs and grabbed her granola bar. "Come on, Merlin. You need to go for a pee."

Merlin got up instantly and ran to the door. When Bay got outside, she smelled the salty ocean air. It was a beautiful day, a day full of possibilities. She ate her breakfast while she waited for Merlin to stop sniffing every bush in the backyard. It had rained during the night, and the small tufts of garden greenery looked fresh and clean nestled in the dark loamy soil. Flo came outside with a container filled with potato peelings and turnip tops from last night's supper to throw in the compost bin. She waved.

"Morning."

"Hi, Flo."

Flo came across the yard. "Do you know what time your sister crawled home last night, or should I say this morning?"

Bay ate the last part of her bar. "I really don't care."

"You don't? God knows what she's up to. People will start to talk."

Bay laughed. "Flo, people talk whether or not there's anything to talk about. You've lived here long enough to know that."

"True. I just don't want her running roughshod over you."

"I'm not the weakling you think I am."

Flo started to smile. "There's my girl."

"And guess what? I'm going to invite Dermot over for supper and then let him take me to a movie."

"Well, it's high time."

"Better dash. Come on, Merlin."

The morning crawled by for Bay as she rehearsed what she would say to Dermot. She wasn't going to take no for an answer. There were cabbage rolls in the freezer and it was only a matter of picking up French bread on the way home. He loved apple pie, so she'd make that too.

Lunchtime arrived and Bay closed up shop for an hour. She got in her car and headed for Dermot's garage, where she parked at the side of the building and went around to the front. The garage doors were open and he was servicing a car that was up on the lift.

"Hi, Dermot."

He looked startled. "Hi."

"How are you?"

"Good."

She watched his face. He was clearly uncomfortable and it was her fault.

"Dermot, I've apologized before, but I don't think you believed me so I'll say it again. I had no right to brush you off like that. You're someone I've cared about for a long time, and I don't want you to be afraid to come near me. I was thoughtless and I want to make amends. Please come for supper tonight and then maybe we can go to the movies. I'd really like that."

He didn't say anything. He looked down at his feet, so she couldn't read his face. Finally he lifted his head.

"Look, Bay, I don't think..."

She walked up to him and put her hand on his arm. "Please, Dermot. I want to be with you."

He looked like he wanted to cry. Not knowing what to do, she reached up and kissed him, but he didn't respond. She pulled her head away. "Please kiss me."

He dropped the rag and put his arms around her, then lowered his head and kissed her hard. It felt incredible. She wanted to take him into the office and be with him right there and then. He had the same idea, because he lifted her off her feet and walked into the back of the garage, keeping his mouth on her the whole time. He kicked the office door shut and sat her on his desk before he lifted his head and held her face.

"Do you know how long I've waited for you to say that?"

"I know," she said breathlessly. "I've been—"

Dermot shut her up with another kiss and reached for her blouse to undo the buttons. She helped him. He pulled it away from her shoulders and leaned her over the desk, kissing under her chin, and then her throat, and then the soft space where her necklace rested. She pulled at his overalls, wanting to feel his skin under her fingers. She forgot where she was. Nothing mattered but this man and his body and how he made her feel.

A voice from out front shouted, "Is anybody here?"

Bay lifted her head. "Oh, God…"

Dermot clamped his hand over her mouth. "Shh. Be quiet, they'll go away." They held their breath while they looked into each other's eyes.

"Hello? Hello? Do you want me to pay for this gas, or what?"

Dermot gritted his teeth. "Shit." He lifted himself off her. Bay sat up on the desk and fumbled to close her blouse. He reached out and held her chin in his hand. "Let's finish what we started tonight, okay?"

She couldn't speak, only nodded her head. Dermot disappeared out the door and she sat there not believing what had happened. She never did things like this.

It was a good day.

No one was home when she got there, so she went straight upstairs and had a hot shower, and then hurried about the kitchen in her bathrobe while she made the apple pie. The phone rang.

"Hello?"

"Hi, Mom. Maribeth's mother asked me if I wanted to stay for supper. Is that okay?"

"Fine, honey. Do you know where your aunt is?"

"She went into town to buy some new clothes."

"Like she doesn't have enough. All right, thanks for calling."

"Bye, Mom."

Bay fairly hopped around the kitchen. No one was home. The minute Dermot walked through that door, she planned to pounce on him. She hoped Tansy would stay away long enough for them to be together.

She took her time getting ready and wore her blue sweater set and grey skirt, putting her hair up with a rhinestone clip. The table was set, the food ready. The kitchen looked cozy and welcoming. All she needed was for him to come through the back door. She paced back and forth to the living room window, peeking out the curtains every time she heard a vehicle out front. Finally his truck pulled into the driveway. He got out carrying a bouquet of flowers. She bit her lip and ran into the kitchen so she could greet him.

When he came through the door, he gave her a smile and didn't say a word, simply handed her the flowers and gathered her in his arms. He kissed her for a long time before he let her go.

"You look beautiful tonight."

She smiled. "Thank you."

"I'm sorry about this afternoon. I wanted to kill that idiot."

She laughed and slipped out of his arms to put her flowers in a vase of water. She placed it on the table. "Sometimes, when you have to wait for something..."

"Get over here."

She complied. He kissed her again before he whispered, "Is anyone home?"

"No."

"Let's go to your room."

She nodded. He took her by the hand and they started up the stairs. That's when another car pulled into the driveway.

Bay craned her neck to look out the window. "Oh, damn. It's my sister."

"Your sister?" Dermot groaned. "For God's sake, this gets better and better."

"We'll have dinner and then I'll ask her to leave. She won't mind. She's always telling me I have to get out more."

"Okay, but then that's it. I'm not waiting a minute longer."

They went back into the kitchen and that's when Tansy pushed the back door open.

"Hi, hi. I'm home. You're not going to believe..." She stopped dead the minute she saw Dermot, the colour draining from her cheeks.

"Tansy, this is my friend Dermot." Bay looked back and was startled by the expression on Dermot's face. "What's wrong? Is something the matter?"

He didn't answer her.

"Dermot?"

Tansy recovered first. She put down her parcels. "Oh dear, he's surprised to see me again, that's all."

Bay was confused. "Again?"

"We met the other day when I went for gas. I was a little mouthy. You know patience isn't my strong suit. I apologize for being rude, Dermot. You have every right to be annoyed with me."

"No worries," he croaked.

Bay was relieved. "Oh, well. Let's put it behind us and start over. Tansy, would you like something to eat? We were about to sit down for supper."

"I don't want to intrude."

"Don't be silly. I'd like the two of you to get to know each other. Why don't we sit and I'll serve dinner?"

"Okay, but I have a few parcels in the car. Would you mind helping me bring them in, Dermot?"

"Sure."

The two of them went out the back door and around the side of the house. Tansy spun around to face him. "Are you joking? This is the girl you love, the one who doesn't love you back?"

"How the hell was I supposed to know who you were?"

"This isn't good, Dermot. It's not good at all."

"No shit. For God's sake, don't tell her. She'd be devastated."

"Oh, I see. So we're only worried about what Bay thinks? I'll be thrown out like yesterday's trash? The first time was a one-off, Dermot. I could've handled that. But last night was something else entirely. That was beyond sex and you know it."

"No."

"Don't lie to me. What you and I did was—"

"Wrong. It was wrong. I was going to stop it anyway. And now, after today…"

"What about today?"

"Bay told me she wants me, and I want her. You said you gave your heart away a long time ago. I told you from the beginning that I was in love with her, so don't mess this up for me."

"I didn't know you meant my sister!" Tansy held her head in her hands. "I can't believe this is happening. Not again."

"What do you mean?"

"Shut up." She got right in his face. "You're a liar, Dermot. We connected last night. You know we did. Am I really that forgettable?"

She marched to her car, got in, and started it up with a roar, peeling out of the driveway.

Dermot wiped the sweat off his face and loosened his collar. He heard Bay call from the porch. "You guys are taking your time."

He walked around to the back of the house. "Sorry. Tansy realized she'd left a parcel at the store. She's gone back to get it and said to go ahead and eat without her."

Bay smiled. "She said that so we could be alone. She's thoughtful when she wants to be."

Dermot walked back into the kitchen. Bay put her arms around his neck. "Where were we?"

He didn't say anything. She waited, but he didn't move. Her arms dropped. "Have I done something wrong?"

"No, of course not. Sorry, Bay. I'm not feeling well."

"Oh dear, can I get you anything?"

He wiped his brow. "I better get home."

She felt his head. "You're burning up. Maybe there's a bug going around."

"I'm sorry. I wanted this evening to be perfect."

"There will be other evenings."

He kissed her cheek. "Thanks for understanding. I'll call you soon." He turned and walked out of the kitchen. Bay stood alone and looked at her nice table setting and her dinner on the counter waiting to be eaten.

What had happened?

CHAPTER SEVEN

Tansy came home around ten. Bay was at the kitchen table doing a crossword puzzle, waiting for Ashley to get back. She looked up when Tansy walked through the door.

"Are you coming down with something too? You're awfully pale."

Tansy put down her parcels. "It's been a long day." She sat opposite her sister. "So, how did it go with Dermot?"

"It didn't."

"What do you mean?"

Bay shrugged. "He wasn't feeling well and had to go home, so it looks like your nice gesture was for nothing."

"Nice gesture?"

"Making up that story about going back for a parcel so we could have some time alone. I appreciate it anyway."

"Right. Oh well." Tansy got up from the chair, went over to the cupboard, and took out a glass, holding it under the cold-water tap. "That was fast. Last night you didn't want to be with anyone and tonight you looked like you wanted to eat him up."

Bay laughed. "You were right; I'm not getting any younger. Dermot's always been nice to me and he's wanted to go out with me for a long time. I decided to meet him halfway."

"I see." Tansy drained the water.

"Can I tell you a secret?"

"Sure." Tansy put the glass on the counter.

"We had this *moment* this afternoon. I didn't recognize myself. I was this crazy, wanton woman."

"You were with him?"

"In his office."

Tansy turned around and folded her arms. "Oh yeah?"

"We were interrupted, unfortunately, and that's why I was looking forward to being with him tonight."

"A guy who thinks his office is a place to romance women doesn't sound like much of a gentleman."

"He doesn't think that."

"Are you sure? Because you're worth more than a quick fuck in a back room."

Bay stood up. "Don't be crude. It wasn't like that."

"It doesn't sound very romantic to me. You have to remember, Bay, you haven't been with a man in a long time. Maybe you forget you're supposed to be wooed."

Bay dropped into her chair and stared at nothing. Tansy walked over and sat beside her. "I'm sorry. I didn't mean to be that blunt."

"I thought it was sort of romantic."

Tansy put her hand on Bay's arm. "It was a little rushed. When someone likes you, even if it's been for a long time, it doesn't mean you give him what he wants right away. Make him work for it."

Bay chewed her bottom lip. "You're right. What should I do?"

"Well, I'm no expert..."

"Yes, you are."

"Take it slow. Don't let him paw at you right away. Men like it when women make them wait."

Bay sat back in her chair and let out a big sigh. "Thanks, Tansy. I'm glad you're here. As crazy as it sounds, I'm almost relieved. I don't have anyone I can talk to about these things. I couldn't talk to Mom, and Gertie's not exactly experienced when it comes to men."

Tansy reached over and took her hand. "You can come to me anytime."

Ashley arrived home and the conversation ended. When Dermot tried to call Bay the next day, she didn't pick up the phone right away. She dithered so long the ringing stopped. Her best bet was to come up with a great excuse not to see him for a while. Trouble was, she couldn't think of one.

The day of the prom, Ashley got out of bed and promptly threw up. Bay worried about her, but Tansy said it was most likely nerves and Ashley agreed. Bay took the day off work so she could accompany Ashley to the hairdresser's. Tansy tagged along and they had a great time discussing what would look best. In the end, Ashley went with something simple instead of a whole head of curls or an elaborate up-do. The front of her hair was pulled back, but the rest fell over her shoulders. Both sisters got quite teary when she got out of the hairdresser's chair.

"What are we going to be like when we see her in the dress?" Bay wondered.

Gertie had finally arrived when that happened, so of course the three women became emotional. Ashley waved her hands in front of her eyes. "Stop or my mascara will run."

They pulled themselves together and took a lot of pictures. At one point, Ashley said, "I wish Nana was here."

Her mother hugged her. "She is, honey. You know why?"

Ashley shook her head.

"Because you and I and Tansy are together, and when we're together we bring her back. I can feel her in this room, can't you?"

"Yes, I think so."

Tansy turned her head away.

Matt arrived at the door a few moments later and looked handsome in his tuxedo—more a man than a kid. Matt and Ashley together were quite a sight as they posed for even more pictures. When they were ready to go, Tansy spoke up.

"Matt, why don't you take Ashley to the prom in my car?"

Matt's eyes got big. "Are you serious?"

"Sure, why not?"

Bay frowned. "Do you think that's a good idea?"

"I'm sure he'll be careful with it." Tansy went to pass him the keys but Ashley grabbed them out of her hand. "Wait a minute. Why can't I drive it? You're my aunt, not his."

"That'll look stupid," Matt said. "The guy is supposed to drive."

"Who says?"

"I say."

"Tough bananas."

Tansy laughed. "Shall we do rock, paper, scissors?"

Both Ashley and Matt put their hands out in front of them. Bay counted. "One, two, three."

Matt held out a fist and Ashley had her palm flat. "I win! Paper covers rock!"

Matt made a face as Ashley shook the keys in victory.

Bay kissed them both. "Okay, you better get going. We'll see you at the grand march."

The three women hurried out to the front step to watch Ashley and Matt run to Tansy's car, but they didn't get far; Flo and the neighbours were out on the lawn and they insisted on getting a few pictures. Matt and Ashley happily obliged.

Flo shouted, "God, girl, I can't believe it. Your nana would be so proud."

❈

Ashley and Matt saw their relatives in the bleachers of the County Arena as they slowly marched with their classmates, a parade of lovely young men and women showing off their finery. Every time Ashley looked up to where her mother sat, flashbulbs went off. She chuckled; Gertie was a camera freak. She'd have a hundred pictures taken by the time the march ended.

Then came the announcement Ashley had been dreading—a dance with their parents. Boys would dance with their mothers, and girls with their fathers. Obviously Matt had to go and find his mother. He gave her a quick kiss and a sympathetic look and left her standing alone. Without a father, grandfather, or uncle, she knew she'd have to step to the side until it was over. Families crowded the arena floor to take pictures. Her mother, Tansy, and Gertie descended from on high and surrounded her.

"I'll dance with you," her mother said.

"Mom, that'll look dumb." The look of distress on her mom's face didn't help matters, but at that moment Ashley's best friend Maribeth zoomed towards them, her father in tow. "I've danced half of my dance with Dad, and now my grandfather wants a turn."

Mr. Munroe held out his hand. "Ashley, would you care to dance? I feel as if you're my daughter after all these years."

Ashley smiled and took his hand. She tried not to look at her mother and aunt as he pulled her into his arms and slowly waltzed with her. More flashbulbs, more snivelling, more tissue passed around.

The music ended and Mr. Munroe gave her a kiss. "You look beautiful tonight."

"Thank you."

Mr. Munroe walked over to Bay. "You must be proud of her, Bay. What a wonderful girl."

Bay took his hand. "Thank you for dancing with her. You've made her night."

"I don't know about that. If I recall my own prom, the night didn't start until the parents left."

They all laughed.

And so the grand march was over. Parents swarmed their children once more, warning them about being careful, no drinking and driving, don't do anything foolish, and finally, have a good time.

They promised they would and gave a big sigh of relief when the adults departed.

The prom was on.

❊

The sun came up and bright rays filtered in through the old curtains of the bungalow where Matt and Ashley spent the night. It belonged to Matt's uncle, who lived in Toronto and never used it until August. It wasn't hard to find the key in his mother's junk drawer.

They finally slept a little, blissfully happy in each other's arms.

Matt was awake and looking at her when Ashley opened her eyes. "Hi."

"Good morning." He kissed the tip of her nose.

She turned on her side and snuggled up to him. "I want to stay here forever."

"Let's do it."

She laughed. "Okay."

They were quiet for a few moments before Ashley suddenly leapt out of bed.

"What's wrong?"

She couldn't answer him as she pushed the doorway curtain aside and ran to the toilet, lifting the lid just before she threw up.

Matt got out of bed and hurried to the bathroom doorway. "You didn't have anything to drink. What's the matter?"

"Go for a minute."

"But—"

"Please." She shut the door, flushed the toilet, and turned on the cold-water tap, rinsing her face over and over, and then washed her mouth out. Grabbing a towel, she rubbed her face raw as she glanced in the mirror.

Her reflection showed a girl who looked frightened, and then she noticed something else. Something she hadn't seen before, because she hadn't wanted to look. Her breasts were bigger, with fine blue veins running along the surface of her milky skin. She'd read in a magazine once that that was a sign.

Oh my God.

Ashley had hoped she was late because of the excitement about the prom. It had happened before. Her periods were never regular, which ticked her off; Maribeth always got them like clockwork.

But Ashley was never this late.

Her hand found its way to her belly. "Oh, no."

She was in there so long that Matt called out, "What's wrong, Ashley? You have to tell me."

Ashley took a deep breath and walked out of the bathroom. Matt put his hands on her shoulders. "Are you all right?"

"I don't feel good." She began to shiver.

Matt gathered her in his arms. "It's okay. I'll take you home."

"Yes," she said faintly. "I need to go home."

It was eight in the morning when he dropped her off. He exchanged cars in the driveway. She gathered up her prom dress, shoes, and change of clothes.

"I'll see you soon," Matt said.

"Yes."

He tried to kiss her, but she turned her head. "You don't want my germs."

"I can hug you." He did, whispering, "I had the best night of my life last night. I love you so much."

"Me too." She turned and ran towards the backyard.

"Feel better. I'll call you later."

Ashley didn't answer him as she disappeared around the corner of the house. She ran up the back steps and through the screen door.

Merlin greeted her first. Her mom would be up early, and sure enough, there she was making porridge. The smell made her sick.

"Hi, honey. How was your night? Was it fun?"

Ashley nodded but didn't open her mouth. The look on her mother's face changed.

"What's the matter? You look dreadful. Please say you didn't get drunk."

"No, I think I'm sick. I feel really bad."

Her mother felt her head. "Why didn't you come home sooner? You should be tucked up in bed."

Ashley dropped her things and hung onto her mother. Bay held her close. "What is it, sweetheart? What's wrong?"

She kept her face hidden in her mother's bathrobe. Ashley wanted desperately to tell her, but she couldn't. She couldn't do it to her.

Her mom stroked her hair. "You can tell me anything. That's what I'm here for."

Ashley shook her head. Her life, as she knew it, was over.

❋

Gertie stayed away from the Gillis household for a while after Bay called her to say that Ashley had the flu or maybe even mono. She wasn't herself. Gertie couldn't afford to get sick and miss work, so she spent her evenings alone. Tansy continued to show up at the crack of dawn to drag Gertie's butt up and down Main Street, but she wasn't very good company, and eventually Gertie told her so.

"Who put the burr under your saddle?"

Tansy didn't break her stride. "What are you talking about?"

"Why are you so damn cranky? I'm the one who's dying here. I can't breathe."

"Stop bellyaching, Gertie."

Gertie stopped to mop her brow. "You see? If you're this unhappy, why are you here?"

Tansy stopped and put her hands on her hips. "You know what? I have no clue."

Gertie bent forward as far as she could and put her hands on her knees. She took deep breaths in and out. "Let me rest for a minute."

Tansy crossed her arms and put her weight on one foot. She looked out over the water. "Can I ask you something?"

Gertie straightened up and reached into her pocket for more tissue. "Sure, as long as it doesn't involve running or doing sit-ups."

"What's going on between Bay and Dermot?"

Gertie blew her nose and started to walk. Tansy joined her. "Nothing, that's the problem."

"And why's that?"

"I don't know. Sometimes I think Bay feels she doesn't deserve to be happy."

"Would Dermot make her happy?"

"Everyone knows he thinks the world of her."

Tansy cleared her throat. "That doesn't mean he's right for her."

Gertie stood still. "You're joking. He's a great-looking guy who runs his own business, has his own home, is unattached, isn't gay, and he's mad about her. I mean, come on."

"I think she can do better."

"Like you, you mean?"

Tansy stopped. "Sorry?"

"Are you married with a great husband and lots of kids? Do you have it figured out?"

Tansy glared at her but didn't say anything.

Gertie pointed her finger. "You're as messed up as the rest of us, so don't pretend like you're not."

Tansy walked away.

"I'm sorry," Gertie sighed. "I didn't mean that."

Tansy looked over her shoulder. "See you tomorrow, Gertie."

"Yeah, see you."

Gertie walked home with a limp. She had a bad blister and the Band-aid she covered it up with had obviously shifted to a different position. Drat and darn that Tansy for making her life miserable. She finally made it up her front steps and into the house. Jeffrey was there to welcome her.

"Don't even ask, Jeff. I've had it with that woman."

She pried off her sneakers with her toes and headed for the fridge to get some water. While she was there she reached in and grabbed a leftover piece of pie. Then she put it back. Then she took it out. This went on for a minute before Gertie screamed and threw the pie in the garbage, plate and all.

She marched over to the computer to distract herself. Not that she dared hope she'd have any email. She hadn't told anyone that she'd joined a Big and Beautiful dating service. It was more of a lark than anything. That's what she told herself, anyway, but her heart skipped a beat when she logged on and there were five letters in her inbox, all from B & B. Holy cow.

❧

Bay was worried about Ashley. She spent three or four days in bed but refused to go to the doctor; said it was a waste of time, she was tired, that's all. She didn't even want to talk to Matt when he called.

Bay was at work telling Marjorie Scott about it. Marjorie was a small, feisty woman who had eight kids. She'd seen it all.

"She won't go to the doctor."

Marjorie rolled her eyes as she filled out her money order. "Of course not, she might have to show an inch of skin. They don't mind showing it to every Tom, Dick, and Harry on the school bus, mind you, but God forbid the doctor take a peek at 'em."

"She's not eating and she's pale as a ghost."

"She's pale because she's not eating. Give her a good dose of cod liver oil. That'll set her to rights."

"Cod liver oil? Yuck, I remember that stuff."

"Listen, honey, all them new fangled packages of expensive purple and pink pills don't do a thing when it comes down to it. There ain't nothing that cod liver oil, goose grease, and a blazin' hot poultice can't cure in a jiffy."

Bay felt sorry for Marjorie's kids.

She was so preoccupied she didn't see Dermot approaching the building. She glanced up and gave a start when he came to the counter.

"Hi, Bay."

Bay stammered for something to say. She hadn't thought of a clever way to seem more aloof. Fretting about Ashley was the only thing on her mind. Tansy's words, *make him wait*, ran through her head.

"Hi...how are you feeling?"

Dermot smiled. "I'm fine now." He looked behind him to make sure no one was around and leaned closer to the counter. She couldn't help noticing the green flecks in his brown eyes, and the way his dimple deepened when he smiled.

"I've missed you."

She cleared her throat and straightened up. "Is that so?"

Dermot looked puzzled. "I thought maybe you missed me too. I can't stop thinking about that day in my office."

He waited for her to speak.

Stay cool. She tucked her hair behind her ear. "Really?"

Now he straightened up. "Yes, really. Has something happened? Has someone said something to you?"

She wrinkled up her face. "Like who?"

"I don't know. You don't seem the same."

"I'm worried about Ashley."

Dermot looked relieved. "Oh, is that all?"

"What do you mean, 'Is that all'? It's not easy to be worried about your child."

He put his hands up in front of him. "I'm sorry. I didn't mean it like that."

"It sure sounded like it."

"Forgive me. Is she sick?"

"Yes. No. I don't know. That's the problem; I'm not sure what's going on."

They were interrupted then by Wendell Bonaparte, who crashed through the door and kept coming. If Dermot hadn't caught him, he'd have careened right into the counter.

"For pity's sake, man!" Dermot shouted. "You'll break your neck one of these days." He pulled Wendell upright by his coat lapels. "Now stay still for a minute."

Wendell gave him a salute. "Aye aye, Captain Kirk. Spock, reporting for duty."

Dermot and Bay laughed, which was all Wendell needed. He pushed his thumbs behind his suspenders and held them out like a clown. "I can't hold on, Jim. I don't have the powa!"

Dermot shook his head. "You look exactly like Stan Laurel when you do that, Wendell."

"I know that bugger. He's me cousin."

They sobered up quickly when Bay spied the United Church minister coming up the walk. "It's the reverend. Be on your best behaviour, Wendell."

"Lord tunderin' jesus. That fella will have me in detox quicker than a snake bite. I gotta get outta here."

"Go out the back door." Bay pointed the way. Wendell tipped his cap and staggered out.

The reverend opened the front door, checked his box, and gave them a wave. "Morning."

"Good morning," Bay and Dermot said together.

The good man went back out just in time to see Wendell hightailing it up the street. He gave chase, waving his mail in the air, trying to flag Wendell down.

Bay and Dermot looked at each other and smiled, the awkwardness between them forgotten. He reached out his hand and took hers. "I want you to be with me."

Bay looked at her hand. "I know, but I don't think we should rush into anything."

He looked up. "What?"

"I think we went overboard the other day. I'm not that kind of girl, you know."

"What kind of girl are you talking about? Are we in high school?"

Bay yanked her hand away. "Don't make fun of me. I don't want you to think I'm cheap and easy."

"I'd never think that in a million years. Who put this foolishness in your head? Was it your sister?"

"Don't be ridiculous. I have a mind of my own."

"Well, one minute you want me and the next you're brushing me off. Something's changed, and blowing hot and cold gets tiresome very quickly, Bay."

"Is that so?" Bay spied someone else coming up the walk. "Look, we can't talk now. You'd better go."

"Fine." Dermot turned around and walked towards the door.

"Dermot…"

He was gone.

✿

Dermot got into his truck and slammed his hand on the steering wheel. He had no doubt that Tansy was behind this "good girl, bad girl" stuff.

It was too dangerous to go near Bay's house. Flo would squawk the minute Bay got home, so he drove back to the garage and called her number, hoping against hope that Tansy would answer instead of Ashley.

She did. "Hello?"

"Tansy, it's Dermot."

"Well, well. How are you, Dermot?"

"I'd be better if you kept your nose out of my business."

"I have no interest in running a gas station."

"What?"

"I could break a nail—or worse, a sweat."

"Stop it."

"Stop what?"

"Trying to make me laugh."

"Sorry."

"I'm annoyed with you."

"Whatever for?"

"You've been talking to Bay."

"I'm allowed to talk to her. She's my sister."

"Suddenly she's not talking to me. I wonder who put that idea in her head."

"I don't have a clue. Why don't I come over and have a chat in your garage office. Isn't that where you take your women?"

He slammed down the phone.

✿

Ashley lay in bed with her arms wrapped around the panda bear Matt won for her at the circus. Here she was, about to be a mother herself, and she still needed to sleep with stuffed animals. That's when the misery of her situation overwhelmed her. She sat up and looked at the things in her room: pink walls, movie posters, ballet slippers, a basketball shoved in the corner, her skating ribbons, her collection of *Winnie the Pooh* figurines.

How was she supposed to bring a baby into the world? She never played with dolls as a kid. She hated dressing them up and carrying them around. It was all too boring.

How had this happened? They'd been careful—but not careful enough, apparently. She thought of her friends, who talked non-stop about getting ready for university in the fall. They were already packing and buying new outfits, picking up microwaves for their dorm rooms and cellphones so their parents could keep in touch.

She'd be buying diapers and baby wipes.

When the phone rang, she cringed, but it wasn't for her or Tansy would've said so. When it rang again ten minutes later, Tansy called up the stairs. "Ashley, it's Matt." She could pretend to be asleep, but she couldn't sleep for the rest of her life. She took a deep breath and picked up the phone.

"Hi."

"Ashley, are you all right?"

"No."

"What's wrong? I'm going crazy here. I haven't seen you since prom and I feel like you're avoiding me. Aren't you glad we were together? Don't you want to be again?"

"Stop."

"Stop what?"

"Stop asking me so many questions. I can't think."

"There's something going on that you're not telling me."

"What do you want to be when you grow up, Matt?"

"What?"

"You heard me. What do you want to do? And don't say you want to be the most famous hockey player in the world. Tell me the truth."

He hesitated. "I don't know."

"You must know."

"I don't. My mother is breathing down my neck to go to university, but I'm not sure I want to. If I wanted to be anything, I guess a cop or a firefighter."

Ashley sighed. "You'd have to go away for that."

"Yeah, but it wouldn't be for long. Not as long as getting some stupid degree."

She lay down on the bed and cradled the phone against her ear. "You'd make a great firefighter."

"I'd take my ladder to come and rescue you. I might have to if you don't come out of your room soon. I miss you. I want to be with you again."

"I know."

"What do you want to be when you grow up?"

Ashley put her hand over her mouth.

"Ashley?"

"I wish I knew," she whispered.

"Get better, baby."

"I will."

"I love you."

"I love you too." She hung up the phone and pressed her face into the sheets.

❀

Gertie was raring to go when Tansy showed up at her door the next Saturday morning. It was a glorious day, perfect for going to the beach, though the water didn't warm up in this part of the world until mid to late July. Still, it looked tempting.

They were off, walking down the main street of town, with its corner stores, gift shops, and the odd motel. A few large homes sat inches from the sidewalk, and cars were parked on both sides of the street. Already large trailer homes and caravans lumbered through the main drag on their way to the fortress. License plates from across Canada and the States were clues as to how far these people had travelled to see this famous site.

Typically for a local, Gertie hadn't been to the fortress in years. But she imagined most New Yorkers didn't visit the Empire State Building, either, unless their relatives were in town.

She wasn't aware that she was walking quickly until Tansy pointed it out.

"You're doing a lot better, Gertie. Have you weighed yourself lately?"

"Nah, I don't believe in that horseshit."

Tansy chuckled. "You're a riot."

"If I spent my entire life chained to a scale I'd never get out of bed. Do I need to be told every single morning I'm a fat slob before I even brush my teeth?"

"I never thought of it that way."

"Let's walk to Bay's."

"Are you sure? It's a long walk."

"I can do anything."

"Good for you."

By the time they got to Bay's street, Gertie was winded. Tansy urged her on. "Keep going. You only have fifty feet left."

Gertie nodded but stopped. Flo, who was out front washing her porch windows, put her hands on her hips. "Leave that poor child alone. Do you want to kill her?"

Before Gertie could say anything, Tansy shouted, "Why don't you mind your own business?"

"It is my business if Gertie has a heart attack on my front lawn. Do you know CPR? Because I sure don't."

"I'm surprised. I thought you were full of hot air."

Gertie pushed Tansy up the driveway, with Flo yelling at her the entire time. "In all my born days, I've never heard a saucier mouth than yours, Tansy Gillis. Why your mother…"

They disappeared around the corner and went into the house.

"Why do you provoke that woman?"

Tansy shrugged. "She called me a brat when I was a kid."

Bay was by the stove making pancakes. "What are you two doing here? Don't tell me you walked over here, Gertie."

"I did indeed. Now all I need is an intravenous drip and new feet."

Bay hurried to the fridge, pulled out a pitcher of water, got a glass, and put them in front of her friend. "You're doing really well, Gertie. You only started this—what, about a week, maybe ten days ago?"

"That's right." She poured her water into the glass and chugged it down.

Tansy walked over to the electric frying pan. "We should be having fruit and cottage cheese, not pancakes."

"I'm trying to entice Ashley to eat something."

"She's still moping around?" Gertie asked.

"Mmm. I'm going to insist she see a doctor, even if I have to drag her out of that room."

Gertie sat at the table with a big sigh. "Sit down, girls. I have some news."

Bay and Tansy looked at each other, but did as they were told.

Gertie tried not to look too pleased. "I have a date."

"That's great." Bay smiled.

"You see?" Tansy grinned. "All this hard work is paying off."

"It's got nothing to do with exercise, unless typing counts."

"You met him online?" Tansy asked.

"Yep."

"You went on that site Ashley told you about?" Bay wondered.

"I went on a Big and Beautiful site."

"Do you think it's safe?"

"Well, I didn't join the one called Chubby Chaser. And besides, you told me that people do it all the time."

"I know, but that doesn't mean there aren't risks involved. Who is this guy? He could be a lunatic for all you know."

Tansy folded her arms across her chest and gave Bay a look. "What is wrong with you? Why do you have to throw cold water on this?"

"People get fooled all the time. You never know what you're dealing with."

"I'm sure Gertie can handle herself, right, Gertie?" Tansy said.

"Right. If he's a maniac, all I have to do is sit on him until the police arrive."

❀

The next day Bay told Ashley she was taking her to the doctor after work and didn't want to hear another word about it. Ashley knew if she kept this secret much longer she'd likely burst forth like a volcano, and she didn't want it to happen in front of Dr. White.

She called Maribeth instead.

Maribeth came flying upstairs and didn't bother knocking, just opened the door and barged right in. Ashley was in her pyjamas on the bed, hugging her panda.

"What are you doing in your PJs? Get dressed and let's go to the mall. My mom gave me the car." She plunked herself beside Ashley and pulled out a pack of gum from her purse. "Want some?"

Ashley shook her head.

Maribeth shoved the gum in her mouth and took a good look at her friend. "If you don't mind my saying so, you look like shit."

"Thanks."

"All right, spill the beans. Did you and Matt break up or something?"

At the word "Matt," Ashley let go of the bear and covered her face with her hands. "I don't know what to do."

Maribeth crawled over the bed to put her arms around her friend. "Did he do something to you? God, he's not cheating on you, is he? I'll kill him."

Ashley shook her head. "It's worse."

Maribeth took Ashley's hands away from her face. "I can't hear you. Tell me."

Ashley couldn't get her breath.

"Calm down, it's okay."

"I'm pregnant."

Maribeth's hand flew up to her mouth. "Oh, shit."

"What am I going to do?"

"Are you sure?"

Ashley got cross. "Of course I'm sure."

"Did you take a test?"

"No, but I don't need one. My boobs are huge and I haven't had my period in three months. I'm throwing up every morning and I can't keep anything down. Doesn't that sound like pregnant to you?"

Maribeth nodded as she chewed her gum rapidly. "I still think you should take a test."

"And I'm going to pick it up where? I know someone who works at every drugstore within a forty-mile radius of here."

"True." Maribeth blew a bubble. "Didn't you...you know...use anything?"

"Of course we did." Ashley looked away. "Except maybe once."

"Trust you to hit the jackpot. Does Matt know?"

"No. I can't tell him. His mother will kill him and blame me for trapping her precious son. You watch, she'll make him hate me by this time next week."

"Don't be crazy. Matt would never hate you, and besides, it's his baby too. You didn't do this all by yourself. He needs to know."

"He's got his whole life ahead of him. He's not going to be eighteen until next month."

Maribeth gave her a look. "You're not going to be eighteen until Christmas, and you have your whole life ahead of you too. Why are you making it more of a tragedy for him than for you?"

Ashley sighed. "I don't know. I can't think. Tell me what to do. What would you do?"

"I'd leave town and get an abortion real quick."

Ashley looked up with a shocked expression on her face. "Are you serious?"

"Sure, I'm serious. I'd take my birthday money and get on a bus to Halifax and go to a clinic and no one would be the wiser."

"But I couldn't. This is Matt's baby."

Maribeth shook her head. "Don't get all girly, Ashley. It's not *any-thing* right now. It's a problem that's going to ruin your life, and if you're smart, you'll get rid of it."

Ashley sat back against her headboard and hugged her pillow. "Wow. I never thought you'd say that."

"Why?"

Ashley shrugged.

"I'm not a softie. I know what I want. I'm going to be an occupa-tional therapist. They make tons of money and I'll be in the right spot to meet a lot of handsome rich doctors. End of story."

"Wouldn't you feel guilty your whole life if you got rid of it?"

Now it was Maribeth's turn to shrug. "Maybe. But I'd have other kids someday. You need to look out for number one. Don't let a five-minute mistake cost you everything."

"I don't think I could do it."

"I'll go with you, if you like. We can tell our moms we're going on a shopping expedition and we'll stay with my sister. She's got an apartment in Halifax and she won't blab."

Ashley frowned. "I'll have to think about it."

"Well, you can't afford to wait too much longer. Just know I'm here if you need me."

Ashley nodded.

❄

Tansy went to the corner store that afternoon and ran into an old classmate. Tansy didn't recognize her at first; she looked ten years older than she actually was, with greying hair in a ponytail and jogging pants hanging off her ass, but she knew Tansy in an instant.

"My God, is that you, Tansy? Well, blow me down. You look fantastic."

"Uh, hi."

"You don't remember me, do you?"

Tansy didn't get a chance to answer because the woman kept talking as if Tansy wasn't there. "I'm Annette Birk, remember? I sat behind you in grade eleven. I was on the school newspaper."

It still didn't ring any bells, but Tansy pretended otherwise. "Right. How are you, Annette?"

"Oh, don't ask." She shifted her purse to her other shoulder. They were standing in the aisle by the chocolate bars and a few people had to squeeze past them to get to the cash. "You look fabulous. Are you back for good? Where do you live? I'm stuck here. I ended up marrying Derek. You remember him, the guy with the big glasses who sat in front of you in Chemistry."

Tansy did remember him. Derek was always passing her notes that said he was madly in love with her and wanted her more than life itself. She'd set them on fire with her Bunsen burner and get into trouble with the teacher.

"Oh, right…"

"He's a complete schmuck, of course, but what can you do. I've got four kids and no job, so I can't leave the son-of-a-bitch."

Tansy realized she had a willing snitch about village life in front of her, and it was too good an opportunity to pass up. "Would you like to get a coffee, Annette?"

Annette looked like she had won the lottery. "Well, sure! That would be great." She rooted in her purse. "I'm not sure if I have any cash, though."

"Don't worry about it. My treat."

They walked out of the store and over to the local diner. Once Tansy placed their order, poor old Annette couldn't wipe the grin off her face. "This is so neat. You always were the coolest girl in school. We all wanted to be like you. Remember Lois Brewer? She tried to dye her hair your colour and ended up having to chop it all off when it turned green instead."

Tansy laughed. "Oh, dear."

"And then there was Karen Musgrave. She ended up calling her daughter Tansy. Naturally she pretended you had nothing to do with it, but I know different."

"Tell me, Annette. Are there any eligible bachelors in town?"

Annette's chin dropped. "Are you looking for a man? You?"

"No, I'm thinking of someone for my sister. She must get lonely at times. I worry about her."

"Well, you don't have to bother, because she has Dermot Fraser wrapped around her little finger. I don't know why he likes her. She ignores him half the time."

"Is he a nice guy?"

"Oh yeah. I wouldn't kick him out of bed for eatin' crackers."

"If he's so special, why isn't he married?"

"I think he got his heart broke once. That was the story, anyhow, when he moved back to town. Something about his girlfriend going for a walk along the beach and disappearing into thin air."

"That's awful."

Annette nodded. "Just my luck Derek never takes a walk on the beach."

"No one ever found her?"

"Nope. Some say she drowned, and some say she ran off with someone else. There are even a few nuts around here who think he murdered her, but that's crazy. Nothing exciting like that happens around here."

"Murder isn't exciting."

Annette waved her hand around, as if to erase the words. "I don't mean it like that. I lead such a boring life. The only excitement I get is watching the soaps, and they murder people left, right, and centre. Only their victims come back from the dead on a regular basis, suffering from amnesia."

Tansy had had enough of Annette Birk. She rose to her feet. "I'm sorry, Annette, I have an appointment and I'd better dash." She took a ten-dollar bill out of her wallet and handed it to Annette. "If you wouldn't mind paying the waitress?"

"But what about our coffee?"

"Sorry. Maybe another time." Tansy walked away.

True to her word, Bay took Ashley to the doctor. She wanted to go into the office with her, but Ashley gave her such a look of incredulity that she backed off. The doctor asked her all sorts of questions and she lied through her teeth for most of them. Was she sexually active? No. When was her last period? Two weeks ago. Was she sleeping all right? Like a log. Eating? Yes.

He felt her glands and listened to her heart and took her blood pressure and all the things doctors do. He ordered blood work.

"Why?"

"Just to be on the safe side. I suggest you take some multivitamins in the meantime. It can't hurt. I hope you're not dieting?"

"No."

"Your mother said you've been throwing up. You aren't bingeing and purging, are you?"

"Of course not. That's stupid."

"I'm glad you think so. As soon as I get your reports back, I'll be in touch."

Ashley turned to go. Before her hand reached the doorknob, he said, "Anything you say to me is private. I can't tell your mother, do you understand?"

She nodded.

"I'm here if you need me."

"Thanks." She left.

Her mother got out of her chair in the waiting room as soon as Ashley emerged from the office. "Well?"

"He says I should take vitamins."

"Is that all?"

Ashley nodded. "He wants me to have some blood work, too."

"Well, let's go to the hospital right now."

"No, Mom. I'm tired. I want to go home."

"But we're in town—"

"Please. Can I get it done tomorrow?"

"I suppose so," Bay frowned. "Although why you don't—"

Ashley turned to face her mother. "Will you stop treating me like a five-year-old? I'm tired and I'd rather do it tomorrow. Don't make a federal case out of it."

Bay pressed her lips together. "Fine. Let's go home."

It was a deadly quiet car ride.

Tansy was at the stove when they came in the door. "How did it go?"

"Okay, I guess," Bay said. "Are you cooking?"

"Even I can't ruin Kraft Dinner."

"I'm not hungry, I'll eat later," Ashley said before she disappeared up the stairs to her room.

Mother and aunt looked at each other.

"What did the doctor say?"

"How should I know? I wasn't allowed in the office with her. He told her to take some vitamins and get blood work done, I guess to rule out anything horrible."

Tansy gave the pot a stir. "You might be barking up the wrong tree."

Bay sat at the table. "What do you mean?"

"Maybe she and Matt had a fight and she doesn't want you to know about it. She hasn't been hankering to see him lately."

Bay folded her arms. "You may have a point. Well, if that's the case, I'm staying out of it. I'd only make things worse. I can't seem to do anything right these days."

Tansy gave her a smile and knocked the wooden spoon against the side of the pot. "That's not true."

"Oh, yes it is. Dermot's annoyed with me."

"Oh?" Tansy walked over and sat in the opposite kitchen chair. "What happened?"

Bay put her elbow on the table and cupped her chin in her hand. "The usual. I said something and he got mad and then he said something and I got mad."

"What did you say?"

"I told him we should take things slow. You'd think I'd asked him to become a monk."

"I see."

"So much for your great advice. Now what?"

Tansy got back up and took some plates out of the cupboard. "Now nothing. He can't manipulate you like that. If he likes you so much, he should be prepared to do things your way. Keep away from him until he gets over his little hissy fit." She placed the plates on the table. "Are you ready to eat?"

"I guess so. You know, you're right. Why am I always the one who has to play by other people's rules? He can stew for all I care. I have more important things to worry about."

It occurred to Ashley in the middle of the night that the blood test would give away the fact that she was pregnant. That's why the doctor had ordered it. The way he'd looked at her made her think he knew what was up. She wouldn't get away with not having it done, so she had no choice.

She had to tell Matt.

Her mother poked her head around the bedroom door before she left for work. "Good morning. Must be nice to sleep in now that you're not in school."

"I'm not sleeping in. You're talking to me."

Bay crossed the room and sat on her bed. "That's true. When are you going to hand out your resumés? You'll need a job soon. You shouldn't have left it so late."

Ashley closed her eyes. "Yes, Mother, I know."

"I'll leave you the car and you can go in and get your blood work done. Don't forget."

"I won't."

"You and Matt aren't having problems, are you?"

Ashley's eyes flew open. "What?"

"You've been reluctant to see him and I wondered if anything was up."

"I haven't been feeling well and he's busy working for his uncle, that's all."

"Good."

"Good? I thought you'd be happy if Matt and I broke up."

Bay frowned. "When did I say that?"

"All the time. It drives me nuts."

"Well, you're wrong. All I said was—"

"Never mind, Mom, I've heard it before." Ashley sat up and crawled out from under the sheets on the other side of the bed. "I'd better take a shower."

Bay sighed. "All right, I'll see you later." She got up and started for the door, but turned around and took Ashley in her arms. "I love you, you know. I only worry about you because I love you."

Ashley stood as stiff as a board, waiting to be released. "Fine. Mom, I have to go."

Bay dropped her arms. Ashley walked out of the room and into the bathroom, shutting the door behind her. Bay looked around at the mess. She wandered over to a picture tacked up on the bulletin board. They'd taken it in a booth at the mall. Ashley had her tongue sticking out and Bay had her eyes crossed. She reached up and touched the picture. She stood there for a long time, thinking about that day. They'd gone to the movies and had ice cream from the Tasty Treat. Ashley had said she was the best mom in the whole world.

Where did that little girl go?

CHAPTER EIGHT

Ashley drove up to Matt's house and blew the horn. She called him before she left the house, so he was expecting her. There was no way she was going near his front door and running into his mother. She was afraid Ruth would look into her eyes and know instantly that she was carrying her grandchild.

Matt came out the door on the run. He had a big smile on his face as he approached the car. At that moment, everything in his world was fine.

And she was the one who was going to ruin it.

He opened the door and hopped in. "Hey, gorgeous. I missed you." He leaned over and gave her a kiss. She pulled back quickly. "Not here. Your mother's probably watching."

"Then let's go, because I've been going crazy without you."

Matt thought he was going with her to get blood work, and chatted happily about his new job before they even left his street. He was so busy telling her about everything, he didn't notice until the last minute that she'd turned off the main highway and driven down a dirt road that led to a point overlooking the harbour.

He smirked. "You want to go parking first, do ya? Then get over here."

Ashley let him kiss her for a while, because it felt good to be with him again, but when his hand disappeared up the back of her blouse, she stopped him.

"We need to talk. Not here."

She got out of the car before he could say anything. He quickly followed her and yelled into the wind that whistled from across the headland. "Just a sec. Wait."

Instead of stopping, she tramped over the rocks and grass that edged the bank. There was a large boulder. This would have to do.

She sat but didn't look at him; instead she kept her gaze out over the water. He scrambled up beside her, out of breath.

"What's going on? Why did you want to come here?"

"Sit down."

Matt gave her a funny look but did as he was told. "You're making me nervous. Have I done something wrong? You don't want to break up with me, do you?"

She shook her head. Her hair whipped around her face because of the wind, and she had a hard time keeping it out of her eyes.

"Then talk to me."

When she turned and looked at his sweet, earnest face, so full of love and concern, it broke her heart. "I have something to tell you and I don't want to."

Matt reached over and took her hand. "You can tell me anything."

Ashley looked at their hands, trying to will the words to come.

"Oh my God, you're not seriously sick, are you? Please tell me you're all right."

"I'm not all right..."

"God, what is it?"

"I'm having a baby."

Matt's head snapped back as if she'd slapped him. "What? What do you mean?"

"It's true. I can't believe it, but it's true."

Matt stood up and put his hands on his head, as if trying to keep this shocking revelation inside his brain. He looked one way, then the other, and finally back at her. "For sure?"

She nodded.

He sank down on the boulder beside her and put his arms around her shoulders. For the first time since the morning she first knew, she let herself cry out loud. No more hiding her face in the sheets or in the shower or into a towel. She cried as if her heart would break, and let her wails be carried off by the ocean breeze.

Matt rocked her and held her close. He said nothing. There wasn't anything to say.

After a while she had no tears left, but Ashley kept her arms around his waist and her face hidden against the soft fleece of his hoodie. He rested his chin on the top of her head. She heard his heart thud in his chest. If only she could stay like this for the rest of her life. Then the world wouldn't be so frightening.

Finally she spoke. "What are we going to do?"

"I don't know."

She lifted her head and let him go. She reached into her pocket for some tissue to wipe her eyes, then crumpled it up and started to shred it in her hands. "Maribeth thinks I should go to Halifax and have an abortion."

"You told Maribeth before you told me?"

"I'm sorry. I didn't know what to do. I didn't know how to tell you and I needed to talk to someone."

Matt rested his elbows on his knees and put his face in his hands.

"Don't be mad at me."

He turned his head to look at her. "I'm not mad at you. I just wish you trusted me enough to come to me first. How do you know she isn't going to blab this all over town?"

"She's my best friend. Best friends don't do stuff like that."

"You better hope not."

Ashley frowned. "At some point everyone's going to know about it, no matter how hush-hush we are. That is, unless you want me to take her advice and get on a bus to Halifax and get it over with."

"Is that what you want?"

Ashley jumped up and held her arms across her chest. "No, that's not what I want. It's our baby. Is that what you want?"

"I don't know what the fuck I want. I can't think straight. All I keep wondering is how we can raise this baby when neither of us has any money, or full-time jobs, for that matter."

"You have your uncle's job."

Now it was Matt's turn to stand up. "I'm an errand boy! I make minimum wage. And what about you? What are you going to do?"

"It doesn't matter, does it, since your mother's going to kill me anyway."

"What about *your* mother?" Matt yelled back. "You think she's going to be happy about it?"

"Of course not. Don't yell at me."

"Well, don't yell at *me*."

Ashley flicked her hand in exasperation. "Listen to us. We sound like kids."

"We are kids."

"Then we're kids who've done a pretty good job pretending we're adults."

Matt ran his hand through his hair. "This is nuts. I don't know what to do."

Ashley started to walk past him. "Never mind, then. I'll figure it out on my own. Tell your mommy to send you to university in September and you can forget all about me and my big belly."

Matt reached out and grabbed her arm. "Hey, that's not fair. You've been living with this for a while. I'm five minutes into it. I'm scared, okay? But that doesn't mean I'm going to leave you in the lurch. This baby's mine too. I do love you, y'know. Don't you love me? Or am I just the creep who knocked you up?"

Ashley reached out and walked right into his arms. "I love you, Matt. I'll always love you. You're my baby's father."

He rubbed her back and kissed the top of her head. "Then we'll figure it out. We don't have to solve it this minute. Let's stop being so frantic. We have to stick together, because when this comes out, we're going to need each other."

❋

All was quiet that evening. Ashley went to her room after supper and spent the night on her computer, instant messaging Matt. Gertie came over and she and Bay played cards at the kitchen table. They asked Tansy to join them, but she refused.

"I hate cards."

"You hate everything," Gertie laughed. "I have yet to hear you say you love something."

"I love sex."

Gertie put her cards down. "Do tell."

Tansy sat down at the table. "There's nothing to tell. Doesn't everyone?"

"How the hell would I know?" Gertie yelled. "I've been felt up maybe twice in my life. But I'm sure hoping that will change by this time next week."

Bay shuffled the cards. "Don't look at me. I've been withering on the vine for years."

Gertie lowered her voice. "Have you had a lot of lovers, Tansy?"

Tansy shrugged. "I guess."

Bay tsked. "Don't you worry about disease?"

"I'm not stupid."

Gertie looked behind her, afraid Ashley would show up. "If you don't mind my asking, where was the craziest place you've ever done it?"

Bay slapped Gertie's arm. "For heaven's sake, don't get her started."

Tansy leaned back in her chair and folded her arms across her chest. "Let's see. There was that time in the elevator, and then there was the revolving door, and oh, I know, once up in an apple tree."

Gertie's mouth hung open. "You're joking."

Tansy got up with a laugh. "Of course I'm joking. Can you imagine trying to do it in a revolving door?"

"Or up a tree," Bay smiled.

The three of them giggled. Then Tansy put on her sweater that had been hanging over the doorknob in the hall. "I'm going for a walk."

"Take Merlin, will ya?" her sister asked.

"Okay. Come on, boy." Merlin jumped up from his mat and rushed over to the door. Tansy grabbed his leash and put it on him. "You guys want me to pick something up at the corner store?"

"Yeah. A bag of Dorit—"

"What was that, Gertie?"

"A bag of oranges."

"Oranges it is." She went out the door.

It was nice out, warm, with no wind. The sun was disappearing over the horizon and the sky was a blaze of pink and mauve. Tansy couldn't remember sunsets like this in New York. She'd forgotten how breathtaking they could be.

Even though it was early in the evening, there weren't many people about. Little kids who'd been racing around on their bikes or playing street hockey were now corralled indoors. Tansy imagined that most mothers on the street were putting little ones to bed or parking older ones in front of a video.

As she rounded the corner, she smelled someone's barbeque going and heard laughter coming from behind a fence. Friends over for a beer, no doubt—all normal, everyday activities that she had never taken part in. It made her sad.

She headed down towards the wharf, a perfect spot to sit and look out over the water. Merlin was happy with this long adventure. Tansy could have sworn he was smiling at her, with his goofy, hairy face. "Thank you, Merlin. At least someone loves me."

On the park bench she stopped and breathed in the fishy air. The fog rolled in from offshore. It wouldn't be long before it crept over rooftops and enveloped the town, muting sounds and making shapes a hazy blur.

Tansy sat there, not registering what was going on around her. If she had, she would've noticed Dermot pass her in his truck, brake, and then pull over to the side of the road. He hopped out, slammed the door, and headed straight for her. He was almost on top of her before she realized someone was approaching, and that was only because Merlin sat up and started to wiggle with excitement.

"I want to talk to you," Dermot said.

Tansy turned her head. "Don't sneak up on a person like that."

"I'm hardly sneaking." He stood in front of her. "What do you think you're playing at?"

"Excuse me?"

He pointed his finger at her. "Don't be all mealy-mouthed and give me that 'I don't know what you're talking about' stuff. You know damn well why I'm annoyed."

Tansy gave a big sigh and looked away. "Everyone's always upset at me about something. Join the crowd."

"Is it any wonder, the way you carry on?"

Tansy glanced back at him. "Don't stand in front of me. I can't look up that long. If you have something to say, sit next to me and maybe we can talk like two adults."

Dermot looked wary for a moment and then did as she asked. She pivoted around to face him and put her arm on the back of the bench. "So what have I done that has you riled up?"

"You've talked to Bay about me. And she's talked to you, obviously."

"Shouldn't you be mad at her too?"

"As a matter of fact, I am mad at her, but since you're here, you'll do."

Tansy smiled.

"What's so funny?"

"'Since you're here, you'll do.' Isn't that exactly it? Isn't that what you wanted? Bay wasn't with you, so I was. And now because I was, you're angry with me. I didn't twist your arm to sleep with me, as I recall."

"I told you I loved her."

"And a minute later you loved me. You aren't better than me, Dermot. You were in that bed too."

"But I didn't know who you were."

"I didn't know who you were either. Why are you mad at me? Shouldn't you be mad at yourself? If I'm getting it in the neck, why aren't you?"

Dermot looked flustered. Tansy knew she'd scored a point, so she waited.

He finally spoke. "All right, we didn't know. We're on equal footing as far as that goes, but I'm annoyed that you told Bay to cool it with me. She was more than ready to be with me the other day and then she changes her mind. I know you're behind it."

Tansy turned away from him. "I'm behind nothing. All I said was that she's been alone for a long time and she's forgotten that she should be wooed by a man."

"You're a great one to be giving that advice."

"I'm aware of my own double standard, Dermot. I'm not my sister. You have to realize that just because you've liked her for years, that doesn't give you the right to undress her in your back room. She's worth more than that, and I told her so. Why is that wrong? I'm worried about her. I don't want her to rush into something she may not be able to handle."

"I'm not some jerk who just wants to get in her pants. I care deeply about her."

Tansy turned back to him. "Then do me a favour and slow down. She's had a horrible time of it. I think she's depressed, and that's why she can't get her life back together. She's not the Bay I remember. She's uncertain and scared and vulnerable. I want you to understand that before you demand things of her."

Dermot stared at the ground.

"I'd better go."

Dermot looked at her. "I'm sorry. I jumped to the wrong conclusion."

She faced him. "I'm not innocent. I love my sister, but if I thought she'd never find out, I'd be with you tonight. You do something to me, and I haven't felt that in a long time. I think you feel it too. Or am I wrong?"

Dermot looked away. She watched his profile and willed him to say it. He cleared his throat. "No, you're not wrong."

They looked at each other.

"So what do we do?"

He shook his head. "I don't know."

"If you're going to be in Bay's life, I'll always be around."

"Maybe you'll go away and never come back."

She looked back out over the water. "I think my sister needs me for a while." When Tansy stood up, so did he. She gave him a sad smile. "We can't undo what we've done. But I know I'll never forget it. I don't want to forget it."

"Neither do I."

"I have to go." When she walked away from him, he called out. "Why don't I drive you home?"

She hesitated. "All right."

They walked together to the truck and Merlin jumped in first. He sat at Tansy's feet. Dermot started the truck but didn't move. He kept his hands on the wheel and looked as if he was struggling for words.

"Don't say anything."

He put the truck in drive and stepped on the gas. They drove in silence until they got to the end of Bay's street.

"You can drop me off here."

He pulled over and stopped the truck.

She looked at him. "Goodbye, Dermot."

He quickly reached over and took her face in his hands. "I'll never forget you." He kissed her before she could say anything.

Tansy had to get out of there. She pulled away and opened the door. Merlin hopped out and she jumped down and slammed the door behind her. She didn't look back as the truck made a U-turn and drove off. As she wiped her eyes and walked towards home she noticed Flo standing in someone's driveway carrying a bag from the corner store.

"Well, well, missy. I knew you was trouble from the very beginning. Stealing your sister's boyfriend. What kind of woman are you?"

Tansy shot daggers at her. "I may be a lot of things, but at least I'm not you."

She pushed past Flo and kept going.

"You'll get yours someday, girlie. You mark my words."

CHAPTER NINE

When Bay went downstairs the next morning, she was surprised to see Tansy sitting at the kitchen table. She had a mug of coffee in front of her.

"Good morning. Couldn't sleep?"

Tansy shook her head. "No, it was stuffy in my room last night. I should get a fan."

"Good idea."

"There's coffee in the pot."

Bay walked across the kitchen and opened the cupboard. She took out a mug and filled it, taking it back to the table to pour in the cream. "I've only got ten minutes." She sat at the table and took a big swig.

"You should eat breakfast. A granola bar isn't enough."

"You sound like Mom."

Tansy frowned and rubbed the outside of her mug. "I suppose she wanted you to eat oatmeal every morning, like we did when we were kids."

"Of course. I make it from time to time, but I couldn't for months after she died."

Tansy folded her arms on the table, laid down her head, and began to weep. Bay stayed quiet; Tansy didn't cry often and Bay knew she needed to.

"I miss her. It's hard to be here."

"But we're here. You have us."

Tansy lifted her head. "And what use am I to you? I only cause heartache for this family."

Bay shook her head. "That's not true. Everything wasn't your fault."

"Yes it was. It was all my fault."

"You were a kid, Tansy."

"Bay, do you know how hard this is?"

"I can't imagine."

"I'm afraid of what I might say."

Bay felt a knot in her stomach. "You wouldn't."

"No. But I'm..."

"You're what?"

Tansy wiped her eyes. "Nothing. I'm sad."

"Is it better to be with us and be sad than to *not* be with us and be sad?"

"Yes. I'm sorry. I had a lousy sleep."

Bay got up and put her mug in the sink. Then she walked back to where her sister sat and cradled Tansy's head against her chest. Tansy's arms went around Bay's waist. "As long as we stick together, it'll be all right. As long as we remember who we're doing this for, it'll be okay."

Tansy nodded.

"I'll see you tonight. Try and get Ashley to eat something."

"I will."

Bay left the house and walked to the post office, but her heart was back in that kitchen with her sister. For the first time in a long time, she saw Tansy as someone who wasn't as strong as she let on. What if it did become too hard for her to be here? What would they do then?

All these questions crowded into her mind and she panicked a little. Her first thought was to call Gertie, but she remembered that Gertie was excited about her mystery date, and she didn't want to ruin that. Then she thought of Dermot.

She took the cellphone out of her purse and called Anne, the woman who subbed for her when she was off sick. Anne lived a block away from the post office, which came in mighty handy.

"Anne? It's me. I'm running a little late. Would you mind holding the fort until I get there? Maybe an hour at most...Thanks, you're a doll. See you."

She wondered if she'd catch Dermot at home. It was still early. She called his number but there was no answer, so she hurried back up the street and jumped in her car. She didn't bother telling Tansy but drove straight to the garage and parked next to Dermot's red truck at the side of the building. She got out of the car and walked through the open garage doors. Dermot had his back to her, writing on a clipboard.

"Dermot?"

He spun around. "Bay? What are you doing here? Is something wrong?"

"Well, yes and no. Can I talk to you for a moment?"

He put down the clipboard. "Sure. Come in my...on second thought, let's go in here." He pointed to the chairs by the cash register in the other room.

"Thanks." She went ahead of him and sat down. He sat beside her and waited.

"I'm not sure why I'm here," she confessed. "I got a little panicky and needed to talk to someone."

"Sure."

"I'm worried about Tansy."

"Oh?"

"I'm afraid it's very hard for her to be here without Mom. It might be so hard that she'll leave and I'm not sure I'll be able to cope if that happens."

"She said she was leaving?"

"No. But she was crying this morning and she hardly ever cries."

Dermot glanced away.

"I'm not feeling strong at the moment and it hit me that if Tansy leaves I may fall apart. And that scares me to death."

He looked at her. "You won't fall apart, Bay, because you're a mother and Ashley needs you. If you feel this way, you should go to the doctor and let him help you with this anxiety. Believe me, I know how it feels."

"Yes, I'd forgotten that. Did you have to go on pills when Jane... left?"

"As a matter of fact, I did. No one knows that, but they saved my life."

She gave a big sigh. "I'd better go to the doctor. This past year I've been lost in a fog. I'm only realizing now that I need help to find my way out."

He smiled at her. "You're a strong woman, Bay. You'll be able to overcome this. I know you will."

She reached for his hand. "Thank you. I wasn't sure where to turn."

"You can always talk to me."

"I know that."

They looked at each other.

"I've missed you these past few days. Are you still mad at me? I'm sorry I've been childish."

"I'm not mad at you, Bay. I've done a lot of thinking, and you're right. We shouldn't rush anything. If it's meant to be, it'll happen."

"Okay. But am I allowed a kiss?"

He leaned over and kissed her. It was nice. They both got up and Bay reached for him again. "One more, please." She kissed him harder but he pulled away first. "Sorry, company's here."

His assistant mechanic Jason was arriving for work.

"I'd better go."

"Okay."

"Would you like to come to dinner tonight?"

Dermot hesitated. "Sorry, I've got plans. A friend from out of town is coming over. I haven't seen him in a while."

"Oh, sure. Another time, then."

"Yeah."

Bay waved and said hi to Jason as she walked back to the car. She got in and started it up. Then it was back to the post office, where she parked her vehicle at the back of the building and went in the side door. Flo was talking to Anne out front, and when Bay heard Tansy's name, she stood still.

"I'm going to murder that Tansy Gillis, I swear to God."

"What did she do now?" Anne asked.

"She was only sittin' in Dermot's truck last night, so she was, necking up a storm with him for everyone to see. Has she no shame? And there's dear little Bay, runnin' around oblivious to all of it. I tried to warn her, but I guess blood's thicker than water, because she can't see her sister for what she is. A no-good tramp."

Bay went ice cold. She couldn't move. The longer she stood there the colder she got. Then she was aware of her heart pounding. She was sure Anne and Flo would hear it. It took all her willpower to move to the side door and slip out, closing it gently behind her. She got back in her car and fought the urge to vomit.

And then she started the engine.

❀

When Ashley came downstairs that morning, Tansy was sitting on the swing by the vegetable garden. She wanted to run outside and fling herself into her aunt's arms. The only reason she didn't was that she knew she had to tell her mother first. And she was going to do it today, when her mother came home for supper.

She and Matt had talked about it endlessly, both on the computer and face to face. They decided they'd tell their mothers at exactly the same moment, so one couldn't get on the phone with the other and spill the beans.

Ashley poured herself a bowl of corn flakes and filled it with milk. She had to drink lots of milk, she told herself. There were so many rules now. She wouldn't be able to have a cooler or a beer at a party, she wouldn't be able to have the odd cigarette or toke of someone's joint. She'd have to eat vegetables, and she hated vegetables. What if she got stretch marks? What would Matt think of that?

And what about sex? Was she allowed to have it? She couldn't bear to think about not being with him for nine months. It was all too difficult. She took the bowl and poured it into Merlin's dish. Let him have soggy corn flakes for breakfast.

As she went out the door and down the steps, Merlin ran to greet her. She stopped to give his big old head a kiss. "Morning, Merly." He licked her hands.

Tansy called to her. "Hi, honey, did you sleep okay?"

Ashley walked over to her aunt and sat beside her. They pushed the swing with their feet.

"Yeah, I guess."

"Are you feeling better?"

"Not really."

"That's too bad. Maybe your blood work will tell us something."

"Yeah, maybe."

"What are your plans for today?"

Ashley looked at her fingernails and pushed the cuticles back. "Nothing."

"You and Maribeth aren't doing anything?"

"Maribeth has a job. She's working at the mall."

"Did you put an application in any of the stores there?"

"No. I should have."

Tansy didn't say anything, and because she didn't, Ashley began to talk. "It's like I couldn't get my act together this year. I was late for everything. I didn't try out for basketball. I was supposed to join the drama club but I never did. I didn't send out any applications for September either. What's the point? I don't want to go to university here."

"What would you like to do?"

Ashley kept her head down and stared at her hands. "Maybe take a cosmetology course in North Sydney. It's less than a year and at least you can get a job."

"That sounds fun."

"Yeah," she said quietly. "It does."

"Talk to your mother about it. If she knows you're interested, she'll help you."

Ashley nodded but didn't say anything.

"I always wanted to do something like that," Tansy confessed. "At one point I thought I'd like to be a hairdresser, but Mom and Dad didn't think that was good enough."

"What did they want you to do?"

"Become a brain surgeon."

Ashley looked up quickly and Tansy laughed at her expression. "I'm kidding. They wanted me to be something boring like a teacher or a nurse. I'd rather be boiled alive."

"So what did you do?"

Tansy looked out at the water. "That was around the time Dad and Bobby died, and none of us could do anything then. It was like a bad dream. We went and stayed with Mom's cousin in Fredericton for a while, to get away from the heartache. You were born there. And then it was time to go home, but I couldn't face it. I knew my heart would break if I had to stare out at this water day after day. I don't know how your mother did it."

"She was busy with me."

Tansy smiled at her. "You're right."

"She was lucky I came along, wasn't she?"

Tansy put her arms around her niece and kissed the top of her head. "She was the luckiest woman in the world. Still is."

"I'm glad you're here."

"Me too."

They continued to rock the swing back and forth, content in each other's company. They listened to the crows cawing to each other from atop the fir trees on the other side of the field. Tansy looked at them. "Is it my imagination or do they sound like Flo?"

"Well, she is an old buzzard," Ashley said.

They laughed together.

Bay went back to the garage first. She tore up the highway and squealed into the station, stopping on a dime. She got out of the car and slammed the door in time to see Dermot and Jason poke their heads out of the garage doors to see what the noise was about.

"Send Jason for coffee," she hollered.

Dermot came towards her. "What's the matter?"

"Send Jason for coffee, unless you want the whole town to know who you are."

Dermot looked confused but he did as he was told. "Scram for a while, Jason."

"Uh, sure." Jason laid his wrench on the top of the gas pump and walked towards his car. The minute he left Dermot said, "What's going on?"

"You tell me."

"What do you mean?"

"Get in here." She walked through the garage doors and into the back room. Memories of the last time she was there filled her head. Bay turned to face him. "When were you going to tell me?"

Dermot paled. "Tell you what?"

"That you've been screwing my sister!" Bay reached for the first thing she saw and threw it at him. He ducked and the stapler hit the wall behind him. She reached for something else, but he was too quick and grabbed her wrists. "Wait. Calm down."

She pulled against him. "You can go to hell, Dermot. Let me go."

He shook her. "*Calm down.*"

"Did you have fun making a fool out of me?"

"It wasn't like that. What did she say?"

"*She* hasn't told me anything. I had to overhear my nosy neighbour telling my coworker you were parked in a truck last night necking like teenagers on my own street. How do you think that makes me feel?"

"Terrible, I know. But that doesn't mean I've been with her."

"Are you serious? I saw your faces the night you supposedly met. I didn't put two and two together then, but no one looks that guilty when they've only been kissing. Now let go of me." She yanked her arms and escaped his grip, wiping her hair out of her eyes with her shirtsleeve. "Are you going to tell me the truth, Dermot, or placate me with more lies?"

He didn't say anything at first. "The truth. I didn't know she was your sister. And she didn't know who I was, either. We met when she stopped for gas."

Bay folded her arms across her chest. "And with her usual speedy charm, she asked you to take her to bed, and naturally, since you're in love with me, you did."

Dermot's face turned angry. She'd never seen him like that before. As he stepped closer to her, she took a step back. His voice was low. "Yes, Bay, I did. And the funny thing is, I told her about you before I did."

"She knew?"

"I told her I was in love with someone who didn't love me back."

"That's not true."

He shouted in her face. "It is true! I've been hanging around you like a lovesick puppy for years now and all I get is an occasional pat on the head."

"You're wrong. I've had a hard time. I'm trying to get better."

He started to pace. "Guess what. You're not the only one. I lost someone too, only I don't know where she is. I don't have the luxury of taking flowers to her grave on Sunday afternoons. She could be in a ditch or at the bottom of the ocean. Or she might be living it up on a tropical island. You're not the only one who's had their heart broken, Bay."

She looked away.

He stopped then and put his hands on the back of the chair in front of him. "And then this woman drops by and she makes it clear from the first moment she lays eyes on me that she thinks I'm special. She flirts with me, makes me feel like a man. And I haven't felt that for a long time. So yes, Bay, when she asked me to sleep with her that night, I did. And guess what?"

She didn't answer him.

"She came to me again, and it was heaven."

"Stop."

"No, you wanted to know the truth. And then you arrived at the garage that day and threw yourself at me. I couldn't believe it."

"Was that heaven?"

"Yes. Yes, it was. I came over that night to be with you. I didn't want to think about what I'd done with Tansy. I hoped you'd never find out. And then she walked in the door. We both nearly died. It was too awful for words."

"So why were you kissing her last night?"

"We were saying goodbye."

"How touching, the two of you doing me this big favour, pretending it never happened, keeping me in the dark. No wonder you won't come for supper. And no wonder Tansy's crying in my kitchen. Only is she crying for me or is she crying for you? What do you think?"

"I don't know what to think anymore."

"Well, why don't I ask her?" Bay started for the door. He came around from behind the chair and hurried to catch her. He held her arm and made her look at him. "Don't go off at her, Bay. The minute she found out who I was, she stayed away from me. It's not fair to get upset with her."

"It isn't? You might think you know my sister, Dermot, but you don't. She's capable of lots of things, things people have to run around and undo, things that need to be kept quiet—so quiet that the silence is unbearable. So don't tell me how to deal with my sister, okay?"

He let her go. "What about us?"

"Us? You're kidding, right?"

She walked away.

❀

Bay called Anne from the car and told her she wasn't feeling well and she was spending the day in bed. Anne told her it was no problem. When she hung up, Bay fought the urge to go to the cemetery and talk to her mother. It was nonsense anyway. Her mother never talked to her. It was her imagination.

She was alone. She was always alone.

Bay started the car and drove back to the house. As she pulled in the driveway, Flo was walking up the sidewalk. Bay got out of the car and ignored her.

"Morning, Bay. Fine day."

Bay turned around and walked over to her. "How can you talk about me behind my back one minute and then give me a big grin five minutes later like butter wouldn't melt?"

Flo's mouth dropped open. "What are you on about?"

"Telling everyone who'll listen that my sister is a tramp. Where do you get off talking about my family like that?"

Flo looked shocked. "I didn't mean no harm. I was only stickin' up for ya."

"Well, do me a big favour and keep your nose out of my business from now on."

She turned around and marched down the driveway and into the house. There was no one in the kitchen.

"Tansy?"

"I'm in here. What are you doing home?"

Bay walked into the living room. Tansy was on the couch reading a *Vogue* magazine.

"Where's Ashley?"

"She's in the shower. Is something wrong?"

Bay threw herself into the armchair by the picture window. She crossed her arms and then her legs and stared at her sister. "You could say that."

Tansy closed the magazine and tossed it onto the coffee table. "Okay. Are you going to tell me what?"

"You know what it's about."

"I do?"

Bay nodded.

"I'm afraid I don't. Enlighten me."

"Dermot."

Tansy went white. She sat very still and kept her eyes on Bay. "Who told you?"

"Does it matter?"

"Yes, it does. Because I know for a fact it wouldn't have been him."

"My wonderful neighbour Flo couldn't keep her mouth shut this morning at the post office."

Tansy closed her eyes.

"Were you going to tell me?"

She opened them again. "No, I wasn't, because it's over."

"You sat in that kitchen and told me I needed to behave like a lady and keep my hands off him. I thought you were looking out for me. But all the while you were making sure you had him to yourself. What kind of a woman does that?"

"I know that's how it looks—"

Bay stood up. "That's how it is! I know you, Tansy. I know what you're capable of."

Tansy stood up too. "And what's that?"

"Creating a huge mess and making the rest of us clean it up."

Tansy said nothing.

"So here it is again. Dermot and I are finished. Any chance we might have had has been wiped out by you."

Tansy raised her voice. "Why weren't you with him in the first place?"

"I had other things to worry about, like raising a headstrong daughter alone and dealing with the loss of everyone I loved, including you."

Tansy turned away and walked towards the window. "It hasn't been easy for me either."

"You drive a Porsche. How difficult was it?"

Tansy turned around. "I have a car. You have a daughter. Who's the lucky one?"

Bay didn't say anything, so Tansy continued. "I met a guy who looked as lonely as I felt and we got together, that's all. It wasn't a big conspiracy against you. It happened. I'm sorry you got hurt."

"You're always sorry."

"What do you want from me, Bay? What else can I say?"

"That you're getting the hell out of my life and never coming back. I thought I wanted you to come home, but I've been miserable since you arrived and I can't take it anymore…"

"Mom?"

They looked up and saw Ashley standing on the stairs, wearing a bathrobe and a towel wrapped around her hair.

"What's going on?"

The sisters looked at each other. Bay spoke first. "Nothing. It's nothing to worry about."

Ashley came down the last of the stairs. "Nothing to worry about? You just told Tansy to get the hell out of your life. Were you going to consult me about it? Or don't I matter?"

"Of course you matter."

"It doesn't sound like it. Why do you hate her so much?"

"I don't hate her."

"That's not how it sounds from here." Ashley looked at Tansy. "And do you want to go?"

"I can't stay if your mother doesn't want me here. It's her house."

"It's my house too!" Ashley shouted. "How come no one listens to me and what I want?"

"I do, honey."

"Mom, that's a lie. I don't want Tansy to go. Are you listening now? I don't want her to go."

"This is between Tansy and—"

Ashley's voice became too high. "No! She can't go. I need her!"

Tansy walked over and put her hands on Ashley's shoulders. "Why do you need me?"

Ashley's face crumbled. "I'm pregnant."

Tansy immediately took her in her arms as Ashley sobbed against her.

Bay's hand covered her mouth. "No. Oh, no."

She ran out of the room.

CHAPTER TEN

Tansy finally sent Ashley upstairs to get some clothes on. She told her to wait in her room, because her mother would be up to speak to her in a minute. Then she went into the kitchen and looked out the back door. Bay was on the swing, just as Tansy suspected.

She took a deep breath and walked outside. Bay was looking out over the water and didn't notice her approach. It wasn't until she sat down that Bay turned and saw her.

They looked at each other for a long moment. Tansy reached over and took Bay's hand. Bay let her.

"We'll figure this out together. I won't leave you; you won't be alone with this, Bay. You have to let me help you. You have to let me help her. She's the only thing that matters."

Bay nodded.

"The issues you and I have mean nothing in the wake of this. We need to put them on the back burner and present a united front, okay?"

Bay nodded again.

"You have to go upstairs and tell her you love her. She's frightened and she needs you."

"This is my fault, you know."

Tansy squeezed her hand. "That's not true. How is it your fault?"

"I've been preoccupied with Mom's death and I didn't pay enough attention to her, so she went and found it somewhere else."

"Nonsense. She fell in love with a boy, that's all."

Tears fell down Bay's cheeks. "She's only a baby. Her life is ruined."

"It's not ruined. We'll figure it out. Go and talk to her."

Bay stood and wiped her face with her hands, then looked down at Tansy. "I'll let you help me with this because I'm smart enough to know I need help, but don't for one minute think I've forgiven you for what you've done to Dermot and me."

She walked back into the house.

As Bay climbed the stairs, her mind went blank and her feet got heavier with every step. She had to rest before she reached the landing. Tansy told her to talk to Ashley. And say what, exactly? All the words would be wrong, because nothing about this was right.

She knocked on her daughter's bedroom door and opened it. Ashley sat cross-legged in the middle of the bed, her face streaked with tears. She broke down the minute she saw her mother. "I'm sorry," she cried. "Don't hate me. Don't hate Matt."

Bay sat on the bed and gathered Ashley in her arms. "I could never hate you."

Ashley cried for a long time as Bay rocked her. When she quieted down, Bay reached for a box of tissues and passed it to her.

Ashley dried her eyes. "I don't know what to do."

"Have you told Matt?"

She nodded. "He's telling his mother today."

Bay rubbed the back of her own neck. "Oh, God."

"I know. She's going to kill me."

"She'll have to get through me first."

That put a small smile on Ashley's face.

"She should be concerned with her own child," Bay sighed. "And you are children, despite what's happened."

"I love him."

"So you say."

"I do!"

"I know you do. But with love comes responsibility—"

Ashley jumped up from the bed. "I don't need a lecture about how irresponsible I am. It's not going to help, Mom. I need someone to tell me what to do."

"All right. Sit down. It's not going to help either of us if you think I'm the enemy. I'm your mother and I want to support you, but this is a shock. It's going to take me a little time to absorb it."

Ashley sat on the edge of the bed. "My whole life is over. I can't go to school in September, I can't be with my friends, I can't go to parties and hang out because I'll have a little baby to take care of and I have no idea how to do it. I'm so stupid."

Bay reached out and pushed her daughter's hair behind her ear. "Listen, sweetheart, you're not the first and you certainly won't be the last girl to find herself in this position. And it took two people to make this baby, so don't take all the blame. Matt has just as much to answer for."

"He's so upset."

"He should be. Why didn't you use protection?"

"We did...except maybe once."

Bay gave a big sigh. "Once is all you need. Oh God, Ashley. I can't believe it."

"That makes two of us."

They sat together and didn't say anything for a few minutes. Finally Bay asked, "Have you given any thought to your options?"

Ashley bit her fingers. "I don't think I could have an abortion. I'd feel so guilty. But I don't think I can take care of it, either. What if I dropped it?"

"It's not an it. It will be a real live baby girl or boy. That's a huge responsibility. Once you're a mother, you never stop being a mother. It's a never-ending job."

"You think I should give it up for adoption?"

"I don't know." Bay got up from the bed and walked over to the window. She pulled the curtains aside and looked out over the street. Everything looked the same and yet everything was completely different. It was like being in some weird time warp. Last time she'd looked out this window her daughter had been a young carefree girl with nothing to worry about. Now Ashley would be someone's mother, and that made Bay a grandmother. Wasn't she too young to be a grandmother? She turned away from the window. "We can't think straight right now. I think we need some time before we make any decisions."

"Please don't make Tansy leave. I don't want us to be alone. I feel better when she's in the house. I feel safer, don't you?"

Bay bit her lip before she answered. "I won't make her leave. We do need her. I know that."

"Why were you fighting? She's your sister. I don't understand it."

"It's complicated." Bay walked to the door. "I'm going to make you an appointment with the doctor."

"Do I have to?"

Bay turned around. "Ashley, you don't have the luxury of being a whiny teenager anymore. You're about to be someone's mother. You have to take care of yourself and that little life you carry inside you. I'm sorry that this has happened to you, but now that it has, you have to live up to what's needed of you. I hate to say it, but you really should have thought about this before you slept with Matt."

Ashley fell back on the bed and grabbed her pillow to cover her face. And as much as Bay wanted to take her in her arms, she knew that her daughter needed to face the truth alone.

Closing the bedroom door quietly behind her, Bay headed straight for the bathroom and locked herself in. She stripped off her clothes and stepped into the shower. As soon as the water hit her face, she started to cry. Her shoulders shook with her sobbing. How had this happened? What was she going to do? Why wasn't her mom here to help her? All she wanted was to close her eyes and never wake up. This was all too much. Much too much.

If Bay thought the first few moments after Ashley's confession were bad, she was sadly mistaken. They were nothing compared to the confrontation with Matt's mother, Ruth. When her car zoomed into the driveway, the three Gillis women were at the kitchen table. Tansy had finally convinced them that they needed to eat something; she heated up a couple of cans of tomato soup and served it with crackers and cheese. To sit together and have lunch did help, but it couldn't completely erase the sensation of being hit by a freight train.

Ashley kept a comforter around her as she ate. She did that when she had a bad day or was home sick from school. It made her look about ten years old. When she heard the car tires scrunch the gravel outside the kitchen window, she looked at her mother with big eyes.

"Oh no, that's her. I know it is. I can't see her."

Tansy grabbed Ashley's arm as she tried to get out of the chair. "Don't you go anywhere."

"I can't face her..."

"You don't have to hide and you have nothing be ashamed of. Hold your head up. Your mother and I are here with you."

Bay gave Tansy a grateful look. "She's right, honey. Be calm."

Ashley sat back down and hugged the comforter closer to her body. They heard the car door slam and then seconds later Ruth was at the screen door.

"Come in, Ruth. It's open," Bay said.

Ruth walked into the kitchen breathing fire. Merlin took one look at her and cowered on his mat. "I can't believe it. I can't *believe* it. Didn't I tell you they were up to no good? Didn't I tell you to get your daughter on birth control pills?"

"Ruth..."

"His life is ruined. *Ruined!* And it's all because of this little madam." She pointed at Ashley.

Bay stood up. "Stop it right now, Ruth. I don't intend to trade insults with you."

Ruth looked at Ashley. "How could you do this? You knew he wanted to go away to university. You did this so he wouldn't leave, didn't you? Matt was going to make something of himself, and now what's he going to do? How's he supposed to support a child? How's he supposed to be a father at seventeen?"

Ashley trembled. "I'm sorry."

"Sorry doesn't fix it, does it?"

Now it was Tansy's turn to stand up. "I suggest you leave before you say something you'll regret."

Ruth gave Tansy a filthy look. "Who are you?"

"I'm Ashley's aunt—"

"Tansy?" Ruth looked incredulous. "Well, well, isn't this interesting. I see that behaving like an alley cat runs in the family."

Bay slammed her fist on the table. "Get out of my house. How dare you come in here and say such mean things? Believe it or not, Ruth, we're in shock too, but you don't see us insulting Matt. How is this going to make anything better, for any of us?"

Before Ruth could answer they heard another car pull into the driveway, only this time two doors slammed and a moment later Matt ran into the kitchen, his father on his heels. He pushed past his mother and put his arms around Ashley, who stood up the minute she saw him.

"I told you not to come here, Mom. Why don't you listen? You have no business making everyone miserable."

"I'm not the one who's made our lives miserable," Ruth shouted. "That's all thanks to you and this little tramp."

"*Ruth.*" Matt's father, Ian, grabbed his wife's arm. "Apologize this instant."

Ruth sobbed into her husband's shirt. He looked over her head at the others.

"Please forgive her, she's distraught. She shouldn't have come here. I'll take her home."

"Good," Tansy answered. "And keep her away from us. We're having a hard enough time as it is without being bullied and insulted by your wife."

Ian started for the back door, with Ruth still sobbing in his arms, but he turned his head. "I want you to come home too, Matt."

"Can't he stay?" Ashley cried. "I need him."

"Not tonight," Bay said. "I think both of our families need some alone time together. We'll obviously be in touch, Ian."

"Yes. Thanks, Bay."

Matt gave Ashley a big hug before he let her go. "I'll call you when I get home."

She nodded and dried her face with the corner of her comforter. "I love you."

He smiled but didn't say anything, obviously embarrassed to repeat it in front of their parents, so he gave her a quick wave.

When the MacLeans left, the three Gillis women collapsed back into their kitchen chairs. They were dazed, as if they'd been boxing for a couple of rounds. Merlin hurried over and put his head in Bay's lap. She rubbed his ears.

"I should've sicced Merlin on her."

They grimaced at each other, comrades together after the first battle.

Just then Gertie appeared at the back door. "Yoohoo, only me. Can you believe I'm now walking on my lunch hour?" She came into the kitchen holding a paper bag. "Someone give me a medal and put the kettle on."

The three of them stared at her.

Gertie stared back. "What's wrong?"

"I'm having a baby," said Ashley.

"Oh, hardy har har." Gertie sat at the table and looked at them all. "So are you going to tell me or what?"

No one spoke.

Gertie's eyes got wider and wider. "For real?"

They nodded.

Gertie burst into tears. She howled so loud Merlin ran around the table and barked at her. The other three jumped up and began to wring their hands.

"Gertie, stop it!" Tansy said. "You're not helping."

"I'm sorry! Oh my God!"

"Even I had a better reaction than that," Bay shouted at her.

"Gertie, please don't hate me!" Ashley cried.

"Hate you? I love you." She jumped up from the table and smothered Ashley in her generous bosom. "I'll help. I'm available for babysitting every night of the week and you never have to pay me."

Dermot spent a long and wearying day at the garage trying to keep his mind off Tansy and Bay. He still couldn't believe everything had gone so wrong. And now there was no way he could talk to either of them, because he didn't dare call the house. He'd have to sit and cool his heels until one or both of them got in touch. That wouldn't help his mood any.

He finally headed for home after locking up the garage. All that awaited him was a couple of tins of beans, but he was in no mood to go grocery shopping. As he drove up Main Street he was aware of Bay's street up ahead. He told himself to keep looking straight but he didn't. As he passed the road he strained to see Bay's house. A rush of relief went through him when he saw that Tansy's Porsche was still in the driveway. But the fact that he was relieved was disturbing.

He and Tansy had no future. Not in this town. And who said he wanted one with her anyway?

When he got home he put the kettle on to make a pot of tea but soon realized he didn't have a tea bag in the house, so he grabbed his keys and wallet and hightailed it up to the corner store. It was a lovely warm summer night, perfect for a stroll. There were plenty of tourists about. You could always pick them out, with their fanny packs and sunhats on. They were the town's lifeblood in the summer and helped local businesses weather the long, quiet winters.

Dermot entered the store and went to the back where the teabags were. He started to walk back up the aisle when who walked into the store but Tansy. Without thinking, he ducked behind some shelves, which was ridiculous, because didn't he want to speak to her?

He watched her from his vantage point. Her face was pale and she looked weary, with her beautiful blonde hair held back haphazardly with an elastic. Obviously Bay had raked her over the coals, and that made him angry. He wondered what he should do, but before he could figure it out, Tansy looked in his direction. Startled, she turned around and walked right out of the store. Without thinking, he left the box of teabags on the shelf in front of him and rushed after her. She was halfway down the block by the time he got outside.

"Tansy, wait!"

She kept walking, so he had to run to catch up with her. He put his hand on her shoulder as he came up behind her. She shrugged it off. "Leave me alone."

"Just a minute, please."

Tansy stopped and faced him. "There is nothing that you and I have to talk about. It's all over. Bay knows and I don't plan on causing her any more pain. So stay away from me, Dermot."

"I want to know if you're all right. Bay was so angry when she left. I worried about you all day."

"I can take care of myself."

He glanced up the road towards Bay's street. "What did she say? I suppose she hates me now."

"I think she hates both of us at the moment."

Dermot looked back at her. "She won't make you leave town, will she?"

Tansy hesitated.

"Don't leave."

"Why?"

He hung his head. "I don't want to be the reason that you and Bay are apart. I think she needs someone. I thought that someone was me. I don't want her to be alone."

Tansy looked out towards the water. "She's not going to be alone. I'm staying here, as awkward as that may be for all of us."

"Do you think there will ever be a chance of..."

"...you and Bay together? Of course there's a chance. Be patient and let her calm down. She'll come around in the end. I have to go, Dermot. I'll see you around."

She walked away quickly before he could say another word.

❀

A couple of days later, Tansy sat on the swing, Merlin at her feet. Her eyes lingered on the bright greenery of the vegetables growing in straight, neat rows in the garden. She could pick out the lacy carrot tops and the tangled leaves of runner beans, but she wasn't sure about the rest. Why didn't she listen when her mother told her about the garden? She could see her mom now, on her knees, humming as she worked the soil. Bay would stay beside her and watch, but Tansy was always too restless. She'd flit and dance around the edges instead. If only she'd stopped and learned. Now it seemed rather a miracle that one could plant a tiny seed and have it ripen into a fat red tomato or a pod of tiny perfect peas.

A screen door slammed and out marched Flo to hang up her dish-towels on the clothesline. Tansy ignored her, which only made Flo's muttering louder. Tansy finally looked at her. "If you've got something to say, say it."

"Well, it's a poor house that can't keep one lady," Flo scowled.

"What's that supposed to mean?"

"Get off your arse and weed the garden for your sister."

Tansy would have if she knew what was a weed and what was an actual vegetable, but she wasn't going to tell Flo that.

"You're a joy to be around, Flo. No wonder Ira loves you so much."

Flo flicked her apron and stalked off. "Saucy brats will be the death of me."

Tansy sighed as she continued to wait for Bay and Ashley to come back from the doctor's office. She'd offered to go with them, but Bay said she wasn't needed, and Ashley was too preoccupied to care. When she finally heard the car pull in the driveway, she got up and headed for the house with Merlin beside her. They met at the back door.

"How did it go?" She held the door open for them and naturally Merlin went in first.

"It was awful." Ashley brushed past her and walked into the kitchen. "Awful?"

"Don't listen to her." Bay went in as well. Tansy brought up the rear and closed the screen door behind her.

Ashley sat at the kitchen table and cupped her chin in her hand. "There are so many things to remember. I don't know what he was talking about."

Tansy sat beside her. "What kind of things?"

"I don't know. Pills and stuff."

Bay sat down as well, and rooted through her purse. "I've written it down. All we have to get are some prenatal vitamins and folic acid."

"Did he say when the baby's due?"

Mother and daughter glanced at each other. "Christmas," they said at the same time.

Tansy smiled. "Maybe it will be born on your birthday."

Ashley frowned. "I'm going to put it up for adoption."

Tansy and Bay stared at her. It was Bay who spoke. "When did you decide this? Is it something you and Matt talked about?"

"When that doctor kept harping about what I have to do. It suddenly hit me. I'm not going to remember any of it; ultrasounds and appointments. There's too much to do and the baby isn't even here. What's it going to be like when it does get here? It's terrifying."

Tansy put her hand out and placed it over Ashley's. "You're overwhelmed at the moment. You don't have to remember everything at once. You'll be fine."

"What do you know about it?" Ashley said. "You never had a kid."

Tansy pulled her hand away.

Bay spoke up. "There's no need to take it out on us, Ashley. It doesn't help."

"Sorry." Ashley folded her arms on the table and laid her head on top of them. "I feel like jumping out of my skin."

"It's called hormones," Tansy informed her. "They're running amok at the moment."

"Do you really want to give this baby away?" Bay asked her.

Ashley hid her face. She didn't say anything for a few moments and then came a muffled "No."

"What does Matt think?" her mother asked.

She sat up. "He says it's up to me. Which is stupid, because why do I have to decide everything?"

"It's no doubt hard for him to know what to say," Tansy said. "He knows it's your body, and so it's ultimately your decision."

"I know his mother thinks I should have an abortion. Just flush it away like it never existed. So even if I wanted to, I'd never do it, just to bug her."

They sat in silence for a while. That's when Tansy brought up something she'd been mulling over. "I'm going to sell the Porsche. It's nuts to have such a fancy car in this neck of the woods. We'll need the money when the baby comes."

"You don't have to do that," Ashley said.

"I'd like to."

Bay picked at her thumbnail and didn't look at her sister. "So you're going to stay, then?"

"Well, of course I'm going to stay. I told you that."

"You say a lot of things you don't mean."

"*Mom.*"

Tansy patted her niece's hand but looked at Bay. "Well, I mean this. We're going to have to stick together. You don't make a lot of money, and Ashley won't be working until the baby is older, and we'll need money for their future. I have a few other things I can sell, and I plan on looking for a job, too."

"A job? What on earth do you do besides sidle up to rich men?"

Tansy rose from her chair. "You can insult me all day, but you're not going to make me run away so you can have the satisfaction of saying 'I told you so.' I'm in this to the end, Bay, like it or lump it."

Tansy turned around and went upstairs to her room.

Ashley gave her mother an incredulous look. "What is wrong with you? Why are you so mean to her all the time? She's only trying to help."

Bay looked away.

"You know what, Mom? Right now, I feel like the adult in this room." Ashley rose from the table and followed her aunt upstairs.

Bay got up and went outdoors to the swing. Looking at the garden made her feel better. Then she closed her eyes and imagined her mother sitting beside her. *What do you think, Mom? Did I do a good job with the vegetables this year? Am I doing anything right? Anything at all?*

She didn't know how long she sat there, but when she finally opened her eyes, the sun had set and there was a definite chill in the air. Her limbs were stiff as she got off the swing and walked back into the kitchen. She heard the television on in the living room, so she poked her head in. Tansy sat on the couch and Ashley was fast asleep, wrapped in her blanket, with her head in Tansy's lap.

Tansy looked up at her. "We were watching TV and she fell asleep. She's emotionally exhausted, the poor kid."

Bay walked over to the wing chair and sat down heavily. "She's not the only one. I'm sorry about what I said earlier. It's like I say things without thinking."

"That's okay."

"What a mess." Bay rubbed her forehead. "I can't believe we're in this predicament."

Tansy shrugged and absent-mindedly brushed Ashley's hair off her face. "Life is about lurching from crisis to crisis."

There was something in Tansy's face that touched Bay. "Is that how it's been for you all these years?"

Tansy shrugged again. "Sort of."

"Why didn't you get married and settle down?"

"I don't know. I always thought I would someday, but that day never came."

Bay looked at the floor. "I know I've been angry at you, for all kinds of things…"

"You've had reason to be."

Bay groaned and put her hands up through her hair. "If only you knew how tired I am of being angry. I don't recognize myself anymore. I'm either numb or furious with everything and everyone. I think I need help."

"You're right."

They sat in silence for a few minutes. Out of the blue Bay asked, "Were you serious about getting a job?"

"I have to. We're going to need the money. My nest egg is becoming a little sparse."

"Thanks. That would help."

❀

Even though Tansy knew she needed to find work, she wasn't optimistic about her chances. What on earth was she going to do here in the middle of nowhere? Not much call for modelling or acting in Louisbourg, which is what she did to make ends meet for quite a few years, before she met the first of her gentlemen friends. And when she sold the Porsche, they'd only have Bay's older car between them, so a job in Sydney wasn't ideal.

There was nothing for it. She'd have to hit the streets and beg someone to take her on as a waitress in one of the restaurants in town. It was that or become an animator at the fortress and dress up in period costumes all day. Wearing an itchy petticoat and bonnet on her head was not an option. She'd rather starve.

But then she remembered who she was doing it for and reconsidered, only to find out that there was a long waiting list to be an animator for the season, so that came to nothing. She even asked Gertie if they needed a typist at her insurance office. Gertie said she liked her, but since *she* was the only typist in the office, that would make her unemployed and she didn't relish the thought.

So Tansy went to all the restaurants in town, but that venture didn't start out with much promise. As luck would have it, the first restaurant was owned by Kay Cathcart of the dog doo-doo incident. Tansy was sent packing with her tail between her legs. Two other restaurants had all the staff they needed, while another one asked for references, which Tansy didn't have. Her own sister didn't trust her as far as she could throw her and no one else in town knew her. Not really.

Well, one man did, but she tried hard not to think about him.

Finally the local greasy spoon said they needed someone to start immediately since the waitress had quit in a snit that very morning and they supposed Tansy would do.

Tansy looked down at her summer dress. "Can I go home to change?"

The cook, a man named Lauchie with a huge beer belly, looked her up and down. "Nah. Keep that on. Might bring in some customers."

"But I'll get grease on it."

"Do you want the friggin' job or not?"

"Fine. Do you have an apron?"

He pointed to a large dishtowel, and with nothing better to use, Tansy wrapped it around her waist and tied it in the back.

It was the start of the longest day of her life.

She limped home in her high-heeled sandals, finally taking them off and walking in her bare feet the rest of the way. Her pretty polka-dot wraparound dress was covered in grease stains and a large mustard stain as well, thanks to an overzealous customer smacking the bottom of the container with undue force.

When she walked into the kitchen, she found Bay with her arms around Ashley. They were having a mother and daughter moment, but that moment was shattered when they turned around and saw her. Their faces registered shock.

"Are you all right?" Bay asked. "What happened?"

"I got a job."

"Doing what?" Ashley squealed. "Picking through garbage?"

"I'm a waitress at Sonny's Snack Bar."

It was so ludicrous. Bay and Ashley stood there with their mouths open.

Tansy smirked. "I think I'll drive the Porsche to work tomorrow. My feet are killing me."

The three of them started to laugh and couldn't stop. Bay reached out and grabbed her sister in a big bear hug. She buried her face in Tansy's neck. They held each other for a long time. Tansy said to Ashley, "Group hug."

Ashley ran over and the three of them embraced, rocking back and forth slightly.

"All for one and one for all," Tansy whispered. "We're going to get through this. And we're going to be fine."

Ashley was booked for an ultrasound and Matt took the day off work to go with her. Bay wanted to accompany them, but Ashley asked her not to. She and Matt didn't have much time alone anymore and she wanted it to be a private moment. So reluctantly Bay waved them goodbye and waited to hear all about it.

Ashley held Matt's hand in the waiting room and wiggled in her seat. "I wish they'd hurry up. I need to pee. What's taking so long?"

Matt looked around, as if that would make things happen quicker. "I don't know. Do you want me to go ask?"

She kept his hand in a death grip. "No, don't leave me."

"I'm right here."

A nurse approached with a clipboard. "Ashley Gillis."

They rose as one. "Matt's coming with me."

"That's fine. It's this way." She indicated the hall to the left and walked ahead of them. "I'll take you to the dressing room. Undress from the waist up and put on a Johnny shirt and robe. Matt, you can wait here for now."

Matt did as he was told. Ashley looked to him for reassurance and he gave her a thumbs up before she disappeared behind the closed door. A couple of minutes later both she and the nurse reappeared and they continued down the hall. Ashley knew she looked ridiculous in the horrid green robe that was ten times too big for her. She hoped she didn't run into anyone she knew.

The nurse opened another door and led the two of them into a darkened room. "Matt, you sit here, and Ashley, you make yourself comfortable on the examination table and the technician will be right in. Did you drink the required amount of water before you came?"

"Yes. I'm not going to be able to hold it much longer."

"Everyone says that," the nurse laughed. "She won't be a moment."

Once she left, Ashley looked at Matt. "I'm nervous."

"They say it doesn't hurt."

"It's not that. I'm afraid to see the baby on the screen."

"Why?"

"Because then it will be real."

Matt nodded and looked at the floor.

The technician walked into the room and greeted them warmly. "There's nothing to be afraid of," she said. "I'm going to put some jelly on your belly...sorry, hospital humour...and then you'll see your baby. Look at the screen and I'll show you when I have something. If you'd like to get closer, Dad, feel free."

Matt looked confused for a moment. Then he rose from his chair and went over to the other side of the table, taking Ashley's hand in his own. They watched in silence as the blurry black-and-white images flickered on the screen.

Ashley couldn't make anything out. "I don't know where to look."

The technician kept her eyes on the screen as she pressed against Ashley's abdomen in a circular motion. "Look right in the middle of the screen. Do you see the pulsing? That's your baby's heart."

Ashley's own heart skipped a beat. "Look, Matt! Do you see?"

A grin broke out on Matt's face. "Yes, I see it. That's cool."

"And here's the baby's head." She pointed with a finger on the screen. "And look here, you can see the fingers."

The young parents were speechless. They looked at the screen in wonder.

"I don't think I want to know what the baby is," Ashley said. "Do you?"

"It doesn't matter to me. We'll call it Fred."

"Fred? After your dog?"

"I love Fred."

"What about Merlin?" Ashley laughed. "He might get jealous."

"Don't tell him."

"All right, Fred it is."

A sudden peace came over Ashley. This pregnancy had been nothing but anxiety, fear, and remorse until this moment. As she watched her baby's fingers open and close, she was filled with an overwhelming love for this tiny being, brought into the world by her and Matt's love.

When Matt dropped her off, he took another look at the picture the technician gave them before they left.

"I wish I could take this home and show Mom. Maybe she'd change her tune."

"If you'd like to take it, you can."

"No, you show it to your mom first. She deserves to see it."

"I better go. I love you."

Matt kissed her and then put his hand on her belly. "Bye, Fred."

Ashley got out of the car and practically skipped into the house. Her mother was waiting for her at the kitchen table, a worried expression on her face.

"How did it go? Are you all right?"

"I'm more than all right. Do you want to see Fred?"

"Fred? My God, is it a boy?"

"We don't know. We just named the baby Fred. It's better than calling it Bump."

Bay held out her hand. "Oh, gosh, let me see."

Ashley sat beside her mother and handed over the picture. Bay looked at it closely. "What am I looking at?"

Ashley pointed out the round shape of the baby's head. "This is a side view. Look closely and you can see the nose."

The vague image suddenly became clear. "Oh, my, look at that. That's your nose!"

"Is it?" Ashley squealed.

Bay shook her head, as if in disbelief. "Isn't that something? Dear little soul."

"Is this what you felt when you had me? Suddenly feeling so happy?"

Her mother didn't answer her. She stared at the picture.

"Mom?"

"Yes, honey. I was very happy."

The back door opened and Tansy walked in, coming home from work and looking done in as usual.

"Look, Tansy, come and see Fred."

"Fred?"

"My baby. They gave me a picture to keep." Ashley held it up for

Tansy to see. "This is the head and there's the nose. Mom says Fred has my nose. Isn't that amazing?"

Tansy stared at the picture. When she didn't say anything, Ashley looked at her. "What do you think?"

"It's overwhelming..." She handed back the picture. "Sorry." She walked out of the kitchen and went upstairs.

"What's wrong with her?"

"I think she's tired."

CHAPTER ELEVEN

Gertie knew she shouldn't bother Bay with trifling matters when Bay had so much going on, but she was starting to have second thoughts about her blind date. What if he was a lunatic? She showed up at Bay's one night at suppertime. Bay was delighted. She was trying to get rid of her endless supply of zucchini. She filled a plate and placed it in front of Gertie.

"Thank you. So what should I do?" Gertie asked.

"Don't go to an out-of-the-way spot, for one thing," Ashley said between bites of breaded haddock.

"I know," Tansy said. "Take him to the diner for coffee. That way I'll be there and if he does anything inappropriate I can brain him with a frying pan."

Gertie made a face. "That dive?"

"I'm only offering a suggestion. You're the one who's worried about going somewhere alone."

"That's a good idea," Ashley said. "Do it on Saturday. That way Matt and I could sit in the next booth and size him up."

"If that's the case, I can come too," Bay added. "We'll give you our opinion."

"I'll be too nervous with all of you there."

"Make up your mind, woman," Tansy almost shouted.

"Okay, okay. The diner it is."

The big day finally arrived. Peter Sullivan agreed to meet Gertie at Sonny's Snack Bar. Gertie arrived a whole hour before the appointed time and Tansy ended up serving her four cups of coffee, which wasn't such a hot idea. She was high on caffeine and had to go to the john every five minutes. Bay, Matt, and Ashley showed up ten minutes before Peter was expected to arrive. They sat in the booth across the aisle, all of them smirking and giving Gertie thumbs up.

"How do I look?" Gertie whispered.

They whispered back, "You look great!"

And she did. She'd been to the hairdresser's earlier in the day and had on a new pantsuit from the Sears catalogue.

They counted down the minutes. Peter was arriving at four o'clock, so Tansy served Gertie another coffee and put a plate of French fries in front of the other three, who sipped their soft drinks, making them last.

At twenty after four the coffee, fries, and soft drinks were long gone. Everyone looked at their watches. Gertie turned a brighter shade of red as time went on.

"This is stupid," she hissed at them. "He's not coming. I never should've done this."

"Maybe he got lost," Bay said.

"How can you get lost in Louisbourg? There's only one Main Street."

At four-thirty, Gertie started to rise out of her seat. "That's it, I'm going home."

Just then, the door of the diner blew open, bringing in with it a giant, overweight Harry Potter. He filled the doorway, his dark hair on end and his round black glasses askew. His trench coat looked as if he might have slept in it. He looked around in a panic.

"Is Gertie here?!" he boomed.

Tansy, Bay, Matt, and Ashley were too surprised to speak. They pointed at Gertie, who was frozen in her seat.

"Gertie!" Harry Potter gave her a huge smile and produced a man-handled bunch of daisies from behind his back. "I'm sorry I'm late. I had to take my mother to choir practice."

The five of them fell madly in love with him at that moment.

The worst part of Dermot's day was going to the post office to pick up his mail. He had a knot in his stomach every time he walked up to the door and opened it to get to the mailboxes. For weeks Bay made a point of not looking in his direction, and it was only as the summer was drawing to a close that she'd nod or give him a quick wave.

Then came the day when he had to mail off a money order, meaning he had to go into the main part of the post office and speak to Bay across the counter. He gritted his teeth and did just that.

"Hi, Bay."

She glanced at him and then down at her feet. "How are things?"

"Okay, I guess. Can I get a money order?"

"Sure." She went about official business and had it done in no time. "Is that all?"

Dermot passed her the money and took the receipt. "No."

She looked up at him and brushed her hair off her face. "What else can I do for you?"

"You can start speaking to me again. We were good friends, and I miss that."

She surprised him. "I've missed you too."

"I feel as if I've been cut off and set adrift. I don't know how to approach you, because of...well, you know why."

"You can say her name, Dermot. I'm not going to throw another stapler at your head."

They smiled at each other.

"How's your summer been?" he asked.

"Long and hot. But one good thing has happened."

"Oh?"

"I've started seeing a therapist. I remembered what you said, and I needed someone to talk to since..."

"I wasn't available." He finished her sentence for her.

"Yes," she smiled. "A lot of the things I had to get off my chest weren't stuff my sister or daughter needed to hear."

"No, I don't imagine. How is Ashley, anyway?"

Bay frowned. "You've heard the rumours, then."

"What rumours?"

"I forget you're a man. Men don't gossip as much as women do. I might as well tell you, since everyone knows anyway, thanks to Matt's bigmouthed mother." She paused. "Ashley's pregnant."

That was the last thing he'd expected her to say. He tried to hide his dismay but didn't do a good job.

"I know," she sighed. "She's had a rough go. We all have."

"I'm sorry, Bay. That must be a terrible worry. Do you know what you're going to do yet?"

She shrugged. "What can we do? She doesn't want to give it up for adoption and I wouldn't want her to anyway. It's not quite the stigma it was years ago. People aren't going to stone her in the street, although Matt's mother might. That woman refuses to even discuss it. Apparently, it's *our* problem and we can deal with it."

"That must be hard on Matt."

"Ashley tells me he broods about it. His mother's harping at him to go to university and forget all about it, as if he didn't have anything to do with it. What a woman."

"Often anger is fright."

"You sound like my shrink," Bay laughed.

"Is he going to university in September?"

"No. His uncle suggested he keep working for him until he can figure something out. Who knows what's going to happen? Even if they don't stay together, Matt will always be the baby's father, so I know he'll be in our lives. But he's a good kid. It's just too bad his mother is part of the package."

At that point they were interrupted with other customers coming through the door.

"I'd better go," Dermot smiled. "Perhaps we can meet for coffee one of these days?"

Bay smiled back. "Okay. See you later."

Dermot walked back to his truck feeling a whole lot better about everything.

❁

Tansy had to get rid of the Porsche. She'd delayed long enough. Every time she went to put an ad in the paper, she'd chicken out. Luckily Bay never asked her when she planned on getting rid of it, but maybe she should have. It might have been the shove Tansy needed.

To sell that car was to turn her back on her old life once and for all. She'd never be able to escape if things got bad. And she knew that things could get bad very quickly if she wasn't careful. It wasn't about losing a car. It was about losing everything.

"Quit daydreamin'," her boss shouted. "Table four needs cleanin' up."

She didn't know where she was for a moment, but the mess at table four soon brought her back to reality. Was there anything worse than picking up someone else's dirty napkin? She needed to get herself another job. Maybe she could be a chambermaid—but that involved grimy tubs and filthy sheets. She wrinkled her nose in disgust.

When Dermot said, "Don't be so glad to see me," she nearly jumped out of her skin. He stood only a few feet away from her with a bemused look on his face. She was aware of her heart pounding too fast.

"Lord, you scared me. What are you doing here?" She grabbed a handful of dirty dishes and walked by him.

He sat down at the lunch counter. "I could ask you the same thing. Do you work here?"

Tansy looked down at her non-descript black slacks, white cotton blouse, and sensible shoes. "Do you think I'd be wearing this if I wasn't?"

"But why here? Surely you can find a better job?"

She took the cutlery from the plates and wiped off the leftovers into a trash pail. "Let me know when there's a fashion shoot in town. I'll apply immediately."

He didn't say anything and she was sorry she'd shot her mouth off. His dark eyes met hers and he didn't look away.

Stop that.

She wiped the counter in front of him. "Do you want some coffee?"

"Yes, please."

Taking a cup and saucer from a plastic tray, she put it in front of him. She poured the coffee into his cup, spilling a little as she did.

"I saw Bay last week," he said. "She actually talked to me."

"How nice. Can I get you anything else?"

"I'll have a cheeseburger, no fries."

Tansy turned her head to the back of the shop. "One cheeseburger, solo."

"She seems much better," Dermot observed. "Said she'd go out for coffee with me someday. I think she's forgiven me."

"Don't bring her here."

There was a long silence. "Why not?"

Tansy kept her mouth shut.

Dermot took a sip of his coffee. "You don't want to see us together?"

She continued to putter around behind the counter.

"Admit it."

She was desperate to change the subject. "Will you sell my Porsche for me?"

He frowned. "What?"

"You heard me. I need to sell my car and I don't know how much to ask for it. I figure you know more about it than I do."

"Are you sure you want to part with it?"

She stopped wiping. "We need the money, okay? Can you do it?"

"Sure. I can ask around."

"Thank you."

A bell went off. The cheeseburger was done. She went over, collected the plate, and passed it to Dermot. He grabbed her hand. "Are you okay?"

"Let me go." She pulled her hand away and went to serve another customer.

❈

Ashley spent the summer as a camp counsellor in Mira. It kept her busy, and being busy was vitally important, because then she could stop thinking. She'd had it with thinking. If she never had another thought in her head for the rest of her life she'd be okay with that.

All her friends were busy with their summer jobs, so no one got together as often. Thank God Maribeth went out of her way to go shopping with her from time to time. When they hung out in each other's bedrooms, Ashley almost felt normal. But the few parties that she did go to were awkward affairs. Some girls only wanted to talk about what it was like to be pregnant, and others didn't say anything, just gave her pitying looks. The guys steered well clear of her.

The first time she waved her hand to get rid of the cigarette smoke around her, she could tell the smokers were annoyed, and when she said no to a beer, she felt like a freak. It was more than obvious that she wasn't much fun to be with. Matt wasn't available all that often either. He worked every hour he could to make money for them both, and while she appreciated his efforts, she still missed him a lot.

And then it was September and everyone was going away. Maribeth came over to say goodbye. She was leaving for St. Mary's in the morning. Ashley sat on the bed and tried not to cry at the thought of her best friend leaving her. Maribeth handed her a small gift wrapped with ribbon.

"What's this for?"

Maribeth shrugged. "Something I want you to have."

Ashley smiled. "You didn't have to do that."

"I know."

She tore off the wrapping paper and opened the little box. Inside was a baby-buggy charm for her charm bracelet.

Maribeth reached over and hugged Ashley. "Remember when we bought our bracelets? How happy we were? I always want you to be that happy."

They held onto one another for a few moments before Ashley pulled away. "It's so *cute*. Thank you, I love it."

"Good."

Ashley put the charm to one side and leaned back on her pillows. "I can't believe you're leaving tomorrow. I'm already lonely."

"You have Matt."

"What if he leaves me? What if he finds some skinny girl and dumps me?"

Maribeth got up from the bed and wandered over to Ashley's makeup table. She sat down and started opening eye shadow containers and then clicking them shut. Because she didn't say anything, Ashley got worried. "You think he will?"

She shrugged. "I don't know. He might."

"You said you wanted me to be happy and now you're telling me that Matt might break up with me?"

Her friend came back and sat on the bed. "I'm worried that you're going to wrap yourself around Matt and whatever he does is going to determine your destiny."

"Huh?"

"Stop thinking in terms of what Matt is going to do. In all likelihood you two are not going to stay together. So you need to think about what *you're* going to do and how *you're* going to raise your baby in spite of him."

"Did my mother send you up here? She said the same damn thing to me yesterday."

"No, of course not. I just don't want you to stop being you. Remember how we were going to go on a road trip to Vancouver, and travel in Europe and surf in Costa Rica? I don't want that girl to disappear when this baby comes."

"I'm always going to be me, aren't I?"

Maribeth lay back on the bed. "Remember Pam whatshername, who graduated two years ago? She's barely nineteen and she's got two kids. I saw her the other day and for a minute I thought she was her mother. She looked trapped."

"You worry too much."

"All right, lecture over. Mom wanted to know if you'd like to have dinner with us tonight. She's invited a ton of relatives over. You'd think I was going to the other side of the moon. It's only Halifax, for heaven's sake."

"It'll feel like a million miles away tomorrow."

Maribeth gave her a quick shove. "Let's go." They scrambled from the bed and went out the door.

❁

Dermot put out feelers among his colleagues in the auto industry to see if anyone would be interested in buying Tansy's Porsche privately. It didn't take long to get results. A man called him at home one evening wondering if it would be possible to take the car out for a test drive. Dermot said that could be arranged and he'd get back to him.

Dermot made the call. Whoever picked up the phone would be the one he'd talk to. It turned out it was Bay.

"Hi, Dermot, nice to hear from you. Are you calling to take me out for coffee?"

"Well..."

"Oh sorry, I shouldn't have assumed that."

"No, not at all. I'd love to take you for coffee. How about tonight?"

"Okay. I can be ready in ten minutes."

"Great. I'll be right over."

After he hung up, he stood there. He was going out with Bay. How did that happen? And he forgot to mention the car. He reached up to feel his face. A shave was the first order of business, so he bounded up the stairs.

About twenty minutes later he knocked on Bay's back door.

"Come in."

Dermot entered the kitchen. Tansy was at the sink, with her sleeves rolled up, an apron around her waist. When she looked up and saw him, the first thing she did was brush her hair away from her forehead, which left a small deposit of soap bubbles by her right ear. "What are you doing here?"

He stared at the small exotic flower bubbles caught in her hair.

"Dermot?"

He pointed and came towards her. "Sorry, you have some bubbles..." Reaching out, he brushed them away with his thumb. She didn't say anything as his hand lingered against her cheek. He was aware of the scent of her and couldn't take his eyes off that perfect mouth. He needed to get away from her as fast as possible.

"You haven't answered my question."

Dermot backed up and stood near the kitchen table. "I'm here to tell you that I have someone interested in your car."

"That's great."

"He wants to take it for a test drive."

"Okay. How do I arrange that?"

"I can do it for you."

"All right. Let me know when he wants to do it and I can take it to your garage."

"Sounds like a plan."

There were quick footsteps on the stairs and Bay appeared in the doorway. "Hi, Dermot. I'm ready to go."

"Go where?" Tansy asked.

Bay smiled at Dermot. "We're going out. We won't be late."

Tansy looked taken aback. "Oh." She continued to wash the dishes. "Have fun."

Bay put on her jacket and started for the door. "See you later."

Dermot looked at Tansy. "I'll call you."

She didn't look at him. "You do that."

Dermot walked to the truck and held the door open for Bay. "Where would you like to go?"

"Let's go into Sydney. I need to get out of this town every once in a while."

They had a pleasant evening. They chatted about everything and nothing. Dermot had to admit it was nice to talk to her again and see that great smile. He'd missed her.

All too soon they realized it was after ten and time to head home. They didn't say much on the ride back to Louisbourg, content to be in each other's company. When Dermot drove up to her door, Bay turned to him.

"I've missed you, you know."

"Me too."

"I'm sorry I raked you over the coals about Tansy. You had no idea who she was and now that I'm thinking clearly, I can see I was wrong. Do you forgive me?"

"Of course. I wouldn't be much of a friend if I didn't."

Bay looked down at her hands. "I think I want to be more than friends."

Dermot watched her. "Are you sure? It might be difficult…"

She shrugged. "Life is difficult. We can't get around that, but Tansy and I have come to an agreement. She's been a big help these past months and I believe her when she says she wants me to be happy."

Bay reached for him then and kissed him. She was soft and sweet. At this moment it was easy for him to forget everything else.

Bay pulled away. "Why don't we have dinner at your place one night? It's a little crowded here."

"How about next Friday? I'll cook."

"I'll be there. Goodnight."

He watched her go back in the house. As he pulled out of the driveway, he noticed the darkened living room window. Tansy sat in a chair, her face silhouetted by the television light. Why wouldn't she go? It would be much easier if she left town without a word. Then he and Bay could get on with things. This mess was Tansy's fault. He shoved the truck into gear and backed out of the driveway.

❈

Just his luck, Dermot had to call the house the next night and ask Tansy to bring the Porsche to his garage by seven. The prospective buyer wanted to meet them there for the test drive. Tansy made sure she told Bay what she was doing.

"Fine by me," Bay said nonchalantly. "You don't have to tell me where you're going every second of the day."

"I feel I do where Dermot is concerned."

Bay put down the newspaper she was reading. "That was a stupid episode that won't be repeated."

"Good. I'll be back in a little while."

Tansy started for the door when Bay said, "Tell Dermot I'll be over on Friday around six."

Her sister turned around. "You're going to his place?"

"He's making me dinner."

"Oh."

Bay smiled. "This is déjà vu. It wasn't long ago you were asking me if I was going on a date. Speaking of that, it's not like you to stay home night after night."

"I'm too tired at the end of the day to go anywhere."

The way she said it bothered Bay. "Are you okay?"

"Fine. See you later." Tansy hurried out to the car and tried not to think that this might be one of the last times she'd drive it. She loved this car, and now it was one more thing to give up.

When she arrived at the garage, Dermot stood with two men. She pulled up beside them and got out of the car. Dermot made the introductions.

"Tansy Gillis, this is Bob Morrison and his brother Joe."

Tansy shook their hands. "How are you? Which one is interested in the car?"

"Guilty as charged," laughed Bob. "My, it is a beauty."

"Like its owner," Joe smiled.

Tansy wasn't in the mood for flattery. "It's a '99 Porsche 911 with only fifty-four thousand miles on it."

"How much are you asking?" Bob wanted to know.

Tansy looked to Dermot and he took over. "Sixty-nine thousand. Considering the pristine condition it's in, that's a bargain."

Bob whistled. "That's a lot of money."

"It's a lot of car," Dermot countered.

Tansy passed Bob the keys. "Take it for a run."

"Don't mind if I do. Would it be okay if I went as far as Sydney?"

"Fine."

"We'll be back in an hour." The two men got in the car, started it up, and left the garage behind.

"Do you think he'll pay that kind of money?"

Dermot shrugged. "It's hard to say. Are you willing to compromise?"

She gave him a look. "That's all I ever do."

There was an awkward silence before Dermot jerked his thumb behind him. "Do you want a coffee while we wait?"

"Sure."

They headed for the garage. Dermot led the way into his office and while Tansy made herself comfortable, he busied himself with the coffee.

"Bay wants me to tell you she'll be over at your place on Friday around six."

"Right. Thanks."

"Apparently you're making her dinner."

Dermot kept his face turned away and watched the coffee drip. "That's right."

"Have fun."

Dermot didn't answer her so Tansy stayed quiet. He broke the silence by asking her if she took her coffee black.

"Yes, please."

He poured the coffee into two mugs and brought one over to her. "Thanks."

He sat behind the desk, facing her. They both took a sip of their coffee. Neither one said anything. Finally Dermot blurted, "This is uncomfortable. Maybe it would be better if I drove you home."

"Why? Don't you want me here?"

"It's not that. I'm thinking of you."

Tansy took another sip of coffee. "You don't trust me, do you?"

He looked away.

That's when it dawned on her. She put down the coffee mug. "You don't trust yourself."

"Stop it."

"I assumed when you took Bay out the other night, and made plans for dinner, that you were truly over me. Don't you dare get Bay's hopes up if you can't give her your whole heart."

"Why can't you leave me alone?"

"I *am* leaving you alone. And that's what you can't stand." Tansy got out of her chair. "Go to my sister. Be with her if that's what you want. Just make sure when you're kissing her you're not wishing it was me!"

He came from behind the desk and took her in his arms. "But I do wish it was you, Tansy." Dermot reached up and held her face in his hands before he kissed her. Tansy was out of breath when she whispered against his lips, "Stop. You have to stop."

"I don't want to stop. Be with me. Stay with me." His mouth travelled down the length of her throat before he pushed back her hair and kissed her earlobe. "Please."

"We can't. It's not right."

"Tell me this doesn't feel right." He softly bit her bottom lip and pulled on it before covering her mouth once more with his own. He murmured, "I do want you, more than anything."

She couldn't do it. Tansy pressed against his chest with her open hands. "Is this what you did to my sister?"

Dermot lifted his head and looked at her with hurt in his eyes. "Don't."

"I'm sorry. I wish I'd never come back to this place. It's only ever caused me pain."

"What am I going to do? How am I supposed to be with Bay and not be with you?"

She wouldn't look at him.

His arms were still around her. "I love you, Tansy."

"You don't know me. If you knew me, you wouldn't love me."

"What's that supposed to mean?"

"I have to go." She pushed against him. "We'll pretend this never happened. And once Ashley's baby is here, I'll leave this place and you and Bay can be together. Because you're a good man, Dermot, and Bay needs a good man to love her."

"And what about you? Why do you think you don't deserve to be loved?"

"I gave away that right a long time ago." She started for the door. "Get me the best deal you can for the car. I'll leave it up to you."

"Wait!"

Tansy ran until she was out of sight.

CHAPTER TWELVE

Bay couldn't wait for the end of her shift on Friday. She'd been looking forward to seeing Dermot all week. It was nice to be happy about something for a change. Life was beginning to feel more normal, due in no small way to the medication she was on. Her mood had been changing slowly, but she was aware of her progress and the small glimmer of hope it provided.

She made a real effort to look pretty before she left for the evening. Ashley whistled at her when she came down the stairs.

"Wow, Mom. You look great."

"Thank you."

"Doesn't she look great, Tansy?"

Tansy looked up from the television screen. "Great. Bay, will you ask Dermot if that man is still interested in my car?"

"Sure. I'll see you two later." Out the door she went. It only took five minutes to drive over to Dermot's house. She was nervous as she walked up the porch steps, more nervous than she cared to admit.

Bay knocked on the door, waited about fifteen seconds, and knocked again. She tried to see into the kitchen through the curtains, but there was no sign of life. She wasn't sure what to do. She started down the steps and hurried over to the car. That's when the door opened and Dermot stepped outside.

"Bay! Sorry, I didn't hear you."

"I thought I had the wrong day."

"Please, come in."

She followed him into the kitchen. He'd taken the trouble to set the table and had a casserole in the oven. It smelled good.

"What's for dinner?"

"Shepherd's pie, I'm afraid. It's the only thing I know how to cook."

"Sounds great."

Dermot stood there and looked down at her shoes. He said in a rush, "Would you like a beer? Or I have a couple of coolers if you'd prefer. I meant to buy some wine today, but it got busy at work."

"A cooler would be nice."

Dermot hurried over to the fridge and took out a bottle. "Would you like a glass?"

"Nah, it's only us."

He passed her the bottle and grabbed a beer for himself. "Please, sit down."

Bay sat at the table and took a swig of her drink. "Before I forget, Tansy wanted to know if that man is still interested in the car."

Dermot rubbed his thumbnail over the beer label. "I should've called her. He said he needed some time to sort out his financial affairs, but that was a while ago. I'll give him a shout tomorrow and see where he stands."

"Thanks. So how's everything going with you?"

"Fine."

"What have you been up to?"

"Not much. You?"

"Ashley and I have started to clean out the bedrooms upstairs. We're trying to figure out which room we can use as a nursery and how the sleeping arrangements are going to work."

Dermot shook his head. "I still can't believe you're going to be a grandmother."

"I can't believe it either. This is not the way I imagined her teen years. I try not to let her know how frightened I am."

"Frightened of what?"

Bay shrugged. "Everything. I know what it's like to be a single mother. I never could have done it without my mother, and I'll be there for Ashley, but it's still a struggle."

Dermot took another swallow of beer. "But at least Matt is in the picture."

"He is for now, but will he stay in the baby's life? Who knows? Not if his mother has anything to do with it."

Dermot nodded. When he didn't say anything else, Bay searched for something to say. "Maybe you should check your shepherd's pie."

"Good idea."

He leapt out of his chair as if relieved to have something to do. As it turned out, it was a good thing he took their dinner out of the oven when he did—it already looked burnt around the edges. Bay told him not to worry about it. They busied themselves getting the food on the table. Once they started to eat, the conversation flowed more easily. Unfortunately, when the tea was poured, they were back to looking at each other across the table without a lot to say.

"Why don't we go into the living room?" she suggested. "It's more comfortable."

"Oh. Sure."

Dermot didn't move until she rose from the table, as if he was reluctant to leave his chair. When she sat down at one end of the sofa, he sat at the other end until she patted the cushion in the middle.

"Why don't you sit here?"

He hesitated.

Bay put down her tea. "Dermot, I thought you wanted me to come here tonight. You're acting as if we just met."

"It's been a crummy day, that's all."

"Anything I can do to help?"

He smiled at her. "Yeah, don't get mad at me."

She smiled back. "Okay."

"Bay, I need to—"

Bay's cellphone rang. "Sorry, I'd better get that."

"Leave it," Dermot pleaded. "I need to talk to you."

Bay was tempted to ignore it, but she couldn't. "It might be Ashley. I'll make sure she's all right." Bay got up from the couch and went to her purse. She took out her cell and flipped it open.

"Hello?"

"Bay, I need your help!"

"Gertie?"

"You have to get over here right now. I think Peter's hurt himself but he won't let me call an ambulance."

"What happened?"

"Never mind, just get over here!"

"I'll bring Dermot."

Bay hung up and looked at Dermot.

"Gertie's in trouble. She needs our help."

"Let's go."

They jumped into Bay's car and were at Gertie's in a matter of minutes. She greeted them at the door, dressed in a satin robe. Bay had never seen Gertie in anything but flannel.

"He's in the bedroom."

Gertie dashed up the hall ahead of them. The three of them ran into the bedroom. Peter writhed on the floor in a pair of boxers with red hearts all over them. His leg was at a funny angle.

"I'll be all right," he moaned. "Help me up."

Dermot reached down and tried to hold Peter up by the shoulders, but Peter moaned, sweat pouring off his face. He eased him down again.

"He's broken something. We need to call an ambulance."

"No ambulance. I'm fine."

"Peter, please listen to him," Gertie wailed. "You need help. Oh my God, I can't believe this happened."

Dermot pointed at Bay. "Call 911." When Bay left the room, he turned back to Peter. "I'm sorry, but we have no other choice."

Gertie flapped her arms around. "What should I do?"

"Get me a blanket and a pillow. He's shivering. He's in shock."

She raced around and gathered up the duvet from the bed, throwing a pillow to Dermot who placed it under Peter's head. Bay ran back into the room.

"They're coming."

"What should I do now?!" Gertie panicked.

"Get dressed," Bay said. "We'll follow the ambulance to the hospital."

Gertie ran around and collected her things before heading to the bathroom to get dressed. Bay knelt beside Dermot. She touched Peter's arm. "You're going to be okay, Peter."

Peter, his teeth chattering, whispered, "Take care of Gertie. I don't want her to be upset."

Bay reassured him she would take care of her friend.

The ambulance came and the paramedics had to enlist Dermot's help to manoeuvre such a giant of a man onto the gurney and out the door. They closed the doors of the ambulance and set off for the hospital.

"You two go," Dermot said. "I'll walk back to the house."

Gertie was tearful. "Thank you for your help, Dermot. I don't know what we'd have done without you."

"No problem."

Gertie rushed over to Bay's car, as Bay fumbled in her pockets looking for the car keys. "I'm sorry about our evening, Dermot."

"Don't worry. Take care of Gertie."

Bay gave Dermot a hug. "You're a wonderful friend. I don't know what we'd do without you."

Dermot watched as their car drove away. If he'd been allowed to finish his conversation with her back at his place, she wouldn't think he was wonderful. He'd come to the realization that if he wanted to remain sane, he had to leave this place for good.

Bay drove as fast as she dared behind the ambulance while Gertie sniffed into a wad of tissues.

"What on earth happened?"

"It's my destiny to die a virgin," Gertie wailed.

"That's nonsense. It was an accident."

"And it wouldn't have happened if I hadn't bought silk sheets. He slid off the bed and I landed on top of him."

Bay didn't dare look in her direction.

Gertie snuck a peek at her. "Don't even think about laughing."

Bay kept driving.

"And now he'll probably never want to see me again," Gertie howled. "I'm cursed."

"Stop it, Gertie. It's obvious he's crazy about you."

"Oh, Bay, I think I'm in love with him."

"Well, that's great."

"No, it's not, because when he dumps me I'll be heartbroken!"

Gertie was determined to cry until they arrived at the hospital. It was her way of punishing herself, so Bay didn't bother trying to make her feel better. She let her off at the emergency door and went to park the car. She realized she'd better call home.

Tansy answered.

"I'm going to be late tonight, so don't wait up."

"Fine."

"I'm not with Dermot; I'm at the hospital with Gertie."

"My God, is she all right?"

"She's fine. It's Peter. A tragedy involving silk sheets. I'll explain later."

By the time she got to the waiting room, Gertie was nowhere in sight. Bay settled in for a long wait. She must have dozed off, because it seemed like no time at all before Gertie shook her awake.

"They have to operate on Peter. He's broken his leg in two places."

"Oh dear."

"They're prepping him now. I've got to get back to him."

"Do you want me to come with you?"

"Would you mind?"

"Not at all."

They went to the third floor and tiptoed into the room where Peter lay waiting to be wheeled to surgery. He was hooked up to an IV. Gertie immediately took his free hand and held it up to her cheek. He gave her a weary smile. Bay stood to the side, not wanting to interfere.

"You'll be fine," Gertie whispered to him.

Peter nodded and closed his eyes.

A doctor came through the door wearing surgical scrubs. Bay could've sworn he was George Clooney. She was obviously overtired and took a second look. He wasn't anything like the actor. He was much taller.

The doctor nodded to them and walked over to the patient, putting his hand on Peter's shoulder. "Peter?"

Peter opened his eyes. "Hey, Michael."

"I couldn't believe it when they gave me your chart. Have you been bungee jumping?"

"No, but I did fall for someone. This is Gertie, the girl I told you about. Gertie, this is Michael Williams. He's my brother—well, my half-brother. "

Michael held his hand out across the bed to shake Gertie's. "Peter has talked of no one else since he met you."

Gertie blushed. "Hi." She turned around. "This is my best friend, Bay. I don't know what I would've done without her tonight."

Michael nodded in Bay's direction. "Bay."

"Hello."

"Michael, I don't want you to tell Mom about this until it's over, okay? She'll only worry."

The doctor looked at his patient. "Okay, if you think that's best. Listen, Pete, I've looked at the X-ray. They're going to put a couple of pins in your leg, but once it heals, you'll be as good as new."

"Good to know."

"You've got the best ortho surgeon in town. He happened to be on call tonight, so you lucked out. And now that he knows you're my brother he'll be extra good to you. I let him win at poker the other night."

"You always were lousy at cards."

"Okay, the nurse will be in to give you your shot before you go downstairs, and I'll see you when you get out of surgery." Michael put his hand on Peter's arm and gave it a squeeze.

"I'm glad you're here," Peter said.

"No problem."

"I want to talk to Gertie for a minute," Peter told him.

"Not too long. You need your strength."

Bay took a step forward. "Good luck, Peter."

He smiled at her. "Thanks."

Michael and Bay walked out of the room and let the other two say goodbye in private. Michael pointed down the hall. "You and Gertie can wait in one of the family rooms."

"It must have been a bad break if he needs pins," Bay said.

"It's pretty nasty, but he should recover nicely. If he lost a few pounds it would help him in the long run."

"I know Gertie would do her best to help him with a diet. She's trying too."

"Gertie seems like a nice girl. I know Peter thinks the world of her."

"She thinks he's pretty special too."

"I'm glad. Peter's always been a gentle giant, not one for dating women."

"I bet he left that up to you." The minute she said it, she wanted to rip her tongue out.

Michael gave her a quick look and checked his watch. "Tell Gertie I'll be back to give her an update halfway through the surgery."

And with that he walked away.

Bay leaned against the wall. She banged her head against it once for good measure. A nurse went into the room and a minute later Gertie came out. Bay took her arm and led her down the hall. "We have to wait down here."

They sat down together on a couch in a small room.

"Can I get you something to drink?" Bay asked.

"No, I'm okay. You should go, Bay. I don't expect you to sit here for hours with me."

"Don't be silly. I'm not going to leave you alone."

"I'm so worried. If anything happens to him..."

Bay patted her arm. "Nothing's going to happen. He'll be fine."

Gertie looked at her. "Do you know what he said just now?"

"What?"

"That he loved me."

"Oh, Gertie, that's wonderful."

"I know!" Gertie started to sob.

Michael popped his head in a couple of hours later to say things were going well. He didn't stay long. When he left, Gertie looked at Bay. "He's quite something, isn't he? And he just got divorced to boot."

Bay scowled. "No wonder he can't take a joke."

"Huh?"

"Never mind."

It wasn't until November that Dermot sold the Porsche for Tansy. He'd hoped it would never happen, because then he wouldn't have to see her. He'd been doing a good job of avoiding both Gillis sisters. He had to; leaving town was not as clear-cut as he'd hoped. It wasn't easy selling a house that needed so much work, and his business was thriving. It was hard to walk away.

Fortunately the few times he had talked to Bay, she seemed preoccupied with Ashley and the baby. And as the days grew colder and nights longer, there weren't as many opportunities to run into each other. It was almost as if a time-out had been declared between them.

He wasn't going to risk seeing Tansy alone, which is why he decided to tell her at the diner. On his lunch hour, he ducked in before she saw him and sat at a booth so he could watch her for a few minutes. He didn't like what he saw. She seemed thinner, if that was possible, and pale, with dark circles under her eyes. Certainly not the woman he first met all those months ago. He wanted to walk over, put his arms around her, and protect her from the ogling eyes of the men who came in to chat her up.

She eventually saw him and frowned before walking over with a notepad and pencil.

"What can I get you?"

"Hi, Tansy. How are you?"

"Fine."

"I'll have a club sandwich, no fries."

"To drink?"

"Tea, please."

She started to walk away.

"I sold the Porsche."

That stopped her dead.

"Tansy?"

When she turned around her face looked lost.

"I'm sorry, I thought that's what you wanted."

Tansy shook her head, as if realizing he was still there. "Yes, of course. Thanks."

"If you don't want to do this, it's okay. I'll call him back."

"No. No. We need the money."

"Sit with me for a minute."

"No..."

"Please."

She sat on the edge of the seat, her back to the door. "What do you want?"

Dermot reached across the table and took her hand. "Something's bothering you and you need to tell me. If there's a reason you don't want to part with the car, you don't have to."

She looked away.

"Tell me."

"I can't escape."

"What? What do you mean?"

"I can't leave."

"Do you want to leave?"

"No. Yes. I need the money. I have to invest it for Ashley and the baby. She's too young..."

Why did she seem so frightened? "Tansy, I want to promise you something. I know you're selling the car because you want to help Ashley, and that's fine, but if you ever need a car for anything, whether it's to leave here or for whatever reason, I'll get you one. Okay?"

"You'd do that?"

"Yes."

"Even if I wanted to go and never come back?"

"Even then."

She looked at him and whispered, "Thank you."

He reached over and wiped away a tear that threatened to fall down her cheek. They sat together for a moment longer before they looked up and saw Bay watching them from outside the diner window.

❧

Ashley liked one thing about November: When she went outside she could wear a coat. It saved her from the overt stares people gave her when she walked by. Since she wasn't a big girl, she carried Fred like she'd swallowed a basketball, all out in front.

It was important for her not to get discouraged, because maybe Fred could read her mind and she didn't want the little guy to know that his mother was sort of afraid of him, even though she did love him. But there were times when the situation threatened to overwhelm her. And today was one of those days.

She ran into Matt's mother at the drugstore.

Ruth pretended not to see her, but Ashley knew she damn well did. She and Matt usually avoided the topic of his mother because it only caused friction. Matt was obviously torn between wanting to throttle his mother and feeling the need to defend her. It bothered Ashley no end.

"How can you ignore your own grandchild?"

"I don't know, do I?"

"She's not even curious about the baby at all?"

Matt would roll his eyes. "I don't talk about it with her because it gets her too upset."

"Well, she's not being fair to you, is she? What does your dad think?"

"I think he wants everyone to shut up."

"You'd like that, wouldn't you? I suppose you'd like me to shut up too?"

"That would be nice."

She'd thrown a box of raisins at him.

And now here was his mother, standing at the drug counter pretending to be a nice person.

Ashley wasn't sure how she got so brave. Maybe it was because Fred needed to be protected from miserable cows like Ruth.

She walked over to the counter. "Hi, Mrs. MacLean. How are you?"

Ruth gave her the slightest of glances. "Fine."

"Would you like to know how Fred is doing?"

Ruth looked at her. "Who?"

"Fred. Your grandchild."

"Fred is my dog, not my grandchild."

"Yes, and he's very nice, unlike his owner."

Ashley noticed the pharmacist kept herself busy and didn't look up at them.

Ruth glared at her. "You're a spoiled brat. What you do with your own life is your business, but don't even think of involving me in this fiasco."

"You are involved. You're Matt's mother and he needs you right now. Haven't you even considered what you're doing to him by behaving this way? He loves me. He loves Fred. And he still loves you for some reason. Why are you making him choose between us?"

Ruth stood there like a statue.

"Wonderful. Be like that. But I'll tell you one thing: I'll treat Fred a million times better than you treat your son." And with that she turned around and left the store.

Ashley was still fuming when she got home, and even madder when she realized she'd forgotten the stuff she was supposed to buy. She made herself feel better by hugging Merlin. Looking at his silly face put a smile on hers.

Since no one was home, she thought she'd look at the paint chips she'd brought home a couple of days before to see what colour the baby's room should be, but when she got to the upstairs landing, the stuff they'd taken out of their bedrooms was still in the hallway. She should go through the boxes and decide what to keep and what to throw out. Ashley knew that would be a help, since both her mother and aunt worked long hours and were tuckered out at the end of the day.

As the afternoon wore on, Ashley forgot about the paint chips. She was lost in a haze of her childhood. Everything she took out of a box had a memory attached to it. A toy pig her nana had given her when she broke her arm one summer, a diary she kept in fourth grade. It made her smile to think that Maribeth was her best friend even back then. She put it to one side so she could show Maribeth when she came home for Christmas. Then there were the drawings her mother had kept, and old scribblers filled with math and writing exercises.

At the bottom of one box, she found a bundle of papers and photo albums, old ones she'd never seen before. She took them out and wiped the dust off them, taking them to her bedroom so she could sit on the bed and go through them.

There were pictures of her nana and the grandfather she never knew. Her nana was slim, not like the roly-poly woman she used to hug. Ashley looked closely at her grandfather. He had a nice face, wrinkled even then. She remembered her mother saying that was from being in the sun all day hoisting lobster traps. There were pictures of her mother and Tansy up in a tree fort. They both had long braids and missing teeth and they were smiling at each other. Ashley kept it out to show them later.

She turned the pages and came upon a picture of her mother and father. They looked young and in love. It made her happy to know that her parents had loved each other, but her heart ached to think that they had so little time together. No wonder her mother was sad most of the time. It wasn't fair. Now that she was in love with a baby on the way, Ashley felt her mother's pain for the first time.

She owed her mother a lot.

Ashley kept going through the pictures and then started to root through the bundle of papers and letters. She was so absorbed in this treasure trove she didn't hear her mother and aunt come home.

❊

They happened to arrive at the house within a minute of each other. Bay was busy giving Merlin his supper when Tansy walked in. Bay glanced at her and then looked away.

"You might as well ask me," Tansy sighed.

"Ask you what?"

"Why Dermot held my hand."

Bay shrugged. "I couldn't care less."

"Is that right?"

Bay put fresh water in Merlin's dish and turned to face her. "Yes. I admit defeat. There's no way I can win when you're here, so I've decided to bow out gracefully. It's obvious to me that Dermot prefers you, so I will accept it and move on with my life."

Tansy shook her head. "I like it better when you yell your head off. Being a martyr is unattractive."

"Insult me all you want, Tansy. I'm rising above your little games."

"Dermot came to tell me he sold the Porsche. I don't know why but I got upset about it and he tried to comfort me. That's all."

"Touching."

"I'm telling you the truth, Bay. I haven't seen him. I haven't gone near him and he has made a point of staying away from me. We have done everything we can to make up for our lousy mistake, a mistake we didn't know we made."

"So now you two are the injured parties. Go figure."

Tansy sat heavily on a kitchen chair. "I'm so tired. I can't tell you how tired I am of this. Even when I try to do the right thing, it's wrong. I don't know what else to do. I don't know how to make you happy."

"Now who's being a martyr?"

They weren't aware that Ashley had come into the kitchen until she was almost on top of them. She held a piece of paper in her hand and she was as white as a sheet.

Both Tansy and Bay saw her at the same moment. Ashley tried to speak but nothing came out.

"What is it?" Bay cried. "Is it the baby?"

"When were you going to tell me?"

Bay shook her head. "Tell you what?"

"That you're not my mother."

There was complete silence. Bay and Tansy looked at each other and then back at Ashley.

"Sweetheart..."

"I don't want you to talk," Ashley said in a low voice.

"But—"

"Shut up, Bay!" Ashley yelled before she turned her attention on Tansy. "Why? Why did you leave me here? Why didn't you want me?"

"Oh, Ashley..." Tansy got out of the chair and tried to approach her, but Ashley held her off.

"Don't come near me."

"You need to calm down," Bay said. "We can talk about this. I know it's a horrible shock."

Ashley turned to look at her. "Shock? That's an understatement, isn't it? Tell me something. Did Nana know about this? Was she in on this little conspiracy too?"

Neither Bay nor Tansy said anything.

"So. Betrayed by all three of the women in my life who supposedly love me."

"Ashley, please," Bay implored. "You need to sit down. You don't look well. Think of the baby."

"I am thinking of my baby. I'm thinking about how I'd never leave Fred. *Ever!*"

And with that, she ran out of the house. Tansy sank back into the kitchen chair. Bay held her hand over her mouth to keep herself from screaming.

"What are we going to do?" Tansy whispered.

Bay shook her head. "This is so awful. Why didn't we know how awful this would be? Why did we think we'd get away with it? I can't even remember why. And now she's going to hate me. She's going to hate both of us. I've lost her. I've lost my little girl. Oh my God, I can't bear it!"

Bay sank to her knees. Tansy got down on the floor and held her.

❈

Ashley had to get to Matt, but it was dark, windy, and cold. She was out of breath and completely helpless. Her tears blinded her as she stumbled along the sidewalk. She had to get to Matt. He'd know what to do. She couldn't go home. Home was where people lied to you and people weren't who they said they were. Nana lied—Nana, who always made everything better, knew about this and never said a word.

Ashley got a sharp pain in her side and started to panic. She put both hands on her belly. "It's okay, Fred. You stay right there. You can't come yet." She was freezing. She needed Matt. Finally, there was his street. The porch light was on. If she could get to that light, she'd be all right.

Almost there. Tripping on the steps going up to the door, she pounded on it. "Matt! Help me!"

Everything was blurred and out of focus. The door opened and Matt's mother stood there like a brick wall. Ashley pushed past her. *"Matt."*

"What do you think you're doing?" Ruth cried.

"Where is he?"

"I think you should go home, Ashley, and stop being a drama queen."

Matt ran down the stairs. "Ashley? What's wrong?"

"Help me! Please help me." She started to fall. He caught her in his arms, picked her up, and carried her upstairs.

Ruth was shocked. She called after him. "This is ridiculous, Matt. If she's in trouble we should call her mother."

Matt didn't bother answering. He took Ashley into his room and kicked the door closed behind him before laying her on the bed. He sat beside her and wiped the hair out of her face and brushed away her tears. "Calm down, you're okay. I'm here."

"I don't know what to do," she shivered. "I don't know who I am."

"What do you mean?"

"My mother..."

"Yes?"

"She's not my mom." Just saying the words caused a pain to shoot through her. She clenched her stomach. "Oh my God."

"Is it the baby?"

"I don't know."

"I need to call your mother."

"*No.* Don't! I can't talk to her. I can't look at her. She's not my mom."

"Ashley, you're not making any sense."

"I don't know who my father is. No one wanted me. No one." Another pain hit her. "Oh no." She doubled up on the bed.

Matt yelled for his mother. She and his father rushed into the doorway.

"Call an ambulance. I think she's having the baby."

CHAPTER THIRTEEN

Once more, Bay found herself in the emergency room. Only this time *Gertie* was comforting *her*. After they received the call from Ruth telling them that Ashley had been taken to the hospital, she called Gertie in a panic; Bay knew that neither she nor Tansy were in any shape to drive.

To her credit, Ruth did ask if she and Ian could take them in, but Bay declined. She didn't want to be beholden to a woman who'd made Ashley's life miserable. It was only after she hung up that Bay realized she'd made Ashley's life more miserable than anyone, she and her sister both.

When they arrived, Bay rushed to the desk and said that her daughter had been brought in and she wanted to see her. The woman went to check the status of the situation. She came back and said Bay could go in. Tansy tried to follow her but she was told only one visitor was allowed. As Bay went through the doors, Tansy cried, "Give her my love." Then she hid her face in Gertie's jacket.

The confusion of the emergency department was disconcerting. Bay wasn't sure where she should go, and in her heightened state of upset, she couldn't concentrate enough to read the signs. From behind she saw a man she thought she knew but she couldn't remember his name.

"Could you help me, please?"

The doctor turned around. It was Peter's brother, Michael.

"Bay, isn't it? Gertie's friend? What are you doing here?"

Bay grabbed his sleeve. "Please, my daughter was brought in. She's in early labour. The baby's not supposed to come until Christmas. Please help me."

"Of course, calm down. We'll find her."

Michael talked to someone at the nurses' station. She pointed down the hall.

"Come this way."

Bay followed him. She was grateful to have someone else with her. When they got to the room, the curtain was pulled over. Michael held it to one side. Another doctor and nurse were in the room. Ashley was lying on an examination table while Matt held her hand.

"Excuse me," Michael said. "Her mother's here."

Bay pushed by him and rushed to Ashley's side. "Oh my God, sweetheart, are you all right?"

Ashley took one look at her. "*Get out.* I don't want to see her!"

Everyone was stunned.

"Oh no, Ashley, please let me stay. I love you."

"Go away!"

The attending physician pointed at Michael. "Get her out of here. We're taking her upstairs to try and stop these contractions."

Bay cried out to Matt, who looked completely miserable. "Take care of her...please take care of her!"

"I will. I promise."

Michael took Bay by the shoulders and escorted her out the door. Bay held her face in her hands and cried as if her heart would break. He needed to get her out of the corridor, so he ushered her into an empty room and sat her down, pulling up a chair beside her while he passed her a box of tissues. "You need to calm down or you'll be sick. Do you hear me?" He reached over and poured some water into a small paper cup. "Here, drink this."

Bay did as she was told because she didn't know what else to do. "What if the baby comes and she doesn't want me there? I'm worried about her. She's only a little girl and I've hurt her so badly." Tears welled up again.

"Stop crying. You're not helping yourself, and you're certainly not helping your daughter. You need to pull yourself together. You're the adult here."

His stern manner had the desired affect.

"Are you always this mean?"

"Yes. Now without the drama, tell me what's going on. Why is your daughter distraught? Is there something we should know to help her through this?"

Bay took a deep breath. "She found out tonight that I'm not her mother. My sister is her mother. When she discovered her birth certificate, she ran all the way to her boyfriend's house, where she started having pain. Obviously brought about by the shock of it all. So there's no one else to blame if something happens to her or the baby."

"I'm sure it won't come to that."

"But if she's having contractions…"

"We have ways of stopping contractions, so it's not a done deal yet. And even if the baby did arrive, it would likely be fine after an NICU stay. Right now, they'll concentrate on keeping her calm, for her own sake. If she won't see you, is there another relative she's close to? Her dad?"

"I don't know who her father is."

"I see. Well, that young man seemed a little overwhelmed in there. I assume he's the father of the baby?"

Bay nodded.

"Perhaps we should get his parents involved."

"His parents don't want anything to do with Ashley or the baby."

"Oh."

Bay looked away. "What a miserable situation this is. Ashley has so few people in her life, and now the only two relatives she has left have been taken from her. No wonder she's so frightened. No wonder we're all frightened."

Michael watched Bay. She seemed to have forgotten he was in the room.

"What about Gertie? Is your daughter close to her?"

Bay's face lit up. "Of course, that's a great idea. I'd feel much better if Gertie was with her."

"I'll go upstairs and ask your daughter if that would be all right."

"Thank you."

The two of them walked out of the room and down the corridor. Before Bay pushed open the door to the waiting room, she turned to Michael. "I'm sorry I said you were mean."

"Don't let it happen again."

He gave her a fleeting smile and disappeared into an elevator.

❖

Gertie waited in the hall outside Ashley's room watching nurses and the occasional doctor go in and out. She wasn't allowed in right away. While she stood there, she tried to figure out what was going on; downstairs, neither Bay nor Tansy were able to finish a coherent sentence without getting too emotional. She finally told them it didn't matter. Whatever had gone on made no difference. She reassured them she'd be there for Ashley and they seemed to get some comfort from that.

Just before Gertie left to go upstairs, Matt's parents arrived. She hoped there wouldn't be a scene, but they were subdued and asked how Ashley was. If they thought it was odd that Bay wasn't upstairs with her daughter, they didn't say anything. They sat a couple of rows away, since it was clear Bay and Tansy were too preoccupied to speak to them.

Eventually a nurse came out and said Gertie could go in. Ashley was lying in bed with her eyes closed, looking small and exhausted, her hands covering her belly. Matt was still by her side.

"Hi," Gertie whispered. "What's the latest news?"

"The contractions have stopped, thank God. They're pretty optimistic that they won't start again, but they want to keep her here for a couple of days to make sure. They said she was underweight and needed to go on some kind of protein drink. They're monitoring her blood pressure, too. It's been kind of scary."

Gertie walked over and put her hand on his shoulder. "I'm sure it's been very scary, but Ashley has a strong will. I know she'll be fine and so will the baby."

"I hope so."

"Why don't you get something to drink? I'll stay here with her. You should go down and tell your parents what's going on."

"They're here?"

"They're in the waiting room."

"Okay."

"And make sure you tell Bay and Tansy what you told me. It'll make them feel better."

"Sure."

Matt left the room and Gertie sat in the chair beside Ashley's bed. She put her hand over the side bars and placed it on top of Ashley's small hand, to let her know that someone was with her.

She opened her eyes. "Hi, Gertie."

"Hi, munchkin. You gave us quite a fright."

"Sorry."

"It's not your fault. I guess mister man here decided he couldn't wait to see his mother." She patted Ashley's belly.

At the word *mother*, Ashley put her arm across her eyes. Her shoulders began to shake.

"Honey, please don't get upset. You need to stay quiet for the baby."

Ashley nodded but kept her eyes hidden.

"Tell me what's bothering you."

"Did you know about this too?"

"About what?"

Ashley removed her arm. "That Mom isn't my mom."

Gertie made a face. "What do you mean?"

"Tansy is my mother."

Gertie couldn't speak.

"I know. It's crazy, huh? The two of them have kept this secret for almost eighteen years. Did they think I'd never find out? Why didn't they tell me when I was a kid? Why keep it from me? Because of their ridiculous pact, my whole life is a lie."

Gertie wasn't sure how to handle this disclosure. Her brain was in overdrive, trying to give everyone the benefit of the doubt. She needed to choose her words carefully. Her main goal at this moment was to help Ashley through what must have been a terrible shock. No wonder the baby nearly arrived.

"I can't begin to understand why your mother and Tansy kept this a secret. Maybe I'll never understand it. But I do know one thing, Ashley. They love you madly. There isn't anything they wouldn't do for you."

"Except tell the truth."

"You have every right to be upset and disappointed with their behaviour. I'm not going to try and talk you out of your hurt or your outrage. You need to feel that. You deserve an explanation and once you're ready to hear it, I'm sure they will tell you everything you need to know. Until then, you have to think about yourself and that little baby inside you."

Ashley got upset. "Where am I going to go? I can't go home. And I can't go to Matt's because his mother hates me…"

"That's why you're coming home with me, and I won't take no for an answer."

Gertie got out of the chair and leaned over to give Ashley a hug. Ashley put her arms around Gertie's neck and wouldn't let go.

❀

Ashley's doctor came in shortly after and told Gertie and Matt that they should go home. Ashley and the baby needed their rest. He reassured them that things looked good and if there were any changes they'd be the first to know. They both kissed Ashley goodbye, and she didn't protest at their leaving. In fact, she was asleep before they left the room.

Back down in the waiting room, Tansy and Bay and Matt's parents all stood when Matt and Gertie came through the door. It was Gertie who did the talking.

"She's fine, the baby is fine. She's sound asleep and she's being well taken care of. We can go home and get a good night's rest and come back and see her tomorrow."

Matt's father, Ian, said, "We'll say goodnight then. If there's anything we can do, don't hesitate to call."

Bay grabbed Matt's arm. "Thank you for being so good to her. I'm grateful she has you in her life."

Matt looked done in. He nodded his head. His mother put her arm around his shoulders. "It's been a long night for everyone. It's time we took him home."

The three of them walked away. Gertie looked at the other two, who stood in misery in front of her. "Let's go. I think we need a stiff drink."

No one spoke all the way home, the three of them lost in their own thoughts. Merlin was happy to see them. Tansy said she'd take him out for a pee and immediately went back outdoors. While Bay sat at the kitchen table, Gertie put the kettle on and went into the dining room and came back with a small, unopened bottle of brandy. She took three mugs and the brandy over to the table and when she'd finished making tea, she poured it in the mugs and then added a slosh of brandy to each one. By this time Tansy was back in with the dog. After she gave him a couple of dog treats, she sat at the table with Gertie and Bay. No one said anything. It was finally Gertie who spoke.

"I never suspected. I never suspected in a million years. You two have been carrying around this secret for almost two decades. Were you ever going to tell her, Bay? Didn't she have a right to know?"

Tansy spoke up. "Don't blame Bay. It was my fault. My mother and sister were trying to protect me."

"What were you thinking?"

"We obviously weren't!" Bay cried. "You remember what a terrible time it was. We were grieving. Tansy was Ashley's age with an unwanted pregnancy. She didn't want to keep the baby, and I was a widow. It made sense to go away to a relative's and pretend I was already pregnant with Bobby's child. That way Mom and I could bring the baby home and raise her while Tansy got on with her life. She never wanted to be here. Even when she was a little kid, she dreamed of bigger and better things. It made sense at the time, and quite frankly I needed that child. I needed someone to hold. Bobby was gone. That beautiful boy was gone before we ever had a life together. I would have gone out of my mind without someone to hang onto."

"Did it never occur to you that someday the truth would come out, despite all your secrecy?"

Bay jumped up from the table. "No. Nothing occurred to me. I lived my life one day at a time and that one day led into another day, and another day, and then suddenly Ashley is grown up and now how do I tell her? And then unbelievably, *she* becomes pregnant. *She's* going to be someone's mother. So how do I break it to her now? It's a nightmare, an unending nightmare that I've tried to keep under control, but little by little it's been eating away at my soul and I don't know how much more I can take."

Bay turned and fled the kitchen. They heard her run up the stairs and slam the door to her bedroom. Gertie looked at Tansy, who stared at the placemat in front of her. She looked like a ghost, someone there but not really there. It wouldn't take much to have her break into a million pieces. She turned her sad eyes to Gertie.

"Do you think Ashley will forgive me?"

"She's going to need time. This isn't something that can be fixed in a couple of days. But I have no doubt that someday she'll forgive you."

Tansy nodded.

"I know there's one thing troubling her."

"What?"

"She wants to know who her father is."

Tansy shut her eyes.

"You have to tell her."

"I can't," Tansy whispered.

"Why? She needs to know the truth. You owe it to her."

"Because Bobby is her father."

CHAPTER FOURTEEN

MARCH 1981

All the customers who blew into the store that day complained about the weather outside. And it was miserable. The snow had stopped falling hours before, but the northeast wind continued to whip it off the rooftops and snowbanks, creating almost whiteout conditions on the main street through Louisbourg.

Tansy was on the cash near the front, so every time the door opened, another blast of freezing air came in with the customer. She finally took to putting on a pair of mitts when she wasn't ringing up purchases, and had two sweaters on, though they didn't do much against the cold. She looked at her watch. One more hour and she'd be finished.

The door crashed opened and in came her next-door neighbour, Flo. "That there wind is gonna be the death of me," she sputtered. "It's not fit for man nor beast out there."

Tansy wished the wind would blow Flo out of town. Flo grabbed a metal basket and gave Tansy a begrudging nod before she hightailed it over to Maude Rankin, who stood in the bread aisle muttering to herself.

Tansy conceded it wasn't a bad job working here at the corner store, but she wished Mr. Beaton would let her have a stool to sit on when they weren't busy. He said it wasn't professional to have someone lollygagging behind the cash. All right for him. He was never out of his chair in the back room.

When the door opened again, Tansy silently cursed. Why on earth did people go out in snowstorms? She changed her tune when she turned around and saw who was standing there. She didn't know his name, but a friend had pointed him out one day and told her he was Lester Campbell's nephew from away. She didn't know where. He was in town to help his uncle with some job or other.

He was tall and slim, almost gangly, with straight blonde hair that fell in his eyes. He didn't have a ball cap on, which was a relief; he wore a jean jacket with the collar turned up, no gloves, and only work boots. If he was cold, he didn't let on. Glancing around, he walked up to the counter and nodded his head. "Hey."

"Hey, yourself. Is it getting worse out there?"

He looked behind him through the window. "Is it bad out?"

Tansy smiled. "Anything I can get for you?"

"A pack of Players, please."

Tansy turned around and grabbed a package of cigarettes off the display behind her. She put them on the counter and he put them in his jacket pocket.

"Thanks."

"What's your name?"

"Bobby." He passed her some money.

Tansy took the bill out of his hand and rang up the purchase. "I'm Tansy. Don't you know you shouldn't smoke?" She gave him back his change.

"Yeah."

"But you do it anyway."

He smiled at her. "I'm not that bright." Bobby started to move towards the door.

"I'm sure that's not true," Tansy laughed. "You're from away?"

He hesitated. "Yes, haven't been here too long."

"I hope you won't get bored. This is a small town."

"Which is why I can't go to another store to pick up my lottery tickets," Flo interrupted. "Why don't you stop flirting with the poor guy for five minutes and give someone else a turn?"

Tansy felt her face burn with embarrassment. Bobby gave her a half-wave and hurried out of the store. It was all Tansy could do not to take the carton of eggs Flo was buying and break them over her head.

"Teenagers," Flo muttered to Maude, who stood behind her. "They'll be the death of me yet."

❧

It was well into summer before she saw him again. A bunch of local kids sat on the bluffs out of town, their cars and trucks parked haphazardly. Someone had a stereo perched on the hood of a car, the music blaring. Beer flowed and so did the laughter. Tansy had had a few too many by this point, and enjoyed the attention of most of the males in the group, whether their girlfriends were there or not. The girls knew better than to make it known they were jealous of her. To hang around with Tansy meant you were with the "in" crowd.

Which is why Bay never came along.

Another truck pulled in and Tansy saw a local fellow from down the road get out of the driver's seat. He was older; she was surprised he'd shown up. And then Bobby climbed out of the truck, a cigarette hanging from his lips. He'd filled out, his arms taut with muscles, which wasn't surprising as he'd been on the lobster boats and was now in the woods cutting trees. His face and arms were a caramel brown and his blonde hair was the colour of flax from long days in the sun. He needed a haircut and a shave and his jeans were almost threadbare, but he outshone all the other guys put together.

Tansy made a beeline for him.

Bobby was nice, joking with everyone, accepting a beer and then another. He didn't give Tansy any more attention than he gave anyone else, and she wasn't used to that. She had to wait her turn.

The sun went down and things got rowdy. Everyone had too much to drink. Tansy had wheedled her way over to Bobby and managed to sit beside him on the grass as he leaned against a huge rock. He was glad to see her and put an arm around her, but she could have been anyone. He was trying to tell his buddies a joke, and since he was three sheets to the wind, he kept blowing it—and the more he flubbed it up, the more he laughed.

Soon everyone's attention was drawn to an argument between two of the guys standing over by the vehicles. People got up and left, getting closer to the action. Bobby stayed put. He leaned his head against the rock, grinning like a fool.

"Don't you want to see the fight?" Tansy asked.

Bobby looked at her. "Now why would I want to see a fight?"

"I thought all guys liked fighting."

"Not this guy."

Tansy smiled at him. "What do you like, then?"

"Let's see." The arm he'd draped over her shoulder became tighter as he counted the fingers on his hand. "I really like pancakes."

Tansy giggled.

"And I really like baseball."

"I bet you're good," she said.

"No, I'm terrible. Can't throw a ball to save my life. Now, what else? Umm, I really like steak and...Newfoundland dogs and...Oh Henry! bars..."

"Do you like girls?"

He laughed out loud. "Yes, I like girls. What are you suggesting?"

"Nothing. I just wondered if you liked me."

"Of course I like you." As he looked at her, his head swayed slightly. "You are one beautiful girl."

"So I've been told."

"I'm not surprised."

"Let me hear you say it again."

"What?" he grinned. "That I like girls?"

"Yeah."

"I like girls."

"Show me."

Bobby reached down and gave her a great kiss. Tansy was completely captivated by him. His wonderful laugh and gentle manner were the sexiest things about him. She wanted him. No, she needed him.

Tansy kept kissing Bobby as she manoeuvred herself on top of him. He cradled the back of her neck with one hand while he reached around her waist and held her close.

Tansy had never felt like this before. He knew what to do. It was as effortless as breathing. She never wanted him to stop touching her. She was in a frenzy to feel him against her skin, but soon after he rolled her over on her back there was a sharp whistle. Bobby lifted his head and looked behind him.

"Hey, Romeo," his friend shouted. "It's getting bad. We gotta get out of here before the cops show up."

Bobby lifted himself off the ground and grabbed Tansy's hand, pulling her to her feet. "Come on, let's go."

They ran for his friend's truck, and he helped her in ahead of him. His friend looked annoyed.

"Shit, what are we supposed to do with her?"

"I'm not going to leave her here. Tansy, where do you live?"

She told him.

His friend threw the gear shift in reverse, and they careened over the bumpy dirt road. Bobby put his arm around her so she wouldn't go flying all over the cab. She wanted to melt into the side of his shirt. He was warm and smelled so good. Tansy wanted to talk to him, but the driver insisted on telling him all about the fight. Bobby rolled his eyes and smiled at her as he listened, as if the two of them were sharing a secret.

The drive ended too soon. They stopped the truck in front of the house and Bobby got out. He extended his hand to help her down. Tansy said thanks to the driver and slid off the seat. She stayed near Bobby by the side of the road.

"Thank you for taking me home."

"No problem."

"Kiss me goodbye."

Bobby gave her a smile before he kissed her cheek. "Goodnight, Tansy." Then he got back in the truck and shut the door and his friend took off, tires squealing.

Tansy stood there and wondered if those few minutes in his arms had been a dream. As she touched her lips, she knew that her mouth was red from his stubble. She felt branded by him and knew she'd never want anyone else.

The front door opened and her father stood on the porch. "Tansy, get in the house!"

She was in for it now. She walked up the driveway and over the lawn to the front steps.

"Who the hell was that squealing his tires at this time of night?"

"No one you know."

She tried to walk past him, but he blocked her way with his arm. His old flannel shirt stank of fish and tobacco, a smell that couldn't be removed no matter how hard her mother scrubbed. His lined and tired face looked fed up. "Have you been drinking?"

"I had a couple of beers."

"More than a couple, I'd say. Were you down at that old quarry? I've told you how dangerous it is down there."

Tansy wanted him to shut up so she could run upstairs, close the door, and lie on her bed in the dark remembering what Bobby had done to her.

She heard her mother's voice in the hall. "She's home now, Jack. Let her go up to bed."

Her father let her go by. As she ran up the stairs she heard him say to her mother, "Why can't she be like Bay? We never had this kind of trouble with her."

"Now, Jack…"

Tansy slammed her bedroom door and fell on her unmade bed. She buried her face in the blankets until she could hardly breathe, then rolled over, stared at the ceiling, and hugged herself. "Bobby," she whispered. "Bobby."

She got up to look in the mirror, pressed her lips with her fingers and remembered how his tongue had felt inside her mouth. Her hands touched her body where he had touched her body, but the hollow ache she felt inside would never be filled unless he was with her again.

Tansy was exhausted the next morning; she'd tossed and turned until the sun came up. Her head ached from all that stupid beer. Her father was right on that score. Slipping on her bathrobe, she opened her door and crossed the hall to the bathroom. The door was locked and the shower was on.

She pounded on the door. "Bay!"

"I'm in the shower."

"No shit. Unlock the door, I need to pee."

The door clicked. Tansy opened it in time to see Bay's arm disappear behind the shower curtain. Tansy pushed the door closed behind her but it didn't catch. No matter. She sat on the john.

"What time did you roll in?"

"I have no clue."

"Did you go to the quarry?"

"Yeah."

"Don't you guys get sick of hanging around down there?"

"What else is there to do in this godforsaken town?"

"You make it sound like you live in Siberia."

"I might as well be."

Tansy reached behind and grabbed some toilet paper. When she flushed Bay screeched as the water went cold. "Don't do that, you idiot."

Tansy washed her hands. "Sorry."

"No, you're not. You do it every time."

"One of these days you'll miss these endearing little rituals."

"Don't count on it."

Tansy shut the bathroom door behind her and went downstairs to the kitchen. Her mother was in her usual spot in front of the kitchen stove, with her apron on.

"Morning." Tansy plunked herself down on the nearest kitchen chair.

"Want some oatmeal?"

"Mom, when have I ever wanted oatmeal?"

Her mother put a tray of tea biscuits in the oven and turned on the timer. "You used to love it as a kid."

"I'm not a kid anymore."

Now her mother busied herself taking juice out of the fridge and poured it into a glass. She passed it to Tansy. "Is that why you think you can gallivant around town with ruffians and guzzle beer until two in the morning?"

"Don't start."

"Your father's right. You're too young—"

"Mom, I'm seventeen. I'm not a baby." Tansy drank her juice and wiped the side of her mouth. "Besides, everyone else is allowed to go out with their friends. I don't know what Dad's problem is."

"He's concerned about you and so am I. You know..."

Tansy tuned her out. Her mother continued to walk around the kitchen, wiping a glass here and a plate there, talking the entire time. She had beans in a strainer that needed to be snapped, and a large pot of glass jars boiling away at the back of the stove, almost ready for the strawberry jam she'd made earlier that morning. How she could do all that and still have the energy to give her a lecture boggled Tansy's mind. She figured it was a mom thing.

"...and Flo told me that you were at the top of the street one night, necking away with that Jamison boy. You need to be careful, young lady. You could get a reputation."

Tansy grunted. "Not difficult in this boring town."

Her mother took a bowl and a box of Cheerios out of the cupboard and put them in front of Tansy. She reached down and took Tansy's chin in her hand. "It doesn't matter where you live. Life is what you make it."

Then off she went to stir a bowl of batter.

Tansy poured some Cheerios in the bowl and knew she was going to make her life as exciting as possible. She just had to track down Bobby to do it.

The trouble was, it was next to impossible to find him.

Like all strapping young lads, he was busy from morning to night, and since he was four years older than her, he didn't hang out with her crowd. Her only chance was maybe another night at the quarry, or seeing him down by the wharf on a late summer evening. After a while her friends were fed up with her, because she never wanted to do anything but hang around and wait for something to happen.

She did see him on a few occasions, always with a crowd around him. They talked and laughed, but it was never alone. He always seemed glad to see her, but it ended there. The only thing that made her feel better was that he never seemed to be with a girl. He spent most of his time laughing with his cronies.

Finally, on Labour Day weekend, there was going to be a big bonfire on the beach at the edge of town. A last hurrah to summer, as kids headed back to university or out West or took jobs in Sydney. People started to gather around nine in the evening, and by eleven the party was jumping.

Tansy sat on the hood of a car and pretended to have fun, but her radar was on the road that led to the water. Every time car headlights showed up, she'd wait to see who approached, but it was never him. She'd about given up when she saw him come out of the dark with a couple of boys she didn't know.

Her heart did a flip in her chest and she realized almost too late that she wasn't breathing. She needed to calm down. Bobby walked up to the fire and greeted everyone with his cheerful smile. He glanced at her for a moment and acknowledged her with a wave of his hand, but then grabbed a beer and talked to his buddies.

By midnight she knew she had to do something; her curfew was one at the very latest. She made her way over to him and slid her arm around his waist. He looked down and gave her a squeeze.

"Hey, Tansy, how's it going?"

"Good. Can we talk?"

"Sure." Bobby motioned with his beer bottle to his friends. "Sorry, guys, I need to talk to the lady."

His friends made appreciative noises and one of them yelled, "Can't you talk to me too?!" They laughed as Bobby led her away.

"Don't mind them," he smiled. "They're joking. So how've ya been? I haven't seen you around."

"I've been busy."

"Well, it's good to see you."

They walked towards the edge of the beach.

"Can we sit down?" she asked.

"If you like." He took off his jacket and placed it on the dune grass for her to sit on. He sat beside her and put his arm around her again. "Are you sure you're not too cold? Don't you want to sit by the fire?"

"No. I want to be right here with you."

"I'm flattered."

"Are you seeing someone?"

"You mean do I have a girlfriend?"

"Yeah."

"No, I don't."

"Why not?"

"You could say I'm a loner."

Tansy's eyes widened. "A loner? The only time I ever see you, you've got a crowd of people around you."

"Doesn't matter who's around you. It's a state of being."

"Oh." Tansy was unsure what he meant.

"I just live day to day. Life is an adventure."

"It's not much fun around here."

"Oh, I don't know about that." He looked out over the water. "I love it here."

Tansy couldn't wait anymore. "Bobby?"

"Yes?"

"Please kiss me."

He smiled before he reached over and did as she asked. It was slow and almost lazy, soft and warm. If it was possible, it was better than before. He took his time as he pushed her back onto the grass and lay on top or her. Everything was in slow motion after that. She pulled at his shirt until she got her hands underneath and felt the hard muscles in his back. When he pressed down and moved his body against hers, it was as if she'd melted into the ground and become one with that dark velvet night.

He reached down to unbutton her jeans. She tried to help him. And that's when he groaned and let his head drop, as if he'd remembered something.

"Don't stop. Please don't stop."

He looked at her. "How old are you?"

"What difference does that make?"

"It makes a big difference."

"I'm almost eighteen. I'm old enough."

"Not quite." He rolled away from her and lay on his back.

She was desperate. "I'll never tell anyone. No one has to know."

"I'd know."

She got up on her elbows. "Don't you like me?"

He sat up and rearranged his shirt. "Sure I do. You're a sweet kid."

"I'm not a kid."

He stood and reached his hand towards her. "Come on, now. Let's go back the party."

Taking her hand, he pulled her up and then reached down for his jacket and put it over her shoulders. He put his arm around her and kissed the top of her head, as if she were a little girl.

Tansy wanted to die.

CHAPTER FIFTEEN

Bay and Gertie were in the kitchen helping Bay's mother slice up a whole tub full of small cucumbers so she could make bread-and-butter pickles. They had an assembly line going. One washed, one peeled, and one sliced.

"Once we have enough," Liz said, "we have to put some rock salt in the bowl."

"What does that do?" Gertie wanted to know.

"You leave it overnight and the salt draws the water from the cucumbers. That way you'll get a crisper pickle."

"How did you learn this stuff?" Bay asked.

"My mother, of course," Liz said. "She had me making pickles by the time I was ten years old. There wasn't anything she couldn't do. She won first place for her pickles and chow every year at the fall fair. But I'll never forget the year Mr. Greer entered his pickled beets as a lark, and didn't he win. My mother was heartbroken." Liz smiled at the memory. "My dad took us out for ice cream that night to try and cheer her up." She shook her head. "Silly things you remember."

Bay and Gertie grinned at each other.

Bay's dad came in the back door. He held out a nail and a drill bit. "Bay, could you run down to the hardware store and get me a pound of three-inch galvanized nails and a one-and-a-quarter-inch drill bit? I'm in the middle of something out there and I want to finish it before dark."

"Sure. I need money, though. How much will it be?"

Her mother pointed at her purse. "I have a ten in my wallet. Take that."

"I'll stay here and help your mom," Gertie said.

Bay wiped her hands on a tea towel and went to get the money. Her father gave her the nail and the drill bit. "Show these to Burt and he'll know what to give you, but make sure they're galvanized nails."

"Okay."

"Thanks." Out he went back to the shed.

Bay was almost out the door when her mother said, "Put a sweater on. It's cold out."

Bay took her sweater off the hook in the back porch and put it on as she ran down the back steps. It was one of those September days that made her glad to be alive. Fall was in the air. It smelled like black earth and leaves and McIntosh apples. The air was crisp, and on days like this the light made the far shore past the lighthouse look close enough to touch.

She almost wished she had a skipping rope. This was the time of year little kids headed back to school and sat in their classrooms looking out the window, longing for the dismissal bell to ring. Skipping ropes made her think of thick sidewalk chalk, and hopscotch, and the smell of crayons and Elmer's glue.

"What are you grinnin' about, girlie?" Eldon shouted from his front porch.

"Nothin', Eldon. Need anything at the hardware store?"

"As a matter of fact, I do. A couple of twenty-amp fuses. Here, I'll give you the money."

"I have enough. I'll catch you on the way back."

Eldon raised his hand in thanks.

It was a ten-minute walk, and by the time she got to the store, her cheeks were red from the biting wind and her hair was every which way. The bell tinkled on her way in as she entered a world inhabited by men. Paint cans and tools and brown bags full of nails and screws and washers seemed to be everywhere. Burt was at the back of the store talking to two men who held a piece of equipment, so instead of interrupting him she slowly went up and down the aisles looking for the proper size of drill bit. She picked up packages and measured them against the one she held, because she couldn't remember if her dad said one-and-a-half-inch or one-and-a-quarter.

"Can I help you with that?" a voice said behind her.

She spun around and saw the nicest-looking boy she'd ever seen in her whole life. Flustered, she kept her head down and looked at the package. "My dad wants a drill bit but I forget what size."

"May I see it?" He held out his hand and she placed it on his palm. "Hmm. This is one-and-a-quarter-inch."

"How can you tell right off the bat?"

He smiled at her. "Guys know this stuff."

She smiled back at him. "Oh."

He reached over and took a package off the hook and gave it to her. "Anything else?"

"I need two twenty-amp fuses and a pound of three-inch nails."

"I'll show you where they are."

He led her over to the next aisle. Bay snuck peeks at him, because she couldn't believe he was talking to her. He stopped in front of the nails. "A pound, you say?"

"Yes. I can get it."

"It's no trouble." He reached for a brown bag. "Did your dad happen to mention if he wanted galvanized nails?"

"Yes! I almost forgot. Thanks."

He scooped up the nails in a couple of handfuls and weighed them on the scale.

"I didn't know it was so complicated," she said. "I thought they came in bags."

He smiled at her. "You don't look like the type of girl who spends a lot of time in hardware stores. Now, one more stop." He led her to the fuses and handed her the package.

"There. You're all set."

"I feel as if I should pay you."

"You can. You can let me buy you a soft drink."

"I can't. I have to get back. My dad needs this."

"I understand. I'm Bobby, by the way. Bobby Campbell." He held out his hand.

She put her hand in his. "Bay. Bay Gillis."

"Bay. That's an unusual name."

"It's short for Elizabeth."

"Well, Elizabeth Bay, the least I can do is carry your bags home. A pound of nails is heavier than it looks."

She still couldn't believe he was speaking to her. "You don't have to do that."

"I'd like to."

"All right."

Bay paid for the items and he took the bag. On their way out the door he offered her a stick of Doublemint gum. Afterwards she couldn't remember what they'd talked about, but it was easy, as if she'd been talking to him her whole life.

They stopped at Eldon's and gave him the fuses and she blushed when he told Bobby that she was the nicest girl in town. When Bobby agreed with him she blushed again. They were at the house before she knew it. He looked around. "I think I've been up this street before. Can't remember why." He passed her the bag. "I'm sorry...are you going out with anyone?"

"No."

"Would you like to grab a coffee at the snack bar tomorrow?"

"Okay, what time?"

"Three?"

"All right. Bye, Bobby. Thank you."

"Goodbye, Elizabeth Bay." He gave her a big smile, put his hands in his pockets, and walked away.

She, on the other hand, skipped to the garage and gave her father the bag before she danced across the lawn and up the back steps. When she sashayed into the kitchen, only Gertie noticed, as her mother was up to her elbows in hot vinegar and sugar. Bay gestured for Gertie to come upstairs. The two of them ran into her room. Bay shut the door and hopped up and down.

"What the heck happened to you?"

Bay grabbed her by her shirt. "I met the cutest boy."

"Aww, how come I'm never around when cute boys are being met? Who is it?"

"Bobby Campbell."

"Never heard of him."

"Take one look and you'll never forget him. He wants to meet me for coffee tomorrow at the snack bar."

"I'll be the customer with the fake nose and glasses."

They met for coffee and Bay forgot that Gertie was there, hiding conspicuously behind the dessert menu three stools down. Bay didn't look in her direction once in the forty minutes she was there, so Gertie eventually wandered out. All Bay and Bobby did was talk, anyway. It got boring after a while. And though Bay said they were doing it again the next day and the next, Gertie didn't sit in again.

Bobby tagged along the day she had to take her neighbours' kids to the local library after school and he was there when she went to the laundromat for Flo, to do her extra bedding after her washing machine died. As he walked up her street with green garbage bags full of folded cotton sheets, he stopped and looked at her. "You're a real Holly Hobby, aren't you?"

"What do you mean?"

"Do you ever go anywhere without doing something for someone? If I wanted to go for a walk with you tonight, would you meet me at the wharf and just walk?"

"Sure."

"Thank goodness. I thought I had to share you with the entire population of Louisbourg."

"I'm worth the wait."

That night she put on her prettiest top and washed her hair and opened up the perfume she'd saved for a special occasion. It was warm enough for just her jean jacket. When she left her room, Tansy came out of the shower, towel-drying her hair. "You look nice."

"Thanks."

"You goin' somewhere?"

"Meeting a friend. You?"

"There's another bonfire tonight."

Bay started down the stairs. "Try not to fall over a cliff while you're there."

"Try not to yawn too often at Gertie's," Tansy sassed back.

"You're so clever," Bay's voice drifted up from below.

Bobby waited for her just where he said he'd be. He took her hand and they wandered along the waterfront. They were in no hurry. They talked about what they wanted to do someday and he told her about being an only child and how even though his parents were divorced they still fought with each other and tried make him take sides, which is why his uncle had offered him room and board—to get him out of the situation for a while. He wasn't sure if he'd go back to British Columbia. "I can fish here as well as there."

"Is that all you want to do? Go fishing?"

"I love it out there on the water. When the sun comes up and the whole sky is pink and purple and the water is so still you think it's glass, there's no better place to be. I always want to be right in the middle of all that beauty."

"That must be why my dad likes it. He says he feels close to God on the water. He says that's all the church he needs."

"I think your old man and I would get along just fine."

She smiled at him. "I think so too."

They walked up around the cove and over to the lighthouse. The sun was going down. They watched it as they sat on the rocks that overlooked the harbour.

"I never want to leave this place," Bay said. "My sister can't wait to get out of Louisbourg and see the world, but I think I'd be lost if I left this island."

"You'd never get lost," Bobby said.

She looked at him. "Why?"

"Because I'd come and find you."

He touched her face with his fingers before he leaned over and kissed her. That was the moment they became one.

Tansy came through the back door. A delicious smell permeated the whole kitchen. She shrugged out of her pea jacket and threw it on the back of a kitchen chair. "Yum. What's for supper?"

"Roast chicken and dumplings," her mother informed her. "Hang up your jacket, please. I'm trying to keep the place neat."

"Why? Who's coming?"

"Bay's bringing a friend over for dinner. A boy."

"A boy? Will wonders never cease?"

"Put a comb through your hair. They'll be here shortly."

"Yes, Mother."

Tansy went upstairs and ran into her dad, who came out of his bedroom doing up the top button of his newest flannel shirt.

"She made you change too, huh?"

"A lot of nonsense for nothing," he groused. "This kid should try to impress me, not the other way around.".

"We know you'll dazzle him with your famous wit and charm, Daddy."

He reached out and messed up her hair. "Where you get your cheeky mouth, I'll never know."

"I'm Jack Junior, remember?"

"You were supposed to be my boy. What happened?"

"I changed my mind in the womb just to tick you off."

They grinned at each other. Then they heard voices come through the door downstairs. Jack kept going and Tansy ran into the bathroom to splash water on her face. She wondered who this guy was. Bay hadn't mentioned she was seeing someone. Not that Tansy was ever home to talk to her, but still. If he was special enough to bring to dinner, you think she would have mentioned him before this.

Tansy took off her T-shirt and put on a nicer blouse, but that was as much as she was willing to do. As she headed down the stairs, she stopped in the hall mirror to brush her long hair back with her fingers. She'd pass inspection.

Then she walked into the kitchen.

Afterwards she remembered Bay's face first, how happy and excited she looked when she turned around. Bobby looked happy too, until his eyes fell on her. There was only a split second of fear on his face, but Tansy saw it and Bobby knew it.

"Bobby, this is my sister, Tansy. Tansy, this is my friend Bobby Campbell."

He was good. She had to give him that. He came towards her with a big smile on his face. "Hi, Tansy. It's nice to see you again."

Bay smiled. "I didn't know you knew each other."

Bobby nodded. "Yes, we've met a few times at the beach during those bonfires they had earlier in the summer. I'm surprised I recognized you, Tansy. I'm used to seeing you in the dark."

Two could play this game.

"I'm surprised I recognized you without a beer in your hand."

Bay and her parents gave her a look.

"Oh sorry, that sounded rude. You know what I mean."

Bobby laughed. "Yes, I know what you mean."

"Why don't we sit down?" Liz said. "Dinner's ready. I hope you like chicken and dumplings, Bobby."

"My favourite," he smiled.

Tansy didn't listen to the dinner conversation. She was busy trying to choke down the few bites of food she did manage to eat. No one looked at her anyway. It was obvious her parents were delighted with Bobby. Her mom was thrilled to have a boy to feed, someone who actually wanted a second helping, and her dad was impressed that this young man knew all about lobster fishing. Her father monopolized the conversation, which was totally unlike him. Bay didn't bother to say anything. She looked blissfully stoned, as high as a kite on a drug called love.

As soon as dinner was over, Tansy offered to wash up. Her mother looked pleasantly surprised and quickly took her up on the offer before she hustled the others out to the living room, where she served tea and lemon meringue pie. Tansy listened to the four of them laugh and thought what a smooth operator Bobby was. You'd never know he had anything on his mind other than to try and impress his girl-friend's parents.

That's when it hit her. That's all he *was* doing. He wasn't out there thinking about Tansy as she washed the dishes, wondering what she'd say or do about their situation. There was no situation. She was a girl he necked with and maybe got to second base with, but that was all. Just your typical summer romp in the grass that happens when night falls and beer flows.

After Tansy finished the dishes, she put on her jacket and went outside to sit on the garden swing. It was a warm night for October. The pumpkins in the garden glowed under the light of the moon. Soon her mother would pick them to make pumpkin pie and pumpkin cookies and pumpkin preserves and pumpkin, pumpkin, stupid pumpkin stuff. Didn't she get tired of constantly making something out of nothing? Didn't she ever want to take a pumpkin and smash it to smithereens against a wall?

Tansy had no idea how long she sat on the swing. She gave a start when she heard the back door open as Bobby thanked her parents again for a wonderful evening. They fell over themselves inviting him back whenever he wanted to come. Then he and Bay headed for his truck in the driveway. They obviously didn't see her. That's when her mother poked her head out the back door and asked if Bobby would like to take home some of the leftovers and the rest of the pie. He said he'd be delighted and Bay said she'd run in and get them.

Bobby used the opportunity to take out a cigarette and light it, before he wandered over to the garden and saw her on the swing. He hesitated and then came forward.

"Hey."

"Hey, yourself. Is it getting worse out there?"

"Sorry?"

"Never mind, you don't remember."

"Remember what?"

"The first day we met."

"Sure I do. It was at the quarry."

"No, the corner store, actually."

"Oh right, that nice old lady."

Tansy gestured with her thumb. "She lives right next door."

"Lucky you."

Tansy didn't say anything else. Bobby walked over and sat beside her on the swing.

"Look, I know this is a bit awkward. I didn't know Bay was your sister."

"Well, she is."

"I'm sorry. I know we weren't dating and we have nothing to hide, but I'd prefer it if you didn't mention any of this to your sister. There's no sense in upsetting her."

"Well, you obviously met her after you were with me, so how can she hold it against you? Is she going to have grudges against all your old conquests? I'm sure you have hundreds."

"Not quite. Still, there's no point in bringing it up, is there?"

Tansy pushed the swing with her feet, setting it in motion before she turned and faced him, tucking one leg under her. "Oh, I don't know, Bobby. I guess if it meant nothing to you, then it doesn't make sense to tell her. But since rolling around in the dirt with your tongue down my throat and your hand between my thighs is the highlight of my life, I'd find it difficult not to bring it up at some point."

Bobby stayed very still while he looked in her eyes. "Tansy, I have every faith that you love your sister very much and you'd never want to hurt her like that, so I know I won't have to ask you again."

Bay ran out of the house with a grocery bag full of goodies from her mother. Bobby got up from the swing and went over to take it out of her hands. Bay waved at Tansy. "See ya later. We're going to the drive-in." They jumped in the truck and backed out into the street. Tansy watched the red tail lights disappear into the night.

She stayed on the swing for quite a while before she got up and twisted a small pumpkin off its stalk. Then she walked next door and threw the pumpkin as hard as she could against Flo's clapboard siding.

Under the harvest moon, it looked like blood and guts all over the dirt driveway.

CHAPTER SIXTEEN

Bobby asked Bay's parents for her hand in marriage a few days before Christmas. They were taken aback at first because it all seemed so soon, but Bobby said he couldn't live another minute without her and they believed him. They knew their daughter was the happiest she'd ever been. When they gave their consent, Bobby gave them both a bear hug, startling Jack momentarily.

Tansy had to watch Bobby give Bay her ring on Christmas morning. It was small, but you'd think it was the Hope diamond the way Bay went on about it. Gertie bawled when she heard the news.

God. It was like no one had been married before.

They set a date for the wedding in May, right before lobster season. Jack offered Bobby a job working on his boat and Bobby gladly took it. They got along like a house on fire anyway. Tansy overheard her mom on the phone to her cousin in Fredericton, saying that Bobby was the son Jack never had.

Bobby's uncle had a small rental property at the edge of town and said the young couple could rent one of the apartments and fix it up any way they liked. All that winter, they painted and hung wallpaper and sanded the old hardwood floors. Tansy went with Gertie a few times, on days she knew Bobby wouldn't be there, to help Bay hang curtains or put up blinds. It was too suspicious to avoid going altogether.

And she had to go shopping with her mother, Bay, and Gertie when they went to pick out the wedding and bridesmaid dresses, because sisters always went along on that sort of thing. Tansy was even happy for Bay when she walked out in the dress she eventually chose, because it was obviously meant for her and the look on her face was one of pure joy. It was only when Tansy went home and shut the bedroom door that the mask she'd worn all day crumbled.

Tansy cried every night alone in her room and every morning she'd get up and put the mask back on. She didn't realize what a toll it was taking on her until she went back for a fitting of her bridesmaid's dress and it had to be taken in by several inches.

Her mother took Tansy's face in her hands. She gently rubbed the translucent dark circles under Tansy's eyes. "Are you feeling okay, honey?"

"I'm all right."

"Is there anything you want to tell me?"

"No."

"I'm always here if you do."

"Don't worry about me. Worry about the bride. She's about to overdose on happiness."

Her mother smiled at her. "Never fear, my love. One day it will be your turn."

So while her sister basked in Bobby's love, every day Tansy felt her heart get smaller and smaller. She knew it wouldn't be long before it disappeared altogether and the surprising thing was she almost looked forward to it. Because once it was gone, it wouldn't hurt.

The only thing that kept her from going out of her mind was to spend as much time as she could in the company of boys. They kept her from thinking. Not that she felt anything when they held her in their arms, but it passed the time. Unfortunately for the boys, it was an exercise in frustration, because although they could do most things to her, they couldn't do everything.

Never that. Ever.

Unfortunately, one night her coping mechanism blew up in her face. She had too much to drink and was parked in the local lovers' lane with a guy from high school. There were lots of other cars and people there, so it wasn't like they were totally alone, but in the end that was the problem. While she and this jock were in the back seat practicing their night moves, two of his friends watched the spectacle through the open car windows. They drank their beer and hooted with delight whenever lover boy tried something fancy, and they didn't notice the truck pull up behind them until the last minute.

Tansy didn't know it was her father who pulled her out of the backseat of the car until she stood on the ground with her blouse open and her jeans unzipped. The two spectators were long gone, but the jock wasn't so lucky. He was pulled out of the car next and received a sharp right hook that connected with his jaw. Down he went. Then Tansy's dad grabbed her by the upper arm and marched her over to the truck. He pushed her into the front seat and got behind the wheel and drove off. He didn't say a word to her all the way home.

When he got out of the truck, he went around to the passenger side, opened the door, and took Tansy by the arm and escorted her into the house. Bay and her mother were at the kitchen table. Her mom jumped up.

"Where on earth have you been? It's almost four in the morning! We were worried sick."

"I'll tell you where she's been," her father shouted. "Up on lovers' lane in the back seat of a car, with one guy pawin' at her and an audience watchin' the show."

Her mother looked at her in horror. "What is wrong with you? Is this what your life has turned into? Do you want to be known as the town pump?"

Bay tried to intervene. "Mom, that's not fair."

"Well, that's what will happen if she doesn't stop behaving like a tramp. Your father and I raised you girls better than that and I can't tell you how disappointed I am with your behaviour, Tansy."

"She drinks too damn much," her father yelled before he pointed at Tansy. "I'm telling you, missy, you're grounded for a month. Do you hear me? I want to see you in this house every night after supper and by God, you'd better be here. Now get upstairs. I don't want to see your face until morning."

Tansy walked out of the kitchen, up the stairs, and into her room. Her father shouted about what on earth they were going to do with her and her mother sounded like she was on the verge of tears, while Bay told them to calm down, that it wasn't the end of the world.

Eventually they came upstairs and went to bed. Soon all was quiet. Tansy lay on the bed with her clothes on and stared at the ceiling. She didn't hear the quiet knock on her bedroom door until Bay came in and shut it behind her. Her sister walked over and sat next to her.

"You okay?"

Tansy shrugged.

"You don't look well, Tansy. Are you sure there's nothing wrong?"

Tansy shook her head.

"You can talk to me if there's something you don't want Mom or Dad to know."

"I know that."

"They'll calm down. They forget what it's like to be young."

"You never put on a show in the back seat of someone's car."

"Doesn't mean I didn't want to."

The sisters smiled at each other.

"I'd be too afraid to do something like that, like the police would show up and put me in jail."

"You're a nut."

"Besides," Bay said, "I never had the opportunity. The boys only looked at you."

"You only need the right boy to look at you. All the rest don't matter."

"True."

They sat in silence for a while.

"What's it like, Bay?"

"What's what like?"

"Knowing that Bobby loves you."

Bay looked away for a moment. "It's like when you're freezing cold on a winter morning, so cold you can't bear it, and then you step on the grate in the hallway and a hot blast of air comes up from below and envelopes your whole body and soon you're toasty and warm and happy again. It's kind of like that."

"You're lucky."

"I know I am. One day you'll be lucky too."

Tansy turned her face to the wall.

"While you're incarcerated, Gertie and I can teach you how to play cribbage. How does that sound?"

"Painful."

Bay patted her hand. "Get some sleep. I love you."

"I love you too."

❋

It was a week before the wedding. The whole family was in a height-ened sense of panic. Not frantic panic, but the sort of busyness that makes people put their hands up to their foreheads and say, "What was I doing?" or "Where did I put that list?"

The uproar on this particular day was over the bridal shower Liz was hosting for Bay at the house. She was about to have kittens be-cause the house had to be spotless and she had ten kinds of squares in the oven and was in the middle of making six different types of finger sandwiches.

Tansy was put to work vacuuming and dusting while Gertie had the horrible job of making sure the bathroom was pristine.

"That's all I need," Liz huffed as she passed Gertie the bucket and scrub brush, "Lois Axworthy snooping around the loo. Everyone knows she opens medicine cabinets and looks under the sink, so make sure you get rid of anything that looks scandalous."

"Such as?" Gertie asked.

"I don't know…suppositories and vaginal cream…that sort of thing."

Gertie wrinkled her nose. "Oh goody."

"I think you should stick a vibrator in the toothpaste drawer," Tansy told Gertie as she trudged upstairs.

"As I live and breathe, Tansy Gillis," her mother shouted from the kitchen. "No wonder I have grey hair."

Gertie was back in the kitchen before Tansy finished vacuuming the entire downstairs. She was sweating bullets, and when she walked into the kitchen was greeted with a wall of heat. "It's like the coke ovens in here," she complained. "Have you finished baking yet?"

"Not quite. Gertie, don't ice those coconut squares. They need to cool down."

"Okay."

"Mom, where's Bay? Shouldn't she be here helping us? It's her shower."

"She ran over to the apartment to finish painting the inside of the kitchen cupboards because she won't get a chance before the wedding."

Tansy was about to sit down and take the weight off her feet when her mother remembered something. "Honey, take the car and run over and ask Bay to give you that plastic bag filled with serving trays. I'm running out of places to put this food."

"No wonder. You're feeding the five thousand," Tansy grumped.

She was in a bad mood when she grabbed the car keys and drove over to the apartment; she hated going over to her sister's little love nest. If she never saw it again she'd be quite happy. When she drove up, she cursed. Bobby's truck was there. Maybe she'd honk and get Bay to run out with the trays, but then Bobby would know why she was doing it and that made her cringe.

Tansy got out of the car and walked around the back. Their apartment was on the ground floor. She reached the door, and was about to go inside when she saw them through the kitchen window. They were definitely not painting.

She wanted to look away but she couldn't. He had Bay up against the counter. Her head was back, her eyes were closed, and her mouth was open as she banged against the cupboard door. Tansy couldn't hear them, which made it worse, because she knew the kind of sounds they were making. They were in their own private world, giving and receiving the pleasure she'd never have. She'd always be on the outside looking in at them and their perfect, perfect love.

To make matters worse, her mother hollered at her when she came home without the trays.

❊

She thought the shower would never end. Tansy vowed that she would never attend another bridal shower for as long as she lived. A room full of cackling hens would be less irritating. Keeping busy was the only way to live through it.

Gertie stayed by Bay's side, oohing and aahing over the gifts, taking photos of Bay with a paper plate festooned with gift bows on her head. To the untrained eye, Liz looked like she was having a good time, but Tansy knew her mother's mind was fast at work, calculating how many teabags she'd need for the urn and whether it was time to take the trifle out of the fridge.

Her well-meaning friends hovered around and asked her if there was anything that needed doing, but Liz good-naturedly shooed them out of the kitchen, saying she had plenty of help. Meaning Tansy.

At some point during even the most hectic of showers, there's a general lull in proceedings when appetites and thirsts have been sated and the weary hostess gets to sit down and enjoy her guests. It was during such a period, while Tansy was alone at the sink, that her father came into the kitchen.

"Hello, my little darlin'," he sang as he took off his jacket. "Any of those tiny sandwiches left? I could eat me boots."

"You've been drinking, mister," Tansy smiled.

"Who's a clever girl," Jack laughed as he put his arm around his daughter's shoulder.

"Mom's gonna kill you."

"Never. Your ma loves me."

"I'm not sure why."

"Always with the saucy talk. I wonder who you take after."

"I'm Jack Junior, remember."

"Oh yeah, so you are."

Liz came into the kitchen and put her hands on her hips. "Wonderful. I thought the stag party would be going on a lot longer than this. How am I supposed to get you upstairs without every gossip in town seeing the state of you?"

"Give us a kiss." Jack puckered up.

"Bobby's stag party was tonight?" Tansy asked.

Jack nodded a little more than was necessary. "Too right it was, and a grand time was had by all. The man himself is a little worse for wear, but I left him down in the boat. He'll be fine."

"You left him on the boat?"

"Jack...are you sure he'll be all right? Why didn't you take him home?"

"Look, my love, we ended up drinking down on the boat and none of us was in any shape to drive, and he wasn't in any shape to walk, so I left him there. He's not goin' anywhere. I'll go down and check on him in the morning."

"If you're sure." Liz didn't sound too convinced.

"I want some food, woman!"

Liz shushed him and turned to Tansy. "For God's sake, gather up a plate of sandwiches and sweets and take your father upstairs as quick as you can, before Lois Axworthy sees him."

Tansy did what she was told. Before she left the kitchen, with one hand on her father and the other on a plate of goodies, she said, "Do you need me anymore tonight, Mom? I'm tired. Think I'll have an early night."

Her mother emptied a teapot into the sink. "No, honey. You've been a great help, and I appreciate it. Thank you."

"You're welcome."

She whispered in her father's ear. "As quickly and as quietly as possible, we're going to rush down the hall and tiptoe upstairs. Have you got that?"

More unnecessary nodding.

Anyone who'd been looking would have seen two people walk swiftly and ramrod straight down the hall carrying a mound of food, whereupon they turned on a dime and headed lickety-split up the stairs.

And anyone looking five minutes later would have seen one person come down the stairs, go out the door, and disappear into the night.

Tansy didn't have a thought in her head. She didn't know why she needed to see him. Maybe because she knew this would be the last unguarded moment she'd have with him, given that the wedding was only days away. And somewhere deep down she knew that he was always happy to see her when he'd been drinking.

It didn't take her long to get to the wharf. No one was around, but she did hear drunken singing from way up the road, no doubt guests of the stag party who were still weaving their way home.

She'd been on her father's boat lots of times. *Tansy Bay* and all the other fishing boats in the harbour were ready for the May fifteenth opening of lobster season, their hulls cleaned and newly painted, the buoys bright with neon colours, the traps waiting to be filled.

Tansy climbed down the iron rails of the wharf itself and silently jumped down to the deck. She crossed over to the cabin door, slid it open, and slipped inside before closing it behind her. Her father had left a small deck light on, and she saw Bobby lying on his back on one of the bunks, his arm covering his eyes. The table was covered with empty beer and rum bottles, overflowing ashtrays, and empty chip bags and dip containers. Amazing how easy men were to please when it came to organizing a party.

She tiptoed over to him and gingerly sat on the bunk. His breathing was deep and even. At one point he shifted in his sleep and his arm came down to rest against his chest. Tansy watched him and didn't realize that she was crying until she felt a tear fall down her cheek.

As soon as she could get the money together, she'd leave this place. She'd come to say goodbye in the only way that made sense; to be alone with him and no one else for a few moments.

"I love you," she whispered.

She rose from the bunk and rushed to the door, but in her haste knocked over a rum bottle. It shattered on the floor. She spun around, her hands clamped over her mouth. Bobby sat up on the bunk. "Wha'... who's there?"

She didn't move. He put his feet on the floor and held his head in his hands, before brushing his hair back with his fingers. He shook his head a little. "Christ, where am I?"

Tansy backed up to the door, one small step at a time. He hadn't seen her in the dim light and the thought of him seeing her now scared her to death. What was she thinking? What was she doing?

Bobby stood up and staggered a little. He held out his hand and managed to right himself when he touched the side of the boat. His head was down, looking at his feet, as if he needed to know where they were. "I want..." He didn't finish the sentence, just laughed and threw his head back. That's when he saw her.

A big smile came on his face. "Hey, you! Come here." He gestured with his hand and waved her closer. "Come on, I won't bite."

Tansy didn't move. That's why he came to her, which was a bad idea, because he banged into the table and knocked a chair over before he bumped into her. She tried to steady them both, but he swayed the other way and they ended up sprawled on the bunk.

"Whoa, nelly!" he laughed.

She sat back up and he struggled to sit up with her, his arm finding its way around her.

"Hey there, Tansy," he slurred. "I gotta ask you somethin'. Why don't you talk to me anymore, huh?"

"I talk to you."

"No, you don't. You turn up that pretty little nose whenever I come in the room."

"I'm surprised you noticed. I thought you only had eyes for Bay."

He grinned. "My Bay-by. Get it? Baby. She's beautiful, isn't she? I can't believe she's gonna marry me. How lucky can a guy get?"

"Did you ever like me, even a little?"

He looked hurt, and put his hand up to her face. "Hey now, I always liked you."

"Do you like me now? Right this very minute?"

"Sure I do. Hell, every guy I know wants you."

"But I only want you."

Tansy turned and straddled him as he sat on the edge of the bunk. "Kiss me once. Just once." She didn't wait for an answer, as she found his mouth and kissed him with her whole heart and soul. It went on and on until he groaned, reached for her head, and pulled her away from him.

"Wait now, I don't think this is right."

"Why not?" She kissed him again and rubbed herself against him. "This feels right to me. We're alone and no one will know. I'll never breathe a word to a living soul." When she kissed him again it took him even longer to pull away.

"I love you, Bobby. And I know you love me just a little. You did things to me that told me you did, but you never finished it and I need you to finish it. I'm going away and I'm never coming back. I need you to make love to me once before I go. Give me something to remember."

She moved against him as she waited, breathless, her mouth open.

"Oh God, Tansy…"

"You're getting married. You'll never be with another girl again. You wanted me once. I know you did. And now I'm here."

He kissed her as he pulled her down onto the bunk.

They didn't talk after that.

When it was over, he turned away from her. She lay on the bunk, her chest heaving. He staggered forward and had to reach out to keep from falling over. He kept his back to her as he did up his jeans. Then he turned around and wiped his mouth on his sleeve. "What are you doing here? Why are you with me?"

"I wanted to say goodbye."

"You said it, now *go*."

Tansy got up off the bunk and had to walk by him. He turned away when she did. She was almost at the door when she heard a sob escape his lips. "What have I done?"

"I'm sorry." She opened the door.

"Tansy, stop!"

She stayed still.

"Look at me."

Tansy raised her eyes.

"You can't tell her. Please…"

"I won't."

"Promise me?"

"I promise." She bolted out the door.

Liz's friend Joan was the last to leave the shower. She'd walked over and Liz wouldn't hear of her walking back in the dark, so she threw on a sweater and drove her home. She was returning to the house when the car headlights caught someone walking away from the wharf. Liz had to look twice because she thought she was seeing things. But there was no mistake.

It was Tansy.

Liz lay awake all night, listening to Jack snore.

CHAPTER SEVENTEEN

The wedding was beautiful, as weddings always are. They were married in the local United Church and the reception was in the church hall. It wasn't a big wedding, as the groom only had a few relatives. His friends took up a couple of pews, but that was it. That's why Bay didn't invite as many as she could have. She told everyone she wanted a small and intimate affair.

The morning passed by in a blur. There was the frantic rush to the hairdresser's, followed by Bay's meltdown when she got home. She declared she hated her hair and Bobby wouldn't recognize her, it was that ridiculous, so back in the shower she went and all that money for the up-do went down the drain.

Between them, Gertie and Tansy were able to fix up her hair with hot rollers, a lot of hairspray, and a few bobby pins. Someone had plugged in a curling iron thinking they might need it and someone else unknowingly brushed it off the dressing table. When Tansy stepped on it and screamed "Fuck!" her parents forgave her; it was a nasty burn. Her mother bound up her foot in bandages, which meant the shoes she was supposed to wear with her mauve gown didn't fit. In the end they found a pair of ballet-type slippers for her to wear, which was the best they could do because they were late as it was.

Gertie grabbed the bouquets and ran out of the bedroom, just as their mom flew by looking for her purse. Their dad hollered up from the stairwell that the car taking them to the church had arrived.

Bay looked around the room as if she'd forgotten something while Tansy grabbed a shawl and the dry-cleaning bag that contained Bay's going-away outfit. They happened to see each other in the mirror at the same moment.

"Can you believe I'm standing here in my wedding dress?" Bay laughed. "Remember the times we played dress-up and imagined this day?"

"You look beautiful."

Bay held out her arms. Tansy dropped the things on the bed and hobbled over to her. They put their arms around each other and held on tight.

"I'm going to miss you so much," Bay whispered. "I'm going to miss my room and I'm even going to miss you flushing the toilet when I'm in the shower."

"I'm going to miss you too," Tansy whispered back. "But you and Bobby belong together and I'm glad he makes you happy. I love you."

"I love you too."

They parted and wiped their eyes, laughing a little.

They heard their father's voice shout, "Get the Jesus down here, will ya?" then grumbling, "Girls. What the hell takes so long?" and their mother saying, "Now Jack..."

❀

Tansy and Bobby didn't look at each other. Not once. As she limped her way down the aisle behind Gertie and ahead of Bay and her father, her only goals were to pretend she wasn't limping and that Bobby wasn't there. She looked at the stained-glass window above the minister's head and once she was up at the altar, she turned and stared at the back of Bay's veil.

She didn't hear their vows. The only thing she heard was the sound of her own heartbeat. After what seemed like an eternity, her sister and new brother-in-law kissed each other, turned to face their guests, and proceeded to walk back down the aisle. She automatically took the best man's arm and limped behind them.

No one noticed that they didn't speak to each other. There was no receiving line, which was an enormous relief, and because of her foot Tansy was able to sit on a chair and didn't have to mingle or dance. When people came up to commiserate with her plight she'd say, "I know. Can you believe it? What a stupid thing to do."

It all became a little too much after a while, so she told her dad that her foot was throbbing and she needed to go home. He told her she was a real champ for sticking it out as long as she did and he was proud of her.

Before he helped her out of the hall, her mother came over and kissed her, and then Bay rushed to her side. "Wait a second. I'll tell Bobby you're leaving."

"No, don't bother. I'll see you guys in a week. Have fun in PEI."

"No, he'd want to know. Just a sec."

Tansy tried to stop her, but Bay hurried over to Bobby. "Tansy has to leave."

"Does she?"

"Come and say goodbye." She took him by the hand and brought him over to her sister. "Thanks again for everything, Tansy. You're the world's best sister." Bay hugged her and then smiled encouragingly at Bobby.

Bobby nodded and gave her the briefest of hugs. "Yeah, thanks, Tansy. Hope your foot feels better."

As Tansy left on her father's arm, Bay was upset. "I can't believe she's not sharing this entire night with us."

"I know."

"Why did it have to happen?"

Bobby's distress was evident. "Bay, please don't be sad. It's our wedding day."

She smiled and put her arms around his waist. "I'm sorry. I know how lucky I am."

❁

Tansy's father drove her home and helped her into the house and up to her room. He insisted on removing the bandages to take a look at the wound, whereupon he tsked and said she was going to the doctor in the morning to have that looked at. He wrapped it up again and asked if there was anything else she needed. She said she was fine.

He put his hand on her shoulder, leaned over, and kissed her cheek. "I love you, Jack Junior."

"I love you too, Daddy."

He closed the bedroom door and Tansy took the quilt from the end of her bed and wrapped herself up in it. Then she cried herself to sleep.

❁

It was like playing house. Bay kept their little apartment as clean as a whistle, but she never minded when Bobby came home from the boat, stinking of fish and sweat. He'd shuck off his big work boots and outer gear and leave them on the floor in the small porch, before he'd go to the kitchen sink and wash his hands and face, always drying himself off with one of her brand-new dishtowels instead of the old towel she wanted him to use.

Then he'd grab her around the waist from behind and pick her up off her feet. He'd walk into the bedroom with her kicking and trying to pry his big arms off her. She always protested because she was inevitably in the middle of something, but he wouldn't listen when she said she was too busy to be loving him in the afternoon and why didn't he wait until bedtime like any other normal person.

Bobby would throw her on the bed and shut her up with one of his fabulous kisses and when their lovemaking was over, she was the one who grabbed his arm and asked him where he thought he was going when he'd try to get out of bed. His answer was always, "Nowhere, I guess," before he'd jump back on top of her and tickle her or put his mouth on her neck and blow so hard it made funny noises until she'd pound his back to make him stop.

On the July first weekend Bay told the whole family that she wanted them to come over to their apartment to celebrate Canada Day. Bobby wanted to christen their new barbeque, and she had her menu planned down to the last detail. The table was set for three hours before anyone arrived. Gertie came first, holding a bottle of wine and a little gift, which turned out to be a package of four new dishtowels.

"I hear there isn't a dishtowel in Louisbourg that's safe from your grubby mitts," she laughed at Bobby.

"Hey, you." He grabbed Gertie around the neck and gave her a noogie.

Her parents arrived with a case of beer and a big Tupperware container.

"Mom, I told you I was making everything."

"I brought along a few goodies. You don't have to eat them."

"Are you nuts?" Bobby shouted. "Give me that." He grabbed the container out of Liz's hand and planted a big kiss on his mother-in-law's cheek, which pleased her no end.

"Where's Tansy?" Bay asked.

"She wasn't feeling well. I think she's coming down with something."

"Oh, that's too bad." Bay was disappointed. "She's going to miss my first family dinner."

Bobby looked away.

Her father put his arm around her. "Don't worry, my love. You have your whole life ahead of you making dinners for this bunch. Now, who wants a beer?"

Later that night as they were getting ready for bed, Bay came out of the bathroom with her toothbrush still in her mouth. She removed it long enough to say, "Is it my imagination or does Tansy not want to be around us?"

Bobby was in his pyjama bottoms lying on his side of the bed, reading a book. He laid it down on the mattress. "What do you mean?"

Bay sat on the bed. "I mean that I never see her anymore."

"Well, we're married. It's different now."

"Why should it be different? She only lives a few minutes away. I miss her."

Bay got up and went back into the bathroom. She rinsed her mouth out with water and spat in the sink. After turning off the bathroom light, she crawled into bed beside Bobby. He moved the book aside and put his arms around her.

"When we were little, Tansy and I used to pretend that our fort down in the woods behind the house was a castle. I loved playing with her. She made everything seem magic, even though she was always the princess and I was always the humble servant."

"That doesn't seem fair."

"I didn't mind. I never wanted to be the princess. Tansy was always wailing in the tower about how the prince would never find her. It was more fun to be down in the dirt, pretending to make a magic potion in one of the old pots Mom let us use."

Bobby didn't say anything.

"And whenever we played together Tansy would think of the most outrageous stuff, like the time she put string nooses around our Barbie and Ken dolls and hung them on Flo's clothesline. You should've heard Flo screech. She got in trouble for that one."

"Did she?"

"Yes, but Tansy didn't mean any harm. She's got this wonderful imagination. I've always wanted to be like her. I'm so glad she's my sister. I just wish I could spend more time with her."

Bobby hugged her tight and kissed the top of her head before whispering, "I'm sorry."

She put her hand on his cheek. "Silly boy, it's not your fault."

"I love you so much, Bay," his voice cracked. "You're the sweetest girl in the world."

Bay looked at him. "What's wrong?"

"I'm just…"

"What?"

"Don't ever leave me, Bay. Don't ever leave me."

"I'd never leave you. You're my heart."

She kissed him then and everything was all right.

It was the last day of lobster season, July fifteenth, and as luck would have it, it was a miserable day, with high winds and a big sea. The race was on to get as many traps as possible out of the water before the deadline. The fishermen of Louisbourg had been hard at it since four in the morning and by late afternoon they were weary, but all pushed themselves, knowing that the season was almost over. It had been a good one, with prices that were pretty decent. It had been worth the effort.

Bay was over at her mother's to use her sewing machine. She wanted to repair a couple of Bobby's overalls, but the seams were so thick she had a hard time manoeuvring them underneath the sewing needle.

Tansy was upstairs in her room, sleeping. That was all she did these days. Liz was sure she had mono but so far Tansy had refused to go to a doctor. She said they couldn't do anything about mono anyway so there was no point.

Bay gave up on the sewing machine and decided it would be easier to fix the overalls by hand. She grabbed the sewing basket and went out into the kitchen. Her mother stood by the window looking out. She held her arms, as if she was cold. She was so still it spooked Bay for a moment.

"What's wrong?"

"I don't know. I have a funny feeling."

"What do you mean?"

Liz went to the back door and pushed it open. She walked by the garden and over to the edge of the field. She stopped then and stared out at the water, as if she were searching for someone. Bay's mouth went dry. She ran outside and hurried over to her mother.

"You're making me nervous."

Her mother didn't answer.

Flo ran out of her house. "Liz!"

Liz turned around.

"There's something on the scanner. Men saying something's happened out on the water. Now it's probably nothing, but they mentioned *Tansy Bay.*"

Liz began to run.

"Mommy, what is it? What's happened?"

Bay went after her mom but she couldn't catch her. Her mother ran down the street, her sweater flapping behind her. Bay stumbled as she tried to keep up. She had a hard time breathing. There was a sharp pain in her throat and she couldn't hear anything except a roaring in her ears.

There were other people running towards the wharf. Bay fell as she ran, but she didn't know she'd fallen. The blood on her scraped knees wasn't real, no more real than the people who shouted at her with no sound coming out of their mouths.

She couldn't see her mother anymore. She had to get to her mother. But two women tried to grab her and make her stop. She wrestled with them to let her go. Then two more tried to hold onto her, but Bay kicked her legs and tried to pry their hands from her body, just like she did with Bobby.

Bobby.

She broke free and ran and ran and ran. And then she stopped.

Her mother knelt over her father and Bobby was asleep beside them. Oh. That's good. Bobby's asleep. Then he won't have to be worried when he finds out that something's wrong with Dad.

There were people all around but this time they left her alone. They backed up when she walked over to her husband. She knelt on her bloody knees and touched his beautiful face. He was sleeping. He'd wake up and take her in his arms and smother her with kisses just like he had at three that morning.

And then there was nothing but sound.

People crying, screaming, and shouting. An ambulance siren. Men kneeling by her mother in tears.

"His boot got caught in the line and he went over the side. The young fella tried to save him. We almost got to them. We almost did. But they were tangled in the rope. There was nothin' we could do."

Bay looked up and saw Tansy standing on the wharf, Flo behind her.

They looked at each other.

That's when Tansy fainted.

CHAPTER EIGHTEEN

It was hot and dry that September.

When Bay took bouquets of wildflowers to Bobby's grave, she always took a plastic container of water with her and filled the vase to the brim, and every day she'd go back and the vase would be almost dry. It was hard to imagine that all that water evaporated in twenty-four hours, so she liked to think that maybe a rabbit or a deer stopped by and had a drink; sometimes the flowers looked like something had taken a few bites out of them. She knew Bobby would get a kick out of that. It made her feel better to know that a creature kept him company through the starry nights.

She divided her time between Bobby and her dad. She didn't like to give too much attention to one and not the other. She and her mother would go, but her mother never stayed as long as Bay needed to, so they agreed it would be best to visit their men alone.

Tansy never went.

Bay gave up the apartment, of course. Gertie was the one who saved her life on that score, doing most of the work herself. Every time Bay put something in a box, she'd tell Gertie the story behind it and inevitably break down and cry when she closed the lid.

She gave Bobby's barbeque to his uncle. He objected at first, but Bay insisted. It would make her happy, she said. And it did; every time she drove by his uncle's place, she saw him sitting by the barbeque as he cooked his solitary meals.

Bay was back in her old bedroom, but it didn't feel the same. Although she'd only shared a double bed with Bobby for three months, it was long enough to feel as if she'd been amputated in some way when she lay down at night on her childhood bed.

Nothing felt right at home. It was quiet now, with none of the delicious aroma of Mom's cooking permeating every room. Their mom spent most of her time out on the garden swing looking out over the water. People were kind enough to make meals for them. There was always a casserole left on the kitchen table.

Most of the time they didn't eat together. Mom sat in front of the TV in the living room holding a plate in her hand. Tansy was usually in her room with her small TV on. Bay spent a lot of meals with Gertie. They liked it when Gertie came over because she was the only one with enough energy to talk, and when she talked that meant the Gillis women didn't have to expend any energy talking themselves.

Mom's cousin called and asked if she and the girls would like to come and visit, to get away from everything for a while, but their mother declined. It was too much effort to put one foot in front of the other, let alone pack a suitcase and drive to Fredericton.

But Bay often wondered how they would fill every day for the rest of their lives. All she saw stretched in front of her was a vast yawning emptiness. At least she got to sit with Bobby every day. At least she had that.

❁

Even in the fog of misery that Liz lived in day after day, she slowly became aware that there was something wrong with Tansy, above and beyond the loss of her father and brother-in-law. Her good friend Joan confirmed it when she mentioned Tansy the day she brought over sweet-and-sour meatballs.

"I saw her at the drugstore and I nearly died. She looks terrible, Liz. She's like a stick and she was bundled up as if she was freezing to death. I don't care what she says. You should take her to a doctor, because mono is nothing to sneeze at. It can affect your spleen, you know."

Liz thanked her. When Joan left, Liz walked upstairs and knocked on Tansy's door. There was no answer. She was sure she was in there. "Tansy?"

She heard a muffled "What?"

Liz opened the door and saw that she was napping. She walked over and sat on Tansy's bed. Joan was right, the child looked ill.

"Tansy, this isn't right. You're spending your whole life in this bed."

Tansy didn't answer her.

"You're seeing a doctor."

Liz reached out and felt her forehead and her glands. "I'll get to the bottom of this."

When she left, Tansy curled up in a fetal position. There was nothing she could do about it now. It was over.

❈

Because their regular doctor was on vacation, Liz took Tansy to an evening clinic. They sat and waited for almost two hours. Tansy didn't say a word the entire time. It was as if she'd left and only her body sat beside her mother.

The doctor called Tansy in. Now there was nothing for Liz to do but sit and worry. She was in there for a half an hour, at which point Liz became concerned. It got worse when the nurse came out and said the doctor wanted to see her. Liz hurried into his office. Tansy sat on the examination table wearing a paper gown.

"Are you all right, honey? Is there something wrong?"

Liz turned to the doctor. He took off his glasses. "First, may I say I'm sorry for your loss, Mrs. Gillis. Tansy told me about your situation."

"Thank you."

"Grieving can bring on a lot of symptoms. Excessive sleeping is one of them. Being depressed is another. Not eating is also common. Tansy is underweight and I'm concerned about that, given her condition."

"Condition?"

"Her pregnancy."

Liz wasn't sure she'd heard correctly. "Her pregnancy?"

"Yes. I've examined her and she's four months along. So far everything looks all right, but for this baby to thrive, we need to start taking better care of the mother."

The doctor continued to talk as he took out his prescription pad and wrote out a list of prenatal vitamins and a protein supplement. He suggested she see her family physician on a regular basis and have an ultrasound done to make sure everything was as it should be.

"But the best medicine for Tansy is her mother's TLC," he smiled as he passed Liz the prescriptions.

"Of course." Liz was aware of Tansy's big eyes watching every move she made. She folded the paper and put it in her purse. "Thank you, doctor. I appreciate you seeing us. Tansy, I'll wait in the car."

Liz didn't remember her walk to the car. She didn't remember Tansy walking to the car either. When she got in, however, she remembered saying, "Don't say a word."

After that was a silence so profound it made Liz's ears ache.

When they got home, Liz got out of the car and went into the house. She walked upstairs and looked in Bay's bedroom. She wasn't there. No doubt she was at the cemetery. Liz removed her jacket and laid it on her bed. She waited for Tansy's footsteps on the stairs. Once she heard Tansy close her bedroom door, she walked across the hall and opened it.

Tansy turned around and looked at her.

Liz took two steps forward and slapped her across the face as hard as she could. Tansy stood there and took it. She slapped her again. Tansy didn't move. She slapped her a third time and still Tansy stayed motionless, never taking her eyes off her mother.

"How do you know?" Tansy whispered.

"I saw you that night. I didn't know what it meant, but I saw you."

Tansy looked at the floor.

"I can't believe it. You and Bobby? How could he? How could you? How long was it going on?"

"It was only that one time!"

"And I'm supposed to believe that?"

"It's true! Only that one time!"

"Oh my God. Why?!"

"I loved him! I loved him!"

"Bay loved him! He was supposed to be in love with her."

"He was! He didn't want me. He never wanted me."

"Apparently he did that night!"

"I'm sorry."

Liz couldn't contain her anguish. "Sorry? You're *sorry*?! Do you have any idea what you've done?"

"Yes."

"You've stolen your sister's child!"

Tansy broke down then. She fell to the floor and wailed in a voice so full of despair that her mother started to cry. Tansy keened back and forth as she asked for forgiveness, not seeing her mother, not seeing anything, and when she started to whimper, Liz got down on her hands and knees with her and took her in her arms. She shushed her like a baby and rocked her back and forth, back and forth.

"It's all right, I'm here, Tansy. I'm with you. I won't let anything happen to you. I'll think of something. Don't worry, I'll think of something."

❀

It was almost a week later when Liz asked both her daughters to come down to the kitchen. She made sugar cookies, the first time she'd baked anything. The lovely smell in the kitchen made it feel like home again, if only for a moment.

She poured them all a cup of tea and passed them a cookie. Bay took one. Tansy didn't.

Liz cleared her throat. "Girls, we have something very serious to discuss. It affects all of us."

"Is this about Dad's will?" Bay asked.

"No. I don't want you to worry about finances, your father left us in good shape."

"Okay." Bay sipped her tea.

Liz took a deep breath. "I know this is going to come as a shock, Bay, but your sister is pregnant."

Bay slowly put her mug down. She looked over at Tansy, who stared at her hands. "What?"

Liz answered. "She's four months pregnant, and that's why she hasn't been feeling well."

Bay kept looking at her sister. "Why didn't you tell me?"

For the first time, Tansy raised her eyes. "You had enough to worry about."

"But…I didn't know you were seeing someone. Who is it? Who's the father?"

There was a long moment of silence.

"I don't know."

Bay glanced at her mother.

"It's obviously a painful situation," Liz continued, "and Tansy and I have discussed it endlessly. She's obviously too far along to do anything about it…"

"You would have had an abortion?"

"I didn't, did I?"

"Bay, be quiet for a minute. What we're trying to tell you is that Tansy doesn't want the baby. She's much too young to be saddled with that kind of responsibility, and you know how much she's always wanted to travel and get away from here…"

"You want to give the baby up for adoption?" Bay grabbed her sister's arm. "Are you sure? That might be too hard."

"Everything is hard!" Tansy shouted.

"Tansy." It was her mother's command to stay quiet.

"Adoption is one solution," Liz started again, "but there's another option and we wanted your opinion."

Bay was confused. "What?"

"I talked to Norma in Fredericton and she's offered us a place to stay for as long as we like. If you think this is a good idea, we could go there and stay until the baby is born, and then come back home and tell everyone the baby is yours."

"That the baby is Bobby's?"

Liz cleared her throat. "Yes. We'll tell people that you were pregnant when he died and only found out after he was gone."

"But why would I stay in Fredericton to have the baby?"

"It was too painful to be here. You couldn't handle it."

Bay put her hand through her hair, trying to make sense out of a senseless situation. "But what about Gertie? She'd know."

"You can tell her you're pregnant over the phone. She won't think anything's amiss. She'll be happy for you. Everyone will be happy for you."

"But what about Tansy?" Bay looked at her sister. "How are you going to cope with me bringing up your child? How would it work?"

"She'd be the child's doting aunt, wouldn't she?" Liz explained.

"I'm asking *her*, Mom." Again, Bay put her hand on Tansy's arm. "Do you understand how hard this would be for you? I'm not sure you've thought this through."

Tansy frowned. "It's better than giving the baby away to someone I don't know."

Bay sat back in her chair, her tea forgotten. "I don't know what to say. This is all so..."

"I'm not asking you for an answer right this minute," her mother said. "You have to think it over. It's a huge decision, one that affects all of us."

"Do you really think we'd get away with it?" Bay asked. "That this is the right solution?"

Liz stood up from the table, her nerves frayed. "Bay, you're asking me questions I can't answer. I can only think so far ahead. We're in this terrible mess and I honestly don't know what else to do. I wish to God your father was here to help me, but he's not. I'm doing the best I can, and maybe this is wrong and I'm making it worse, but I don't know anymore. I really don't."

Liz walked away from the table and went out the door. Her daughters watched as she went out to her swing. She looked so alone out there by herself, so small and vulnerable. Bay wanted to protect her from harm, as if Bay were the mother.

The mother.

Bay had to ask. "Are you sure you don't know who the father is? Or are you just not telling Mom?"

"You think I wanted to tell Mom that I don't know who the father is? That it could have been any of two or three boys?"

"Oh, Tansy."

"Don't feel sorry for me. I couldn't bear that."

"I do feel sorry for you, but I'm also angry that you were so stupid."

Bay left her chair and went over to the sink. She leaned against it and looked out the window at the water beyond. "You don't want this baby?"

"No," Tansy lied.

❁

Bay sat on the grass by Bobby's grave. She had to talk it over with him. It was a beautiful day, with big white clouds crossing the blue sky. Every so often a cloud would cover up the sun and the warmth would disappear for a moment, but it always returned. Bay heard the birds in the trees and watched a squirrel scamper up a nearby tree, scolding her as it went. She absent-mindedly picked a nearby daisy and started to pull the petals.

"The thing is, the minute they said it I knew I wanted to do it. Deep in my heart I wanted it. The thought of carrying a baby around and telling everyone it's yours filled me with happiness, something I never thought I'd have again. But then my head kicked in and I thought of a million reasons why I shouldn't, not least of which is that Tansy might change her mind, and where would that leave me? I feel sorry for Mom. She looks terrible. I could choke Tansy for doing this to her. You know how proud Mom is. She'd hate the gossip of Tansy being an unwed mother, but doing it to save the Flos of the world from talking about us is not a good enough reason."

Bay looked at Bobby's name carved in granite. "It would also mean I'd have to leave you for five months, which is the hardest thing of all. But I know Dad's here with you, which makes me feel better. What do you think I should do?"

Bay pulled out the petals one at a time. "Yes. No. Yes. No. Yes. No."

"Yes."

She kissed the ground in front of his stone. "I love you, Bobby. I'll be able to bring the baby to come and visit you. Then it won't be so lonely here."

❊

Gertie was there to wave them off. So were Joan and a few other friends of their mother. They promised to keep an eye on things. Joan said her husband would make sure the furnace was checked and he'd put up the storm windows when the weather got colder. Flo said she and Ira would dig up the potatoes and put them down in the basement. She'd also pick the pumpkins, cut them up, and freeze them.

Gertie made a huge picnic lunch for the trip. The car was packed to the rafters. There were a lot of hugs and kisses.

Joan held onto Liz. "You're doing the right thing. I think you and the girls need to get away for a while. Not that we won't miss you, but sometimes a change of scene helps."

"Thank you for everything. I'll miss you."

Gertie tried to put on a brave face when she hugged Bay. "Don't worry. I'll visit Bobby every chance I get."

"Thanks, Gertie. You're the best."

"Well, hurry up and go, so you can hurry up and get back."

Finally they were in the car. Bay was the driver, with her mother in the front seat and Tansy in the back with the huge hamper of food. Everyone waved and Bay honked the horn as they pulled out of the driveway and headed down the road.

When they arrived at Norma's, she did everything possible to make them comfortable. She was a single woman who lived in a lovely old Victorian home and had more than enough room for them. She'd been a music teacher all her life and still gave piano lessons to children after school.

Norma moved Liz into the cozy front bedroom and got the girls settled in the large bedroom at the back of the house that overlooked the garden. A big turkey dinner waited for them that first night and after they had their fill, Norma told the girls that their mother had explained the situation and she wanted them to know that if this was their decision, she'd take the secret to her grave. She was in their corner.

It was such an enormous relief to have someone else know what they were doing and why. They agreed coming to Fredericton was the best thing that could have happened.

Three days later, they made their phone calls back home.

"I can't believe it," Gertie sobbed. "This is a blessing. Bobby's child! Oh, Bay, I can't tell you how happy I am. I'm thrilled for you."

When Bay didn't say anything, Gertie stopped gushing. "You are happy, aren't you?"

"Of course I'm happy," she whispered. "I just miss him."

"Oh dear, of course you do. Don't worry, Bay. We'll get through it together. We'll all help."

"Thanks, Gertie."

"Did you know you were pregnant when you were here? Of course, you must have. I can't believe you kept it a secret."

"I didn't want to jinx anything, so I waited until the first three months were over. I needed to keep it to myself."

"Of course. So does this mean you'll come home sooner than you thought?"

"I've been thinking I may have the baby here."

"Oh?"

"It's hard. Everywhere I go at home, Bobby is there. I can only face it again when I have someone else to hold in my arms. Does that make sense?"

"Listen, Bay, you need to do whatever feels right. Whatever you decide, I'm a hundred percent behind you. Of course now I have to get to Fredericton. I can't imagine not seeing you preggers! Oh, this is so exciting."

Bay had to think fast. "Actually, Gertie, I have a big favour to ask you."

"Anything."

"Mom and I will send you the money. We need a nursery. Tansy said she'd move into my room with me, since my room is bigger, and her room can be the baby's room. I need you to dismantle Tansy's room and fix it up for the baby. You can paint or wallpaper, whatever you think is best. Buy all the baby equipment and have it ready for when we get home. I trust you to do a fabulous job, and you have five months to do it."

"Oh wow, I'd *love* to."

"You've lifted a huge weight off my shoulders, Gertie, as you always do. I'll never be able to repay you."

"Yes, you will. I expect you to name the baby Gertie."

They laughed. It felt good.

❈

Tansy's contractions started in the middle of the night. She lay in the dark and asked her baby to stay with her a while longer. The baby obliged until sunrise and then Tansy had no choice. She called to Bay, who immediately jumped up from a sound sleep and ran to her bedside. "Is it time?"

Tansy nodded. Bay ran out of the room calling for her mother.

They brought her to the hospital and the staff settled her in a room. The doctor came in and said she was four centimetres dilated, so she still had a long way to go. He said he'd be back later. Bay and her mother started to settle in. That's when Tansy spoke.

"I don't want you here."

They looked at each other and then at her.

"What do you mean?" Bay said. "We can't leave you alone. What if you need us?"

"I won't."

"You don't want me in the delivery room with you?"

"No."

"But—"

"I said no."

"Mom, tell her—"

"If that's what Tansy wants, we should respect that."

Her mother came over to her bed and put her hand on Tansy's head. "You're a brave girl. You're going to be fine. Your sister and I will be waiting for you. I love you very much." She kissed her cheek, squeezed her hand, and quickly left the room. Bay stood there a moment longer.

"Well, all right, then. If you're sure."

Tansy nodded.

Bay also went to her bedside and kissed her. "I love you. Stay safe."

When Bay left the room, Tansy put her hands on her belly. "It's okay now. We're alone."

She was in labour for over fifteen hours. Every time the nurses asked if she wanted something for the pain, she refused it. This was the last time she and her baby would be together and she wanted to feel every second of it. They couldn't know that contractions were nothing compared to the mental torture she'd been through the last nine months.

They asked if she wanted her family with her, but she'd shake her head no. She saw them look at each other with pity in their eyes. One of them told her it was all right to scream, but Tansy didn't make a sound. Her whole being was with her baby and she needed to be calm and not miss a moment of it.

On the delivery table they told her to push. She didn't want to. She tried not to, but that primal urge took over and she had to do it. She wanted to scream then.

When the doctor told her she had a daughter, everything receded into the background. The only thing she saw was her little girl. They put her on her chest and Tansy wrapped her arms around her. The baby opened her eyes and looked at her. She gave a little cry but settled when Tansy kissed her head.

If the doctor and nurses thought it strange that Tansy never said a word, she wasn't aware of it. She'd forgotten they were in the room.

She only had words for her daughter. She lifted her baby closer and held her lips up to her ear. "Mommy will always love you. Please remember that. Know that I wanted you. And know that I loved your daddy."

❀

When her mother and sister came into the room, Tansy's baby was tucked into the baby cart beside her bed. Tansy had her hand on her daughter's back, because she knew she couldn't hold her when Bay first saw her.

They immediately started to cry, her mother in particular. They gathered around the baby and made all those noises women make when a beautiful infant is within their grasp. Her mother came around the other side of the bed so she could put her arms around Tansy. She held her like that for a long time. There were no words.

And then Bay said, "May I hold her?"

Tansy nodded.

Bay picked up her niece and held her against her heart. "Hello, sweetheart. Oh, Tansy, she's utterly beautiful." Bay touched her cheek. "Did you pick a name?"

"Ashley Elizabeth."

Bay looked up and smiled. "Really? After me and Mom?"

Tansy nodded again.

"That's sweet," her mother said. "May I have a turn?"

She sat in the chair beside the bed and Bay put Ashley in her grandmother's arms. "Oh, girls, how I wish your dad could see her."

Tansy looked away.

Bay sat on the bed and held Tansy's hand. "Was it hard?"

"No."

"Is this hard?"

"Yes."

So hard, in fact, that when the time came for the Gillis women to go home to Louisbourg, Tansy told them she wasn't going back with them. Norma had a friend in Ottawa who could get her a sales job in a department store, and who'd agreed to let Tansy stay with her until she got on her feet.

It was a dreadful goodbye.

CHAPTER NINETEEN

1986

Three years later, Tansy lived in Toronto and had a roommate. She'd met Cecily when she worked in Ottawa and before too long they decided that Toronto would be a more exciting place to be. They ended up working at the Eaton Centre, Tansy at a high-end boutique and Cecily in the trenches at Reitman's. Their apartment was downtown, which always impressed people until they visited. It was awful, but since it was cheap and they were never home anyway, they didn't care.

Tansy liked Cecily because she was never serious about anything. Everything was a good time. They always laughed together, and at night when their shifts were over, they'd head down to one of their favourite dance clubs and stay there until closing time. It was great entertainment and it cost them nothing; they never bought their own drinks.

But they did try to look out for each other, especially after one night when Cecily went back to some guy's place after closing time, returning in the morning with a black eye and bruises all over her arms. She didn't want to talk about it.

Tansy didn't worry as much about that sort of thing. She tended to stay away from guys her own age. She'd gravitate towards the men in suits, the business types from the financial district who came down for a couple of drinks before they headed back to the suburbs and their wives.

That's how she got her first modelling gig. A man who'd chatted her up for weeks gave her the business card of a friend who was looking for girls. Tansy told him she wasn't stupid and didn't do porn. He said the guy was legitimate and it turned out he was. He got Tansy a lot of work over the years. She was always sorry she hadn't been nicer to the guy who gave her the card.

And then one night, after a shitty day at work, she found herself drunk and alone at the club. She couldn't find Cecily for some reason, and the two guys she was dancing with were too close for comfort. They constantly rubbed themselves up against her. She tried to leave the dance floor, but they boxed her in and she became frightened. She kneed the jerk in front of her and when he bent over in pain, she slipped away, but his friend caught up with her near the bathrooms. He pushed her into the men's room, took her by the throat, and shoved her up against the wall.

"Who do you think you are, hurting my friend like that?"

Tansy couldn't speak.

He knocked her head back one more time and squeezed her neck. "How would you like it if I hurt you?" He rammed his hand between her legs. "I can think of lots of ways to hurt you, bitch."

Tansy couldn't breathe.

The door opened and a couple of men came in. They quickly grabbed the guy and threw him to the floor, asking if she was okay. She nodded and ran out the door into the ladies room, only just reaching the toilet before she was sick.

She took a cab home and was treated to the spectacle of Cecily having sex with a stranger on their couch.

"Where were you?" Tansy cried.

Cecily was drunk. She didn't have the decency to be embarrassed. "Who are you, my mother?"

The guy thought that was a riot.

Tansy ran to her room and slammed the door. She didn't sleep all night, going over and over how it felt to have that man's hand around her neck. Any one of those men could snap it like a twig. What the hell was she doing, putting herself in that kind of danger?

She had the next day off, which was helpful because she was hungover and exhausted. Cecily didn't speak to her on her way out the door in the morning and Tansy didn't speak to her either. She took her coffee into her bedroom; she never wanted to sit on that damn couch again. As she sat in bed and looked out the window at the brick building next door, she wished she was a smoker. This was a scenario that called for at least a half a pack.

Tansy put the mug down on her bureau and saw the mail she'd brought in the day before but hadn't had a chance to look at. Picking it up, her heart skipped a beat when she tossed the power bill aside and saw her mother's handwriting. The envelope was thick. That meant there were pictures of Ashley inside.

There were times when she looked forward to gazing at her daughter's face. And there were other times when it damn near killed her. And this was one of those times. Did she really want to see Ashley on the swing with Bay? Eating an ice cream cone? Dressed up as a bunny for Halloween?

She debated whether she should open it. If she weren't so lonely, she would have put it aside for another day, but she found herself running her thumb under the flap of the envelope.

Ashley was three now. That adorable age. In the first picture she sat at the kitchen table on a booster seat in a pair of pyjamas with feet. She was obviously just out of the tub; her blonde curls were damp. She had a milk mustache on her upper lip and held a graham cracker in her hand. Mom or Bay must have told her to say cheese, because she had a silly grin that showed all her teeth. Her perfect little teeth.

In the next one she held her favourite toy duck. She'd carried that thing around ever since she could walk. With every picture the duck was flatter and flatter and sometimes it was dirty and sometimes it was clean. Her mother told her they washed it at night after Ashley was in bed so she wouldn't miss it.

But there was always one picture that tore her guts out. She was never sure why some pictures were so painful. There was no way to brace for it as she looked through them. The minute she saw the next one, she knew this was the one. Her mother had taken a photo of Bay and Ashley as they walked down the road. They must have been off to the store for milk, or maybe Bay was taking her to feed the ducks. They were a little too far away from the camera, so they looked like shadows on the sunny street. Bay held Ashley's hand and looked down at her as Ashley looked up.

A mother and daughter moment.

Tansy traced the picture. Because it was a shadow it was easy to imagine that it was her in the picture. It looked like her. And from that moment, it was. She took a safety pin and pinned the picture to the wall exactly at eye level, where she lay on her pillow. She'd be able to lie on her side and stare at it until she went to sleep. There was no point in looking at the other photos. They could wait. But she did open her mother's letter, and was sorry she did.

> Dear Tansy,
>
> How are you, honey? I haven't heard from you in a while. I know you're busy but if you could call a little more often I'd appreciate it. Whenever I call your apartment you're not there. I hope that means you're having fun in the big city…but not too much fun!
>
> As you can see, Ashley is doing well. She bumped her head last week on the pantry door so she had a bit of a bruise, but she's fine now. She was very excited the other day when Gertie came over with finger puppets she'd made for her. She pranced around all morning with them on and cried when she had to take them off to eat her lunch.
>
> We have some news. Bay got a job at the post office. It's only part-time, but you never know where it might lead. Bev Murrant isn't getting any younger and once she retires there will be an opening, unless they give it to someone with more seniority who works somewhere else, but we'll keep our fingers crossed.
>
> I'm feeling good, although I had to go on blood pressure medication. But it's nothing to worry about.
>
> The reason I'm writing is your sister. Bay's been down lately and I know it's because she's missing you. She never says anything, because she knows how hard it must be for you to see her with Ashley, even in the pictures we send. She understands the reasons you stay away, but I know she never thought you'd stay away for years at a time. And quite frankly, I didn't think that would happen either.
>
> When we decided to do this, I assumed you'd be here more often. Obviously young people go away to get jobs, especially around here, but they do come home for holidays and family occasions and I thought that's the way it would work for us. We're such a little family now. When you didn't come home for Christmas last year, there was a real sense of loss. And if I'm being perfectly honest, people are starting to talk. Even Gertie asked me the other day when you'd be home to see your niece.

I'm not trying to make you feel guilty, dear. I just wanted you to know how it is. I was hoping that maybe you'd consider coming home this Christmas. I've enclosed a cheque for you to buy a plane ticket, and I've given you a little extra. It's not a bribe! I spend money on your sister and the baby and I miss spending money on you. I worry that you need money but you're too proud to tell me. You know your father wouldn't want to see you without, and in three years you've never asked me for anything, so please take this and sock it away in case you ever need it.

I love you, Tansy. And I miss you. We all do.

Mom xoxox

Tansy pulled out the cheque. It was for ten thousand dollars.

"Oh, Mom, what have you done?"

❁

She didn't tell them she was coming home for Christmas.

When she called her mom to thank her for the money, her mother never mentioned Christmas, and Tansy didn't bring it up either, because then it would seem like a bribe. When Bay got on the phone she was cheerful. A little too cheerful. She asked about Toronto and Tansy asked about the new job. They talked a little bit about Ashley, but not much. Tansy liked to hear about her daughter from her mother, that way it was not as personal. Bay must have sensed that, and she never said more than she had to.

Tansy decided that if she had to do this thing, she would fly in the day before. The days leading up to Christmas had always been her favourite time of the holidays. She didn't want to be around for the baking and wrapping and decorating. She'd arrive in the afternoon and they could go to the Christmas Eve church service so everyone in town would see that they were a "normal" family that did get together for the holidays. Then surely a three-year-old would go to bed early. Christmas morning would be a blur. She'd be able to choke down Christmas dinner and stay for one more day to make it seem like she really wanted to be there, but then use the excuse that she had to get back to work. That was as much as she would do. If her mother wanted more than that, she'd have to slit her wrists.

And that was exactly what Tansy wanted to do when she realized she'd have to buy Christmas presents for her daughter instead of sending gift certificates.

❀

The taxi pulled up to the house around two in the afternoon. She'd forgotten how pretty the house looked when it snowed. Like a gingerbread house. Her mother had her favourite wreath on the door and single battery-operated candles in all the windows. There were no Christmas lights on the spruce tree in the front yard. Dad always did that, and either her mother didn't want to get up on a ladder or she didn't have the heart to do it.

Tansy had one small suitcase and a carryall. She paid the driver and walked to the back door. Should she knock? That seemed silly, so she took a deep breath and walked in.

Her childhood hit her in the face. The smell of shortbreads and mincemeat tarts and gingerbread were mixed in with the scent of evergreen and cedar, cinnamon and apple cider.

She almost turned around and walked out. She couldn't do this.

And then she saw Ashley.

Her daughter ran into the kitchen wearing a red velvet dress with a white Peter Pan collar, tied in the back with a big bow. She had on white tights and black patent leather shoes and a green velvet ribbon around her head, keeping back her curls.

As soon as Ashley saw her, she stopped running and looked uncertain. Her hand immediately went to the back of her hair and twisted a curl around her finger.

"Hello."

Ashley didn't say anything.

"You're very pretty."

Bay stuck her head around the hall entrance as if afraid of what she'd see. The minute she laid eyes on Tansy her face lit up. She never said a word, simply ran into Tansy's arms. Tansy had to drop her bags to hug her back.

Ashley twisted around and yelled, "Nana!"

Mom came down the stairs and put her hand on her heart. "Oh, my girls."

It was nice.

Gertie came over when Bay called to say Tansy was home. And as usual, it was better when she was there because they were distracted from bigger issues. They did end up going to church and the only thing Tansy remembered afterwards was a buzz of voices in the vestibule all sounding delighted when they realized Tansy was in their midst. She almost laughed. Most of these people had talked behind her back her whole life, and here they were pretending to be as pleased as punch to see her.

Then she realized they were pleased for her mother and she didn't have anything to do with it.

Ashley was overtired and cranky by the time they got home. She cried and called out for her mommy. Bay almost hesitated before she picked her up. She asked Tansy if she wanted to help put her to bed, or read Ashley *The Night Before Christmas*. Tansy said no.

The worst moment of the day was when the three of them sat together and placed gifts under the Christmas tree. To keep from talking about anything important, they reminisced about Christmases past, but that's a dangerous thing to do when emotions are raw. Mom got teary as she talked about Dad and Bay wept when she remembered it was four years ago tonight that Bobby had asked her to marry him. Tansy made damn sure she didn't cry about anything.

Tansy didn't sleep. She told them she was tired and went to bed, but was still awake when she heard her sister's deep, even breathing and her mother's occasional snore from her bedroom.

She got up and went out into the hall. Ashley's door was almost closed, but not quite. Trying not to make any noise, she slowly opened the door and hoped it wouldn't squeak. She crept over to the baby bed Ashley now slept in. It was disappointing. Tansy had expected a crib and felt cheated somehow.

A nightlight gave the room a glow and provided enough light for Tansy to see Ashley sleeping. She knelt by the bed so she could get closer. What a perfect little face. She wondered if Bay noticed how much like Bobby she was. But of course Bay wasn't looking for any of his features and so obviously didn't notice how they had the same shaped eyebrows and bottom lip. Her hairline was the same, too, and the shape of her ear. Tansy wanted to touch her, but she didn't dare wake her up. It was enough to look at that angelic face and know that Bobby lived in her.

She didn't see Bay watching her from the doorway.

In the morning, Tansy pretended Ashley was anyone's little girl. It was the only way she could get through it. Fortunately, a three-year-old is entertaining around Christmas presents, so there was a lot of laughter as she opened her gifts. Ashley insisted on sticking the gift bows on her nightgown and soon she was covered from head to toe. That provided more fun than anything, until she got the rocking horse from her nana.

It gave Tansy a small stab of satisfaction when Ashley spent more time looking at the picture books she'd bought than with the doll Bay gave her. But she wasn't prepared when Ashley came over with a book and plunked herself on Tansy's lap while she sat cross-legged on the floor.

"Read."

They went through the storybook, but the entire time Tansy was only aware of the smell of Ashley's hair and how delightfully solid she felt in her arms. She'd imagined little girls were light and airy when you picked them up. But Ashley took up space. Tansy felt her legs get tired with the weight of her when Ashley insisted on her reading the book again.

Tansy looked up at one point and noticed that both her mother and sister had left the room. Whether that was for their benefit or hers, she didn't know.

She tried to pay attention to every detail of how this felt so that when she left she could replay this moment over and over. At one point she bent down and laid her cheek on the top of Ashley's head.

Ashley wiggled and brushed her away with her hand. "Don't."

That was a thrill. Ashley was a person, not a doll. It was nice to know that her daughter liked what she liked and knew what she didn't. Good for her. She had her mother's spunk.

Christmas dinner also turned out to be a complete surprise. Tansy imagined she wouldn't be able to eat, but she ate non-stop. She hadn't tasted her mother's cooking for a long time and that was a hole that needed filling. Her mom was delighted to see her shovel it in.

"You're too thin," Mom said. "Do you ever cook a decent meal for yourself?"

"What do you think?" she said with her mouth full.

Mom tsked. "You have to promise me that you'll take better care of yourself."

"I promise."

"I don't believe you."

"You shouldn't."

"Oh, you!"

Ashley fell asleep at the table, with her messy bib still on, her head over to one side, and a piece of cookie in her hand.

"She's exhausted," her nana said.

Bay got out of her chair. "I'll put her to bed."

"No. I will."

Bay and Mom looked at her.

"If you don't mind?"

They rushed to say they didn't mind at all, but it wouldn't have mattered because Tansy was going to do it anyway. She wanted that heaviness against her again. The last time she'd held her daughter in her arms Ashley had weighed six and a half pounds. Now there were three years of life stuffed into those dimpled cheeks and knees.

Tansy picked her up as if she'd been doing it all her life. Ashley's head fell against her shoulder and the bib covered with bits of mashed potato and gravy adhered to Tansy's silk blouse. Tansy took her time going upstairs and once she was in Ashley's room she stood and swayed back and forth, drinking in her little body as she hugged her tight. She hummed the song that her mother used to sing to her at bedtime. She hadn't thought of that song in twenty years, but instantly it appeared from the deep recesses of her mind. Is this what all mothers felt or was it just her? Had leaving Ashley behind caused this exquisite, torturous love? Was it magnified a hundredfold because they weren't together?

All Tansy knew as Ashley's heart beat against her own was that this little girl was meant to be and Tansy was her mother.

❖

The next day Mom asked if she was going to visit her father's grave. Tansy knew she was expected to. It was one thing not to visit a cemetery after a death because of profound grief. It was another to completely ignore the deceased for years.

Mom said she'd watch Ashley if Bay wanted to go too. Tansy was aware of what her mom was doing. She wanted her daughters to spend time alone together in the middle of nowhere. Did she think they'd scream and yell at each other, that they'd have "the talk"? The one that made it all better, made everyone behave as they should? The look on Bay's face suggested she'd rather not do it either, but a mother's gift for instilling guilt is a powerful thing and they both knew they had to obey.

Their mother happened to have a Christmas arrangement all ready to take up there. Of course she did. They put on their coats and boots and both of them turned around when Ashley yelled, "Bye, Mommy!" before she ran back into the living room to watch cartoons.

The cemetery was in a secluded spot, which was nice. There was nothing worse than trying to visit a loved one when the whole town could see you from the highway. They got out of the car and Bay led the way to their father's plot. Tansy kept her eyes averted from Bobby's grave a little further on.

Bay knelt and placed the artfully arranged bowl of cedar, evergreen, holly berries, and pine cones snug against the marker while Tansy watched. When she stood up she brushed the snow from her mitts.

"That looks nice," she said.

"Very. But wasn't Dad allergic to cedar?"

"Only if he touched it."

"Oh, that's all right, then."

They tried not to laugh because you're not supposed to crack up standing over people's graves, but the harder they tried, the worse it got, and when Bay snorted that did them in.

Bay put her arms around her sister. "Oh God, I've missed you. You have no idea how much."

"I've missed you too."

They looked at their father's grave with their arms around each other.

"I miss Dad," Tansy sighed, "even if he was an old crank most of the time."

"He wasn't cranky all the time."

Tansy laughed. "He was around me. No wonder. I wore him out with all my nonsense."

"Remember that time he hauled you out of the back seat of that car?"

"How can I forget? Whenever I walked down the street after that Donnie Murphy would run the other way."

"You were with Donnie that night? He was good looking."

They stopped talking. The silence was acute in this remote place. Their breath mingled in the cold air in front of them. Tansy waited for it.

"Tansy, I have to ask you something now that we're alone. Are you staying away from us because you resent me raising your daughter?"

Tansy looked away before she faced her sister. "It's hard, Bay. Everything is hard. I come back here and I see the mistakes I've made in my life. I was never truly happy here. I find it physically painful to look out at the water...the water that took Dad's life and Bobby's life."

"But you forget, Dad and Bobby loved being on the water. It was their home."

"I wish I could see it like that. Maybe someday I will, but not now."

"Tansy, I never would've gone along with this if I'd known I was going to lose you in the process."

Tansy took her hands. "Whether I stay or whether I go, you'll never lose me. My leaving wasn't your fault. Don't ever think that."

They spent a quiet evening together. It was subdued; the thought of saying goodbye in the morning was hard for them. Fortunately Ashley was in rare form and entertained them with her antics. She said she was a bumblebee and she wanted them to be the flowers. She buzzed all over the living room and flitted from one to the other, pretending to gather pollen. She laughed so much she had a hard time buzzing, and by the time she got to Tansy, she jumped in her lap, put her chubby little arms around her, and nuzzled into her neck.

Tansy put her arms around her, whereupon Ashley lifted her head, put her hands on Tansy's cheeks, and said, "I love you."

"And I love..." Tansy closed her eyes and whispered, "Take her. Take her."

Bay rushed over and lifted Ashley out of Tansy's arms. "Let's go get an animal cracker." She whisked her out of the room.

Tansy felt rather than saw her mother approach. "Don't. Leave me."

Her mother hesitated before doing what she asked. The minute she was gone Tansy ran upstairs and hid in the bathroom.

❀

Tansy knew what she had to do. She called a cab company when the other two were upstairs putting Ashley to bed and told them to wait at the end of the street at two in the morning. She made sure they knew to wait for her, as it might not be exactly two o'clock. They said they would.

Her bags were already packed in anticipation of tomorrow's flight. When Bay was in the tub and Mom was downstairs locking up, Tansy quickly went into Ashley's room and grabbed a few outfits and her snowsuit. She wouldn't be able to put it on her until she was in the cab. Her mom was walking up the stairs when she realized she needed the duck. It was by the bed. Tansy ran and grabbed it just in time to disappear into Bay's room before Mom got to the top of the stairs. She stuffed everything in the carryall she'd brought full of Christmas presents, now given away.

She and Bay said goodnight and talked a little in the dark, but finally fell silent. It was torture waiting. Was Bay really asleep or was she lying there worrying about tomorrow? At 1:45 she heard Bay talk in her sleep, like she did as a kid. She obviously never outgrew it.

Tansy took off her nightgown. She was dressed underneath; her wallet was in her pocket. She'd brought her boots up earlier and hidden them under the bed. Her coat was still downstairs, but she'd grab it on the way out and put that on in the cab too. At least Ashley slept like a log once she was asleep.

She picked up the two bags and slipped out of Bay's bedroom, leaving the luggage on the landing. Opening the door to Ashley's room ever so slowly, she tiptoed in and didn't hesitate. She picked her baby up in her arms and wrapped a small quilt around her body.

Then, holding Ashley with one arm, she grabbed the two bags with the other hand and ran downstairs as fast as she dared. She hurried down the hall into the kitchen.

The light came on when she was halfway across the kitchen floor.

The shock of it stopped her in her tracks. She blinked and out of the corner of her eye saw her mother sitting at the kitchen table, next to the light switch.

They stared at each other.

"Put her down."

"No."

"Put her down, Tansy. She's not yours."

"She *is* mine. She's mine."

"You gave away the right to have her when you agreed Bay would bring her up."

Ashley and the bags became unbearably heavy. She hitched her daughter up onto her shoulder a little higher. "I'm not letting her go."

"I'm not a stupid woman and neither are you. You knew Bobby was drunk and people are capable of doing anything when they're drunk. He's dead and I still want to wring his neck for being so weak-minded and foolish. But what's your excuse, Tansy? You were stone sober. You went down there deliberately to crawl into his bed and have him cheat on your sister."

"That's not true! I didn't want him to cheat on her. Bobby had feelings for me too."

"At seventeen a lot of girls mistake sex for love."

"I met him first. He was *mine* first."

"You sound like a child."

Tansy took a deep breath. "I'm not anymore. I'm a woman who has a child, and this child belongs to me."

"We were going to do this together and then you changed the rules."

"How did I know I'd go out of my mind without her?" Tansy hissed. "I didn't know what having a baby was. I didn't know you loved them so much that you'd die without them. No one told me that!"

Her mother stood. "That's why I did what I did! I went crazy trying to think of what would be fair to both my girls. You put me in an impossible situation, Tansy. This is your fault. You have to accept the consequences of your actions. If you're an adult then act like one."

Tansy had to put the bags down. It was easier to hold Ashley with two arms. "I've been acting out of guilt this entire time. But being with her, hearing her laugh, watching her play, has changed everything. I should've kept my mouth shut and denied she was Bobby's until I was blue in the face. Then she'd be with me and no one could take her away. But no, instead you made me feel like a criminal. You accused me of stealing my sister's child."

"And you did."

"And then she stole her right back! And what's worse, I agreed to it. Like a little robot I said go ahead, take her. Well, I don't agree with that anymore."

Tansy picked up her bags and left the kitchen. She almost made it to the back door when her mother grabbed her.

"If you love your daughter as much as you say you do, you'll give her to me. Not for my sake, or even your sister's, but for Ashley's. She's a little girl who's only known Bay as her mother. I'm her nana. She lives with us in this house. She plays with the little boy up the street. She likes to go to the corner store and buy popsicles. She has a life here. Can you imagine the horror of waking up in a cab being hustled onto a plane and flown two thousand miles from everything she's ever known? What kind of mother would do that?"

"You started this, Mom. I knew somewhere deep down inside that I couldn't handle seeing her in person and that's why I stayed away, but you couldn't leave it alone, could you? It was you who bribed me to come here, with your guilt and your money and your love!"

Her mother held her hand over her mouth, shaking her head.

"I'll never forgive you for this. I will never see you again. I will never come back here. I can't. I can't."

"No!"

Tansy put her mouth up to Ashley's ear and whispered, "Mommy will always love you. Please remember that. Know that I wanted you. And know that I loved your daddy."

Tansy pushed her daughter into her mother's arms and ran out of the house.

CHAPTER TWENTY

2000

By the time Tansy finished pouring her heart out, the tea was gone. Gertie drank the three mugs herself and finished off the bottle of brandy to boot. She wasn't sure if her colossal headache was from the confession or the booze. She had a feeling it was the confession.

There wasn't a lot to say. Well, there was, but where did she start?

Tansy still looked as if Gertie could blow her away with one breath, but she at least seemed more at peace. They sat together for a good ten minutes in total silence while Gertie gathered her thoughts.

At last Gertie spoke. "At least now I understand why you never came to visit. I couldn't wrap my head around that. I disliked you for a lot of years because of it. I saw what Bay went through without you and how much she missed you."

"You had every right to dislike me. My only consolation was that you were here for Bay. You've always been her other sister and I'll always love you for that."

"I'm the lucky one," Gertie smiled. "Your mom and sister and even you, with your swift kick, saved my life in more ways than one. I didn't have a close family like you guys, but from the day Bay took me home for cookies, it's like I never left this house. I owe that stupid Bradley kid a thank you."

A wave of exhaustion hit Gertie. She needed to go.

"Listen to me, Tansy. I want you to go upstairs and get some sleep. There's no need for you to talk to Bay at all tonight. I hope to God she's fallen asleep up there. I've told Ashley that when the time comes for her to leave the hospital she can come home with me. I think that would be best for all of you. She needs time to come to terms with this, but she also needs to stay calm for the baby, and I don't think her coming back here at this point would help any of you."

"No, you're right."

"I also don't want either of you to visit her in the hospital, for precisely the same reasons. It'll be hard but I have to insist. I saw the state of her and I think that's best. I'll visit her and let you know how she is. I want you to tell Bay that in the morning."

"Of course."

"Don't say anything to her about what you've told me tonight until I come over. It's going to be ugly. There's no way around it. But I think this wound has festered long enough, and the sooner the truth comes to light the better off we'll be. I'm here for both of you. I will help in any way I can. I promise."

Tansy whispered, "Thank you."

Gertie got up from the table, which wasn't an easy task. She was as stiff as a board and her head pounded. Tansy stood as well and they hugged each other before Tansy walked upstairs and Gertie let herself out.

Once she got in the car and sat for a minute, a thought occurred to her. "Aw, shit." She couldn't drive the car with all that booze in her system. So she struggled out of the front seat, took the old blanket she kept in the trunk, and wrapped it around her coat because it was flippin' freezing out. Then she proceeded to walk home in the dark.

Turned out it was the best thing she could've done. As she trudged along the streets of Louisbourg, she listened to the sounds of the town as it slept, the solitary swish of a car going by, a dog barking in the distance, and the foghorn as it pierced the night with its mournful cry. She thought of the people who were now her family. They had suffered such loss, each of them in their own way, and yet Gertie knew that they loved each other deeply. It was her job in the coming days and weeks to make sure they remembered that.

But she needed help.

Gertie was worn out by the time she reached home. Jeffrey was there by the door as he always was when he heard the key in the lock. When she picked him up and held him close, he licked her cheek with his rough tongue.

"Hey, buddy. I bet you're hungry."

She took him into the kitchen and cleaned out his water and food dish and replenished them both with fresh supplies. Then she walked into her bedroom and picked up the phone. She knew it was the middle of the night and that was the part that made her happy. Peter wouldn't mind. She lay back on her bed as the phone rang in her ear.

"Hello," a sleepy voice said.

"Hello."

"Hey, beautiful." She heard the smile in his voice.

"I'm sorry I woke you."

"No problem. You okay?"

"Yes and no."

"Anything I can do to help?"

"Pray for my family."

❁

When Bay awoke the next morning it felt like a normal day, but only for a moment. A ton of bricks quickly buried her alive as she lay there. She wondered how she'd get up, but then remembered that Ashley was lying in a hospital bed. Even though Ashley might not want to see her, Bay needed to be at the hospital.

When she went to take a shower she noticed Tansy's bedroom door was still closed. She wondered if she was sleeping. The hot water, as it pounded on her skin, reminded her that she was still alive but could do nothing about the numbness around her heart.

When she went downstairs she was surprised to see the kitchen table set. Tansy was at the stove and the smell of coffee filled the air.

"What are you doing?"

Tansy turned at the sound of her voice. "Hi. Would you like some oatmeal?"

"Oatmeal? I can't have oatmeal. I have to get to the hospital."

"No, you don't."

"Excuse me?"

Tansy pointed at a kitchen chair. "Sit."

"Why are you acting like Betty Crocker? Do you not remember what happened yesterday?"

"That's precisely why I think we need Mom with us this morning. Now sit."

Bay opened her mouth to argue, but Tansy gave her a look, so she sat. Then she put a bowl of oatmeal in front of her, gave her the brown sugar, and scooped a bowl of oatmeal for herself. She also poured them both a coffee. It was only when she sat down with the cream and picked up her spoon that she looked at Bay.

"Eat the whole bowl. Then I'll tell you what Gertie wants us to do."

They ate in silence. When they were done Tansy picked up both their bowls and took them to the sink.

"Now what are you doing?"

"Mom always told me to put some water in the bowls as soon as I was finished so it wouldn't stick. Makes it easier to wash up."

"Fine. Now will you tell me what Gertie said?"

Tansy sat back down. "She said we're both to stay away from Ashley until she tells us otherwise."

Bay's mouth dropped open. "What?"

"That's what she said. She insisted upon it."

"But…"

"Think about it. Ashley was in such a state because of us that she almost gave birth six weeks early. That's why she's going home with Gertie when she gets out of the hospital. Ashley doesn't want to see either of us, and Gertie feels this will give her a chance to come to terms with what's happened. She's doing it for our benefit too. Gertie loves Ashley and us, so she's the best one to broker this deal. She'll let us know on a daily or even hourly basis how Ashley is doing. So the best thing we can do is stay here and wait until our child wants to see us again."

Bay didn't say anything.

"You know she's right."

"I know she's right," Bay sighed. "Thank God for her. But I still feel like a big fat failure. I should be in that hospital room holding Ashley's hand, but what am I doing? Eating oatmeal with you."

"Mom would be happy."

"I wish Mom was here."

"Me too."

Bay got up from the table so quickly she spilled her coffee. "That's bullshit! If you missed Mom so much, why did you break her heart by never coming to see her?"

Tansy stayed quiet.

"And while we're on the subject, there's something I always want-ed to know but was too afraid to ask. Why did you leave that night instead of next morning like you were supposed to? Who leaves for the airport eight hours ahead of time with no luggage?"

"What did Mom tell you?"

"That you were upset, so you left."

"She was right."

Bay sat at the table again and crossed her arms. "So upset that you didn't say goodbye to me and stayed away for fifteen years?"

"Yes."

"And then to rub salt in the wound you decided not to come for Mom's funeral."

Again Tansy didn't answer her.

"What in the name of God was so bad that your only recourse was to leave us behind forever?"

"I can't explain that right now. I will. I just can't do it this min-ute."

"Why not? We've got nothing else to do for the next few days or weeks or months or however long it takes for Ashley to stop hating us."

"Mom and I argued, okay? I said things to her that I shouldn't have said. I couldn't come back for her funeral because of my never-ending guilt about it."

"Again, it's all about you. Your guilt. You didn't give a thought to how it felt for Ashley and I to stand at her grave alone and say good-bye to her?"

Now it was Tansy's turn to get up from the table. She paced the floor. "Of course I thought about it! I thought about nothing else. But I worried that I'd make the situation unbearable if I showed up."

"What?"

"I didn't come to see her when she was alive but I suddenly show up when she's dead, when it didn't matter anymore?"

"Well, Mom was past caring, but we weren't."

"I was wrong. I see that now. I'm sorry."

"It's too late, isn't it?"

When Tansy didn't say anything, Bay pressed on. "While we're on the subject of coming and going, why did you come back now? Did someone throw you out or did you suddenly remember you had a sister?"

Tansy laughed. "Wow, you're good. Both answers are correct, actually. I knew Ashley would graduate from high school in June and maybe leave home. I also knew you'd be horribly lonely without her, and since I'm intimately acquainted with how that feels..."

Bay jumped up. "Then why in the name of God did you give her to me? I asked you when you came home that year if you were staying away because I was raising your daughter and you gave me some generic response that didn't answer the question. Why did you lie to me? When you were seventeen, you sat here at this kitchen table and told me that you didn't want the baby. You didn't *want* her. I said you hadn't thought it through, that maybe it would be too hard, and you said it would be better than giving her away to a stranger. I thought I was helping you and instead you hate me for it. You've stayed away all these years because you can't stand the fact I'm her mother and you're not!"

"You're *right*. I can't stand the thought of it! I've never been able to come to terms with it. I wanted her from the moment I knew I was carrying her. That's why I left that night. I was taking Ashley with me. I went into her room and grabbed her while she slept. I had my bags ready and a taxi waiting. I was almost out the door when Mom stopped me. She waited for me in the dark. She told me to put Ashley down, that you were the only mother Ashley knew and if I loved my daughter I wouldn't take her away from you. Well, I love my daughter, so I gave her back, but I told Mom that I would never forgive her and I'd never see her again. So now you know why I couldn't come back here. Are you happy now?"

Tansy rushed out of the kitchen and went upstairs to her room. Last night Gertie had told her to wait until she was there. To be around Bay was dangerous, so Tansy needed to get away from her. If she stayed out of sight and waited in her room until Gertie came over, she'd be safe.

Bay came to her instead.

She opened the door without knocking. "None of this makes any sense. Even twenty years ago an unwed mother wasn't a criminal offense. Sure, Mom would've had to deal with some gossip, and it might have hurt her, but it wouldn't have killed her. So if you knew you wanted this baby so badly why didn't you tell us? We could've helped you raise her. Then we'd have spent our whole lives together instead of living apart. We lost Dad and Bobby. We only had each other left and because of shame or pride or whatever your motivation was, we ended up living separate lives. It didn't have to happen, Tansy. None of this had to happen!"

Tansy looked at her. "Yes, it did."

"*Why?*"

"Because Ashley is Bobby's daughter and Mom knew that."

It was done. It was out. It was over.

Bay had to reach out her hand to steady herself against the closet door. Her face was devoid of emotion, as pale and lifeless as a mannequin in a store window. She had trouble staying on her feet. Tansy reached for her but Bay held her off. She kept her hand in front of her to ward her sister away. With the other hand she felt the wall behind her and took unsteady backward steps out of Tansy's room and into the hall, before she lurched forward and managed to make it to her bedroom. She closed the door.

There was no sound from behind it.

Tansy ran downstairs, picked up the phone, and called Gertie.

"She knows," Tansy whispered.

"I told you not to tell her!"

"It happened. I'm sorry, I'm sorry. Please come."

"I'll be right there."

Tansy threw the phone down and ran to the porch. Poor old Merlin thought he was going for a walk but Tansy didn't even see him. She opened the back door and ran outside with no coat or gloves on. It was a bitterly cold day, but she didn't feel it, nor was she aware of the neighbour's kids in ski jackets and hats waiting for the school bus. They looked at her like she was nuts. She didn't see cars pass by or the milk truck lumber down the road. Some people stopped and watched her and many wondered if she needed help, but she was gone before they could ask her.

She finally arrived at her destination and pounded on the door. She pounded until he opened it.

"I need a car."

❀

Peter had listened to the whole sad story over the phone the night before. By the end of it he knew Gertie was exhausted so he insisted she put down the phone and try and get some sleep, but she worried about who she should deal with first thing in the morning. She wanted to check on Ashley but knew that Tansy and Bay were in a powder-keg situation over at their house. One thing she did know was that she had to take time off work.

Peter solved her dilemma. He told her that since he was recuperating, it was just as easy for him to sit in a chair at the hospital as sit in a chair at home, and he'd go over in the morning by taxi and stay with Ashley. He also knew Michael would be at the hospital so he'd get him to check in on her too. Would that make her feel better?

Gertie had enough energy to tell him she loved him before she began to snore. He had to shout her name and tell her to put down the phone. She did, badly. It sounded like three or four tries before she actually hung up the receiver.

Peter's leg was healing well and life was much easier now that he had a walking cast on, but it was still a major ordeal to get himself ready in the morning. Thank goodness he lived with his mother. Dorothy was a tremendous help while he was in this blasted cast.

Not that he'd always lived with her. Peter had a very nice apartment at one time, one that wasn't too far away from the university where he worked, but when his father had died, Dorothy found it a bit overwhelming to manage the large home they'd lived in on Whitney Avenue in Sydney. It made sense for Peter to move in for a while. Neither one thought it would be a permanent arrangement, maybe a year or so, but they found they enjoyed each other's company and never got in each other's hair. Dorothy wasn't a woman who stayed at home picking up Peter's underwear. She had a large circle of friends and did lots of charity work, and she was the one out gallivanting with her cronies in the evening while Peter stayed at home with his computer and his books.

And much to Peter's delight, his mother thought Gertie was quite a gal. They liked each other instantly. So when Peter mentioned that he was going to the hospital for the day to help Gertie with her little friend Ashley, she immediately packed up a nutritious lunch for them both.

Dorothy also passed him a pile of magazines. "Pixie brought these over to donate to the hospital anyway, so Ashley might as well read them. Pixie says they're her granddaughter's so I imagine this is the stuff teenagers like to read." She picked up a *Seventeen* magazine. "Look here, articles on how to be sexy, look sexy, and have sexy boys look at you. It'll be right up her alley if she's a normal teenager."

"Ashley's having a baby, so I think she's got that covered."

"Oh dear, poor little mite. Is her family behind her? So many aren't and it's such a shame."

Peter did up his jacket. "She's got a lovely family, but they're in crisis mode right now, so Gertie's taking over for the moment."

"Well, if Gertie's there, then I don't have to worry. That girl is the salt of the earth."

Peter grinned. "She is, isn't she?"

Dorothy kissed his cheek. "And you're the pepper."

His mother wanted to drive him to the hospital, but he said he'd be fine. He knew she had a meeting down at the Every Woman's Centre and he didn't want her to be late. The taxi arrived and he had a bit of a job getting in and out of it, but he managed. He put the lunch, the magazines, some books, and a pack of cards in a backpack so his hands were free.

When he got to Ashley's room he knocked softly before going in. It was a double room, but there was no patient in the bed closest to the door. He limped over to the far bed behind the curtain. Ashley had her eyes closed and he thought she was asleep at first, but when he moved closer, she opened her eyes. A big smile came to her face.

"Hi, Peter. What are you doing here?"

"I'm here to babysit for the day. Gertie had some business to attend to, but she'll be in later. She didn't want you to be alone this morning."

"She's so sweet. I'm glad you're here, though. Matt can't come in until this afternoon, but he's called about five times this morning. His uncle might get fed up if he sees him using a cellphone on the job."

"I'm sure his uncle understands that Matt wants to check up on you."

"I guess. What's in the bag?"

Peter stood next to the bed and emptied out the backpack. "I've got a healthy lunch for both of us, courtesy of my mother, and some books and magazines and a pack of cards. How does that sound?"

"Really nice."

He put it all on the table tray at the end of the bed and sat in the chair beside her. It was a tight squeeze.

"Are you sure you're going to be comfortable there?"

"Don't worry about me. I want to know how you're feeling."

Ashley made a face. "I slept on and off all night. I worry that if I move Fred will get fed up and come anyway."

"Fred?"

Ashley put her hands on her belly. "The baby. We call him Fred. We call her Fred too."

"What have the doctors said?"

"That I need bedrest. I think I might be in here for longer than I thought. They're concerned about my weight and my blood pressure."

"Then you're exactly where you should be, and I want you to relax and forget about everything. We have nothing to do and nowhere to go. My idea of heaven."

They chatted quietly for the rest of the morning. Ashley didn't know he was a professor of computer science, or an egghead, as she called him. He said egghead was a perfect description. Nurses came in every so often to check on her, to take her temperature or blood pressure. Her doctor came in once too and confirmed what Ashley had suspected, that she may be in for longer than they first thought but not to worry. It was more of a precaution than anything else.

After that they opened the lunch Dorothy made for them and Ashley was delighted to see she'd put in little chocolate pudding cups, carrot sticks, and yogurt, along with ham and cheese sandwiches and homemade cookies.

"This looks like the lunches my nana used to make for me."

That was the only tricky moment. She got upset after she said that, but Peter soon distracted her with a chocolate bar and a game of Go Fish.

Michael came in and sat on the edge of the bed for a while. He told Ashley about the day he and his friends took Peter's glasses from him and tried to start a grassfire by pointing them at the sun. When they were successful and the neighbour's coalhouse nearly burned down, they all pointed at Peter and said he started it. Then the man chased them around the block.

She had a snooze after that, and so did Peter. It was Matt who woke him up. They both quietly left the room so they could talk, but before that Peter's cellphone rang. It was Gertie.

"How is she?"

"She's fine, just fine. Matt is here now."

"Would you mind staying with her for the rest of the day? I can't leave Bay alone."

"Where's Tansy?"

"I have no clue. She's disappeared, but I can't worry about that right now. Bay is in dreadful shape and she needs me."

"Don't worry about Ashley. The doctors want her to stay here for a while, so she's not going anywhere. She's quite happy, for a sad little girl."

"Thank you, thank you for this."

"It's all good. Stay with Bay and if I have to come here every day for a month, I will."

"You're done for, Peter Sullivan. There's no way in hell another woman is going to get her claws into you. Do you hear me?"

"Message received and understood."

Dermot had to stop the shaking first. He took Tansy into the house, put his arm around her, and led her into the kitchen. He made her sit on a chair. "Wait here." The first thing he grabbed was an afghan off the couch in the living room to wrap around her shoulders. Next he put the kettle on, and after that he looked over at a hamper full of wrinkled clothes and pulled out a pair of thick socks that were fortunately clean. He took off her wet slippers and put the socks on her feet, rubbing them between his hands.

She didn't stop shaking, so he pulled her up and held her tightly in his arms.

"It's okay now, Tansy. I've got you. I'm not going to let anyone hurt you."

She never made a sound. He wasn't even sure if she heard him. The kettle started to boil so he reached over with her still in his arms and poured the water into a mug and added a teabag.

"Come with me. It's okay."

He slowly walked her out of the kitchen and sat her on the couch, adding another throw around her legs. While the tea steeped he kept his arm around her and waited for the shaking to subside. It took a while. He threw the teabag away and put the mug in her hands so it would warm her fingers.

"Take a little sip."

She obeyed him.

"Take a couple more."

She did.

"Now, we'll stay here for a while, okay?"

Tansy nodded.

Dermot's cellphone was within reach, so he picked it up and called Jason to ask him to open the garage and keep an eye on things until he heard from him again, saying it might be a couple of days. Jason said it was no problem.

After that he was content to sit with her. At one point he thought she'd fallen asleep. It was an hour before she stirred a little and opened her eyes. It was the first time she'd looked at him.

"You shouldn't be nice to me."

"That's not possible."

She shook her head. "I'm not a nice person. I do bad things and hurt the people I love."

"I don't believe that."

"My sister will never forgive me. I need a car to get away. Will you help me?"

"I'll help you, Tansy, but you're in no condition to go anywhere at the moment. You're welcome to stay here for as long as you need to."

Her voice shook a little. "I can't. I'm supposed to stay away from you."

Dermot smiled at her. "You can stay as far away from me as you like. I'll fix up one of the bedrooms upstairs and you can stay in there and lock the door behind you, if necessary. This is a safe place for you. Please remember that."

"If you knew what I did you wouldn't want me here."

"Why don't you tell me and let me be the judge of that?"

❄

The first hour Gertie was with Bay, Bay didn't say a word. The next hour she did nothing but cry. The hour after that she shouted and screamed until she was hoarse.

"Am I really that stupid, Gertie? So stupid that I believed him when he said he loved me? How could he love me and have an affair with my sister at the same time? I don't understand it. We were always together, or am I losing my mind?"

"They didn't have an affair—"

"She had his baby! Even I didn't manage that!"

"They only did it once."

"You only have to do it once to betray someone!"

"I know."

"No, you don't! And you know what makes me feel really dumb? I've been living like a nun my whole life, pining away for him, telling myself all these years that no one could ever replace him. But he sure replaced me when it suited him, didn't he?"

"You need to let me tell you what happened."

Bay paced up and down the kitchen. "How do you know about all this? Please don't tell me you knew about this or I really will go out of my mind."

"I knew nothing. Tansy told me at the kitchen table last night."

"Then why didn't you scratch her eyes out? Why didn't you scream at her? I thought you were my friend!"

Gertie remained calm and slowly revealed the story in fits and starts. Bay would only listen when it suited her. She continued to fly off the handle even as Gertie let Merlin out for a pee. When Gertie made them a couple of grilled cheese sandwiches, Bay threw hers at the far wall. Merlin enjoyed it when he came in. At one point Gertie took a basin of hot water and wrung out a facecloth and made Bay apply it to her face a few times. That actually helped, because Bay was so stuffed up from crying that she couldn't breathe. Her face was red and blotchy and swollen.

By the fourth hour she was exhausted. This was the stage Gertie was waiting for. As Bay lay on her bed, wrung out and spent, Gertie brought up a tray. On it was a bottle of water, two extra-strength Tylenol tablets, a mug of creamy hot chocolate, and a plate of oatmeal raisin cookies.

"This is my favourite prescription. I insist you swallow, drink, and eat all of it."

Bay looked at it listlessly. "I can't eat all those cookies."

"I know. I'll finish them for you."

Soon the mug and plate were empty. Gertie saw a slight improvement in her closest friend before Bay nodded off to sleep in spite of herself. Gertie covered her with a quilt and closed the curtains to keep the afternoon daylight from streaming in the window.

Back downstairs, Gertie did some household chores and put on a load of laundry. Then she made goulash and tea biscuits for supper. She wasn't worried about Jeffrey. She'd left three bowls filled to the brim with cat chow and a big bowl of water.

While Bay slept, she and Merlin cozied up together to watch the soaps. This was a rare treat, to be home in the afternoon. She'd called work earlier and said she needed a few days off. Her supervisor didn't sound too impressed, but Gertie knew if there was a problem Peter would come to her rescue. No doubt he'd install himself in her apartment and look after Ashley there if he had to, while she was at work.

She rubbed Merlin's ears. "I'm a lucky woman, Merly. I waited a long time, but this particular man was worth the wait."

She and the dog fell asleep at some point, because when Gertie woke up with a kink in her neck, Bay was bundled up in her quilt on the chair across from her.

Gertie rubbed her neck. "Oh boy, I hate it when this happens. What time is it?"

"Seven."

Gertie sat up. "What?"

"Sit, Gertie. No wonder you fell asleep. I put you through the wringer this morning."

Gertie sat back and wiggled her neck around. "Hell, what are friends for?"

"Gertie, you're more than a friend."

"Right back at ya, kid."

Bay held the quilt up to her chin. "When I woke up, I thought I'd had a nightmare."

"That's understandable," Gertie smiled sadly. "It's going to take a while to process twenty years' worth of history."

"I feel..." Bay searched for the right word, "raw. Like someone's laid me open and trampled on every inch of my body and mind and soul. And now I have to learn to walk again. Everything I knew, I don't know anymore."

Gertie leaned forward on the couch. "Bay, you know the one good thing in all this?"

"There's a good thing?"

"There are a lot of them, but they'll only come to you in stages. For right now, the good thing is that you and your sister and daughter don't have to live with any more lies. What's that hokey old saying? *The truth will set you free.* I truly believe that. You three will be able to remember that this was done in the name of love, not hate. These decisions were misguided, maybe, but think back to when they were being made. You were all nearly dead from grief. I remember those horrible days. It was like a fog of despair lived in this house, a sad energy that sapped the life out of all of you. It was a terrible thing to witness. They were the worst days of my life."

Bay shook her head. "Poor Gertie, I never thought of how it must have been for you. All I remember is that you were always there whenever I needed you."

"My therapy was fixing up Ashley's nursery. I was so happy that a new little life was coming to live in this house."

Bay leaned her head back on the chair. "Bobby's child. Ashley is Bobby's child. It doesn't feel real to me, I can't absorb it. I don't believe it yet. There's no emotion when I say those words. Shouldn't I feel something?"

"No. You're still in shock. It will take days, even weeks before it sinks in. It doesn't matter whose child she is, does it? She's Ashley and you adore her exactly as she is."

"Oh, I do. But Gertie, how do I tell her that Bobby is her father? That sounds silly, but you know what I mean."

"I think it will give her a measure of comfort. She's afraid of who her father might be. To be reassured that Bobby is still her dad can only be a good thing. And don't worry about telling her, because I will when the time is right."

"Did you call the hospital today to see how she was?"

"Yep. She and Fred are fine. Peter spent the day with her and Matt went over in the afternoon."

"Gertie, I keep saying thank you, but it doesn't adequately express…"

Gertie got up. "Enough of that. I gotta pee and then I'm dishing out some grub. I don't know about you, but I'm starving."

Bay ate a little supper and had a cup of tea, but she started to fade soon afterwards. Gertie told her to take a hot bath and she'd do the dishes. She'd just finished when Bay called her upstairs. She was out of the tub and in her pyjamas at the end of her bed.

"Yes, madam?"

"Where's Tansy?"

"I don't have a clue."

"I didn't think of her all day."

"She called me this morning and told me to get over here fast, but she wasn't here when I arrived. I wonder where she'd go."

"Dermot's."

"Dermot's?"

"Oh, she conveniently didn't tell you that part of the story. I'm not surprised. Turns out she and Dermot went to bed together on a couple of occasions before they knew who the other was."

"Oh God."

"So you see? She insists on sleeping with all the men in my life. What a gal."

"Wait a minute. You have that backwards. She was with them first, wasn't she? In a biblical sense?"

Bay started to say something and then stopped. She looked confused.

"Never mind," Gertie said. "We've both had a long day. Let's go to bed and we'll talk about it in the morning."

"You're staying here?"

"If I can find a nightgown that fits me, which I highly doubt."

After they said goodnight, Gertie went downstairs and called Dermot.

"Is she there?" Gertie asked.

"Yes. She was in quite a state when she arrived."

"I can well imagine. Did she tell you what happened?"

"I know the whole story."

"Wonderful, isn't it?"

"I think it's a bloody shame that two young girls were put through that torture for one lousy mistake. And as badly as I feel for Bay, I feel ten times worse for Tansy. She's been an outcast her whole life because of this. Can you imagine how lonely it's been for her all these years? I know Bay is hurting, but she did get to live with her mother and her daughter and that's more than Tansy was allowed to do."

"I know. It's a sad situation, but hopefully between us we can help them recover. Ashley's safe at the hospital and I'm here with Bay. If Tansy can stay with you for a while, that would help."

"I've already got her moved into one of the bedrooms upstairs. She cried for most of the day, but she's finally gone to sleep."

"I have to call Anne tomorrow and tell her Bay won't be at work for a while. Are you able to stay with Tansy or do you want me to drop by?"

"By all means come and see her, but I've arranged it so I can stay here for a few days."

"Perfect. I appreciate it."

"At some point," Dermot sighed, "we need to get Bay and Tansy in the same room."

"Preferably before Fred gets here."

"Fred?"

CHAPTER TWENTY-ONE

Everyone stayed in their own corner of the ring for two weeks. That's how long Ashley spent in the hospital.

Dermot explained the situation to Tansy as they sat together at his kitchen table.

"I've talked to Gertie and she's going to stay with Bay, so don't worry about your sister. I told her that you're going to be here with me."

"What did she say?"

"She thought it was a good idea."

Tansy rubbed her forehead. "There's so much to sort out. I have to call work."

Dermot pointed at her. "There's no way in hell you're going back to that diner."

"But I need money."

"You have the money from your Porsche."

"That's for Ashley and the baby."

"Well, you don't need a damn thing while you're here with me. I'll take care of you."

"I've always looked after myself."

Dermot reached across the table and took her hand. "Listen to me. You've been on your own for far too long. None of us can get by in this world without leaning on someone from time to time. This is your time. Please take it. I'm your friend. Let me help you."

Tansy closed her eyes.

"I only ask one thing."

She looked at him.

"You can't leave without telling me. I've already had a woman I love walk out the door and never come back. I can't live through it again."

Tansy spent most of the first week asleep in her room across the hall from him. There were days when she was asleep when he went to work and was still asleep when he came home. By the beginning of the second week the dishes were done and his bed was made. Near the end of that week, he came home to his dinner on the table. Nothing fancy, mind you, eggs and bacon and toast, but it tasted great to him. The house was tidy and she did a wash one day, his underwear, socks, and shirts folded on the end of his bed, a small gift for him.

One day Gertie brought over some of her clothes. When Tansy saw her she hugged Gertie for a good long time. Eventually Tansy made her a cup of tea.

"How is she?"

"She's quiet," Gertie said. "It was traumatic, but every day she's getting better. Last night Merlin got his head caught in a plastic container and couldn't get it off and Bay laughed out loud, so she's coming along."

"That's good."

"She even brought out some photo albums the other day and we sat on the living room floor remembering old times. It's a journey, but we're making progress."

Tansy nodded.

"How are you?" Gertie asked.

"I'm better."

"You could've told me about Dermot, you know."

"How could I? Your loyalty belongs to Bay, as it should."

"I would've listened."

Tansy smiled. "You're good at that."

Gertie took a sip of tea. "I'm glad you're here. You need a safe haven."

"This is a gift I don't deserve."

Gertie put down the teacup. "The day you realize you do deserve this is the day you truly are better."

❀

Gertie took a total of three days off before the office called in a panic and said they needed her back. She got on the blower and called her man.

"Don't worry about it," Peter said. "I'm at the hospital during the day, Matt's here in the evening, and you can come in when you can."

"You've got this all figured out."

"Yep."

"So you don't need me at all, do you?"

"Gertie, I'll always need you."

"I cannot wait to get you in my arms again, big guy."

"Oh no, I can't afford to fall out of bed a second time."

"Then we'll do it on the floor."

"Deal."

By this time, there was a stack of board games on the hospital window sill a couple of feet high. That's how Peter and Ashley entertained themselves. Their favourite was Monopoly.

"You really are a real-estate czar," Peter complained. "You make Stalin look good."

"Quit your bellyaching and pay up. I've got three hotels on Park Place, so that's…"

"…too much. You win again."

Ashley rubbed her hands together with glee before she patted her belly. "You see, Fred. Your mother's going to be a tycoon some day."

Peter slowly got out of his chair and put the game pieces and money away in the box. "I hope you remember me when you're rich and famous."

"I'll never forget you as long as I live."

They smiled at each other before Peter reached over and put the Monopoly box on top of the pile, whereupon the entire thing came crashing down around his feet. Dice and money, game pieces and cards from every game they had littered the floor. The look of dismay on Peter's face sent Ashley into gales of laughter.

"What's so funny? Keep laughing and Fred will be here in no time to help me clean this up."

At the end of two weeks the doctor reassured Gertie that it was safe for Ashley to go home. At thirty-six weeks, she was close enough to full term that there wouldn't be any problem if she did go into labour. Good old Peter moved into Gertie's apartment to be with her, so it was tight quarters. Jeffrey was mightily ticked.

"That cat is staring at me," Ashley frowned.

"He could be hissing," Gertie said, "so consider yourself fortunate.

Don't forget, you're on his turf."

"Sorry, Jeffrey."

Gertie had it all figured out when they arrived. "Ashley, you sleep in my room, because you need to rest. Peter and I will sleep on the hide-a-bed in the living room."

When Ashley went into Gertie's room with her suitcase, Gertie hugged Peter. "I cannot wait to get you in my arms tonight."

"We'll have to be very quiet."

"Quiet I can do."

But quiet wasn't in the cards. After an endless evening waiting for Ashley to stop watching television and finally go to bed, Gertie rushed over to the hide-a-bed and had it made up in a jiffy. Poor Jeffrey tried to make himself comfortable on the quilt, but he was unceremoniously dumped back on the floor. He took his wounded pride and sat with his back to them on a nearby armchair.

She and Peter took turns in the bathroom getting ready for the big night. They met on either side of the bed. Gertie pointed at his cast.

"You better come on this side. It'll be easier for you to get in."

"You're right."

They switched places.

"Be careful getting on. You go first and make yourself comfortable."

Peter took his time sitting down on the bed. He put one leg up on the mattress and then swung his cast leg up as well before he lay back on the pillows.

"So far so good."

Gertie eased herself into bed as well. She snuggled up beside him and sighed. "At last. This is what I've been waiting for."

There was an enormous crash. The resounding bang sent furball Jeffrey flying out of the room.

"My God! What was that!?" Ashley leapt out of bed in a panic. She hurried to the living room holding her belly. Peter and Gertie were on the floor, sprawled on top of the mattress in a daze.

They looked at each other and burst out laughing.

"Stop!" Ashley cried. "I'm going to pee myself!" She crossed her legs and hopped up and down before rushing down the hall to the bathroom. When she got back, Peter and Gertie were still in hysterics.

Eventually Gertie dragged herself to her feet and held out her arms to Peter. "Let me help you."

"I don't think I can get up." He turned this way and that, but wasn't able to get enough leverage to get to his feet. "This is impossible."

"You can't stay on the floor all night."

But after a good ten minutes of trying, they admitted they were defeated.

"I'm going to call Matt," Ashley said.

"It's too late," Gertie replied.

"He's young, he'll get over it," Peter said. "Call him."

When Matt arrived, he did his best to keep a smirk off his face, but even he couldn't get the big man and his cast off the floor.

"You can't live on the floor," Gertie worried. "What are we going to do?"

"Call Michael," Peter said. "I'm desperate."

Michael arrived with his camera. Peter pointed at him. "Don't you dare."

"Listen here, Peter. You drag me out of a warm bed in the middle of the night and make me drive an hour to come and pick you up off the floor. You owe me, buddy boy."

Michael couldn't stop laughing as he took a few shots, so the other three got down on the floor and joined Peter. They had their arms around the hapless victim and it turned out to be such a great picture they all wanted a copy.

Between them they managed to get Peter upright again. They looked at the mangled hide-a-bed.

"What do we do now?" Peter wondered.

"Why don't you sleep in my room," Gertie said, "and Ashley and I can sleep on the floor tonight."

"I'll go first thing in the morning and buy another hide-a-bed for you—a better one, obviously. They can deliver it in the afternoon," Michael suggested.

"I can't have you buying me furniture."

Michael took Gertie by the shoulders. "That was the best laugh I've had in years. It's worth every penny."

In the end that's how Gertie told Ashley the story of her two mothers and her father—late at night, in the dark, while she held her in her arms. There were tears, of course, and some nights when Ashley still couldn't believe their betrayal. Knowing that her nana had been a party to it still rankled, until Gertie reminded her that her grandmother was an ordinary woman caught up in an extraordinary circumstance, doing the best she could for both her girls. She said that everyone likes to think their grandmothers can do no wrong, but that's not fair. Everyone makes mistakes, even nanas.

"But I'd never give Fred away," she said. "When I feel him kick and move inside me it makes me so happy. Didn't Tansy feel that?"

"Of course she did, but you need to remember something. Tansy and your mom were your age when this happened, like you and Maribeth. What if you fell in love with Matt and suddenly Maribeth came along and took him away from you? You watch as she picks out her wedding dress and fixes up their apartment, and pretend to be happy as you walk down the aisle, knowing Maribeth is his bride.

"And then the unthinkable happens. Matt is dead and you're carrying his child. Your mother accuses you of stealing Maribeth's baby, and wants you to give your baby up.

"When you're in labour with this little bundle, I want you to think about what it must have been like for Tansy, knowing the minute you were born, you belonged to someone else. She had to love you more than life itself to hand you over and let someone else raise you. And then she had to stay away from the only family she has so that you could live in a happy and stable home. Now that's what I call love."

Ashley didn't say anything after that.

One morning Bay got out of bed and called Dermot's house. She knew he'd be at work and she also knew that Tansy wouldn't answer the phone because it wasn't her place. She'd let the answering machine pick up.

Bay left a message.

"Tansy, I'd like to see you. If you don't feel you're ready to talk then you don't have to come. But if you do, I'll have the tea poured at three this afternoon."

She hung up.

Tansy sat there and wondered what she should do. In a way, she didn't want to go. After that first horrible week, she was content within the walls of this old house, like she was wrapped in a bubble and the world outside didn't exist. It was frightening to step back into the minefield that was her life.

But Tansy knew that she and her sister needed to come to terms with the rest of their lives and it needed to be done before Ashley had the baby. The thought of her going through labour and delivery while she was estranged from them didn't bear thinking about.

So at three o'clock she rapped on the back door. Bay opened it and Merlin almost knocked Tansy over, he was that glad to see her.

"Hey, Merlin." She gave him a couple of pats. "I think he missed me."

"He did. Come in."

Bay had the table set with their mother's silver tea service. Tansy looked at her.

"You did oatmeal," Bay reminded her. "I figured Mom better be in on this conversation too."

So they sat down at the kitchen table and Bay poured the tea. She'd even made plate of sandwiches, though the squares were store-bought.

"Eat something," Bay said. "You look like a skeleton."

"Ditto."

They each took a sandwich and ate while they sipped their tea. After they each ate one more, Bay cleared her throat. "I'm not sure where to start..."

"At the beginning is usually best."

"I'm not sure where to start because in one sense I've only just met you, and in another sense, I finally know who you are."

"I can understand why. You've looked at me through a haze of lies for twenty years."

"I can't believe you and Mom were able to pull the wool over my eyes for so long. I can't believe one of you didn't crack."

"I did crack," Tansy said. "The Christmas our daughter was three."

"So you walked out that night knowing you might never see us again?"

"Yes."

"What did that feel like?"

"Death."

"How have you lived your life for the past fifteen years? You never talk about it."

"I don't talk about it because it was my false life. My real life was here."

"Did you ever love another man?"

"No. I had a lot of men to keep me from being lonely, but their faces run together now. I don't remember them. The final relationship lasted two years, but only because he was extremely wealthy and able to buy me luxurious distractions. He was a pig. He used to say, 'Come give Daddy a kiss.'"

"God."

"It turned my stomach when he said that—like the real me that was hidden inside would flare up in protest. I wanted to scream at him that he didn't know how to behave like a real daddy. He wouldn't know what it was to get up in the middle of the night and brave the elements for twelve hours a day, out on the rough seas in the freezing cold, just to keep food on the table for his family, or that a daddy would drive around in the dark and look for you so he could keep you from harm. That a daddy is someone who'd drag you out of a car and punch the boy who had his hands on you."

Tansy fought to stay calm. "You know, it hit me the other day that I was Ashley's age when all these decisions were being made. I look at her now and still see her as a baby. She is in a lot of ways. That was us. We were so young and missing our father and there's Mom trying to do what was right without Dad to lean on. They always talked things over. I remember at night I'd hear them in their room, the low murmuring that told me we were safe because Mom and Dad would take care of it."

Tansy picked up a napkin and dabbed her eyes. "I hope Mom knows that I love her and I've forgiven her."

"She knows. Have you forgiven yourself?"

"No. Not until I hear it from you and I hear it from Ashley."

"Well, that's why I called this family meeting. I'm here to say that I forgive you and Bobby, but only if you forgive me."

"But none of this was your fault, Bay. None of it."

"I want you to forgive me for taking Dermot away from you."

Tansy was still. "What do you mean?"

"I led you to believe that Dermot was someone I loved and that you ruined everything between us. That's not true. There was nothing between us except friendship. We were drawn to each other out of loneliness. We loved the idea of being a couple, but every time we got together we'd argue or make the other person feel bad for one reason or another. If I loved him, I'd have been with him before Mom died. I knew deep down that he wasn't for me but I didn't want to tell him because he's so darn nice.

"But the day I knew for sure was the day I saw the two of you through the diner window. I saw a man and a woman deeply in love with each other. I have no right to keep you from that kind of love. Bobby and I shared that happiness and I know how precious it is. You and Dermot belong together. I don't want you to waste one more day without him."

They rose from the table at the same time and met in the middle of the kitchen floor, where they held each other for a long time.

"Thank you for bringing Bobby back to me," Bay whispered.

Eventually they sat down to finish their tea. All the sandwiches were eaten, even the dreary squares. And then Bay remembered something. "Just a sec."

She went out into the living room and brought back a photo to show Tansy. It was the picture Ashley had found and put aside on the fateful day she'd rooted through old boxes, the one that showed the two of them up in the tree house, with their hair in braids and their grins gap-toothed.

"We looked happy, didn't we?" Tansy smiled.

"We will be again."

It was after six o'clock before Tansy left Bay's house. She walked along the streets of Louisbourg and revelled in the cold north wind. She smiled at people as they passed by and thought how beautiful this little town was, perched on the Atlantic coast. Tansy felt sorry for anyone who wasn't here at this particular moment.

Dermot's house appeared in the distance. There was so much work to do. It really was an old barn of a place, but it was sturdy and welcoming. She knew she'd lost her mind when she wondered what sorts of flowers she might plant along the walkway in the spring. Wouldn't her mother get a kick out of that? She rounded the bend and saw the back of Dermot's truck parked in the yard. That's when she remembered she hadn't left him a note and had unthinkingly erased Bay's message off the machine.

Tansy ran up the porch steps just as he opened the back door. The look of panic in his eyes gave her a fright.

"It's okay, Dermot. I'm home."

He grabbed her by the arm and pulled her to him. As they embraced, she felt his heart beating too fast beneath his jacket.

"I thought you left me."

"I'll never leave you."

Dermot reached up and framed her face with his big hands. "I adore you. You must know that."

"I do."

He rubbed her cheek with his thumb. "We'll take it slow."

"I've been set free, Dermot. We have Bay's blessing. I want you to take me upstairs and let me show you how much I love you."

Dermot picked her up in his arms and carried her across the threshold.

❁

It was only two days later when Fred decided he had had enough and couldn't wait to join this whacked-out family. Naturally it was in the middle of the night, which always heightens the sense of urgency. He was still a few weeks early but the doctor said he was more than happy that Fred had stayed put for as long as he did. But he did warn Ashley that things could get serious in a hurry once it started, as she was already a bit dilated from her first scare.

When Ashley's water broke, she panicked.

"Oh my God."

Gertie sat straight up in bed from a sound sleep. "What? What?"

"My water broke."

Gertie threw the quilt aside and leapt out of bed. "Nobody move. Everyone calm down. Where am I?"

"My water broke on Michael's new mattress! What am I going to do?"

"Forget the fucking mattress."

Ashley was shocked. "Gertie, you never swear."

Gertie ran around in circles. "Of course I do, just not in front of you." She took off like a missile and ran into her bedroom, where poor old Peter was snoring in peace. She shook him awake.

"Peter, the baby's coming on Michael's mattress!"

Peter grunted and shook his head before he wiped the sleep from his eyes. "Michael's mattress?"

"Forget the fucking mattress—Ashley's having the baby!"

"Okay, calm down."

"You calm down!"

"I am calm, Gertie." Peter struggled to sit up in bed. "The baby isn't coming on Michael's mattress because we're going to get dressed and take Ashley to the hospital."

Gertie jumped around. "So what do I do?"

"You get dressed and tell Ashley to get dressed and I'll get dressed and we'll go."

"I'd better call Matt."

Peter put his hand on Gertie's arm. "I'll call Matt. You'll frighten the life out of him."

Ashley appeared at the bedroom door, dressed and carrying her suitcase.

"Why are you two still in your pyjamas?"

When they were ready and about to leave, Gertie looked at Jeffrey. "I forgot to feed the cat!"

"I think we should go," Peter said.

Gertie booted it down the hall and grabbed the mega-sized bag of cat chow, but in her rush, she spilled it all over the kitchen floor. "Oh my God!"

"Forget it. Let's go."

Gertie rushed back down the hall and they trooped out to the car. Peter put Ashley in the front seat and tucked a blanket around her.

"You're not having any pain, are you?" Peter asked quietly.

"Only when I breathe. Is that bad?"

He shut the car door and shouted at Gertie. "Get in the car now!"

She climbed behind the wheel and it was amazing how fast Peter got into the back seat, cast and all. As Gertie sped down the highway, she fretted. "Jeffrey's going to blow up if he eats all that food."

"I'll buy you another cat."

"Peter!"

Ashley cried out and leaned over in her seat. "Oh, this is getting worse."

"It's getting worse!" Gertie repeated.

"You're fine," Peter said. "This is supposed to happen. Take deep breaths in and out."

Ashley began breathing but another pain hit her. Again she cried out and then reached over the seat to grab Peter's hand.

"Call my moms."

❁

When the phone rang, Bay wasn't surprised. She'd had a funny feeling all day and was lying in bed thinking about Ashley. But just because she wasn't surprised didn't mean she was prepared.

"She's having contractions?!" she shouted into the phone at Peter.

"Don't worry, Bay. We're ten minutes out of Sydney. We'll get her there in time."

"What do I do now?"

"Get dressed and come to the hospital."

Bay paced by the bed. "I don't think I can drive. I'm shaking."

"I'll call Dermot. He'll drive you and Tansy to the hospital."

"Yes, yes. Good plan."

Bay ran around her bedroom opening and closing bureau drawers. "What do you wear when you're about to be a grandmother?" Because she couldn't think, she threw on the clothes she'd taken off just hours before. Then into the bathroom to splash water on her face and brush her teeth. A quick brush through her hair and she was ready. She was halfway down the stairs when she realized she'd forgotten her purse. Did she need her purse? Yes. You always need your purse. It was on the dresser and as Bay grabbed it, her eyes fell on the picture of her mother. She reached out and took it with her.

Bay was bundled up outside in the frosty air when she saw head-lights come along the main road. When they turned up her street, she ran down the driveway and jumped up and down until Dermot pulled the truck up to the curb. Tansy opened up the door for her and Bay hopped into the truck.

"It's happening!" Bay said.

"I know!" Tansy said.

They both looked at Dermot. "Hurry up!"

❀

Matt was waiting outside the hospital doors with a wheelchair when Gertie and Peter pulled up in the car. Matt opened the passenger door and was met with a screech from Ashley. "This is all your fault!"

Peter and Gertie got out of the car and helped Matt put her in the chair.

"How did you get here so fast?" Gertie asked him.

"He didn't stop to feed a cat," Ashley yelled. "Peter, don't leave me!"

"I won't." He took Ashley's hand and limped beside her into the hospital, with Matt pushing the chair.

Gertie wrung her hands behind them. "So what do I do?"

Peter looked back. "Go park the car and wait here for Tansy and Bay."

Ashley shouted over her shoulder. "I don't want to see them. Not until I say so. Have you got that?"

"Got it." Gertie ran back to the car.

When a doctor checked Ashley she was almost fully dilated. Matt was with her in the room while Peter paced outside. Then the door opened and Matt appeared wearing a hospital gown, holding Ashley's hand as the medical team wheeled her to the delivery room. He looked like he was about to faint. He mouthed, "Help me."

Once Ashley laid eyes on Peter, she held out her other hand. "You have to come with us! I can't do this without you." She gasped when another pain hit.

A nurse approached him with a hospital gown. "Here, put this on. We don't get many fathers in the delivery room. It's usually the moms."

"She's got three of those downstairs."

"You get all sorts these days." She helped him into the gown.

"I don't know if I can do this."

The nurse patted his back. "Just hold her hand and close your eyes."

When Dermot pulled the truck up to the hospital, Bay and Tansy were out the door before he even stopped. Gertie was there to greet them, stamping her feet to keep warm.

"Why aren't you with her?" Bay shouted.

"She wanted Peter."

"Peter's in the delivery room?"

"I don't know where anyone is at the moment. I've been waiting down here for you."

"We have to get up there." Bay ran to the hospital door with Tansy sprinting behind her.

"Wait!" Gertie shouted.

They kept going.

A sharp whistle from Dermot stopped them in their tracks. They turned around. "Bay, Gertie's trying to tell you something."

Bay looked at her. "What is it?"

"Ashley doesn't want to see either of you until she says so."

Dermot pointed at them. "Have you got that? Now calm down and do as you're told."

At that moment, Ashley was pushing with all her might. Peter was on one side of her head and Matt was on the other, both of them with their eyes closed. She had their hands in a vice grip. Their fingers were turning lovely shades of white and blue.

As the doctor told her to bear down once more, Ashley shouted at Matt, "You're never touching me again, do you hear me!?"

Peter opened one eye to see Matt look at him with dismay. Peter whispered over her head. "She didn't mean that."

"I did so...ooohhhhhhhh!!"

And then it was over.

Fred gave a little cry and the doctor put him in his mother's arms. That made his mother cry and his father cry and his uncle Peter cry. They were one big crying machine. Eventually Peter turned to Matt.

"You should go down to the waiting room and put the mothers out of their misery."

Matt rushed down the hall and the minute he appeared in the waiting room doorway, Bay, Tansy, Gertie, and Dermot rose as one.

"We have a son."

The three women rushed towards Matt like a tidal wave of screeching maternal love. He was enveloped in a sea of arms and lifted right off the ground. He didn't mind one bit.

It was about an hour later that Matt came back in and said Ashley would like to see them. Dermot stayed where he was.

Matt went on ahead. Tansy and Bay held hands as they approached the room, but neither one dared look at the other. Gertie was behind them. They walked in to see their daughter holding her baby as Peter and Matt stood protectively beside her. Before they had a chance to react, Ashley put up her hand.

"I don't want a huge scene. I'm tired and it's too much. I love you guys and I forgive you and I forgive Nana. But you have to promise there are no more lies between us. Ever."

Bay and Tansy promised.

"Now if you can act like normal people, come meet your grandson."

They tiptoed over and all three women squished up their faces in delight as they looked at the most beautiful baby in the world. They gushed quietly and hugged Peter to thank him for all he'd done. Ashley let Bay and Tansy kiss her on the cheek, and she gave Gertie a big hug.

By now Peter couldn't hide the fact that his leg was bothering him, so he sat in the chair by the bed. Ashley handed Matt the baby and he in turn put the baby in Peter's arms. It was quite a sight to see that 280-pound man hold a six-pound newborn.

Matt cleared his throat. "Peter, Ashley and I don't know what we would have done without you and Gertie this past month. You sat in an uncomfortable chair with a cast on your leg, eight hours a day for two weeks, and then sat in an apartment with her for another two weeks. That's why we'd like to name our son after you and ask you and Gertie to be his godparents."

Well, that did it.

Any sense of decorum was forgotten in the melee of hugs and

kisses that followed. Things were just calming down when Ashley made the mistake of telling them Peter's full name.

Peter Robert Ian Gillis.

Baby Peter and his mother went to live at Bay's house. Tansy went to live at Dermot's house. Big Peter went to live at Gertie's house. Matt went to live at his house but spent most of his time over at Bay's house. And Ashley was sick of it.

Not that she didn't want him there all the time, but she knew Matt suffered in silence because of his parents and their head-in-the-sand attitude. They congratulated him, of course, and had seen pictures of Peter, but that's where it stood. Matt told Ashley he heard his father on the phone one night telling a friend the baby's name and he thought his dad sounded rather proud. It confirmed what Ashley knew in her heart. Ruth was the culprit holding up the works.

So one day she bundled Peter up in his snowsuit and packed a diaper bag and two bottles of breastmilk and told her mother she'd be back in a minute. She left before Bay could ask her where she was going. When she got to Matt's house she took Peter out of his car seat, held him in her arms, and walked up to the front door. She rang the bell.

When Matt's mother opened the door, she plunked Peter and the diaper bag into Ruth's arms. "I'll be back in three hours."

Ashley got in the car and went home.

That was the end of the problem.

Two weeks later it was Christmas. Bay invited everyone over to her house for a big Christmas dinner. There were eighteen of them altogether. Bay, Ashley, Matt, and baby Peter. Then there were Tansy and Dermot and Gertie and big Peter and his mother, Dorothy. Also Ruth and Ian and Matt's brother, Adam, and his girlfriend, May Ling. Peter's brother, Michael, and his three children came too, because it was his turn to have them for Christmas and he usually spent it with his brother, but since Peter was coming here, Bay invited Michael and family too. Maribeth and her new boyfriend, Ryan, came for dessert after dinner with her parents, making twenty.

And although it was crowded and noisy and confusing, and Merlin got into the turkey carcass, it was the best Christmas Bay and Tansy could remember.

✻

They waited until June to have Peter christened. It was a glorious Sunday. The weather couldn't have been more perfect. The entire family descended on the church in their finery, having walked to the church en masse. Bay was having everyone back to the house for a summer luncheon afterwards. Dorothy and Michael had cameras at the ready for big Peter's big day and Gertie bought an outfit that wasn't from the Sears catalogue.

During the ceremony, baby Peter was not impressed when the minister poured water on his head. He pouted and cried and held his arms out to big Peter. Of course everyone thought that was adorable.

As they walked home, Michael and Bay found themselves side by side at one point. They smiled at each other.

"You know," Michael said, "I watched Peter and Gertie on the altar today and I had a premonition that someday we'd be at their wedding."

"I don't doubt that for a minute."

He leaned closer. "Actually it's more than a premonition. Peter asked Mom about our grandmother's engagement ring."

Bay grabbed his arm in excitement. "I won't breathe a word. Oh, how wonderful."

"You love her, don't you?" he laughed. "Of course, what's not to love?"

Bay grew pensive. "Gertie was the glue when our world became unglued. She hung in there and wouldn't let us give up on each other. I can never repay her for what she's done for my daughter, my sister, and I. She's living proof that family isn't about bloodlines. It's about one heart connecting to another. It's as simple as that."

"In my line of work," Michael replied, "I see families interact all day under stressful situations and often it's not pretty. But I have to say, I was impressed with the way all of you handled the crisis last winter. I'm proud of my little brother. He's someone I look up to. It hasn't been easy since the divorce, dealing with the hurt and heartache my own kids have gone through. But seeing the way your friends and family rallied around each other gives me hope that my kids and I will weather the storm and not be crushed by it."

"You'll be fine, Michael. I've seen you with your kids. You're a great dad."

"You don't think I'm too mean?"

She looked at him and laughed. "You're never going to let me forget that, are you?"

"Nope. Well, there's one way that might happen."

"Oh?"

"If you agree to have dinner with me one night."

Bay smiled. "I'd like that."

The luncheon was a success. All three of Peter's grandmothers took turns feeding him a tiny bit of vanilla ice cream on a spoon while cameras clicked. Then there was a more formal picture with the happy parents and godparents. It turned out so well that Bay had it enlarged and gave it to Gertie for her birthday.

Ruth and Dorothy offered to do the dishes. Gertie took little Peter upstairs for his nap while Ashley and Maribeth got caught up on the latest gossip. Dermot, big Peter, Michael, Matt, Adam, and Ian settled in front of the television to watch the rest of the ball game.

That left Bay and Tansy free to wander outside, sit on their mother's swing, and enjoy the late afternoon sun.

"Did Ashley tell you that she wants to take that cosmetology course in September?"

"Yes," Tansy replied. "She mentioned it to both Ruth and I. I'll be lucky if I can pry Peter out of Ruth's hands. She wants to babysit him every day. I said I'd be happy to help out, but you know that woman. She's so damn stubborn. For someone who didn't want this baby to come into the world she's awfully glad he's here."

"It's kind of sweet," Bay said. "I know it pleases Matt no end."

"What are his plans now?"

"He's starting at NSCC in September. That two-year electrician course. He'll get plenty of work with his uncle when he's finished.

Ashley told me he'd thought about going away to the police academy, but couldn't bring himself to leave her or the baby behind."

"I'm glad for them both."

"Speaking of leaving, are you and Dermot going away on holiday this summer?"

"No, there's too much work to do around the house. I've nagged him for weeks to start scraping the kitchen cabinets so I can paint them. He's already ripped up the carpet in the hallway and living room. We're going to put hardwood in. I think that will make a big difference."

"Sounds positively domestic."

Tansy grinned. "If only dear old scumbag Charles could see me now, up to my eyeballs in bleach and furniture polish and loving every minute of it."

"The reason I ask is that I wondered if you'd help me plant Mom's garden. She and I did it every year and I hated doing it alone last summer."

"I'd love to, but you can decide what to plant. I'm not good at that kind of thing."

Just then Flo came outside to hang out her towels. She saw the Gillis sisters on their swing.

"Hi, Bay."

"Hi, Flo."

"Hi, Flo," Tansy shouted.

Flo ignored Tansy. Instead she loudly muttered that rude people would be the death of her.

Tansy turned to her sister. "I do have to plant one thing."

"What?"

"I need one pumpkin."

"Just one?"

"Yeah."

"What can you do with one pumpkin?"

Tansy looked at Flo. "I'll think of something."

❀

A READER'S GUIDE TO
Her Mother's Daughter
BY LESLEY CREWE

There are many themes in *Her Mother's Daughter*, but arguably the most important is secrecy and its effect on relationships. What are some of the examples of secrets affecting relationships in this book?

What are some of the other themes Crewe explores in this novel?

The swing and the garden are central motifs in *Her Mother's Daughter*. What do they represent to the Gillis family? What do they signify to the reader?

Who was your favourite character in this novel? Why?

The novel takes place in Louisbourg, Cape Breton. How do you think the setting affected the storyline? What elements might have been different if the Gillis family lived in a big city? What would have stayed the same?

Ashley becomes pregnant as a teenager, and chooses to have and raise her baby. Did she receive good advice and guidance from the adults in her life? Would you have given her different advice?

Tansy was also a pregnant teenager, but her situation was complicated by the fact that she was impregnated by her sister's fiancé. Do you think Liz's solution to the problem was fair? What should she have done differently, if anything? What would you do in her shoes?

From the outside, Bay seems like a textbook "good" person—caring, generous, and loyal. Tansy can be and often is labelled a bad person—impetuous, promiscuous, and materialistic. But both sisters are much more complex than these tidy summaries. What are some of Bay's darker qualities, and some of Tansy's good ones? Are the women unfairly cast by the people in their lives—including their parents—as the "good" sister and the "bad" sister, or is there truth in those assessments? In what ways have their lives been shaped by these labels?

What are the significant friendships in this novel? In what way are they important?

Gertie is often referred to as part of the Gillis family. Do you think we can choose our own families? What does it take for a friend to become part of a family?

❀

AN INTERVIEW WITH LESLEY CREWE

Her Mother's Daughter is your fifth book. How has your writing process changed, if at all, since your first book was published?

These first five books were written in a two-year period, from 2003 to 2005. It was a crazy, mad spurt of storytelling, and it very nearly did me in, but I've always been an all-or-nothing kind of gal.

Now I'm trying to incorporate having a life along with the writing and it's been a bit of a struggle. When I'm in the zone, I can't think of anything else. I find it difficult to live in two worlds at once. When I write I belong to my fictional world, and it takes a lot of energy to drag myself out of it. We'll see what happens with the next book. I have no idea how it's going to go.

What's the hardest part of being published, and what's been the most fun?

There's nothing hard about being published! Except when I don't listen to my inner voice. Lots of people have opinions about what I should and shouldn't do, and I do ask for those opinions, but essentially it always comes back to what feels right for me. Happily, I don't think of my writing as a career. It's just who I am and what I do.

The most fun has been the writing itself, and of course the people I've met along the journey, and the wonderful readers who take time to let me know I've touched them in some way.

And I love the kids that I meet in schools all over Cape Breton. They're the best.

How did you decide on Louisbourg as the setting for *Her Mother's Daughter*? Do you have a particular connection with the town?

My mother lived in Louisbourg as a teenager during the war because her dad (my grampy) was in charge of maintaining the ships that came into port. Mom would tell us about all the fun she had growing up in a small town and it sounded wonderful to me, as I was a city girl.

It was at a dance at the legion (or maybe a church hall) in Louisbourg that she met my dad. The local girls were hosting a dance (with plenty of chaperones) for the visiting sailors, and my dad was in the navy. Mom said she noticed him right away because he was playing "Moonlight Sonata" on an old piano stuck in the corner of the hall. He missed playing music on the ship. He played the most beautiful music by ear. Never had a lesson in his life.

So Louisbourg is a favourite place in my world.

You write a lot about young love. When did you and your husband meet? Was it as romantic as you always write these passionate young lovers?

I do write about young love, don't I? I always say "write what you know," and this is what I know.

I met John when I was barely nineteen and he was twenty-one. It was a Friday. We walked across the field from our bungalow to the old Dillon farmhouse to ask Mom if he could stay for Sunday supper.

Mom said when the two of us walked through the door she knew that was it. As it turned out, John and I brought our first child home to that old farmhouse, seven years later.

I adore John. He's the nicest man in the whole world.

Although there are certainly men in this novel, at its core is a family—biological and chosen—of women. What draws you to writing about women's relationships? What are your most important relationships with women?

I write about women because I am a woman. I don't have a clue how men think...wouldn't want to be one, either!

Growing up, my mother, sister, and grandmother were the most important people in my life. Now that I've grown, my daughter, my sister, my nieces, my cousin, my aunt, my girlfriends, and their girls are my posse. They are like pieces of my heart that can walk around on their own, but they belong to me. I would die if I lost one. I have died when I lost one and then two and then three...

Women share a big secret. We know it and we recognize it in each other. When the world gets big and scary, your girls will gather around you and keep you safe.

Two of your characters, Ava from *Ava Comes Home* and Tansy in *Her Mother's Daughter,* have left Cape Breton and had wildly successful lives from a material perspective, but also suffered a deep loneliness that is only cured by returning home to Cape Breton. Do you think that kind of healing comes to anyone returning home, or is there something special about Cape Breton?

The politically correct answer is that healing of any kind is always made better by going home, wherever home is for you, but since my sensibility is firmly entrenched on Cape Breton Island, I'll say there is definitely something special about this place.

But how difficult is it to describe something you love to a stranger? What few words can you use to bring that spirit to life?

This island is the sum of its parts...the landscape, the water, the people and their connection to each other, family and history and memories and stories, the music and language, the wildlife and beaches, the wind and storms, and the trees and stars all come together to create such an astonishing, beautiful place that your heart grieves when you are separated from it.

When you cross the causeway and leave the island behind, it pulls you back, like a never-ending tide.

You write Bay's depression very realistically. What did you draw on to depict her struggle?

I drew on my own life experience. I only write what I am emotionally connected to, and unfortunately I know depression intimately. It's been my constant companion since I can remember.

I also know how it feels to lose precious members of my family, and how that loss can run so deep that it changes who you are. But none of us escape this world without being wounded and it is inevitably other members of our tribe who pick us up and drag us along until we can find our feet again.

Do you have a favourite character in this book? If so, who is it, and why?

My favourite character is Gertie. I always identify with the big girls!

Gertie is a big mushball of pure love and despite the fact that her life hasn't been easy, she's never bitter and doesn't resent her best friend's happiness with Bobby. That's why I needed someone just as loveable to come into her life. She and Peter are the real deal, two ordinary souls who may not set the world on fire but create magic when they are together.

Finally, can you tell us about the photograph on the back cover?

This is one of my favourite pictures of our daughter, Sarah. She came into our lives when we needed her the most. Her father, brother, and I were still reeling from the death of our little boy Joshua and I honestly thought I would die of grief.

But that sweet, spunky little face and healthy set of lungs convinced me that she was sticking around and was a force to be reckoned with. She is, and always will be, my angel on earth.

❁

Lesley Crewe is the author of *Hit & Mrs.* (2009), *Ava Comes Home* (2008), *Shoot Me* (2006), and *Relative Happiness* (2005), which was shortlisted for the Margaret and John Savage First Book Award. Previously a freelance writer and columnist for *Cape Bretoner Magazine*, she currently writes a column for *Cahoots* online magazine. Born in Montreal, Lesley lives in Homeville, Nova Scotia.

www.lesleycrewe.com